Bugs Bunny
and friends
A COMIC CELEBRATION

Jenette Kahn
PRESIDENT & EDITOR-IN-CHIEF

Paul Levitz
EXECUTIVE VICE PRESIDENT
& PUBLISHER

Martin Pasko
GROUP EDITOR

Bob Kahan • Rick Taylor
EDITORS-COLLECTED EDITION

Constance Baldwin
Dana Kurtin
EDITORS-ORIGINAL SERIES
(LOONEY TUNES (curr. series))

Jim Spivey
ASSOCIATE EDITOR-COLLECTED EDITION

Georg Brewer
DESIGN DIRECTOR

Robbin Brosterman
ART DIRECTOR

Richard Bruning
VP-CREATIVE DIRECTOR

Patrick Caldon
VP-FINANCE & OPERATIONS

Dorothy Crouch
VP-LICENSED PUBLISHING

Terri Cunningham
VP-MANAGING EDITOR

Joel Ehrlich
SENIOR VP-ADVERTISING & PROMOTIONS

Lillian Laserson
VP & GENERAL COUNSEL

Bob Rozakis
EXECUTIVE DIRECTOR-PRODUCTION

Bob Wayne
VP-DIRECT SALES

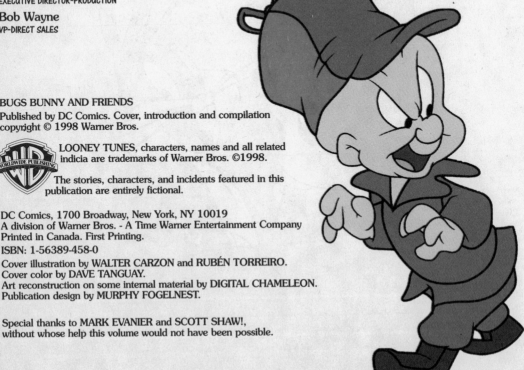

DC Comics, 1700 Broadway, New York, NY 10019
A division of Warner Bros. - A Time Warner Entertainment Company
Printed in Canada. First Printing.
ISBN: 1-56389-458-0
Cover illustration by WALTER CARZON and RUBÉN TORREIRO.
Cover color by DAVE TANGUAY.
Art reconstruction on some internal material by DIGITAL CHAMELEON.
Publication design by MURPHY FOGELNEST.

Special thanks to MARK EVANIER and SCOTT SHAW!,
without whose help this volume would not have been possible.

TABLE OF CONTENTS

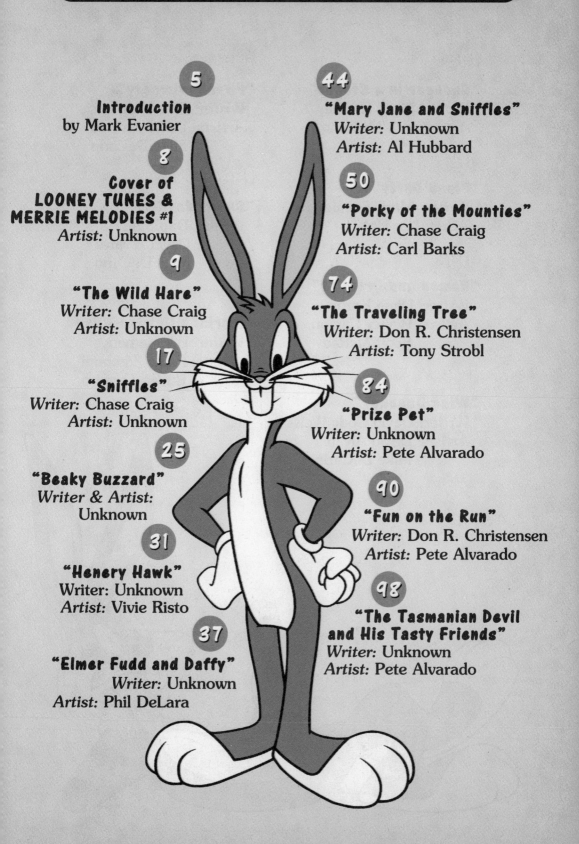

TABLE OF CONTENTS
(continued)

INTRODUCTION

Like any good force of nature, Bugs Bunny sprang from everywhere and nowhere, becoming a star so brilliant he seemed like he'd been around forever. Bugs, Porky Pig, Daffy Duck and over a hundred other stars formed their own separate universe, radiating from a Hollywood animation studio founded by an entrepreneur named Leon Schlesinger.

Everyone at Schlesinger's was keenly talented, but though many of the early comic books were signed with his name as if he'd drawn them himself, Schlesinger was a businessman, not an artist. Warner Bros. distributed his wares and, eventually, he sold Jack Warner the whole operation.

But, before that, he entered into a deal with a firm called Western Printing and Lithographing Co. to create comic books (and coloring books and Little Golden Books and puzzle books, etc.) using his studio's characters. For two decades, the comics were published in tandem with Dell Publishing. Later, Western published them for a time under the banner of Gold Key Comics.

The comics were launched with *Looney Tunes and Merrie Melodies* #1, portions of which are reprinted in this volume. Of special note is the story "A Wild Hare," which adapts the then-recent cartoon of the same name, directed by Fred "Tex" Avery. A key Bugs Bunny cartoon, it was an apt kickoff for his comic-book career as well.

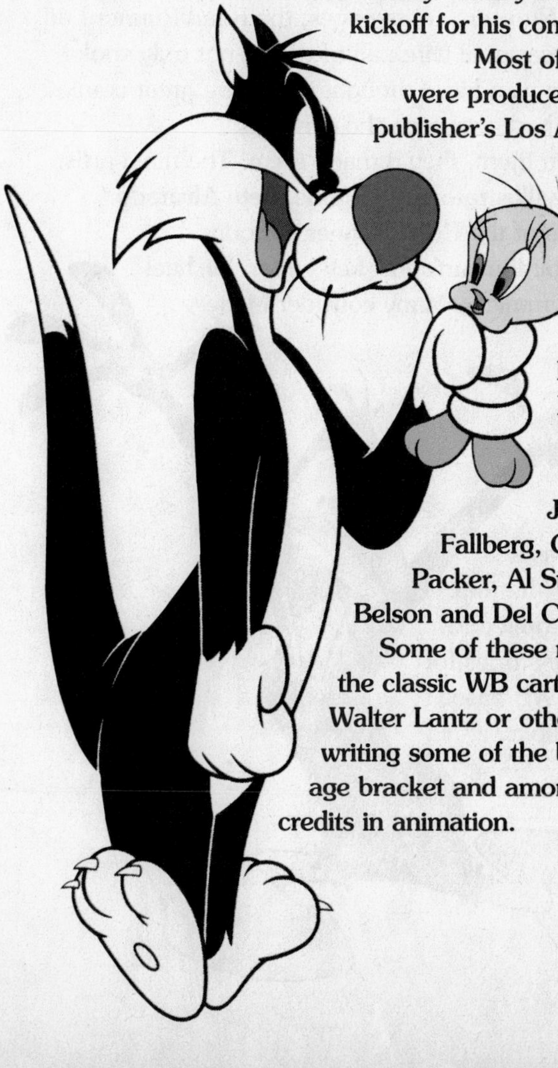

Most of the stories in Western's comics were produced by freelancers working for the publisher's Los Angeles office. Here's a partial list of those who created WB comic stories, many of whom also worked on the cartoons: Vivie Risto, Phil DeLara, Roger Armstrong, John Carey, Don R. Christensen, Vic Lockman, Pete Alvarado, Lloyd Turner, Tom McKimson, Michael Maltese, Tedd Pierce, Bob Ogle, Tony Strobl, Ralph Heimdahl, Jack Manning, Joe Messerli, Lee Holley, Carl Fallberg, Carl Buettner, Sid Marcus, Tom Packer, Al Stoffel, Win Smith, Cecil Beard, Jerry Belson and Del Connell.

Some of these names can be seen in the credits of the classic WB cartoons; others worked for Disney, Walter Lantz or other animation studios. When I began writing some of the books, I was one of the first in my age bracket and among the few without extensive credits in animation.

The overseer for most of the books was Chase Craig, a former storyman (gag writer) for the Lantz and Schlesinger studios. He worked in Tex Avery's unit at Schlesinger and then dabbled in newspaper strips before connecting with Western, where he eventually became editor-in-chief. He turned out to be brilliant at the job.

All the early WB comics are filled with Chase's artwork but are noteworthy for his stories. Some are quite faithful to the cartoons, but in other cases it was deemed necessary to rethink a character for comic-book purposes. Sniffles the Mouse, for example, had appeared in but a half dozen, largely plotless cartoons when Chase was assigned to write the comic-book translation. He added a little girl named Mary Jane — the name of Mrs. Craig — and concocted a charming fantasy format that endured for 20+ years of *Looney Tunes* comics. It didn't have a lot to do with the cartoons directed by Chuck Jones, but a prevailing view throughout Western was that their comics had to succeed as comics, even if that meant deviating from the animated versions.

This philosophy allowed the great Carl Barks — who worked on Western's Disney comics (also edited mainly by Chase Craig) — to retool Donald Duck quite successfully for comic-book purposes. (Barks's one attempt to work for the WB books is reprinted herein. He was not comfy with the characters, and so his renditions of Porky and Bugs were heavily modified by another artist.)

Jones's Road Runner-Wile E. Coyote cartoons were turned into a long-running comic, *Beep Beep The Road Runner*. In its pages, the Road Runner had three (sometimes, four) sons and an occasional wife...all of whom not only spoke, but spoke in rhyme. When I read them as a kid, I thought they were great comics, but I wondered if the guys doing them had ever seen the cartoons.

Turned out they'd not only seen them, they'd made them: The main artist was one of the most prolific funnybook illustrators of all time, Pete Alvarado. Pete had been one of the key designers of the Road Runner cartoons.

And many of the scripts were by the cartoons' key writer, Michael Maltese, who loved the talk/rhyming gimmick. Many consider Maltese the world-class "storyman" of the WB animation team and though his comic-book scripts were funny, they read nothing like cartoons transferred to paper. "You couldn't do the cartoons as a comic book," he told me. That applied to his many stories for all the WB-based comic books.

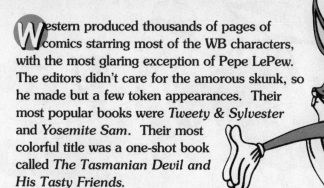

Western produced thousands of pages of comics starring most of the WB characters, with the most glaring exception of Pepe LePew. The editors didn't care for the amorous skunk, so he made but a few token appearances. Their most popular books were *Tweety & Sylvester* and *Yosemite Sam*. Their most colorful title was a one-shot book called *The Tasmanian Devil and His Tasty Friends*.

Reading back over these comics as an adult, I find that some have withstood the test of time better than others. (Not that there's a direct connection but, as the WB cartoon studio withered in the '60s, so did the quality of the WB comics.) For this collection, space permits only the most fractional overview of what Western published.

By the time Western opted out of the comic-book biz, DC Comics had become part of the same corporation that owned Warner Bros. but it wasn't until later, however, that Bugs and crew began appearing under the DC logo.

Interestingly, though the Bugs, Daffy, Porky and company comics are now created by artists and writers who were never involved with the original cartoons, they are generally closer in spirit to the original films. It should come as no surprise, since they are largely the work of writers and artists reared on those shorts, which are now more popular and more widely available in broadcast and video form than ever before.

Either way, it's nice to see the wabbit, the duck, the puddy tat and all the others in good hands. Their cartoons have become an exquisite legacy, enjoyed across four generations. Can their comic books be far behind?

— Mark Evanier

Quick P.S. — Western Publishing did not put credits on its comics, and just a few years ago someone threw out the only records of who'd done what. So credits on the pre-DC stories can be calculated by educated guesswork, supplemented by a few creators' personal records. — M.E.

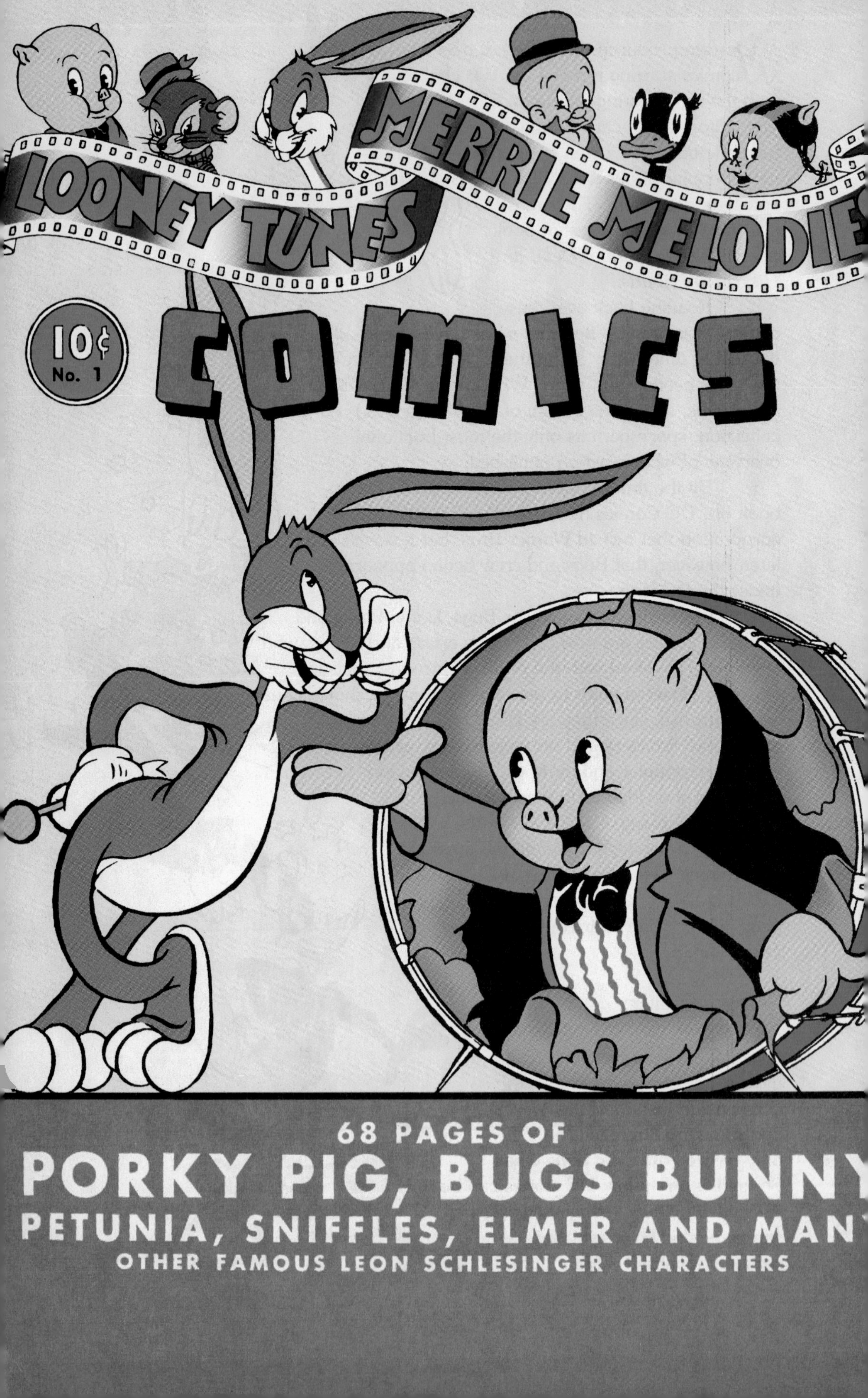
LOONEY TUNES
MERRIE MELODIES
10¢
No. 1
COMICS
68 PAGES OF
PORKY PIG, BUGS BUNNY
PETUNIA, SNIFFLES, ELMER AND MANY
OTHER FAMOUS LEON SCHLESINGER CHARACTERS

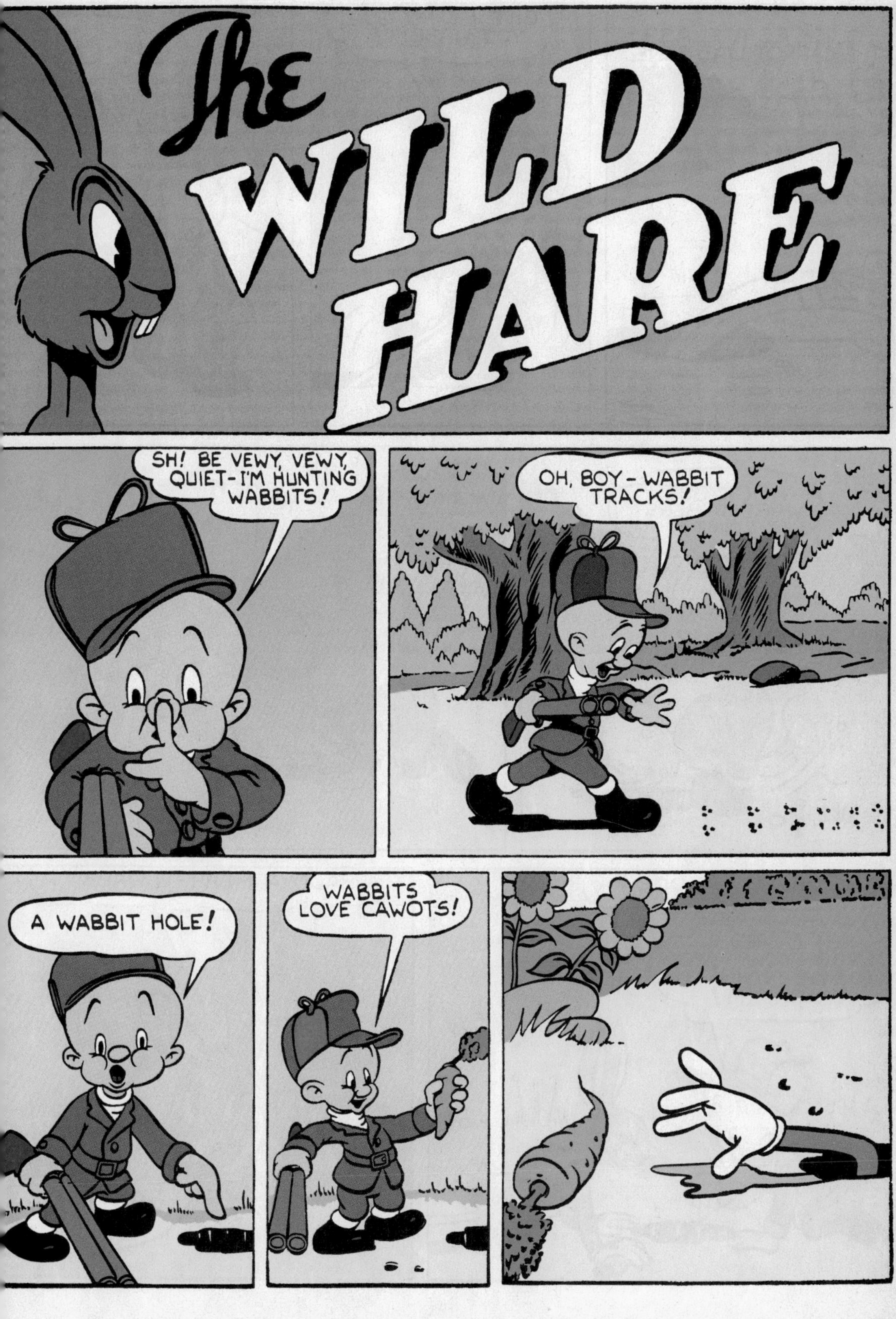
The WILD HARE
SH! BE VEWY, VEWY, QUIET-I'M HUNTING WABBITS!
OH, BOY-WABBIT TRACKS!
A WABBIT HOLE!
WABBITS LOVE CAWOTS!

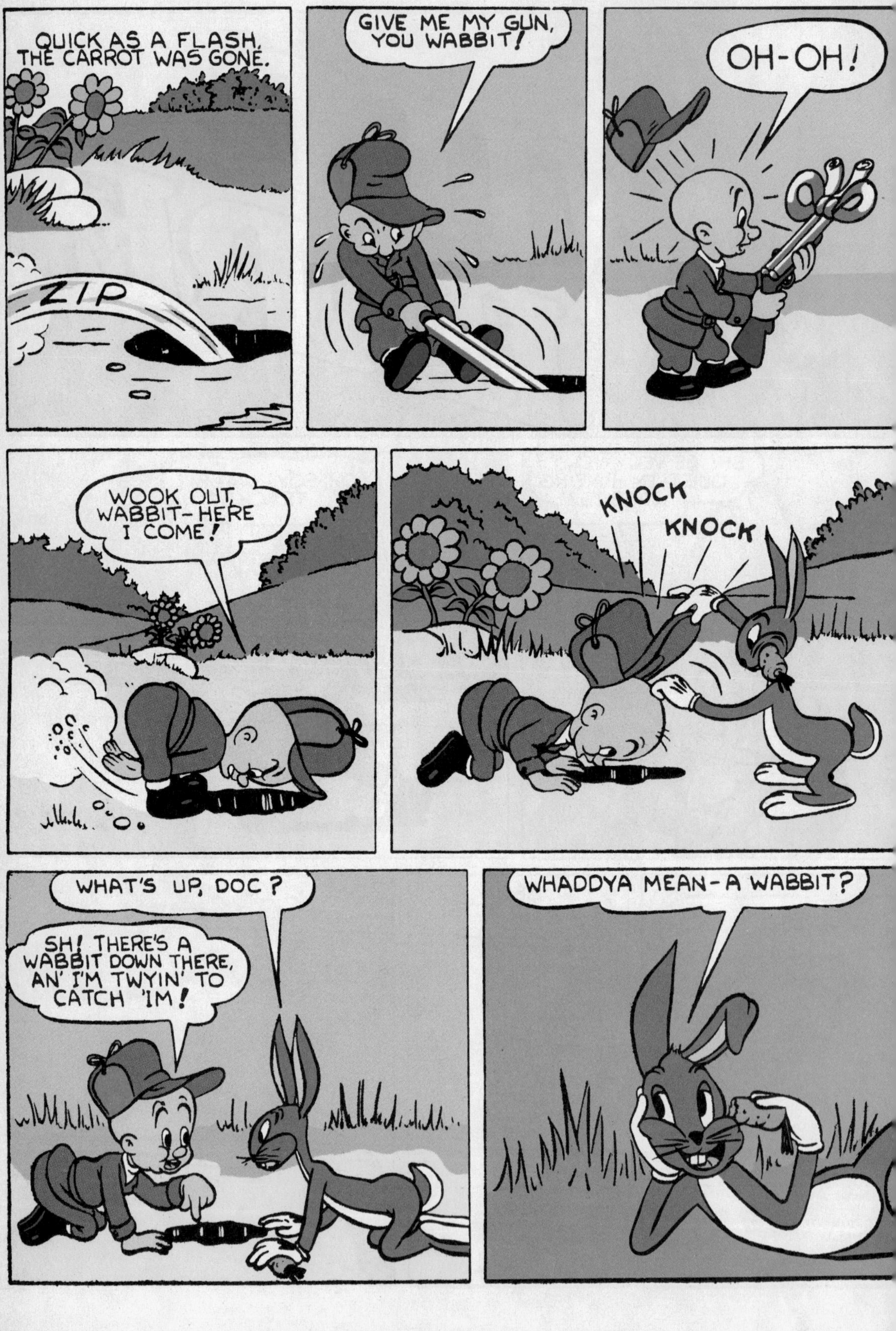

QUICK AS A FLASH, THE CARROT WAS GONE.
ZIP
GIVE ME MY GUN, YOU WABBIT!
OH-OH!
WOOK OUT, WABBIT- HERE I COME!
KNOCK
KNOCK
WHAT'S UP, DOC?
SH! THERE'S A WABBIT DOWN THERE, AN' I'M TWYIN' TO CATCH 'IM!
WHADDYA MEAN- A WABBIT?

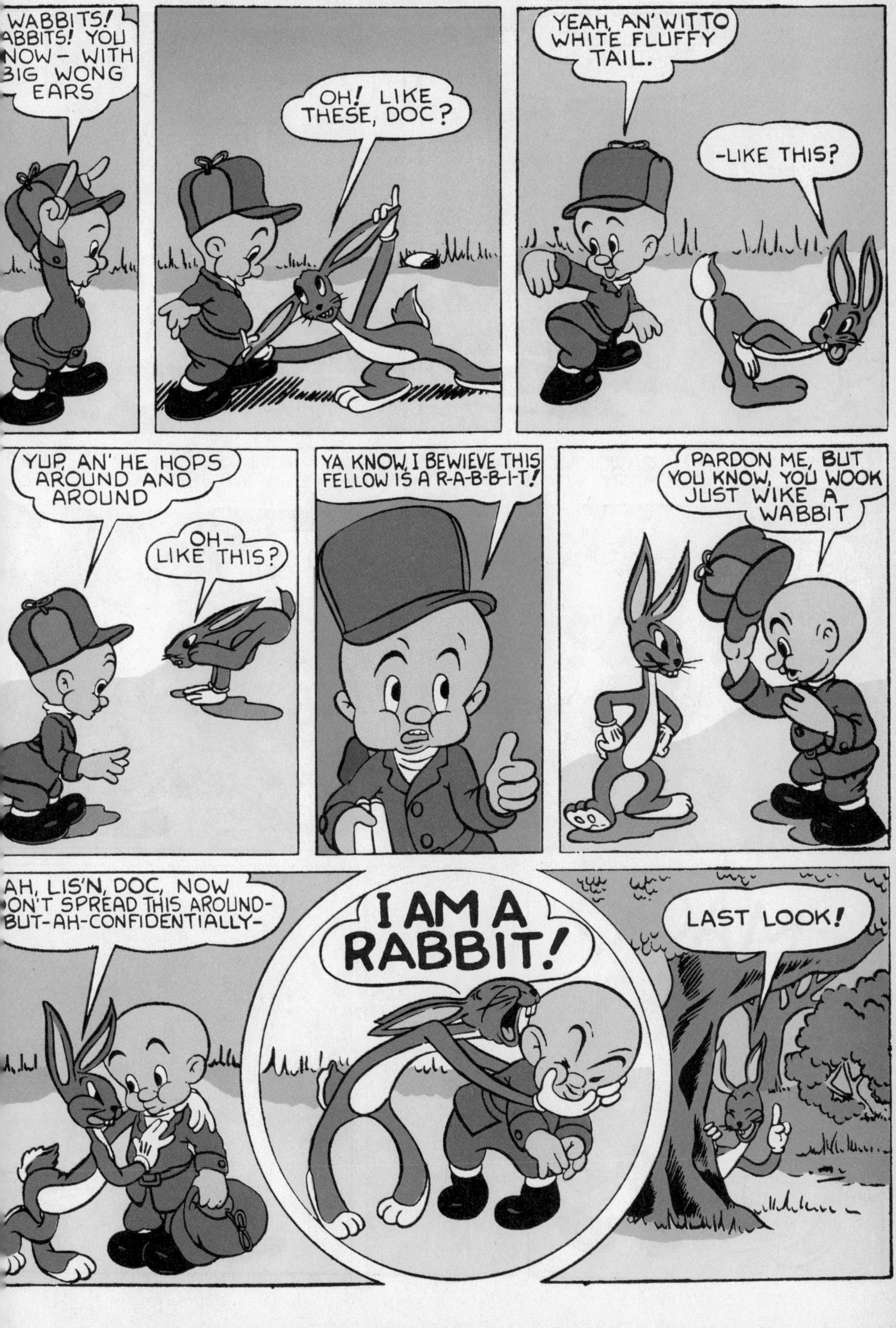
WABBITS! ABBITS! YOU NOW – WITH BIG WONG EARS
OH! LIKE THESE, DOC?
YEAH, AN' WITTO WHITE FLUFFY TAIL.
-LIKE THIS?
YUP, AN' HE HOPS AROUND AND AROUND
OH- LIKE THIS?
YA KNOW, I BEWIEVE THIS FELLOW IS A R-A-B-B-I-T!
PARDON ME, BUT YOU KNOW, YOU WOOK JUST WIKE A WABBIT
AH, LIS'N, DOC, NOW ON'T SPREAD THIS AROUND- BUT-AH-CONFIDENTIALLY-
I AM A RABBIT!
LAST LOOK!

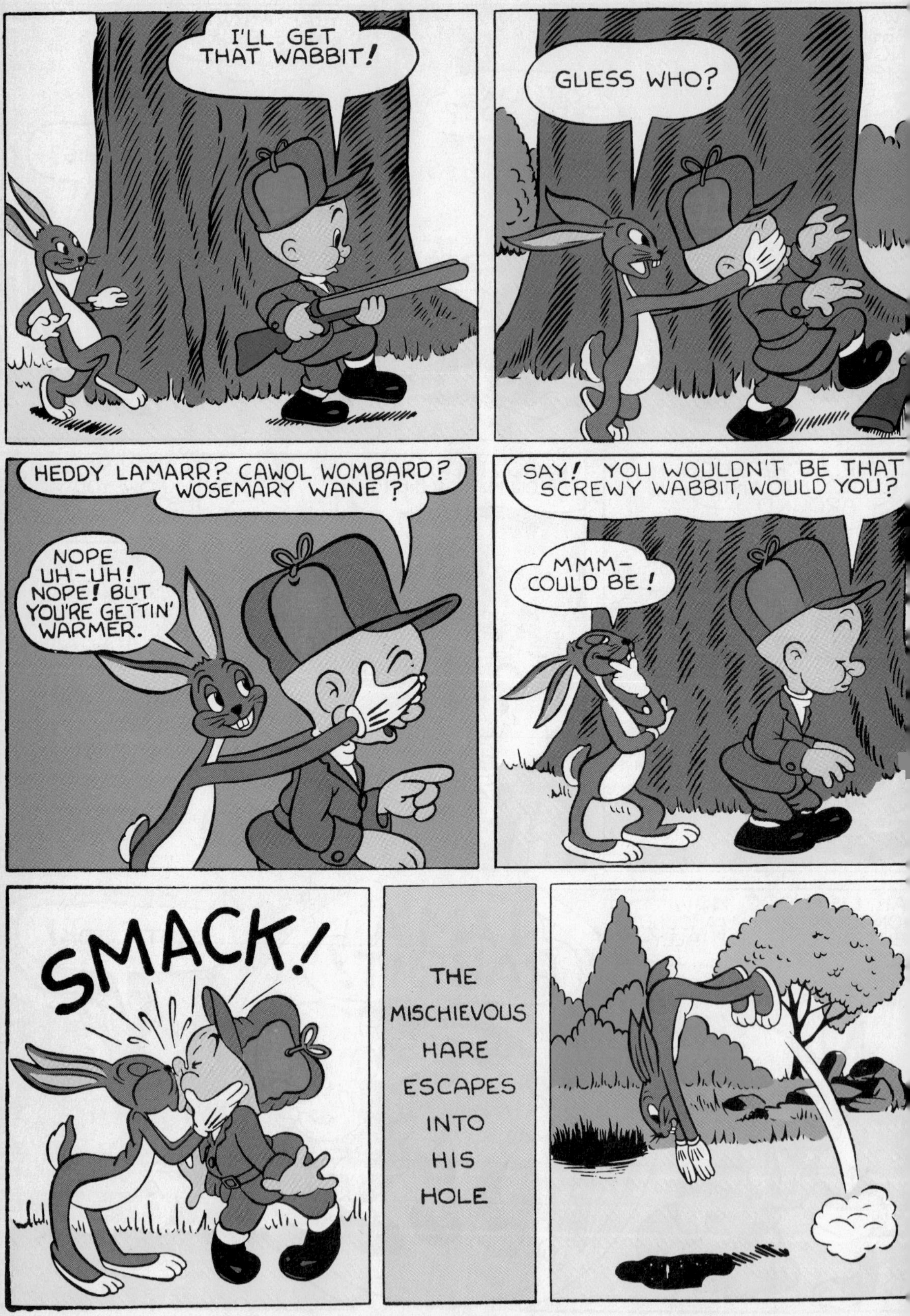
I'LL GET THAT WABBIT!
GUESS WHO?
HEDDY LAMARR? CAWOL WOMBARD? WOSEMARY WANE ?
NOPE UH-UH! NOPE! BUT YOU'RE GETTIN' WARMER.
SAY! YOU WOULDN'T BE THAT SCREWY WABBIT, WOULD YOU?
MMM- COULD BE!
SMACK!
THE MISCHIEVOUS HARE ESCAPES INTO HIS HOLE

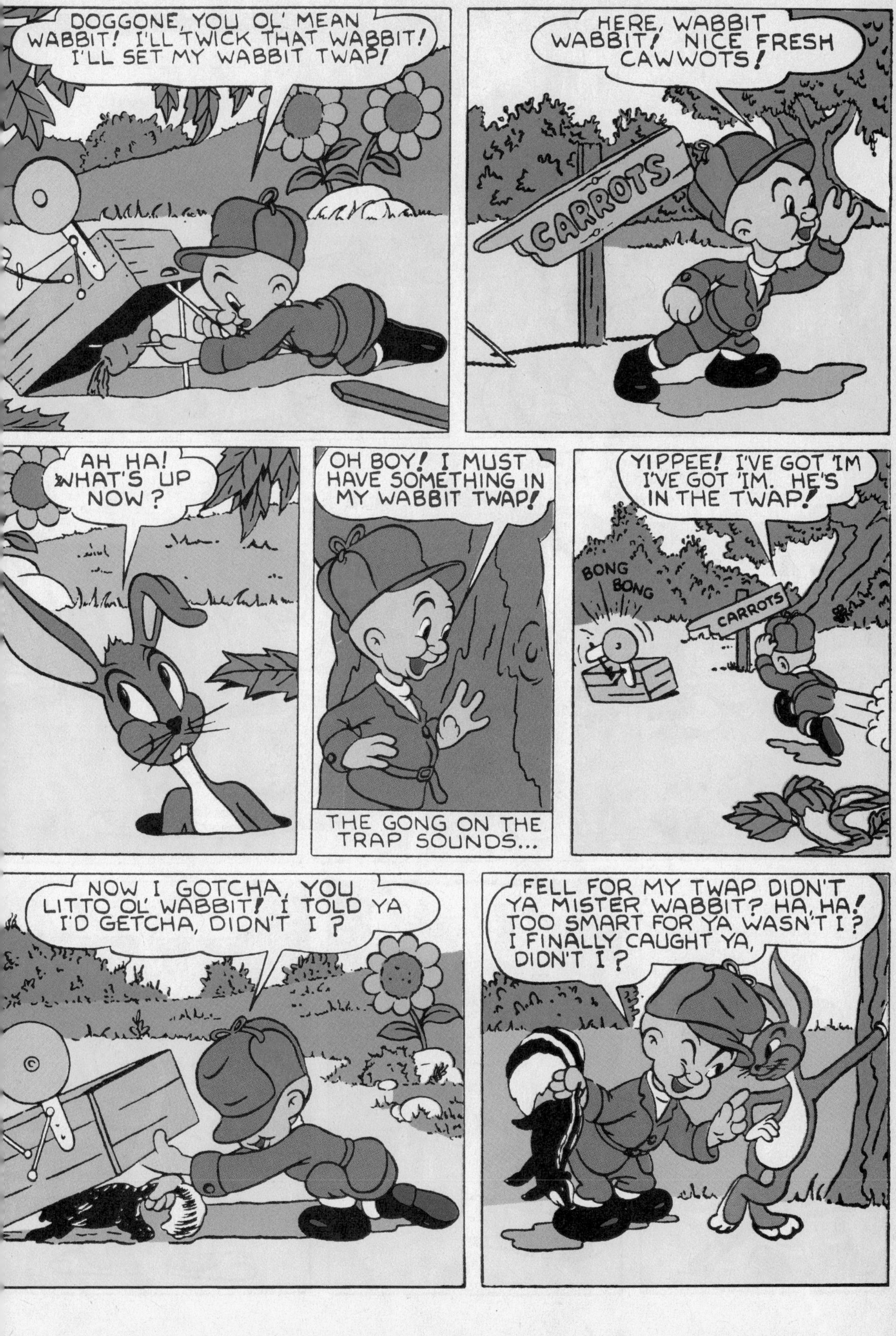

DOGGONE, YOU OL' MEAN WABBIT! I'LL TWICK THAT WABBIT! I'LL SET MY WABBIT TWAP!
HERE, WABBIT WABBIT! NICE FRESH CAWWOTS!
CARROTS
AH HA! WHAT'S UP NOW?
OH BOY! I MUST HAVE SOMETHING IN MY WABBIT TWAP!
THE GONG ON THE TRAP SOUNDS...
YIPPEE! I'VE GOT 'IM I'VE GOT 'IM. HE'S IN THE TWAP!
BONG
BONG
CARROTS
NOW I GOTCHA, YOU LITTO OL' WABBIT! I TOLD YA I'D GETCHA, DIDN'T I?
FELL FOR MY TWAP DIDN'T YA MISTER WABBIT? HA, HA! TOO SMART FOR YA WASN'T I? I FINALLY CAUGHT YA, DIDN'T I?

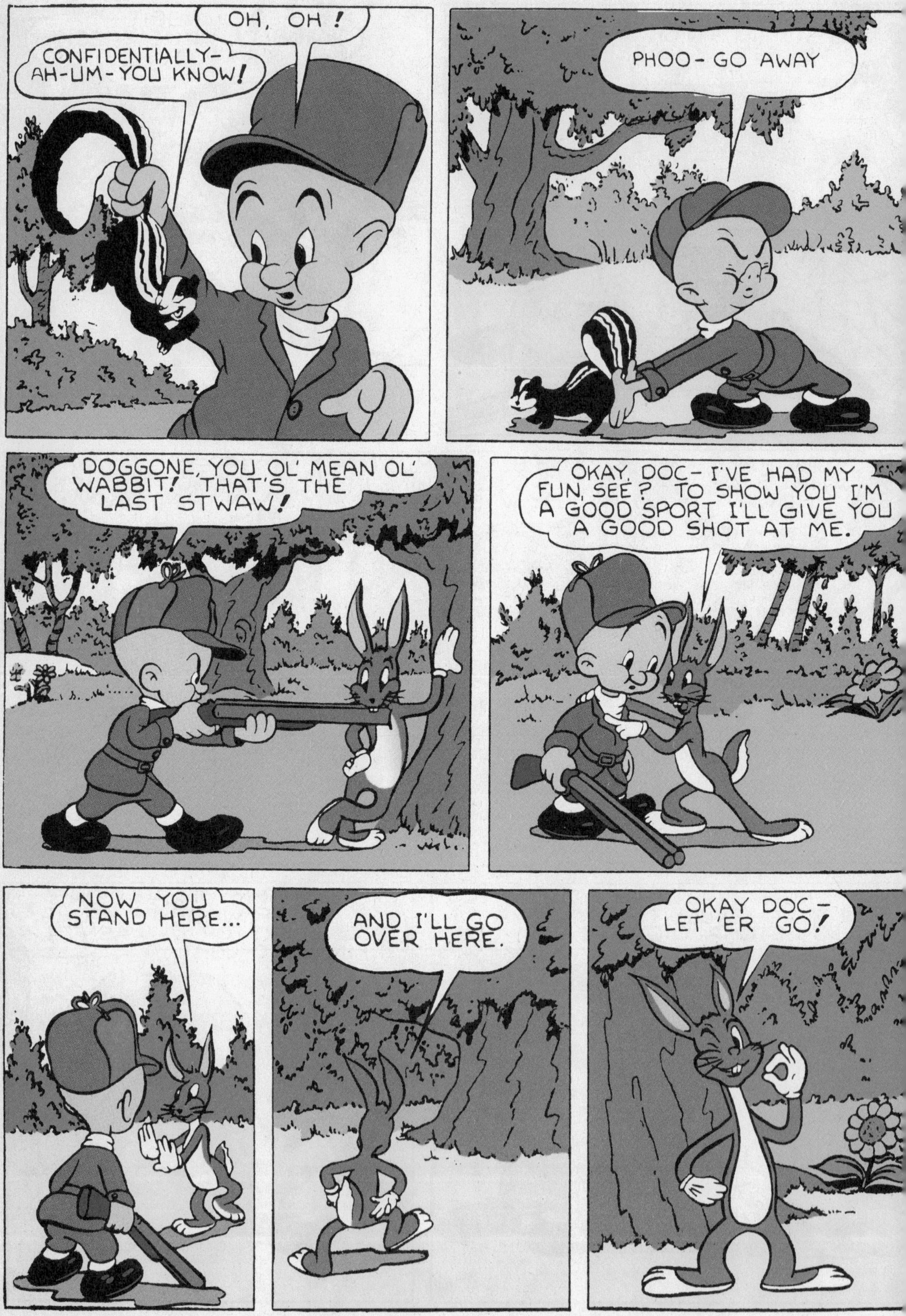
CONFIDENTIALLY-
AH-UM-YOU KNOW!
OH, OH!
PHOO- GO AWAY
DOGGONE, YOU OL' MEAN OL' WABBIT! THAT'S THE LAST STWAW!
OKAY, DOC- I'VE HAD MY FUN, SEE? TO SHOW YOU I'M A GOOD SPORT I'LL GIVE YOU A GOOD SHOT AT ME.
NOW YOU STAND HERE...
AND I'LL GO OVER HERE.
OKAY DOC- LET 'ER GO!

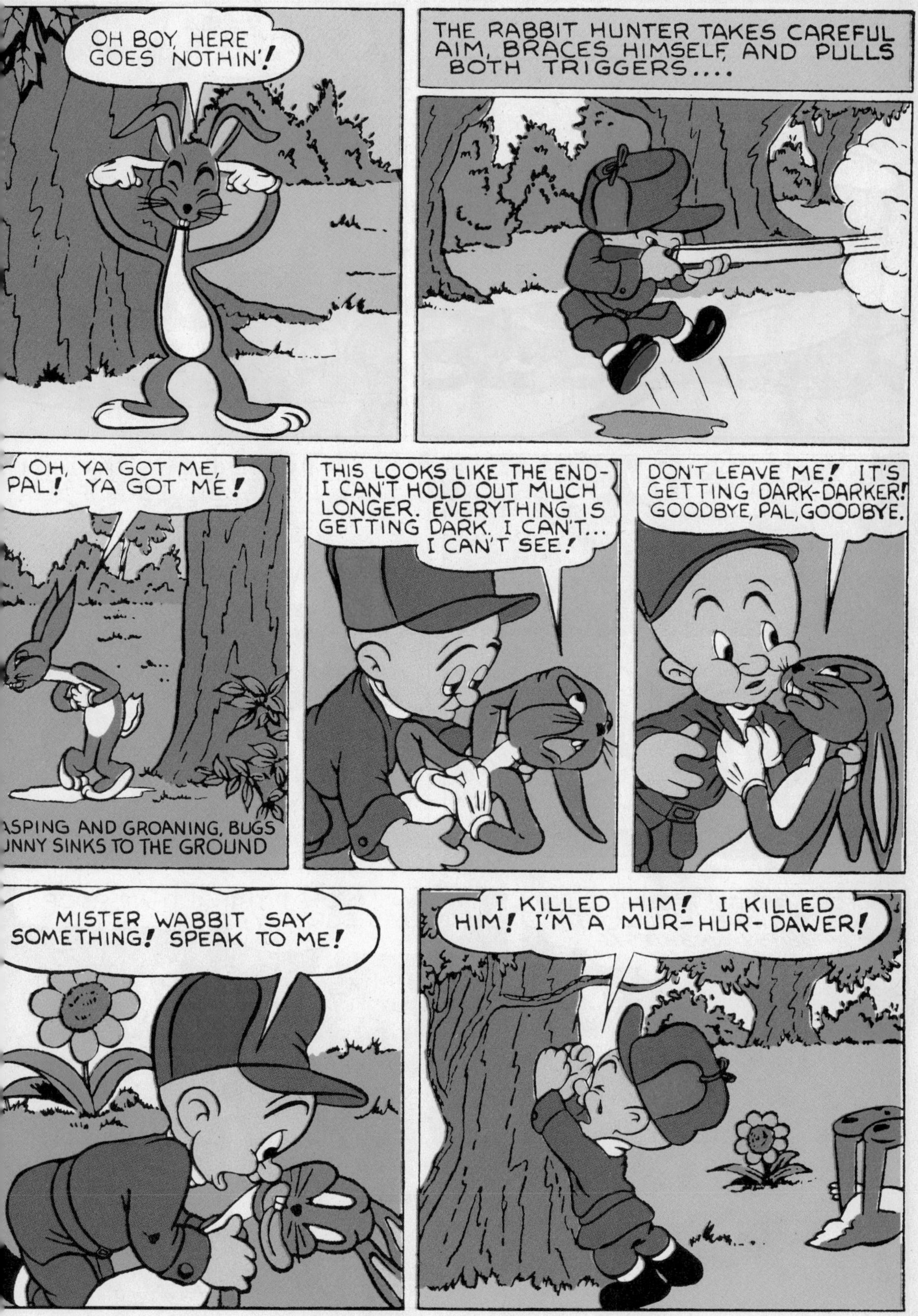
OH BOY, HERE GOES NOTHIN'!
THE RABBIT HUNTER TAKES CAREFUL AIM, BRACES HIMSELF, AND PULLS BOTH TRIGGERS....
OH, YA GOT ME, PAL! YA GOT ME!
ASPING AND GROANING, BUGS UNNY SINKS TO THE GROUND
THIS LOOKS LIKE THE END- I CAN'T HOLD OUT MUCH LONGER. EVERYTHING IS GETTING DARK. I CAN'T... I CAN'T SEE!
DON'T LEAVE ME! IT'S GETTING DARK-DARKER! GOODBYE, PAL, GOODBYE.
MISTER WABBIT SAY SOMETHING! SPEAK TO ME!
I KILLED HIM! I KILLED HIM! I'M A MUR-HUR-DAWER!

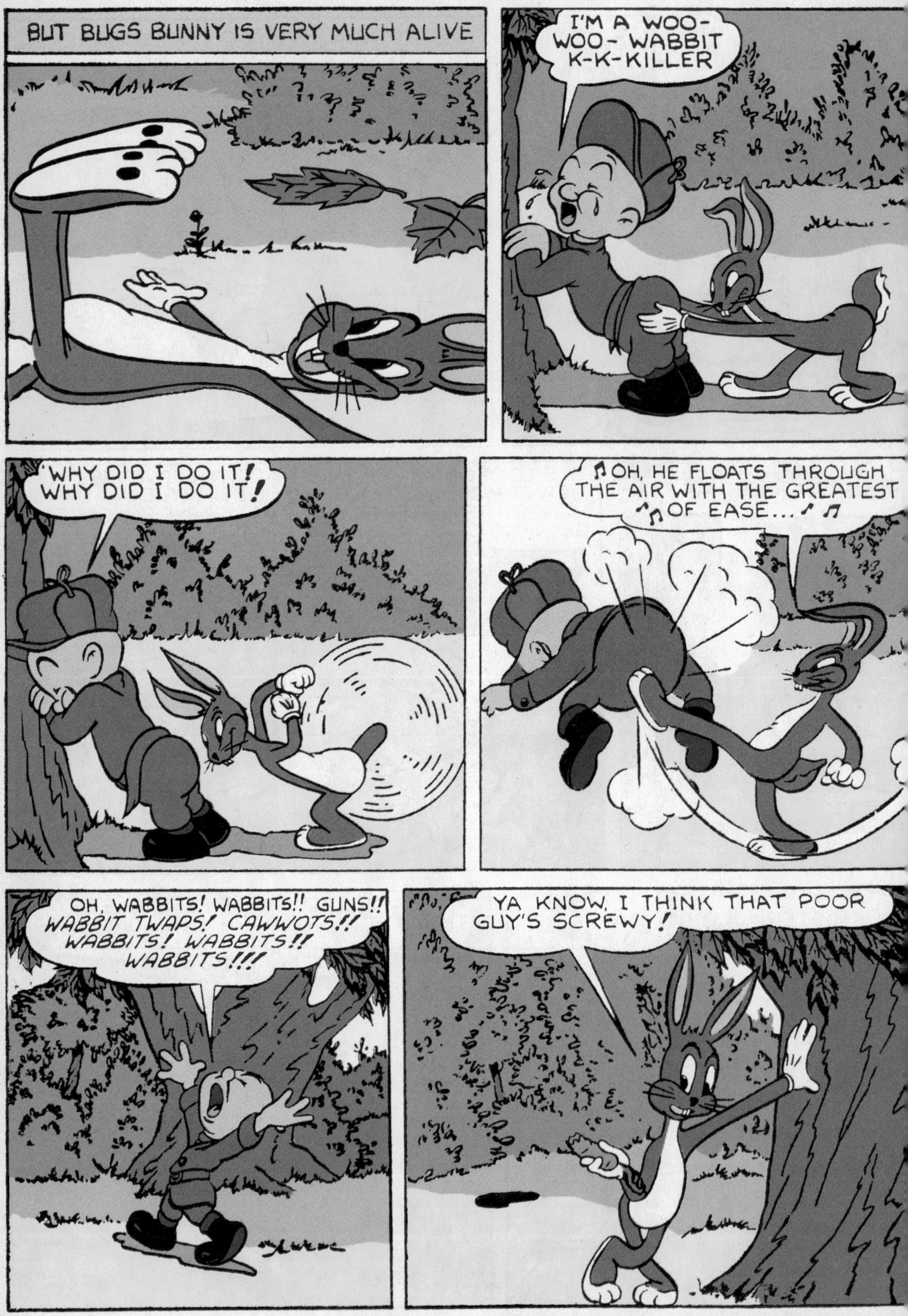
BUT BUGS BUNNY IS VERY MUCH ALIVE
I'M A WOO-WOO- WABBIT K-K-KILLER
WHY DID I DO IT! WHY DID I DO IT!
OH, HE FLOATS THROUGH THE AIR WITH THE GREATEST OF EASE...
OH, WABBITS! WABBITS!! GUNS!! WABBIT TWAPS! CAWWOTS!! WABBITS! WABBITS!! WABBITS!!!
YA KNOW, I THINK THAT POOR GUY'S SCREWY!

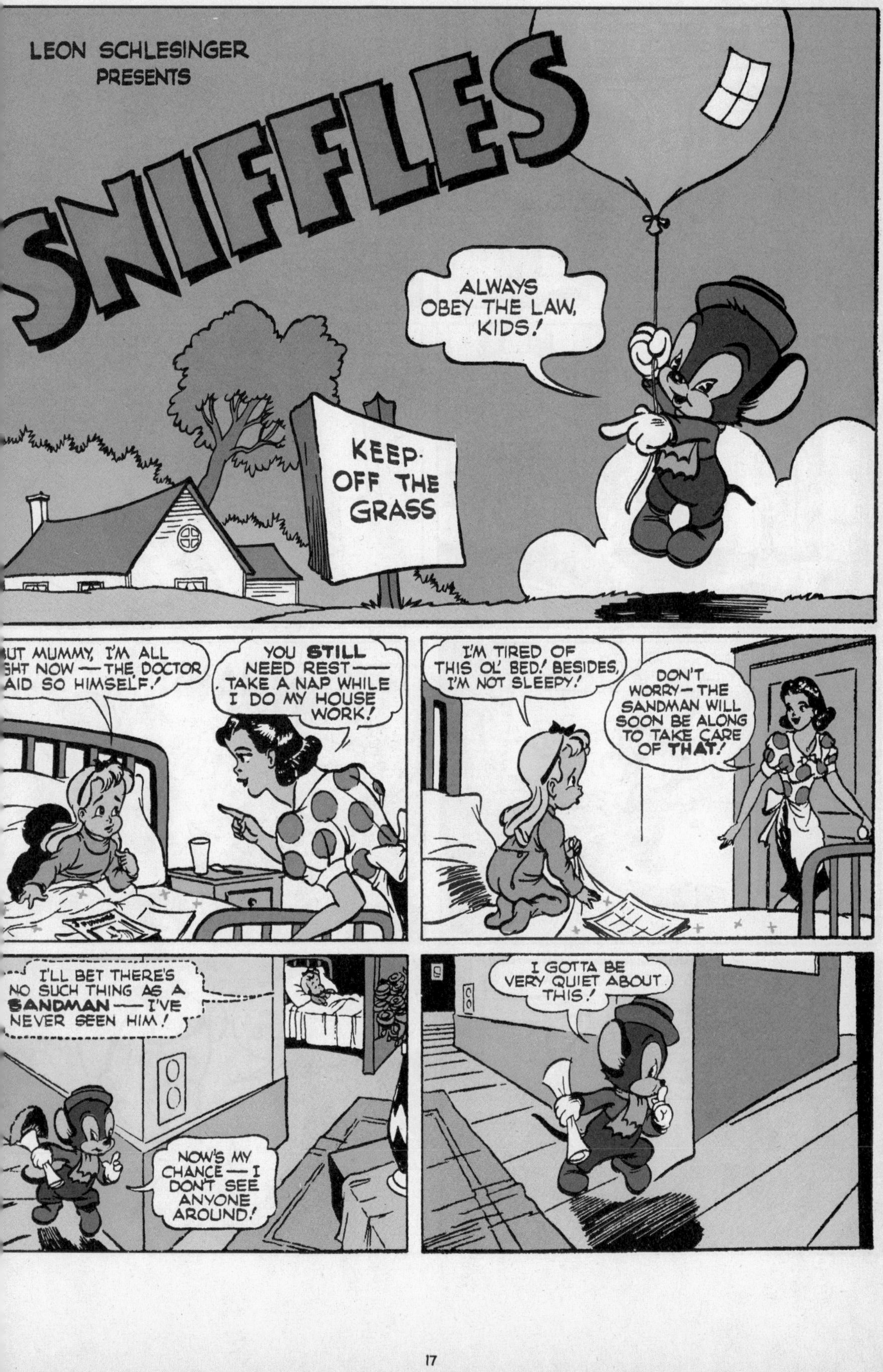
LEON SCHLESINGER PRESENTS
SNIFFLES
ALWAYS OBEY THE LAW, KIDS!
KEEP OFF THE GRASS
UT MUMMY, I'M ALL GHT NOW — THE DOCTOR AID SO HIMSELF!
YOU STILL NEED REST — TAKE A NAP WHILE I DO MY HOUSE WORK!
I'M TIRED OF THIS OL' BED! BESIDES, I'M NOT SLEEPY!
DON'T WORRY — THE SANDMAN WILL SOON BE ALONG TO TAKE CARE OF THAT!
I'LL BET THERE'S NO SUCH THING AS A SANDMAN — I'VE NEVER SEEN HIM!
NOW'S MY CHANCE — I DON'T SEE ANYONE AROUND!
I GOTTA BE VERY QUIET ABOUT THIS!

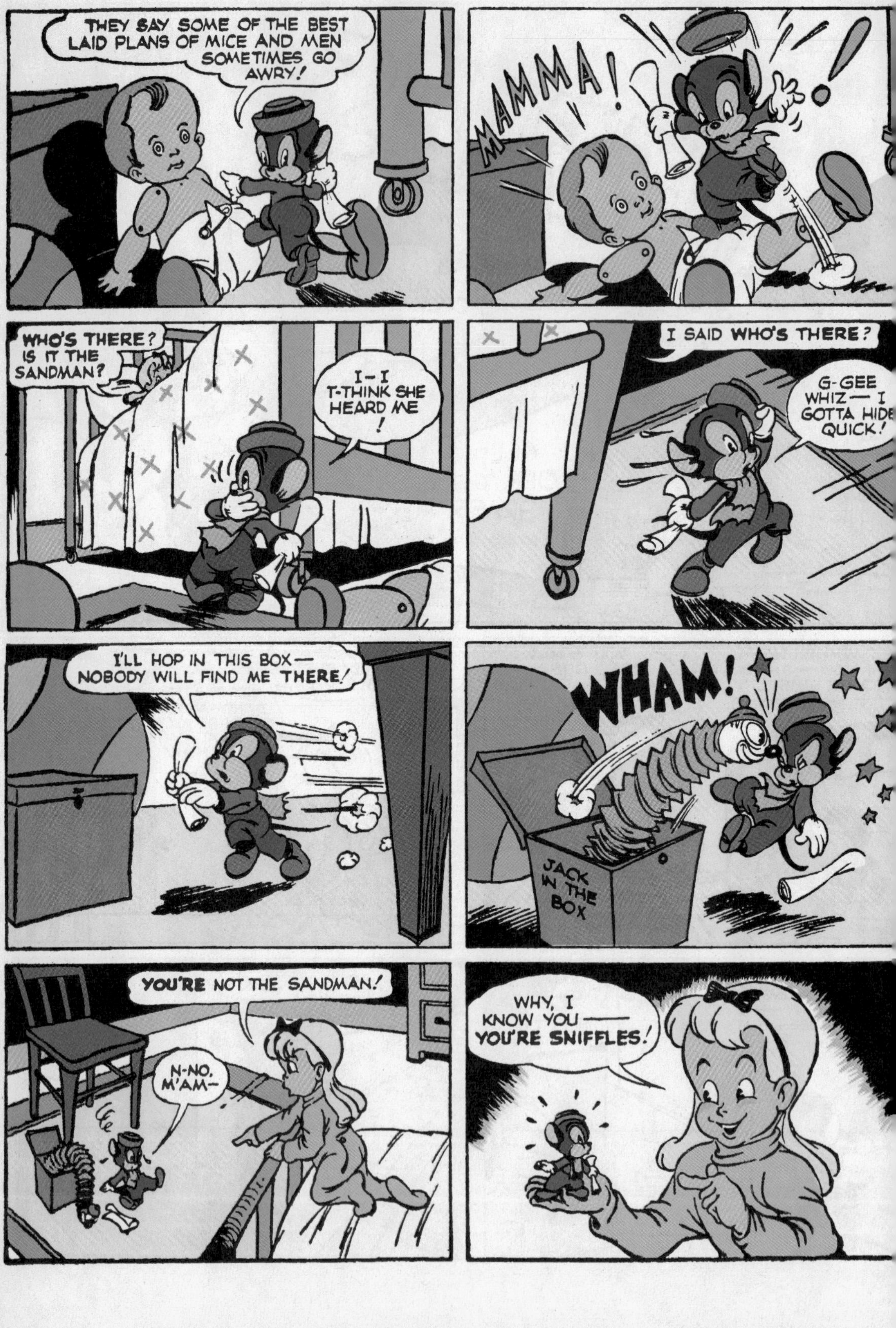
THEY SAY SOME OF THE BEST LAID PLANS OF MICE AND MEN SOMETIMES GO AWRY!
MAMMA!
WHO'S THERE? IS IT THE SANDMAN?
I-I T-THINK SHE HEARD ME!
I SAID WHO'S THERE?
G-GEE WHIZ— I GOTTA HIDE QUICK!
I'LL HOP IN THIS BOX— NOBODY WILL FIND ME THERE!
WHAM!
JACK IN THE BOX
YOU'RE NOT THE SANDMAN!
N-NO, M'AM—
WHY, I KNOW YOU—— YOU'RE SNIFFLES!

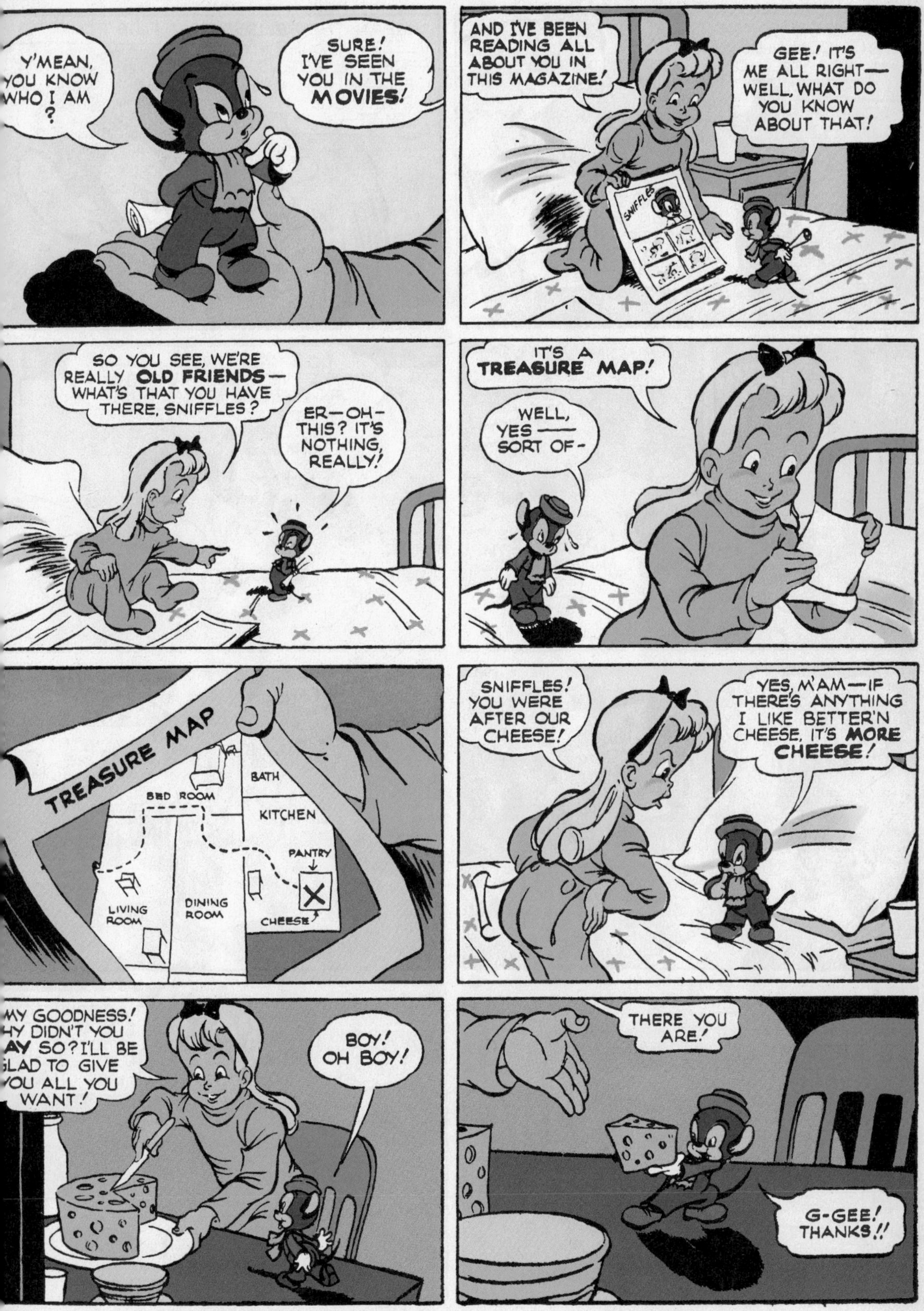
Y'MEAN, YOU KNOW WHO I AM ?
SURE! I'VE SEEN YOU IN THE MOVIES!
AND I'VE BEEN READING ALL ABOUT YOU IN THIS MAGAZINE!
GEE! IT'S ME ALL RIGHT— WELL, WHAT DO YOU KNOW ABOUT THAT!
SNIFFLES
SO YOU SEE, WE'RE REALLY OLD FRIENDS— WHAT'S THAT YOU HAVE THERE, SNIFFLES?
ER—OH— THIS? IT'S NOTHING, REALLY!
IT'S A TREASURE MAP!
WELL, YES—— SORT OF-
TREASURE MAP
BATH
BED ROOM
KITCHEN
PANTRY
LIVING ROOM
DINING ROOM
CHEESE
SNIFFLES! YOU WERE AFTER OUR CHEESE!
YES, M'AM—IF THERE'S ANYTHING I LIKE BETTER'N CHEESE, IT'S MORE CHEESE!
MY GOODNESS! HY DIDN'T YOU AY SO? I'LL BE LAD TO GIVE OU ALL YOU WANT!
BOY! OH BOY!
THERE YOU ARE!
G-GEE! THANKS!!

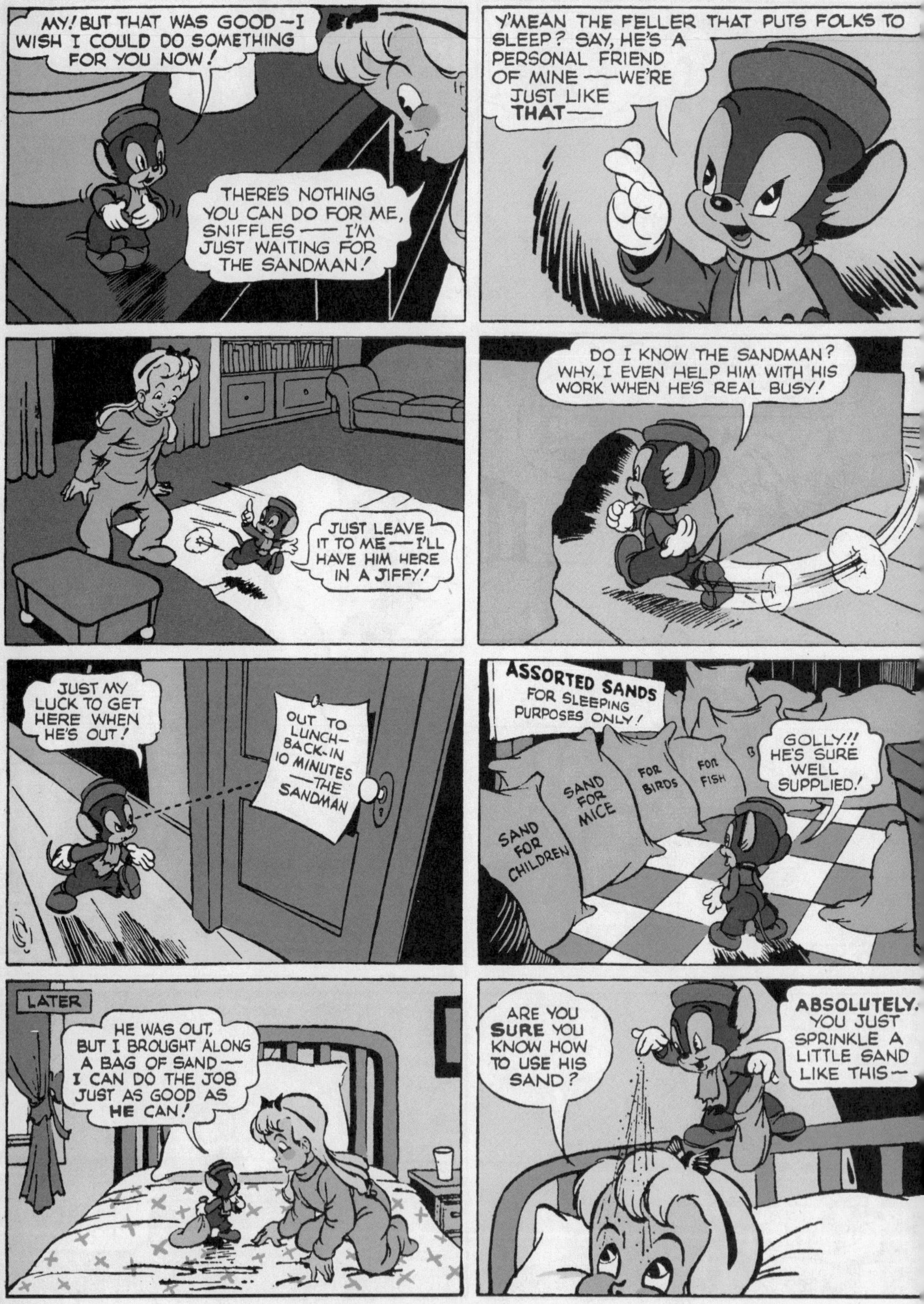

MY! BUT THAT WAS GOOD—I WISH I COULD DO SOMETHING FOR YOU NOW!
THERE'S NOTHING YOU CAN DO FOR ME, SNIFFLES —— I'M JUST WAITING FOR THE SANDMAN!
Y'MEAN THE FELLER THAT PUTS FOLKS TO SLEEP? SAY, HE'S A PERSONAL FRIEND OF MINE ——WE'RE JUST LIKE THAT——
JUST LEAVE IT TO ME——I'LL HAVE HIM HERE IN A JIFFY!
DO I KNOW THE SANDMAN? WHY, I EVEN HELP HIM WITH HIS WORK WHEN HE'S REAL BUSY!
JUST MY LUCK TO GET HERE WHEN HE'S OUT!
OUT TO LUNCH-BACK-IN 10 MINUTES —THE SANDMAN
ASSORTED SANDS FOR SLEEPING PURPOSES ONLY!
SAND FOR CHILDREN
SAND FOR MICE
FOR BIRDS
FOR FISH
GOLLY!! HE'S SURE WELL SUPPLIED!
LATER
HE WAS OUT, BUT I BROUGHT ALONG A BAG OF SAND— I CAN DO THE JOB JUST AS GOOD AS HE CAN!
ARE YOU SURE YOU KNOW HOW TO USE HIS SAND?
ABSOLUTELY. YOU JUST SPRINKLE A LITTLE SAND LIKE THIS—

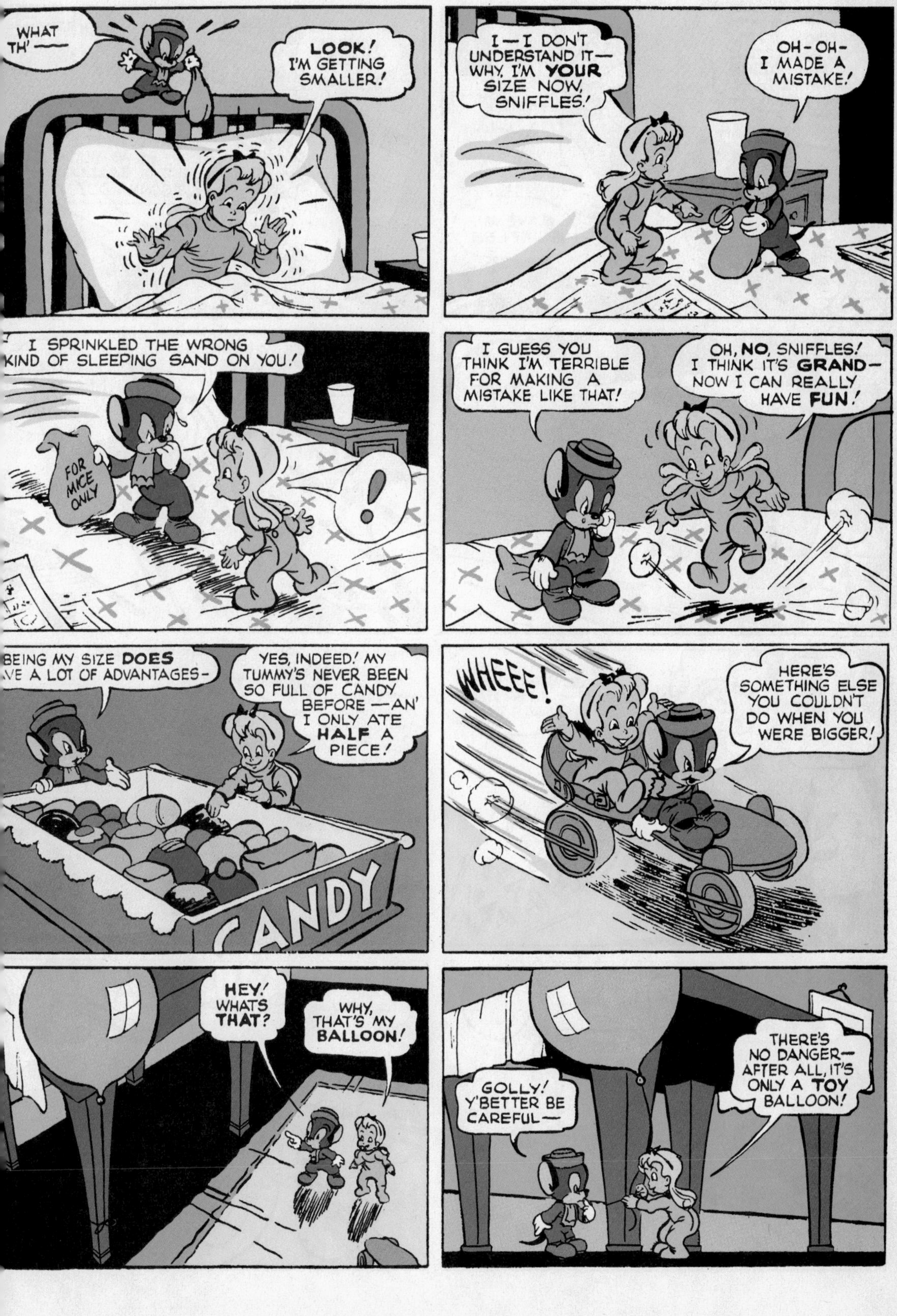

WHAT TH'——
LOOK! I'M GETTING SMALLER!
I—I DON'T UNDERSTAND IT— WHY, I'M YOUR SIZE NOW, SNIFFLES!
OH-OH- I MADE A MISTAKE!
I SPRINKLED THE WRONG KIND OF SLEEPING SAND ON YOU!
FOR MICE ONLY
!
I GUESS YOU THINK I'M TERRIBLE FOR MAKING A MISTAKE LIKE THAT!
OH, NO, SNIFFLES! I THINK IT'S GRAND— NOW I CAN REALLY HAVE FUN!
BEING MY SIZE DOES VE A LOT OF ADVANTAGES-
YES, INDEED! MY TUMMY'S NEVER BEEN SO FULL OF CANDY BEFORE —AN' I ONLY ATE HALF A PIECE!
CANDY
WHEEE!
HERE'S SOMETHING ELSE YOU COULDN'T DO WHEN YOU WERE BIGGER!
HEY! WHATS THAT?
WHY, THAT'S MY BALLOON!
GOLLY! Y'BETTER BE CAREFUL—
THERE'S NO DANGER— AFTER ALL, IT'S ONLY A TOY BALLOON!

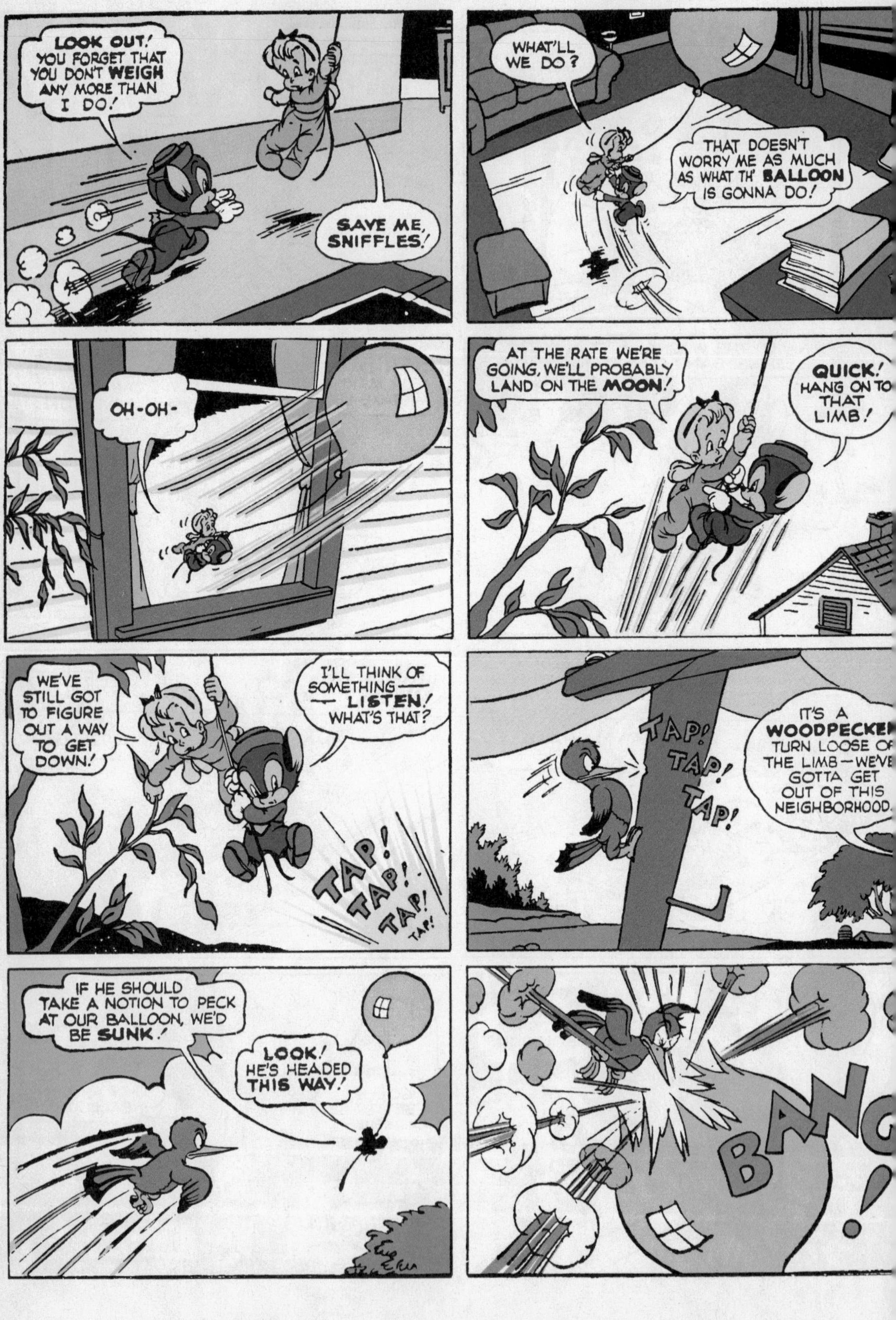
LOOK OUT! YOU FORGET THAT YOU DON'T WEIGH ANY MORE THAN I DO!
SAVE ME, SNIFFLES!
WHAT'LL WE DO?
THAT DOESN'T WORRY ME AS MUCH AS WHAT TH' BALLOON IS GONNA DO!
OH-OH-
AT THE RATE WE'RE GOING, WE'LL PROBABLY LAND ON THE MOON!
QUICK! HANG ON TO THAT LIMB!
WE'VE STILL GOT TO FIGURE OUT A WAY TO GET DOWN!
I'LL THINK OF SOMETHING— —LISTEN! WHAT'S THAT?
TAP! TAP! TAP! TAP!
TAP! TAP! TAP!
IT'S A WOODPECKE
TURN LOOSE O
THE LIMB—WE'V
GOTTA GET
OUT OF THIS
NEIGHBORHOOD
IF HE SHOULD TAKE A NOTION TO PECK AT OUR BALLOON, WE'D BE SUNK!
LOOK! HE'S HEADED THIS WAY!
BANG!

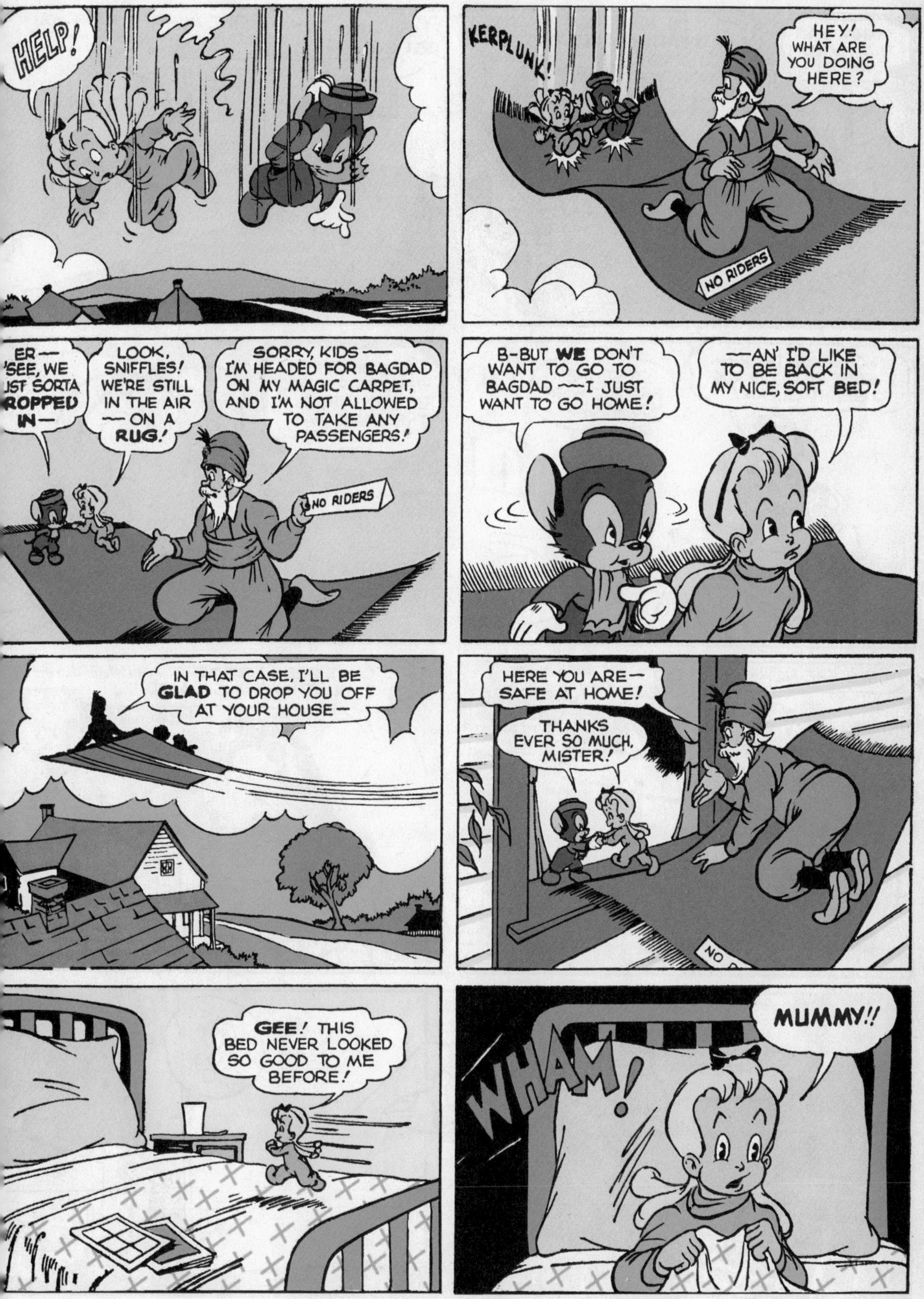
HELP!
KERPLUNK!
HEY! WHAT ARE YOU DOING HERE?
ER— 'SEE, WE JUST SORTA DROPPED IN—
LOOK, SNIFFLES! WE'RE STILL IN THE AIR —ON A RUG!
SORRY, KIDS — I'M HEADED FOR BAGDAD ON MY MAGIC CARPET, AND I'M NOT ALLOWED TO TAKE ANY PASSENGERS!
NO RIDERS
B-BUT WE DON'T WANT TO GO TO BAGDAD —I JUST WANT TO GO HOME!
—AN' I'D LIKE TO BE BACK IN MY NICE, SOFT BED!
IN THAT CASE, I'LL BE GLAD TO DROP YOU OFF AT YOUR HOUSE—
HERE YOU ARE— SAFE AT HOME!
THANKS EVER SO MUCH, MISTER!
GEE! THIS BED NEVER LOOKED SO GOOD TO ME BEFORE!
WHAM!
MUMMY!!

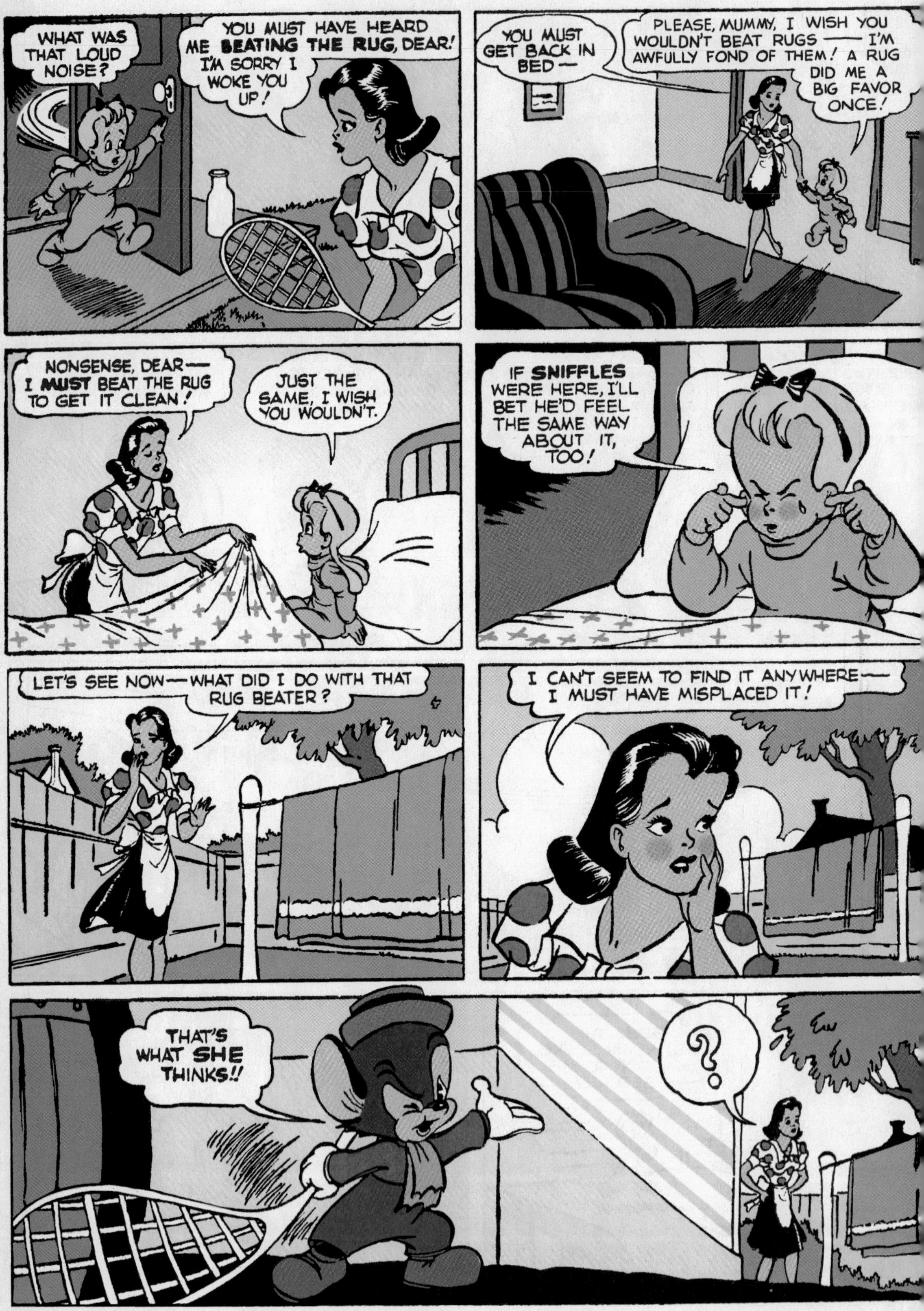
WHAT WAS THAT LOUD NOISE?
YOU MUST HAVE HEARD ME BEATING THE RUG, DEAR!
I'M SORRY I WOKE YOU UP!
YOU MUST GET BACK IN BED—
PLEASE, MUMMY, I WISH YOU WOULDN'T BEAT RUGS —— I'M AWFULLY FOND OF THEM! A RUG DID ME A BIG FAVOR ONCE!
NONSENSE, DEAR— I MUST BEAT THE RUG TO GET IT CLEAN!
JUST THE SAME, I WISH YOU WOULDN'T.
IF SNIFFLES WERE HERE, I'LL BET HE'D FEEL THE SAME WAY ABOUT IT, TOO!
LET'S SEE NOW—WHAT DID I DO WITH THAT RUG BEATER?
I CAN'T SEEM TO FIND IT ANYWHERE— I MUST HAVE MISPLACED IT!
THAT'S WHAT SHE THINKS!!
?

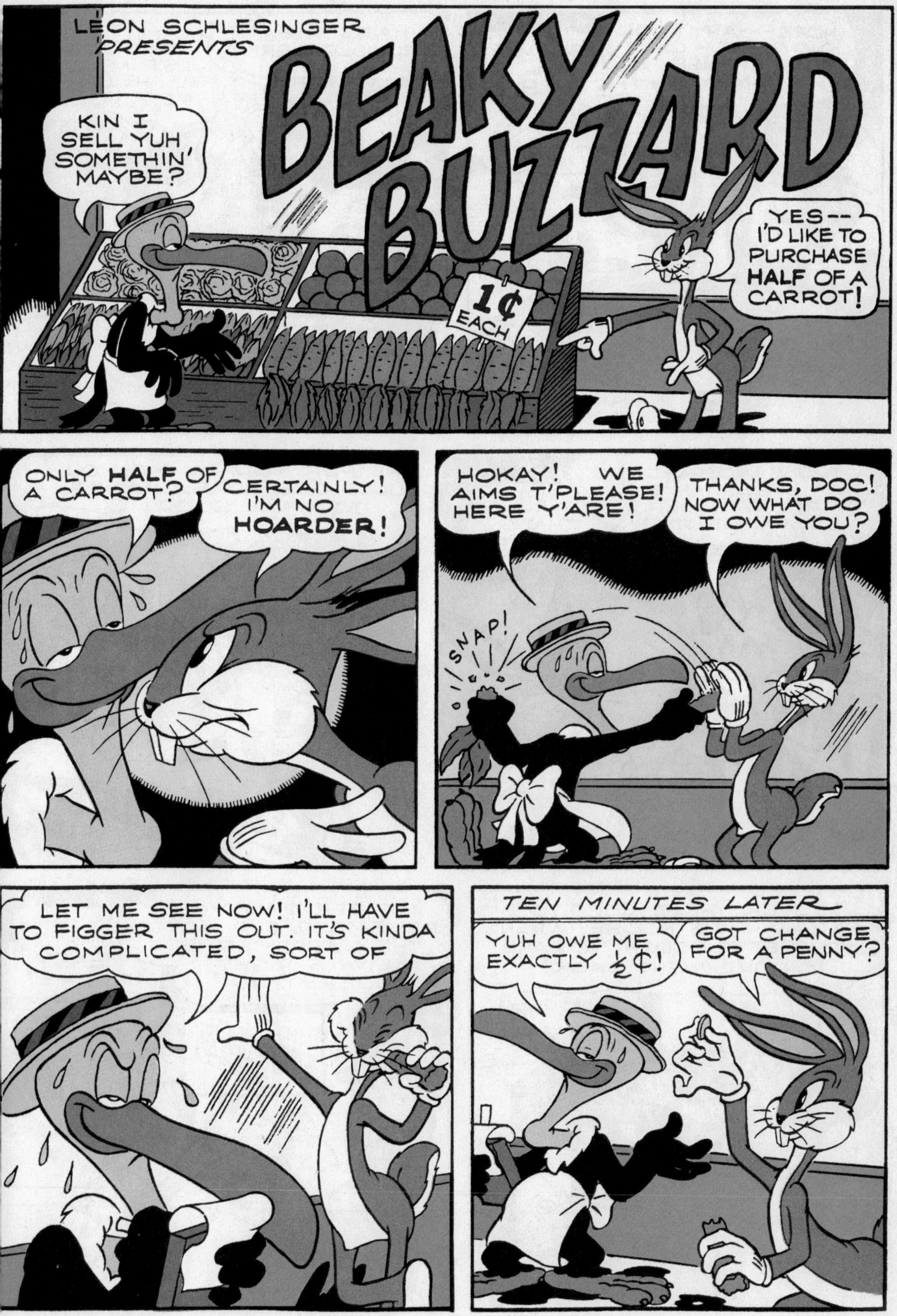
LEON SCHLESINGER PRESENTS
BEAKY BUZZARD
KIN I SELL YUH SOMETHIN' MAYBE?
YES-- I'D LIKE TO PURCHASE HALF OF A CARROT!
1¢ EACH
ONLY HALF OF A CARROT?
CERTAINLY! I'M NO HOARDER!
HOKAY! WE AIMS T'PLEASE! HERE Y'ARE!
SNAP!
THANKS, DOC! NOW WHAT DO I OWE YOU?
LET ME SEE NOW! I'LL HAVE TO FIGGER THIS OUT. IT'S KINDA COMPLICATED, SORT OF
TEN MINUTES LATER
YUH OWE ME EXACTLY ½¢!
GOT CHANGE FOR A PENNY?

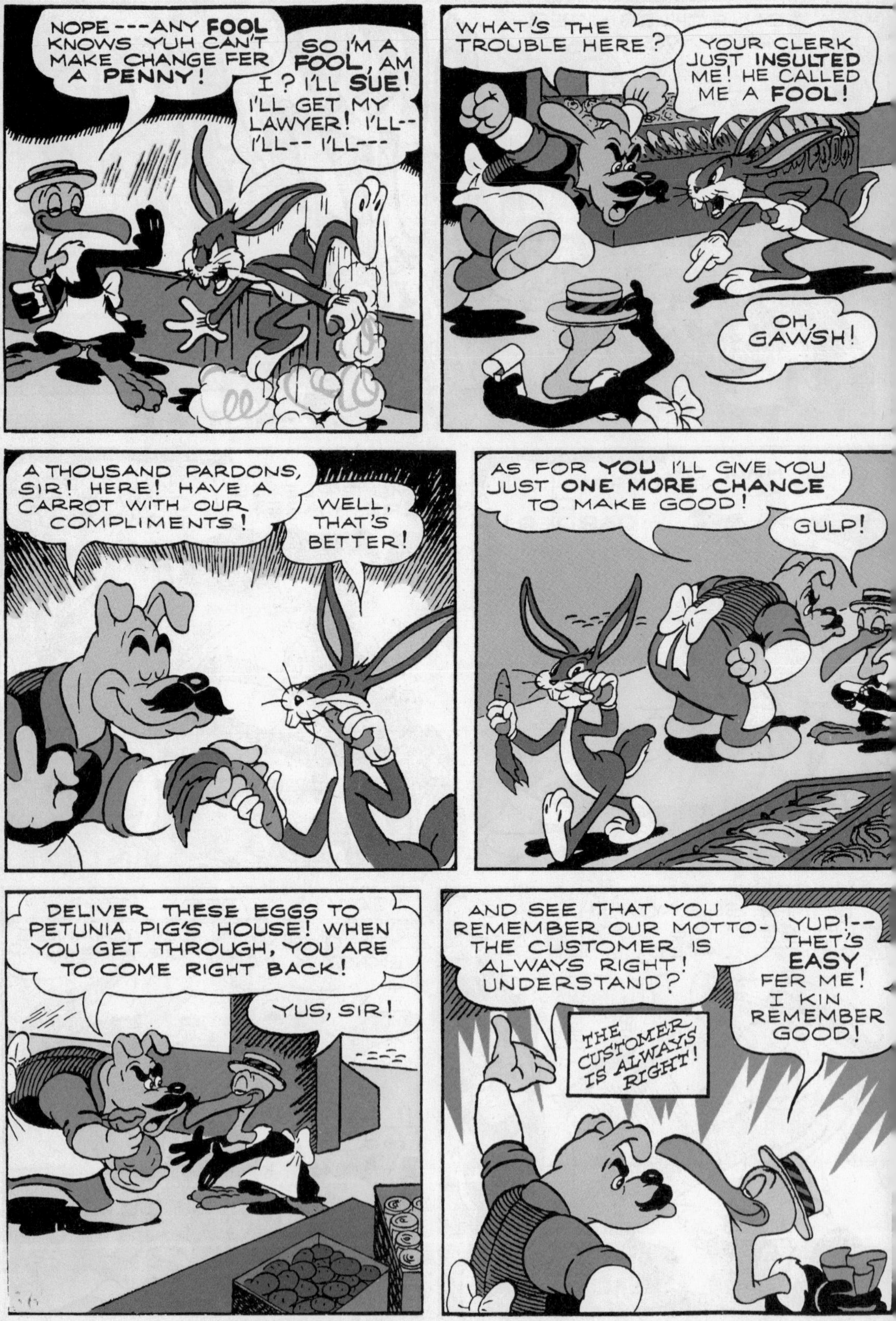
NOPE---ANY FOOL KNOWS YUH CAN'T MAKE CHANGE FER A PENNY!
SO I'M A FOOL, AM I? I'LL SUE! I'LL GET MY LAWYER! I'LL--I'LL-- I'LL---
WHAT'S THE TROUBLE HERE?
YOUR CLERK JUST INSULTED ME! HE CALLED ME A FOOL!
OH, GAWSH!
A THOUSAND PARDONS, SIR! HERE! HAVE A CARROT WITH OUR COMPLIMENTS!
WELL, THAT'S BETTER!
AS FOR YOU I'LL GIVE YOU JUST ONE MORE CHANCE TO MAKE GOOD!
GULP!
DELIVER THESE EGGS TO PETUNIA PIG'S HOUSE! WHEN YOU GET THROUGH, YOU ARE TO COME RIGHT BACK!
YUS, SIR!
AND SEE THAT YOU REMEMBER OUR MOTTO-THE CUSTOMER IS ALWAYS RIGHT! UNDERSTAND?
THE CUSTOMER IS ALWAYS RIGHT!
YUP!--THET'S EASY FER ME! I KIN REMEMBER GOOD!

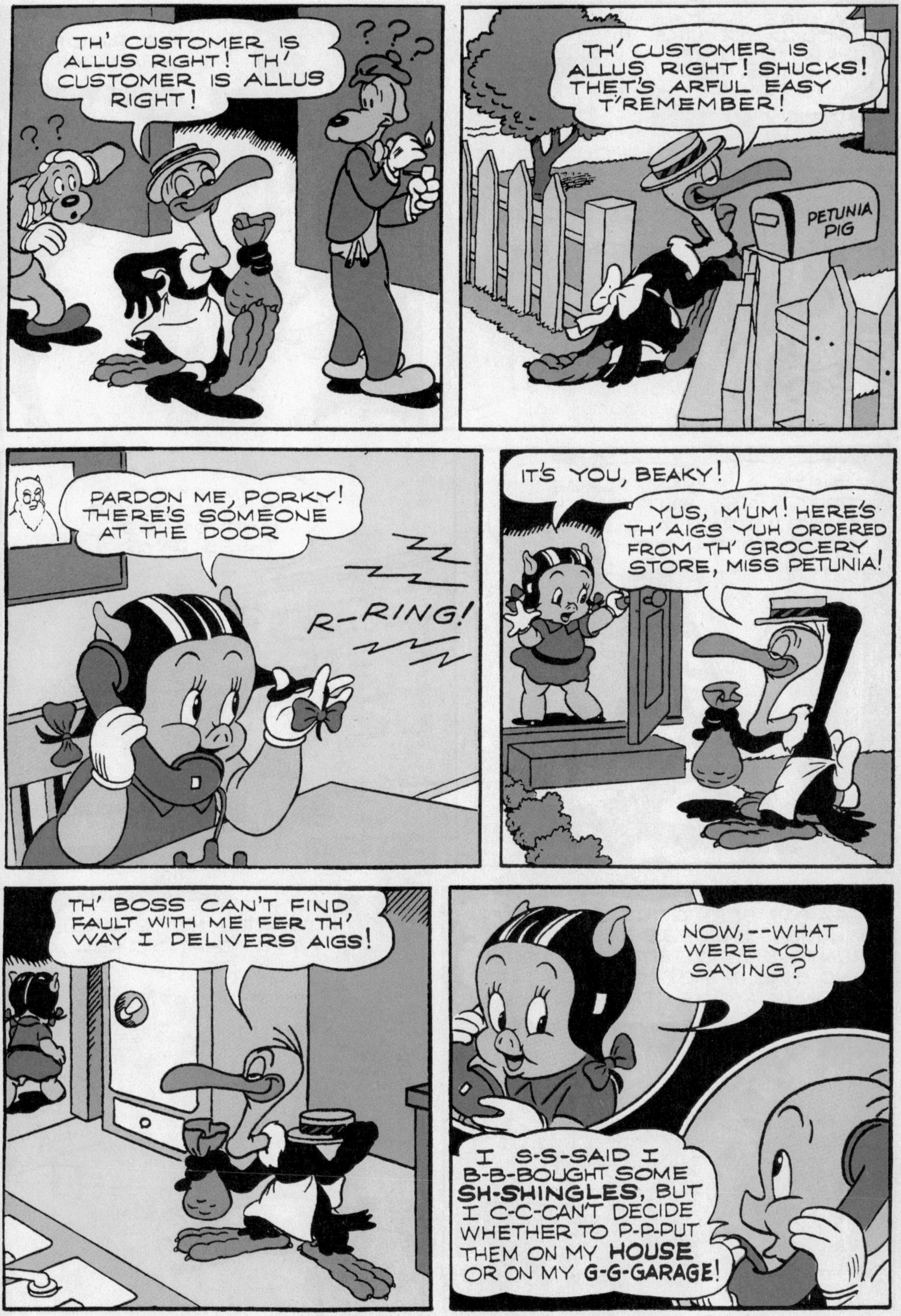
??
??
TH' CUSTOMER IS ALLUS RIGHT! TH' CUSTOMER IS ALLUS RIGHT!
TH' CUSTOMER IS ALLUS RIGHT! SHUCKS! THET'S ARFUL EASY T'REMEMBER!
PETUNIA PIG
PARDON ME, PORKY! THERE'S SOMEONE AT THE DOOR
R-RING!
IT'S YOU, BEAKY!
YUS, M'UM! HERE'S TH' AIGS YUH ORDERED FROM TH' GROCERY STORE, MISS PETUNIA!
TH' BOSS CAN'T FIND FAULT WITH ME FER TH' WAY I DELIVERS AIGS!
NOW,--WHAT WERE YOU SAYING?
I S-S-SAID I B-B-BOUGHT SOME SH-SHINGLES, BUT I C-C-CAN'T DECIDE WHETHER TO P-P-PUT THEM ON MY HOUSE OR ON MY G-G-GARAGE!

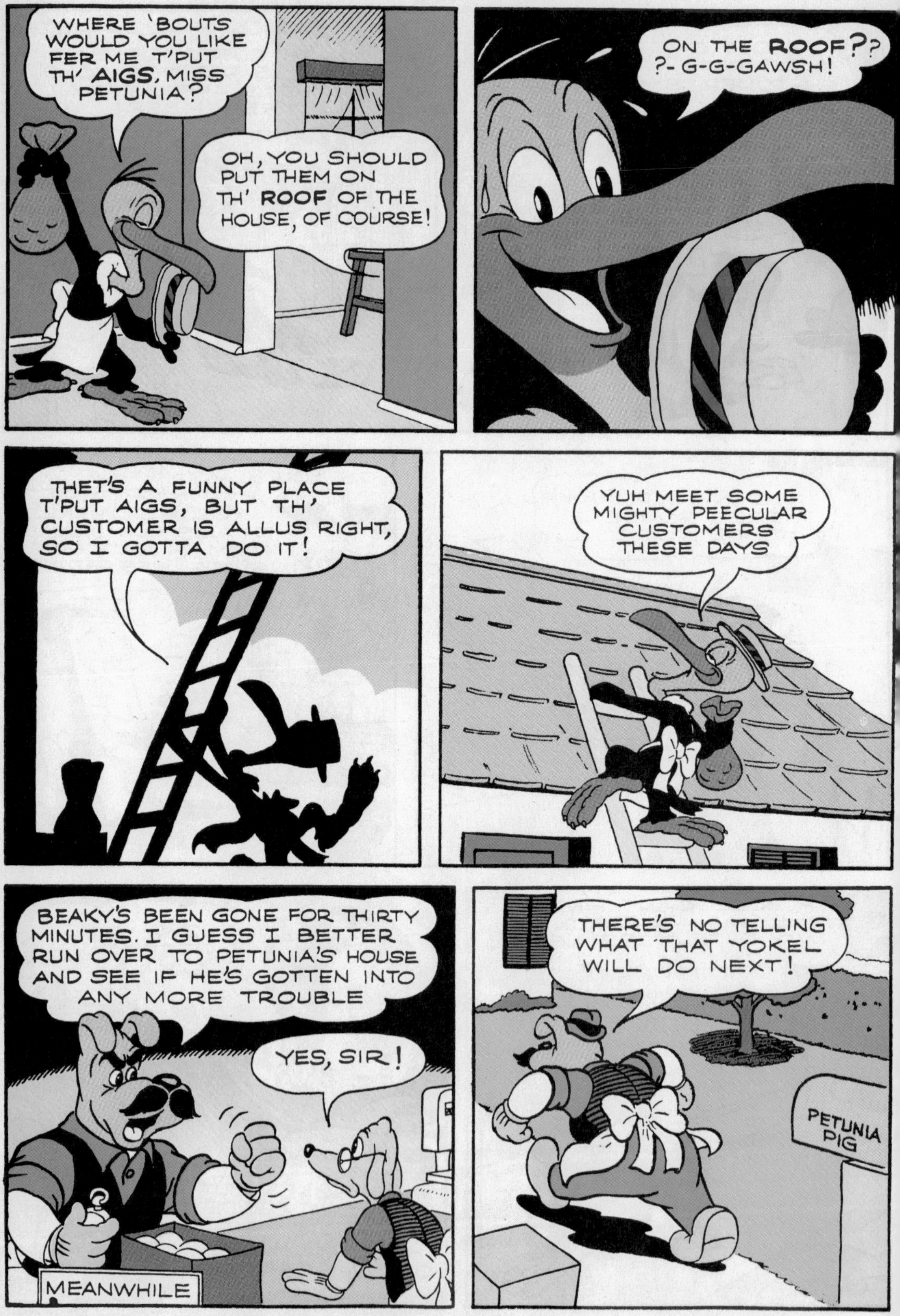

WHERE 'BOUTS WOULD YOU LIKE FER ME T'PUT TH' AIGS, MISS PETUNIA?
OH, YOU SHOULD PUT THEM ON TH' ROOF OF THE HOUSE, OF COURSE!
ON THE ROOF?? ?- G-G-GAWSH!
THET'S A FUNNY PLACE T'PUT AIGS, BUT TH' CUSTOMER IS ALLUS RIGHT, SO I GOTTA DO IT!
YUH MEET SOME MIGHTY PEECULAR CUSTOMERS THESE DAYS
MEANWHILE
BEAKY'S BEEN GONE FOR THIRTY MINUTES. I GUESS I BETTER RUN OVER TO PETUNIA'S HOUSE AND SEE IF HE'S GOTTEN INTO ANY MORE TROUBLE
YES, SIR!
THERE'S NO TELLING WHAT THAT YOKEL WILL DO NEXT!
PETUNIA PIG

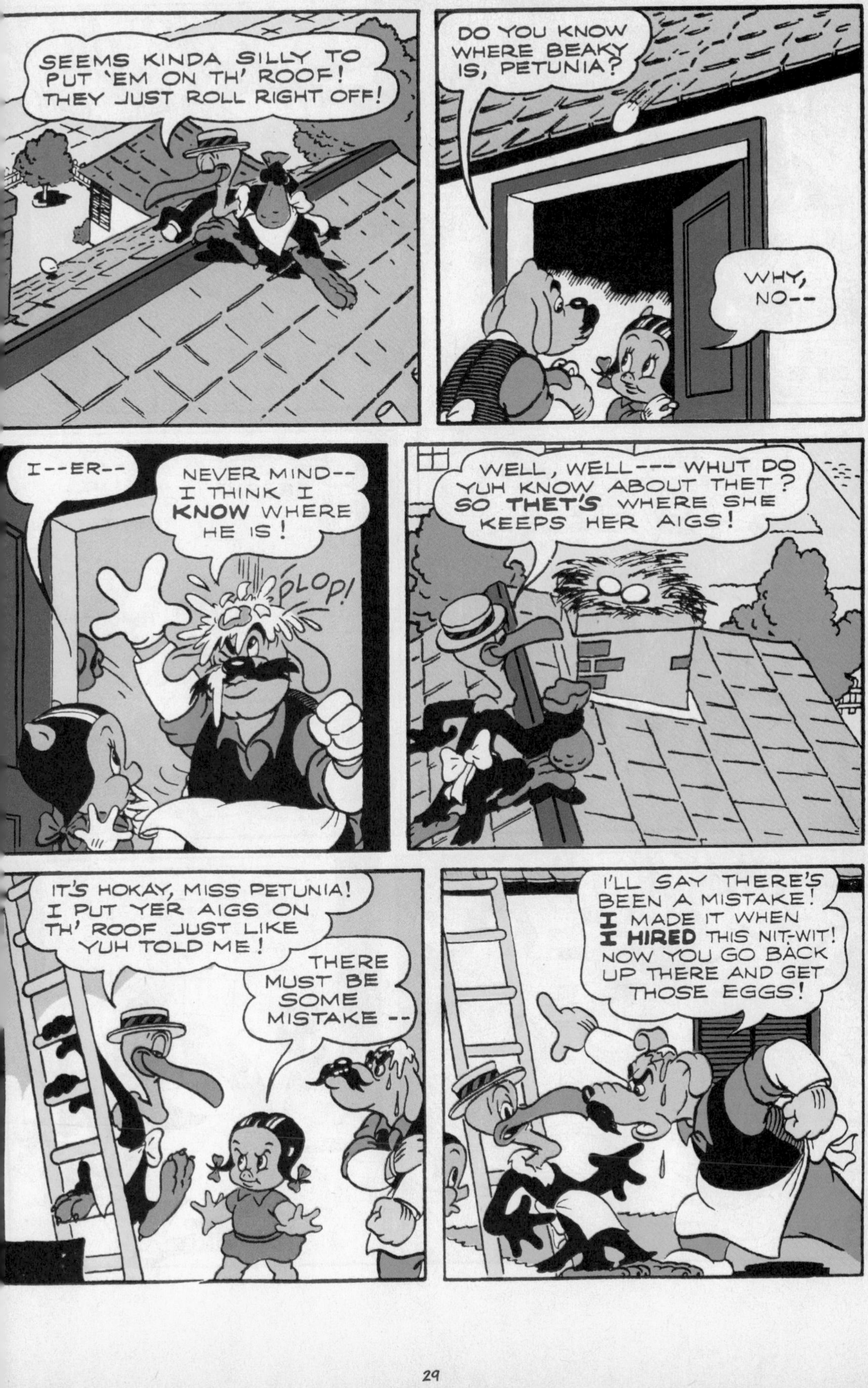
SEEMS KINDA SILLY TO PUT 'EM ON TH' ROOF! THEY JUST ROLL RIGHT OFF!
DO YOU KNOW WHERE BEAKY IS, PETUNIA?
WHY, NO--
I--ER--
NEVER MIND-- I THINK I **KNOW** WHERE HE IS!
PLOP!
WELL, WELL--- WHUT DO YUH KNOW ABOUT THET? SO **THET'S** WHERE SHE KEEPS HER AIGS!
IT'S HOKAY, MISS PETUNIA! I PUT YER AIGS ON TH' ROOF JUST LIKE YUH TOLD ME!
THERE MUST BE SOME MISTAKE --
I'LL SAY THERE'S BEEN A MISTAKE! **I** MADE IT WHEN **I HIRED** THIS NIT-WIT! NOW YOU GO BACK UP THERE AND GET THOSE EGGS!

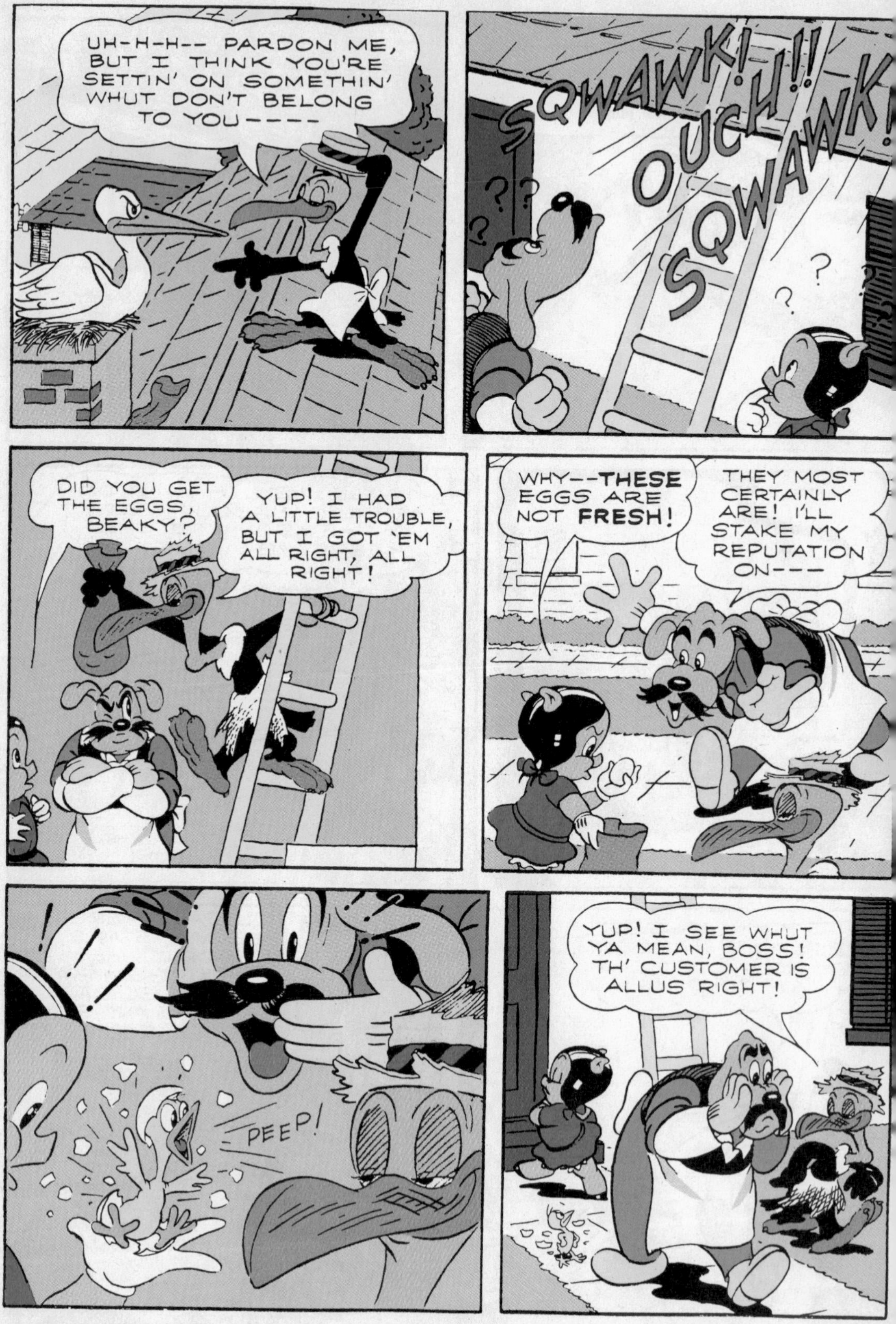
UH-H-H-- PARDON ME, BUT I THINK YOU'RE SETTIN' ON SOMETHIN' WHUT DON'T BELONG TO YOU----
SQWAWK!
OUCH!!
SQWAWK!
SQWAWK!
DID YOU GET THE EGGS, BEAKY?
YUP! I HAD A LITTLE TROUBLE, BUT I GOT 'EM ALL RIGHT, ALL RIGHT!
WHY--THESE EGGS ARE NOT FRESH!
THEY MOST CERTAINLY ARE! I'LL STAKE MY REPUTATION ON---
PEEP!
YUP! I SEE WHUT YA MEAN, BOSS! TH' CUSTOMER IS ALLUS RIGHT!

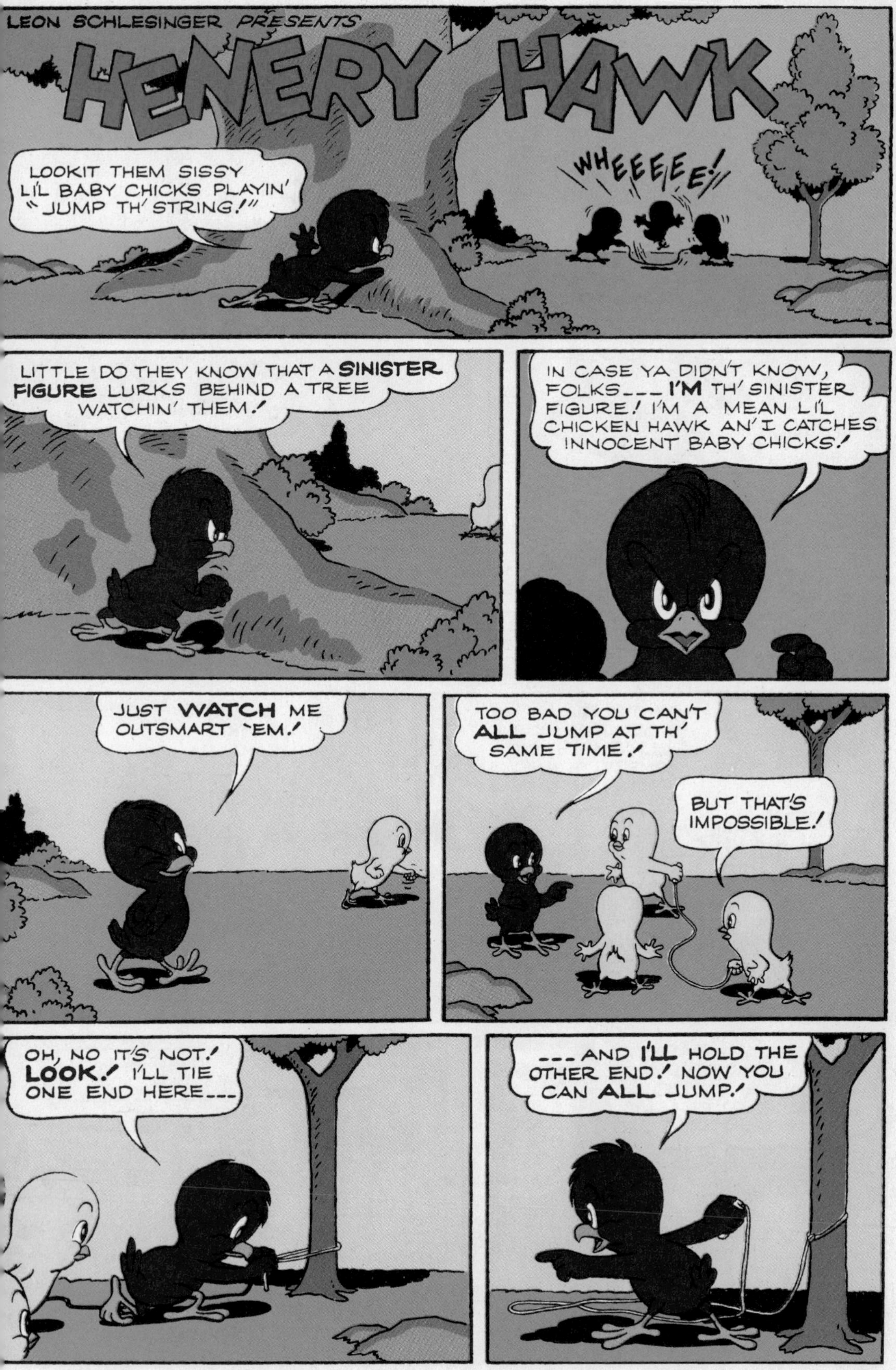
LEON SCHLESINGER PRESENTS
HENERY HAWK
LOOKIT THEM SISSY LI'L BABY CHICKS PLAYIN' "JUMP TH' STRING!"
WHEEEEE!
LITTLE DO THEY KNOW THAT A SINISTER FIGURE LURKS BEHIND A TREE WATCHIN' THEM!
IN CASE YA DIDN'T KNOW, FOLKS--- I'M TH' SINISTER FIGURE! I'M A MEAN LI'L CHICKEN HAWK AN' I CATCHES INNOCENT BABY CHICKS!
JUST WATCH ME OUTSMART 'EM!
TOO BAD YOU CAN'T ALL JUMP AT TH' SAME TIME!
BUT THAT'S IMPOSSIBLE!
OH, NO IT'S NOT! LOOK! I'LL TIE ONE END HERE---
---AND I'LL HOLD THE OTHER END! NOW YOU CAN ALL JUMP!

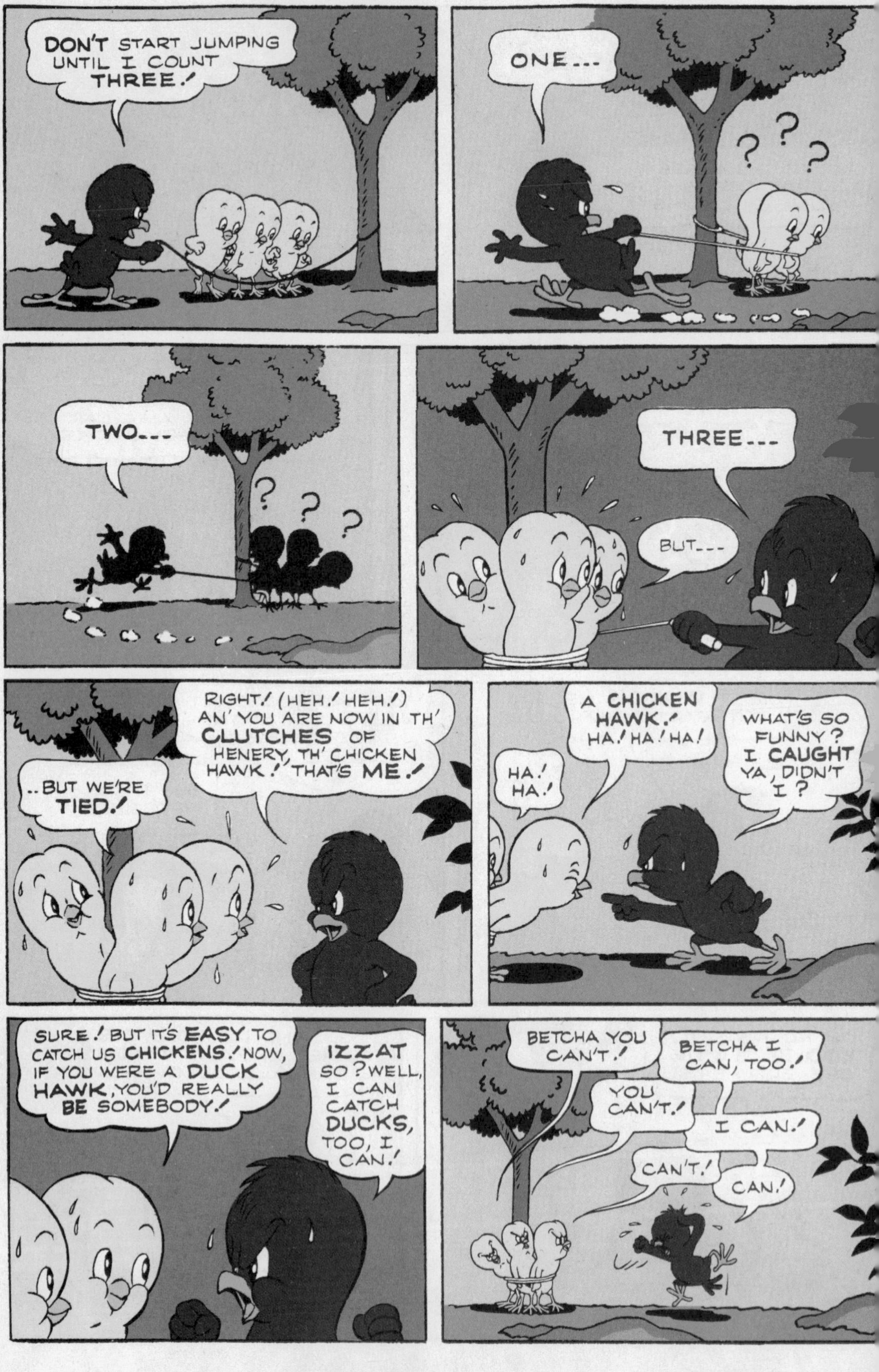
DON'T START JUMPING UNTIL I COUNT THREE.!
ONE...
TWO...
THREE...
BUT...
..BUT WE'RE TIED.!
RIGHT.! (HEH.! HEH.!) AN' YOU ARE NOW IN TH' CLUTCHES OF HENERY, TH' CHICKEN HAWK.! THAT'S ME.!
HA.! HA.!
A CHICKEN HAWK.! HA.! HA.! HA.!
WHAT'S SO FUNNY? I CAUGHT YA, DIDN'T I?
SURE.! BUT IT'S EASY TO CATCH US CHICKENS.! NOW, IF YOU WERE A DUCK HAWK, YOU'D REALLY BE SOMEBODY.!
IZZAT SO? WELL, I CAN CATCH DUCKS, TOO, I CAN.!
BETCHA YOU CAN'T.!
BETCHA I CAN, TOO.!
YOU CAN'T.!
I CAN.!
CAN'T.!
CAN.!

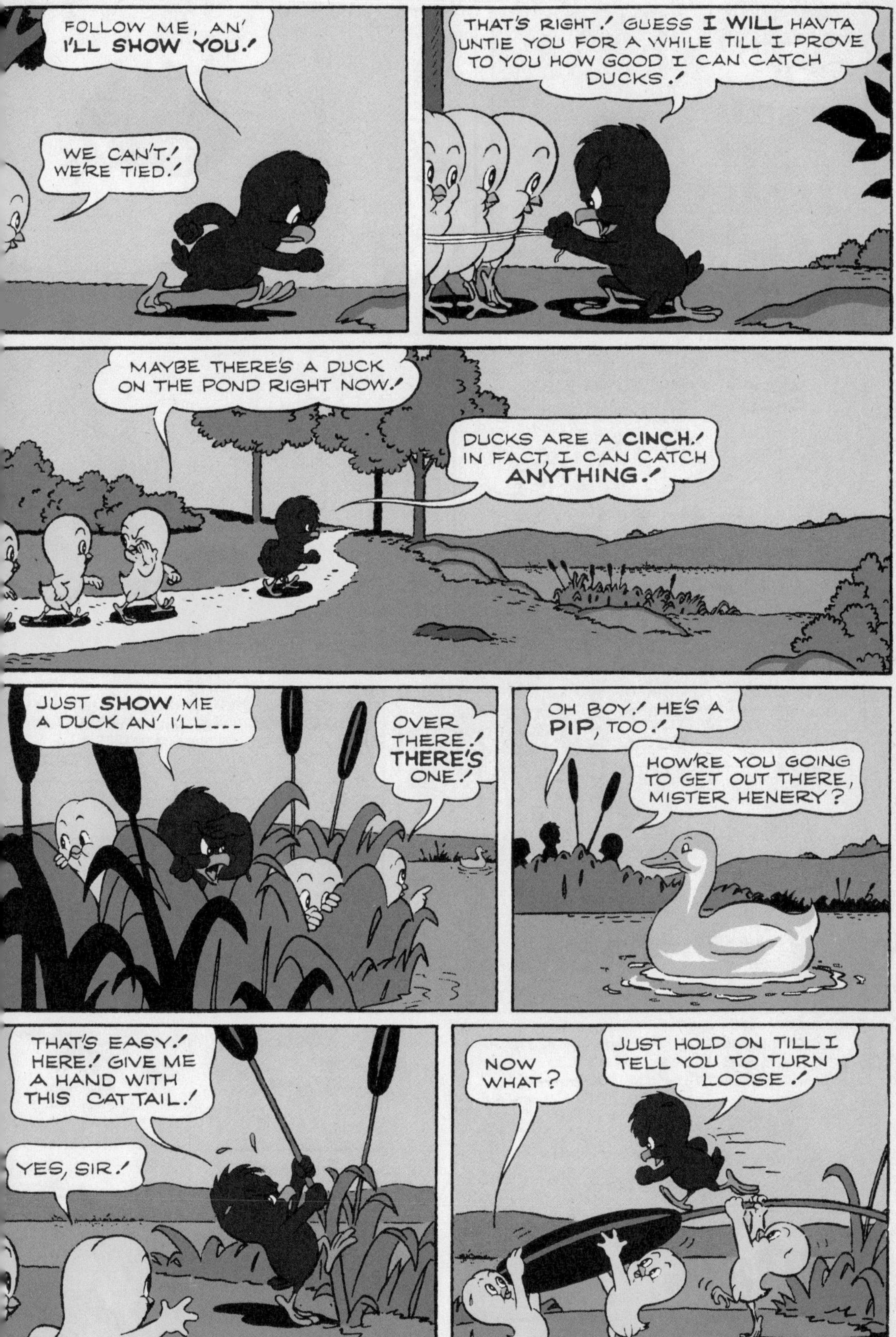
FOLLOW ME, AN' I'LL SHOW YOU.!
WE CAN'T.! WE'RE TIED.!
THAT'S RIGHT.! GUESS I WILL HAVTA UNTIE YOU FOR A WHILE TILL I PROVE TO YOU HOW GOOD I CAN CATCH DUCKS.!
MAYBE THERE'S A DUCK ON THE POND RIGHT NOW.!
DUCKS ARE A CINCH.! IN FACT, I CAN CATCH ANYTHING.!
JUST SHOW ME A DUCK AN' I'LL...
OVER THERE.! THERE'S ONE.!
OH BOY.! HE'S A PIP, TOO.!
HOW'RE YOU GOING TO GET OUT THERE, MISTER HENERY?
THAT'S EASY.! HERE.! GIVE ME A HAND WITH THIS CATTAIL.!
YES, SIR.!
NOW WHAT?
JUST HOLD ON TILL I TELL YOU TO TURN LOOSE.!

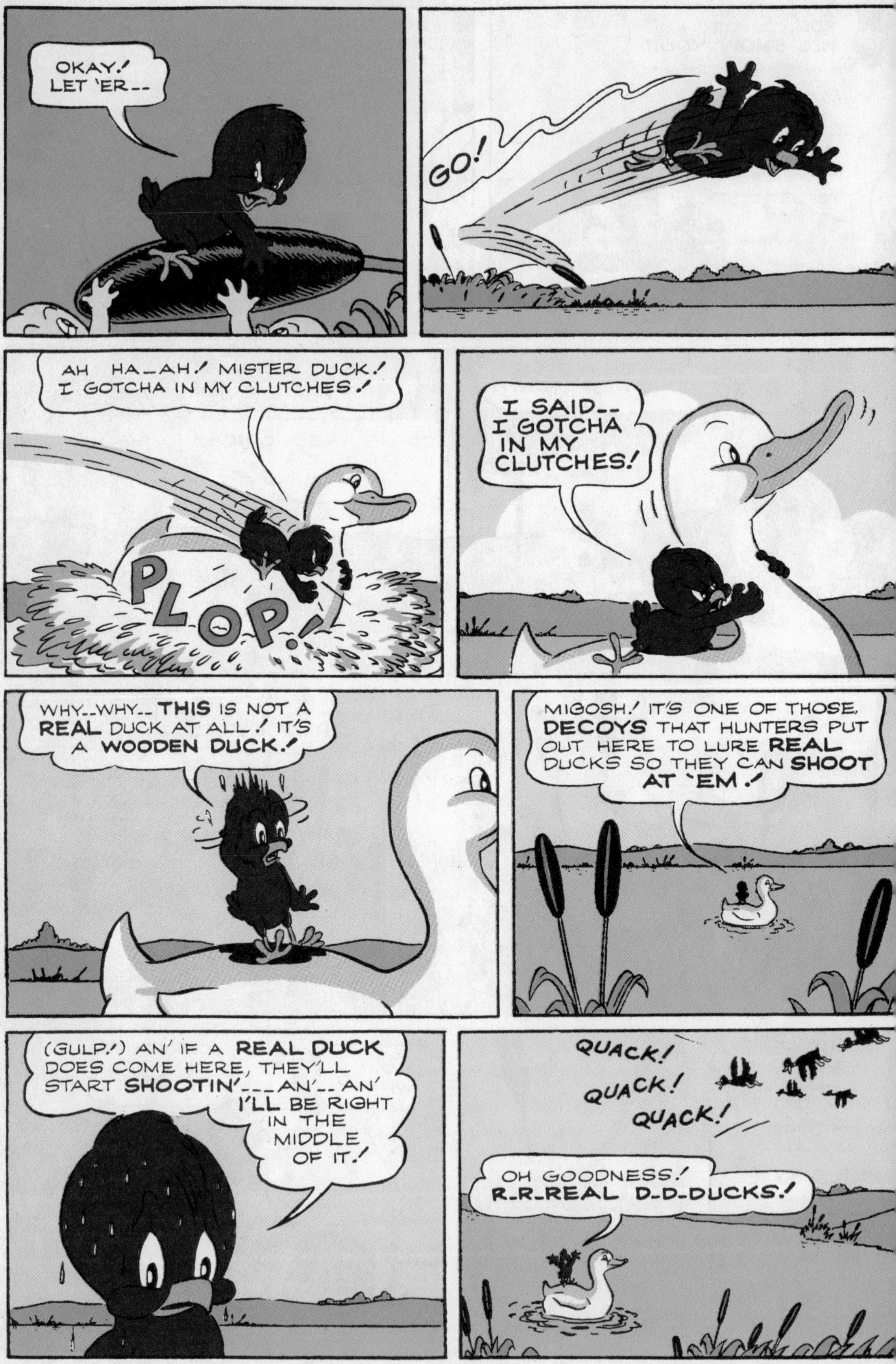
OKAY! LET 'ER--
GO!
AH HA-AH! MISTER DUCK! I GOTCHA IN MY CLUTCHES!
PLOP!
I SAID-- I GOTCHA IN MY CLUTCHES!
WHY--WHY-- THIS IS NOT A REAL DUCK AT ALL! IT'S A WOODEN DUCK!
MIGOSH! IT'S ONE OF THOSE DECOYS THAT HUNTERS PUT OUT HERE TO LURE REAL DUCKS SO THEY CAN SHOOT AT 'EM!
(GULP!) AN' IF A REAL DUCK DOES COME HERE, THEY'LL START SHOOTIN'---AN'--AN' I'LL BE RIGHT IN THE MIDDLE OF IT!
QUACK!
QUACK!
QUACK!
OH GOODNESS! R-R-REAL D-D-DUCKS!

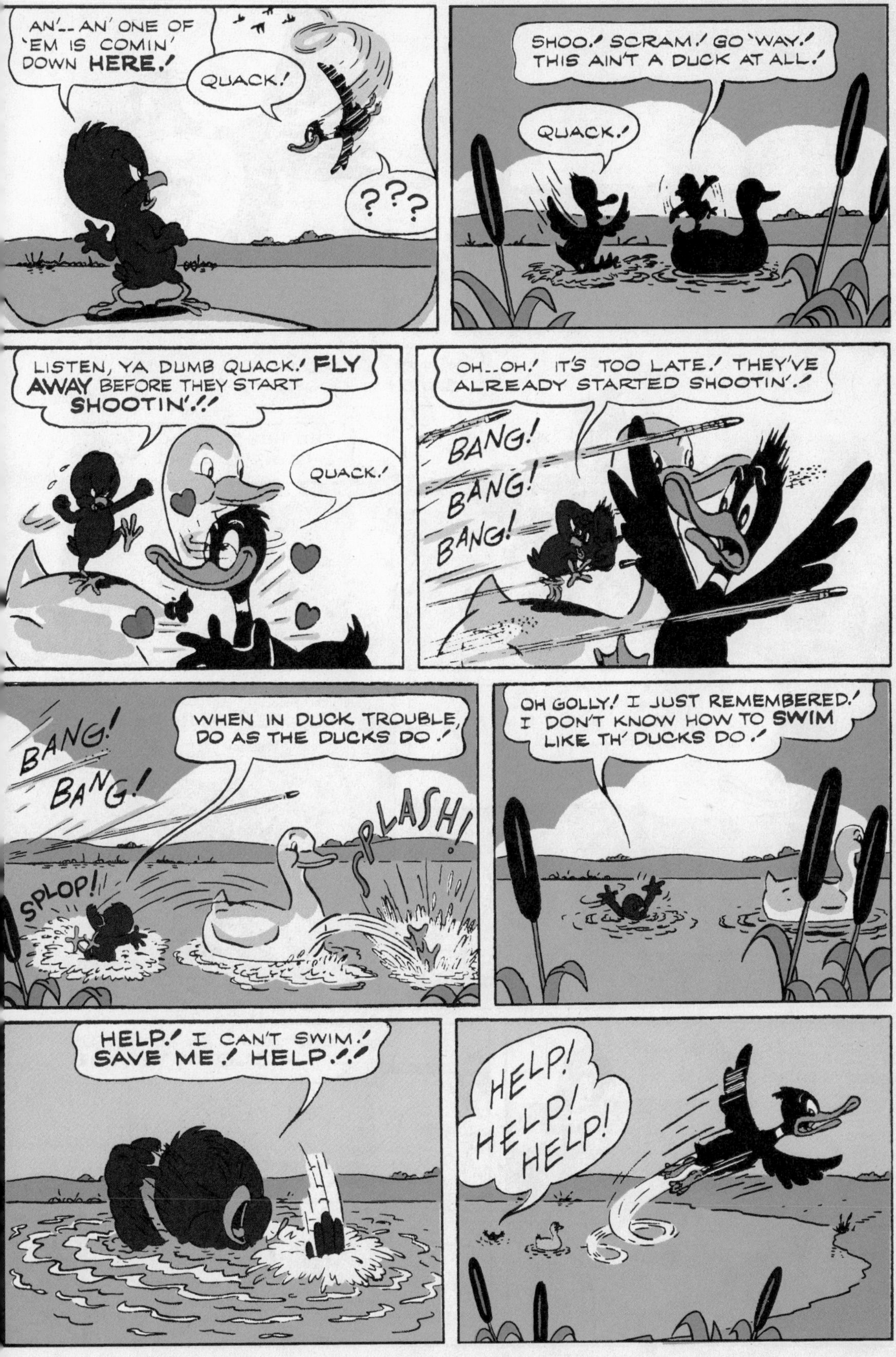
AN'-- AN' ONE OF 'EM IS COMIN' DOWN HERE.!
QUACK.!
???
SHOO.! SCRAM.! GO 'WAY.! THIS AIN'T A DUCK AT ALL.!
QUACK.!
LISTEN, YA DUMB QUACK.! FLY AWAY BEFORE THEY START SHOOTIN'.!!
QUACK.!
OH--OH.! IT'S TOO LATE.! THEY'VE ALREADY STARTED SHOOTIN'.!
BANG! BANG! BANG!
BANG! BANG!
WHEN IN DUCK TROUBLE, DO AS THE DUCKS DO.!
SPLASH!
SPLOP!
OH GOLLY.! I JUST REMEMBERED.! I DON'T KNOW HOW TO SWIM LIKE TH' DUCKS DO.!
HELP.! I CAN'T SWIM.! SAVE ME.! HELP.!.!
HELP! HELP! HELP!

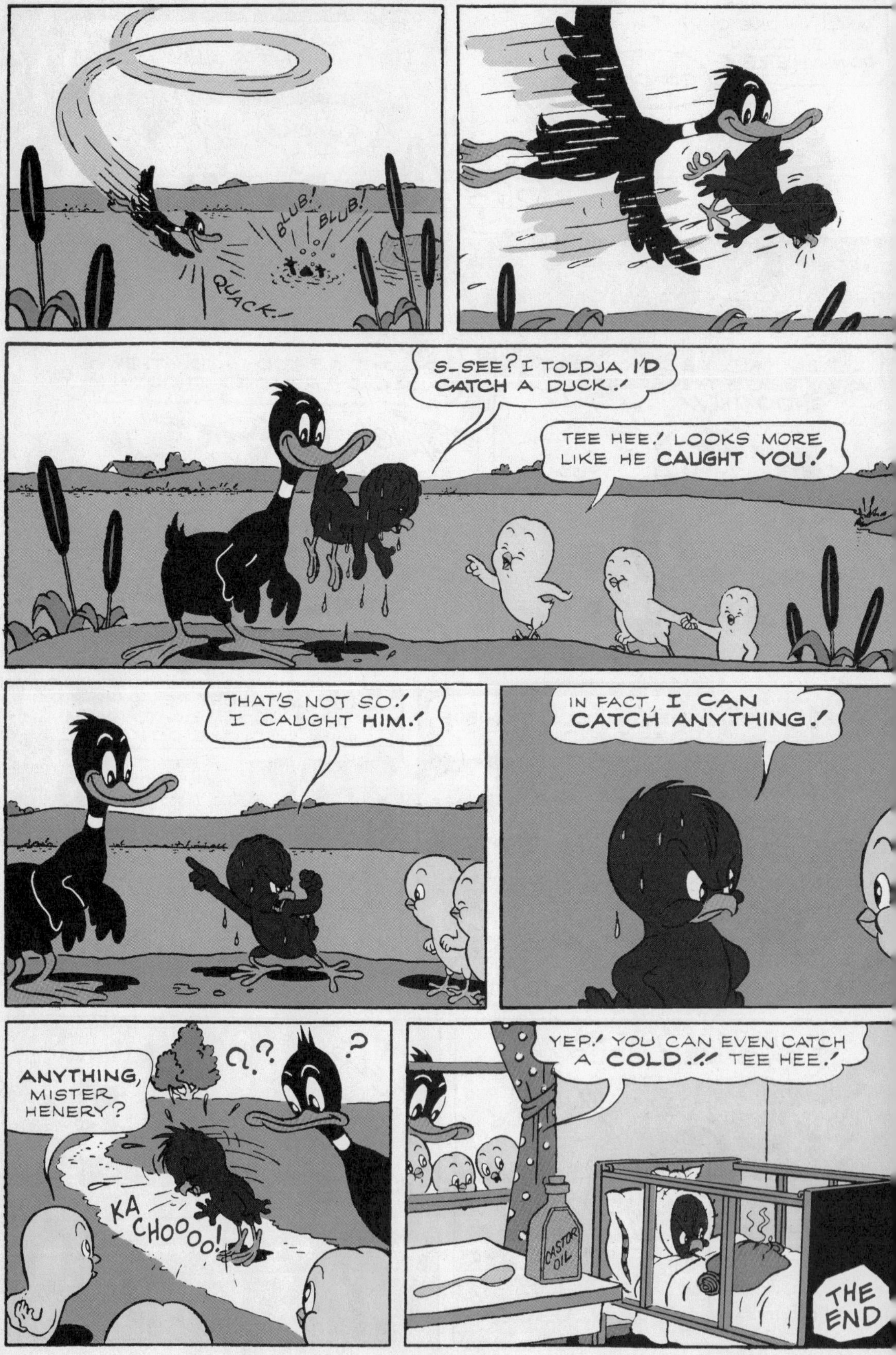
BLUB! BLUB!
QUACK!
S-SEE? I TOLDJA I'D CATCH A DUCK!
TEE HEE! LOOKS MORE LIKE HE CAUGHT YOU!
THAT'S NOT SO! I CAUGHT HIM!
IN FACT, I CAN CATCH ANYTHING!
ANYTHING, MISTER HENERY?
?? ?
KA CHOOOOO!
YEP! YOU CAN EVEN CATCH A COLD!!! TEE HEE!
CASTOR OIL
THE END

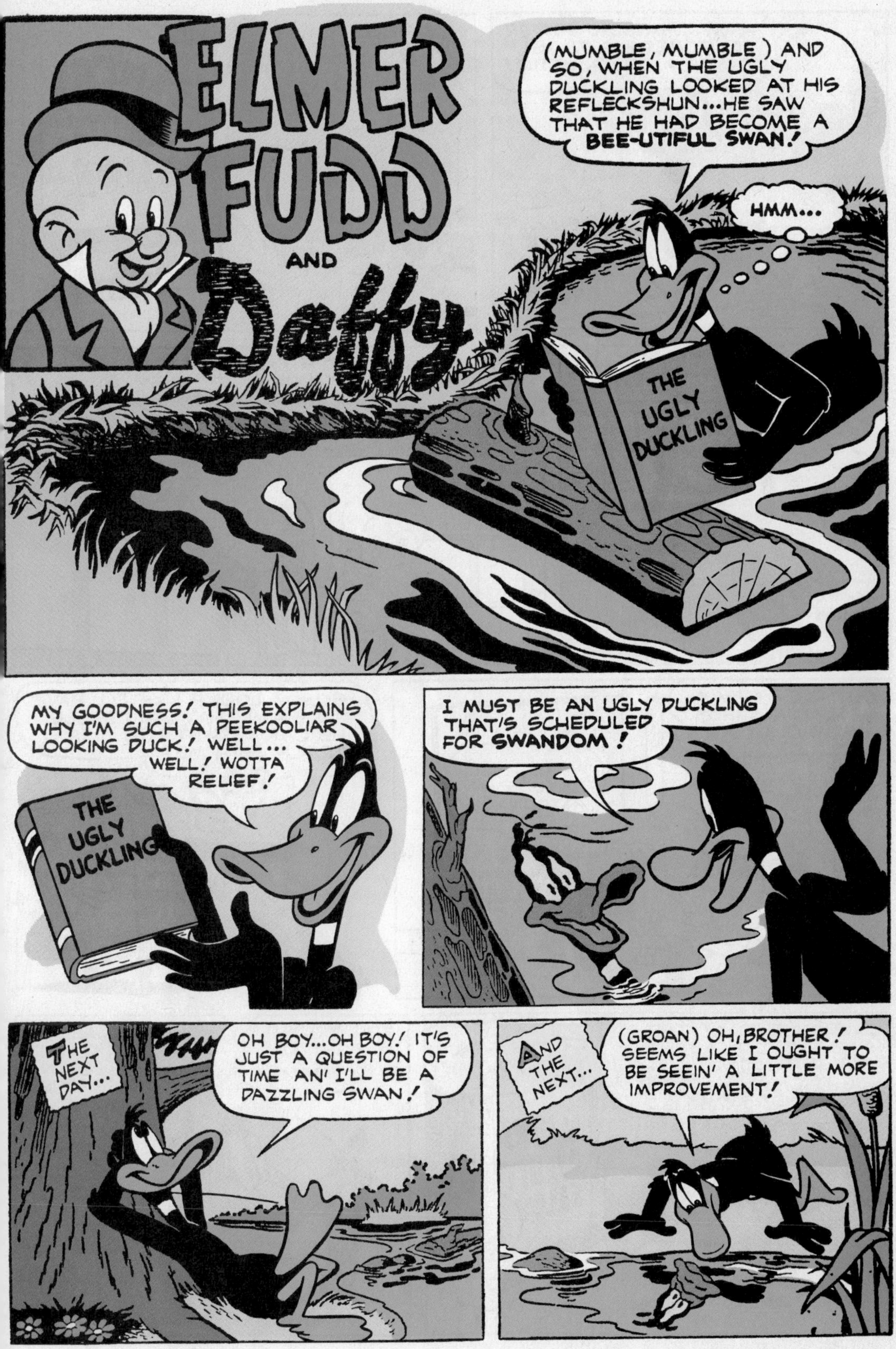
ELMER FUDD
AND
Daffy
(MUMBLE, MUMBLE) AND SO, WHEN THE UGLY DUCKLING LOOKED AT HIS REFLECKSHUN...HE SAW THAT HE HAD BECOME A BEE-UTIFUL SWAN!
HMM...
THE UGLY DUCKLING
MY GOODNESS! THIS EXPLAINS WHY I'M SUCH A PEEKOOLIAR LOOKING DUCK! WELL... WELL! WOTTA RELIEF!
THE UGLY DUCKLING
I MUST BE AN UGLY DUCKLING THAT'S SCHEDULED FOR SWANDOM!
THE NEXT DAY...
OH BOY...OH BOY! IT'S JUST A QUESTION OF TIME AN' I'LL BE A DAZZLING SWAN!
AND THE NEXT...
(GROAN) OH, BROTHER! SEEMS LIKE I OUGHT TO BE SEEIN' A LITTLE MORE IMPROVEMENT!

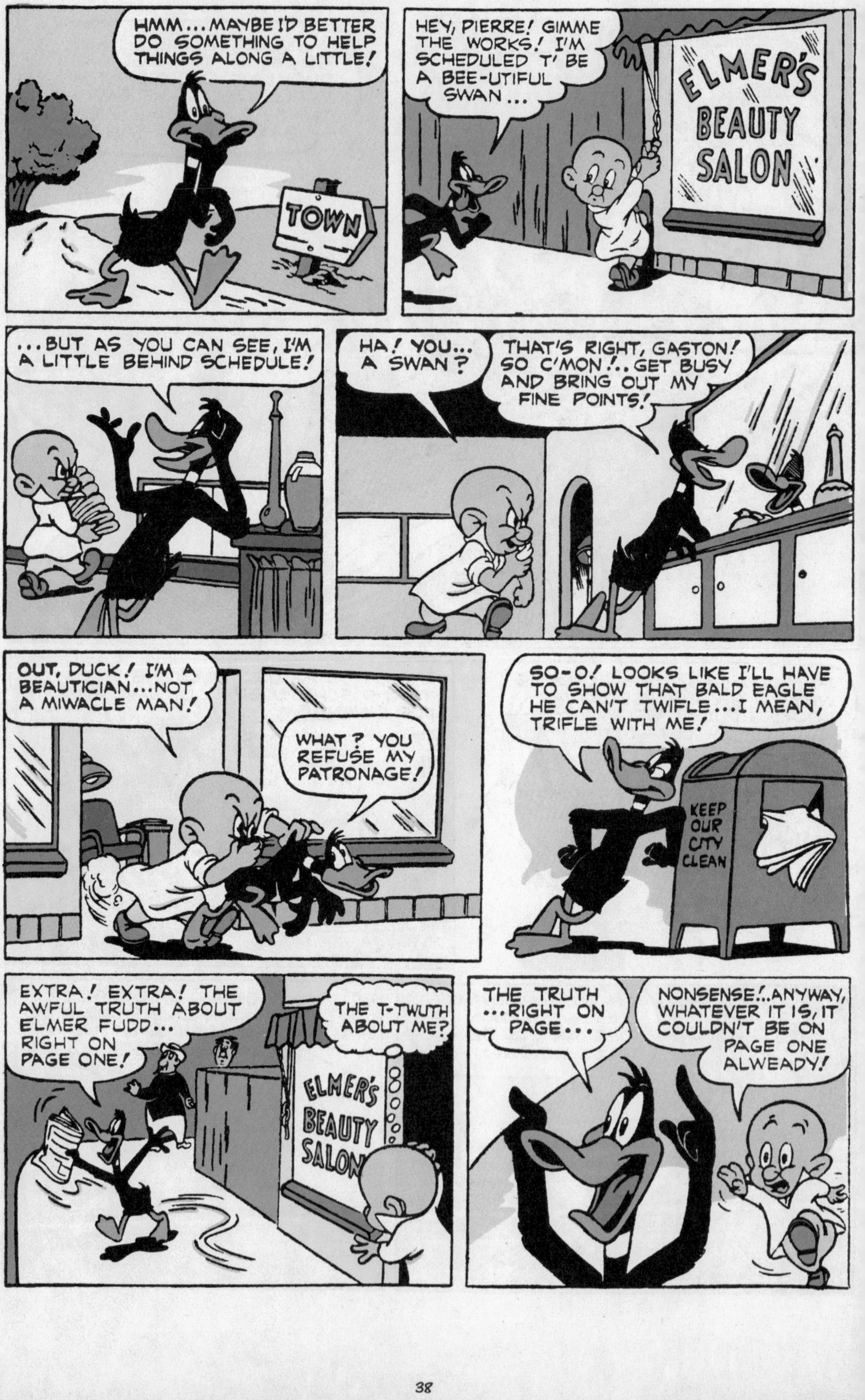
HMM...MAYBE I'D BETTER DO SOMETHING TO HELP THINGS ALONG A LITTLE!
TOWN
HEY, PIERRE! GIMME THE WORKS! I'M SCHEDULED T' BE A BEE-UTIFUL SWAN...
ELMER'S BEAUTY SALON
...BUT AS YOU CAN SEE, I'M A LITTLE BEHIND SCHEDULE!
HA! YOU... A SWAN?
THAT'S RIGHT, GASTON! SO C'MON!..GET BUSY AND BRING OUT MY FINE POINTS!
OUT, DUCK! I'M A BEAUTICIAN...NOT A MIWACLE MAN!
WHAT? YOU REFUSE MY PATRONAGE!
SO-O! LOOKS LIKE I'LL HAVE TO SHOW THAT BALD EAGLE HE CAN'T TWIFLE...I MEAN, TRIFLE WITH ME!
KEEP OUR CITY CLEAN
EXTRA! EXTRA! THE AWFUL TRUTH ABOUT ELMER FUDD... RIGHT ON PAGE ONE!
THE T-TWUTH ABOUT ME?
ELMER'S BEAUTY SALON
THE TRUTH ...RIGHT ON PAGE...
NONSENSE!..ANYWAY, WHATEVER IT IS, IT COULDN'T BE ON PAGE ONE ALWEADY!

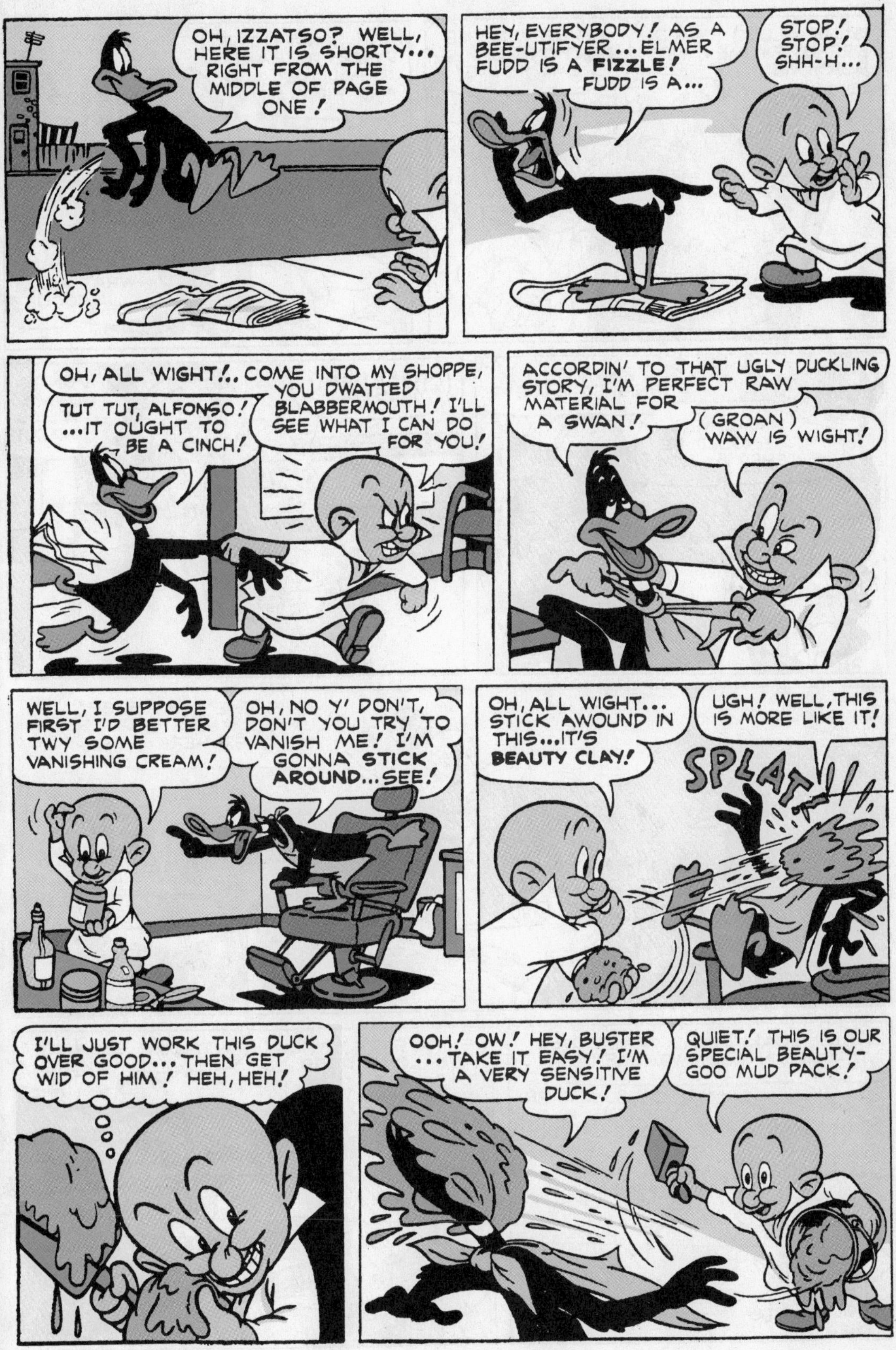

OH, IZZATSO? WELL, HERE IT IS SHORTY... RIGHT FROM THE MIDDLE OF PAGE ONE!
HEY, EVERYBODY! AS A BEE-UTIFYER ... ELMER FUDD IS A **FIZZLE!** FUDD IS A...
STOP! STOP! SHH-H...
OH, ALL WIGHT!.. COME INTO MY SHOPPE, YOU DWATTED BLABBERMOUTH! I'LL SEE WHAT I CAN DO FOR YOU!
TUT TUT, ALFONSO! ...IT OUGHT TO BE A CINCH!
ACCORDIN' TO THAT UGLY DUCKLING STORY, I'M PERFECT RAW MATERIAL FOR A SWAN!
(GROAN) WAW IS WIGHT!
WELL, I SUPPOSE FIRST I'D BETTER TWY SOME VANISHING CREAM!
OH, NO Y' DON'T, DON'T YOU TRY TO VANISH ME! I'M GONNA **STICK AROUND**...SEE!
OH, ALL WIGHT... STICK AWOUND IN THIS...IT'S **BEAUTY CLAY!**
UGH! WELL, THIS IS MORE LIKE IT!
SPLAT
I'LL JUST WORK THIS DUCK OVER GOOD... THEN GET WID OF HIM! HEH, HEH!
OOH! OW! HEY, BUSTER ... TAKE IT EASY! I'M A VERY SENSITIVE DUCK!
QUIET! THIS IS OUR SPECIAL BEAUTY-GOO MUD PACK!

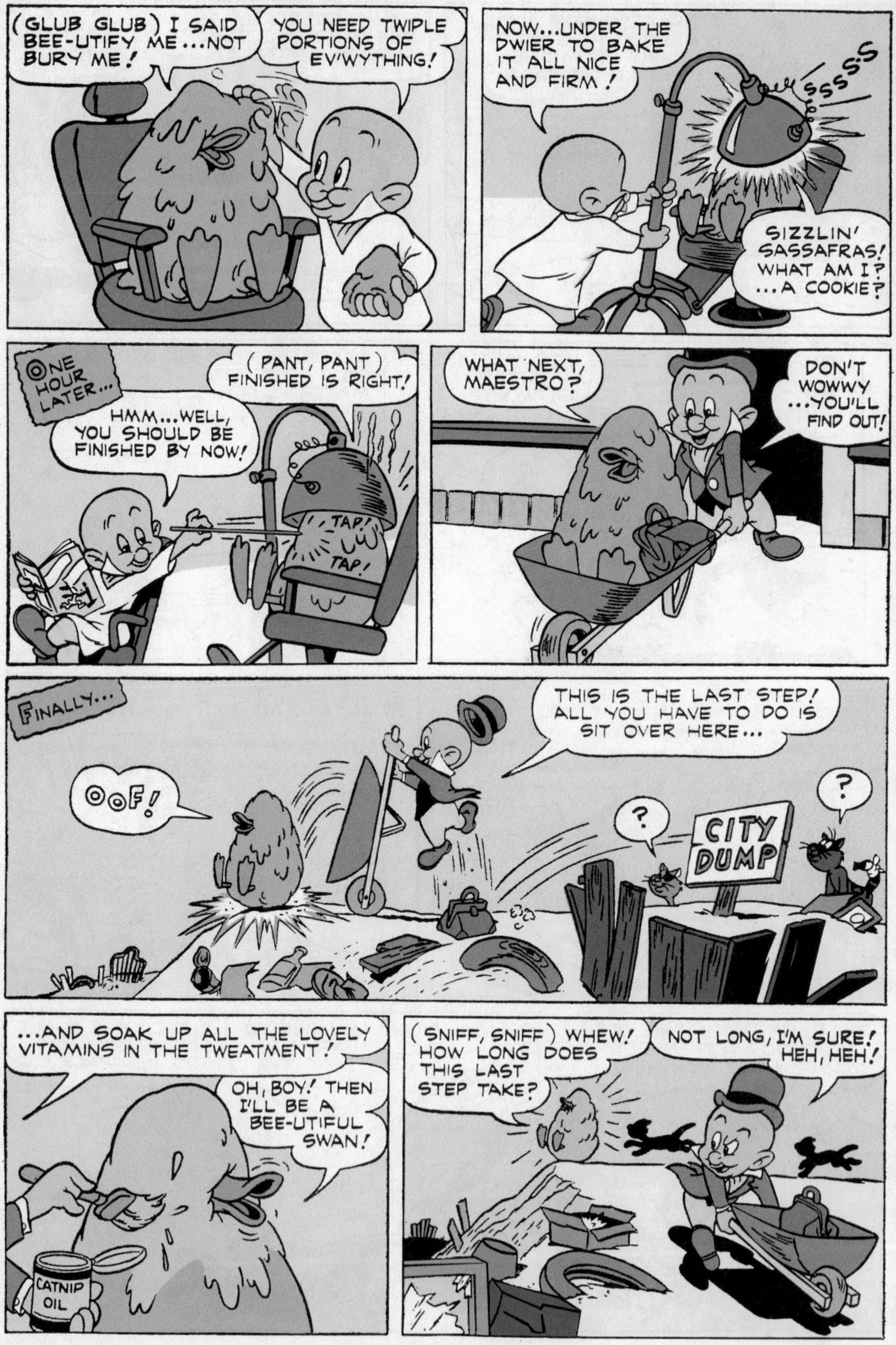
(GLUB GLUB) I SAID BEE-UTIFY ME...NOT BURY ME!
YOU NEED TWIPLE PORTIONS OF EV'WYTHING!
NOW...UNDER THE DWIER TO BAKE IT ALL NICE AND FIRM!
SSSSS
SIZZLIN' SASSAFRAS! WHAT AM I? ...A COOKIE?
ONE HOUR LATER...
HMM...WELL, YOU SHOULD BE FINISHED BY NOW!
(PANT, PANT) FINISHED IS RIGHT!
TAP! TAP!
WHAT NEXT, MAESTRO?
DON'T WOWWY ...YOU'LL FIND OUT!
FINALLY...
THIS IS THE LAST STEP! ALL YOU HAVE TO DO IS SIT OVER HERE...
OOF!
?
?
CITY DUMP
...AND SOAK UP ALL THE LOVELY VITAMINS IN THE TWEATMENT!
OH, BOY! THEN I'LL BE A BEE-UTIFUL SWAN!
CATNIP OIL
(SNIFF, SNIFF) WHEW! HOW LONG DOES THIS LAST STEP TAKE?
NOT LONG, I'M SURE! HEH, HEH!

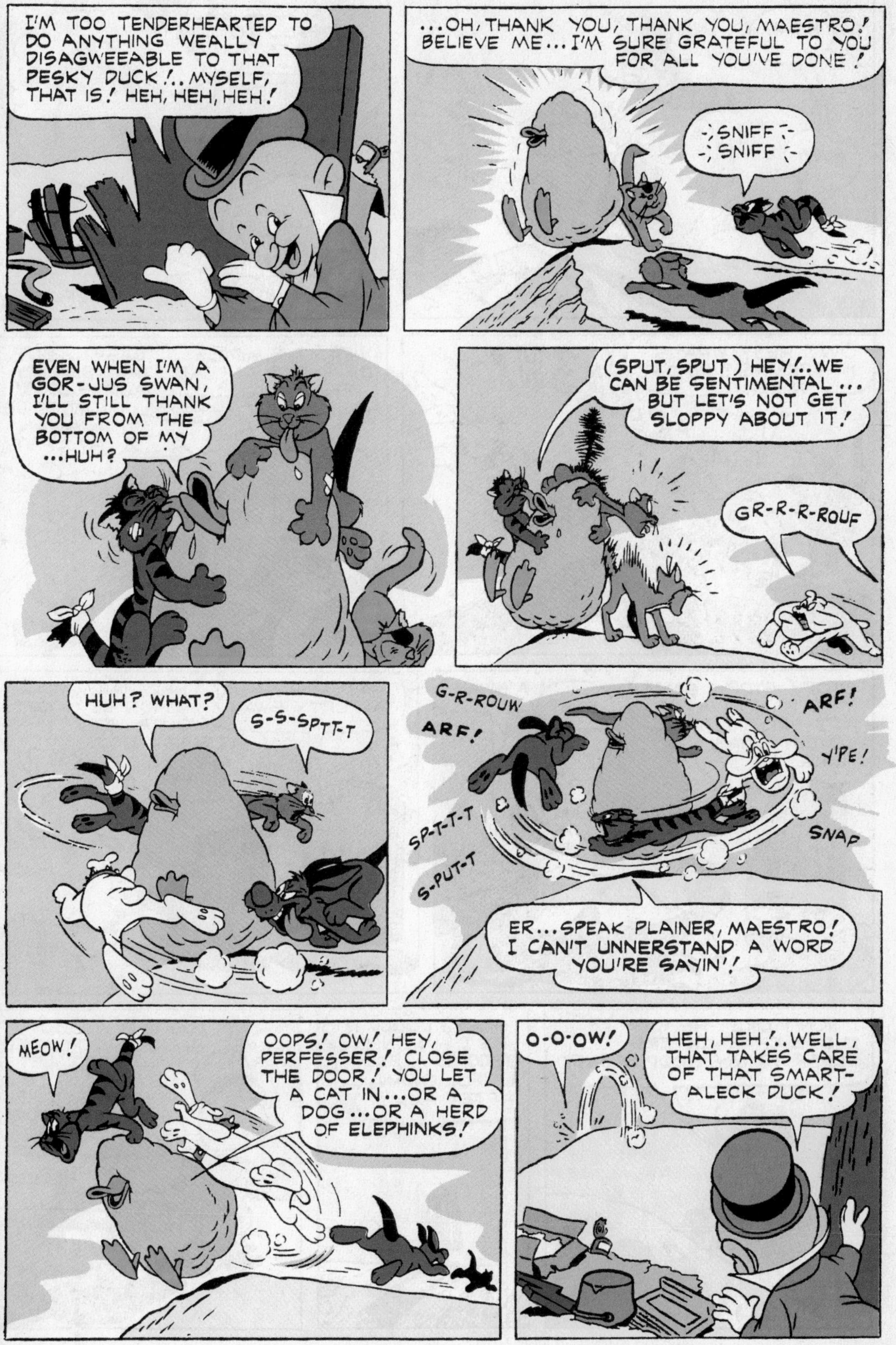
I'M TOO TENDERHEARTED TO DO ANYTHING WEALLY DISAGWEEABLE TO THAT PESKY DUCK!.. MYSELF, THAT IS! HEH, HEH, HEH!
...OH, THANK YOU, THANK YOU, MAESTRO! BELIEVE ME... I'M SURE GRATEFUL TO YOU FOR ALL YOU'VE DONE!
SNIFF SNIFF
EVEN WHEN I'M A GOR-JUS SWAN, I'LL STILL THANK YOU FROM THE BOTTOM OF MY ...HUH?
(SPUT, SPUT) HEY!..WE CAN BE SENTIMENTAL... BUT LET'S NOT GET SLOPPY ABOUT IT!
GR-R-R-ROUF
HUH? WHAT?
S-S-SPTT-T
G-R-ROUW
ARF!
ARF!
Y'PE!
SP-T-T-T
S-PUT-T
SNAP
ER...SPEAK PLAINER, MAESTRO! I CAN'T UNNERSTAND A WORD YOU'RE SAYIN'!
MEOW!
OOPS! OW! HEY, PERFESSER! CLOSE THE DOOR! YOU LET A CAT IN...OR A DOG...OR A HERD OF ELEPHINKS!
O-O-OW!
HEH, HEH!..WELL, THAT TAKES CARE OF THAT SMART-ALECK DUCK!

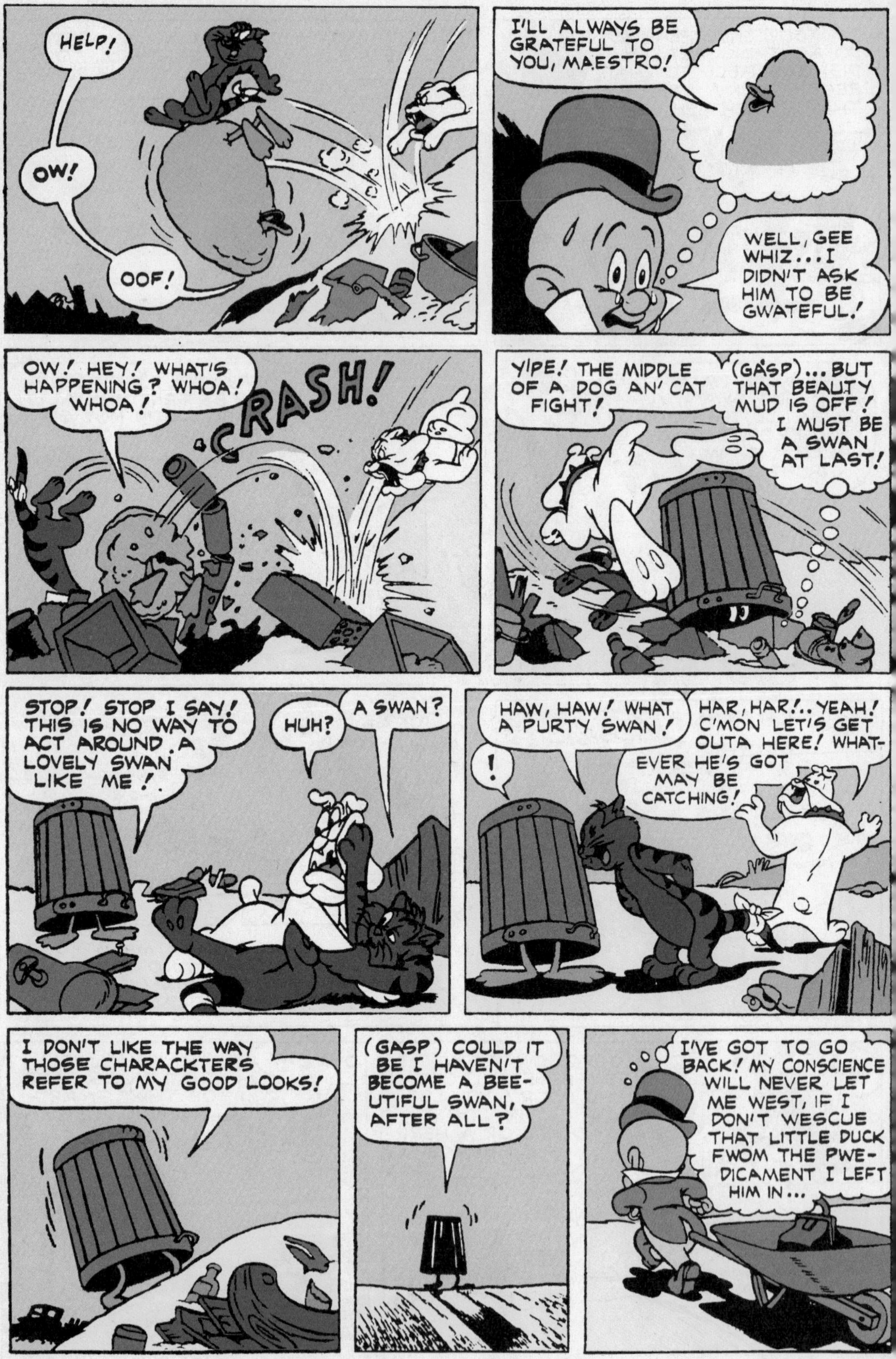
HELP!
OW!
OOF!
I'LL ALWAYS BE GRATEFUL TO YOU, MAESTRO!
WELL, GEE WHIZ... I DIDN'T ASK HIM TO BE GWATEFUL!
OW! HEY! WHAT'S HAPPENING? WHOA! WHOA!
CRASH!
YIPE! THE MIDDLE OF A DOG AN' CAT FIGHT!
(GASP)... BUT THAT BEAUTY MUD IS OFF! I MUST BE A SWAN AT LAST!
STOP! STOP I SAY! THIS IS NO WAY TO ACT AROUND A LOVELY SWAN LIKE ME!
HUH?
A SWAN?
HAW, HAW! WHAT A PURTY SWAN!
HAR, HAR!.. YEAH! C'MON LET'S GET OUTA HERE! WHATEVER HE'S GOT MAY BE CATCHING!
!
I DON'T LIKE THE WAY THOSE CHARACKTERS REFER TO MY GOOD LOOKS!
(GASP) COULD IT BE I HAVEN'T BECOME A BEE-UTIFUL SWAN, AFTER ALL?
I'VE GOT TO GO BACK! MY CONSCIENCE WILL NEVER LET ME WEST, IF I DON'T WESCUE THAT LITTLE DUCK FWOM THE PWE-DICAMENT I LEFT HIM IN...

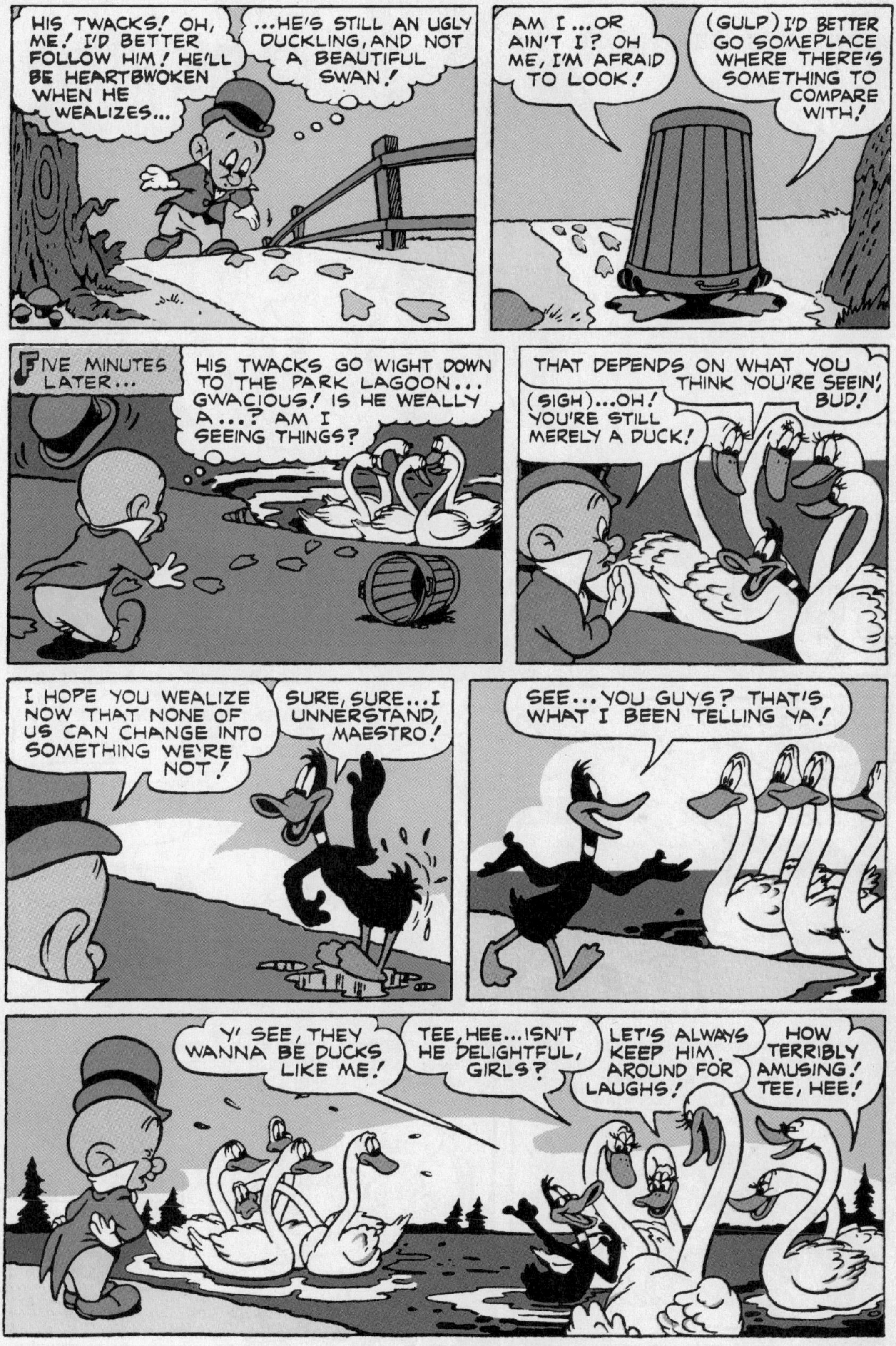
HIS TWACKS! OH, ME! I'D BETTER FOLLOW HIM! HE'LL BE HEARTBWOKEN WHEN HE WEALIZES...
...HE'S STILL AN UGLY DUCKLING, AND NOT A BEAUTIFUL SWAN!
AM I ...OR AIN'T I? OH ME, I'M AFRAID TO LOOK!
(GULP) I'D BETTER GO SOMEPLACE WHERE THERE'S SOMETHING TO COMPARE WITH!
FIVE MINUTES LATER...
HIS TWACKS GO WIGHT DOWN TO THE PARK LAGOON... GWACIOUS! IS HE WEALLY A...? AM I SEEING THINGS?
(SIGH)...OH! YOU'RE STILL MERELY A DUCK!
THAT DEPENDS ON WHAT YOU THINK YOU'RE SEEIN', BUD!
I HOPE YOU WEALIZE NOW THAT NONE OF US CAN CHANGE INTO SOMETHING WE'RE NOT!
SURE, SURE...I UNNERSTAND, MAESTRO!
SEE...YOU GUYS? THAT'S WHAT I BEEN TELLING YA!
Y' SEE, THEY WANNA BE DUCKS LIKE ME!
TEE, HEE...ISN'T HE DELIGHTFUL, GIRLS?
LET'S ALWAYS KEEP HIM AROUND FOR LAUGHS!
HOW TERRIBLY AMUSING! TEE, HEE!

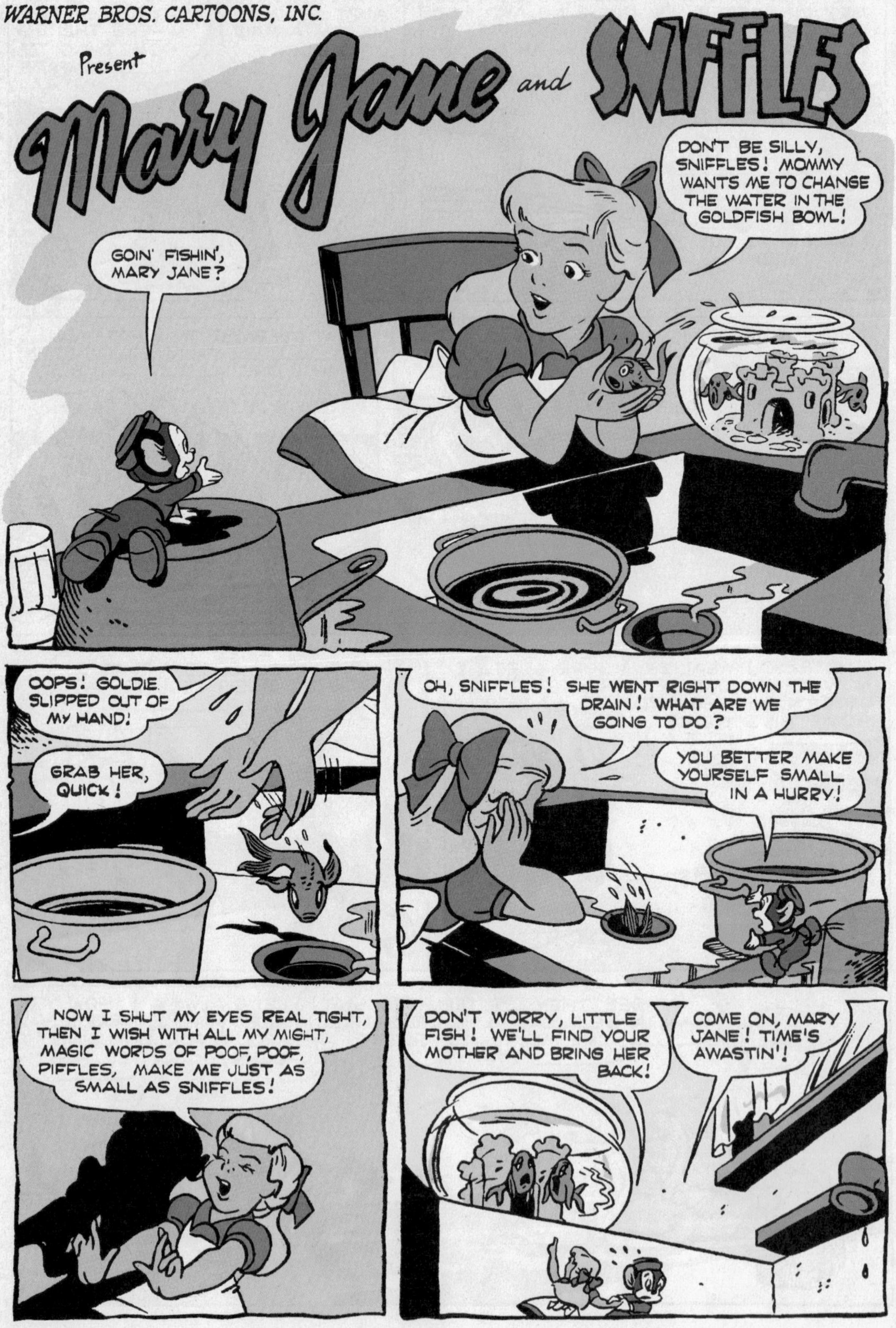
WARNER BROS. CARTOONS, INC.
Present
Mary Jane and SNIFFLES
GOIN' FISHIN', MARY JANE?
DON'T BE SILLY, SNIFFLES! MOMMY WANTS ME TO CHANGE THE WATER IN THE GOLDFISH BOWL!
OOPS! GOLDIE SLIPPED OUT OF MY HAND!
GRAB HER, QUICK!
OH, SNIFFLES! SHE WENT RIGHT DOWN THE DRAIN! WHAT ARE WE GOING TO DO?
YOU BETTER MAKE YOURSELF SMALL IN A HURRY!
NOW I SHUT MY EYES REAL TIGHT, THEN I WISH WITH ALL MY MIGHT, MAGIC WORDS OF POOF, POOF, PIFFLES, MAKE ME JUST AS SMALL AS SNIFFLES!
DON'T WORRY, LITTLE FISH! WE'LL FIND YOUR MOTHER AND BRING HER BACK!
COME ON, MARY JANE! TIME'S AWASTIN'!

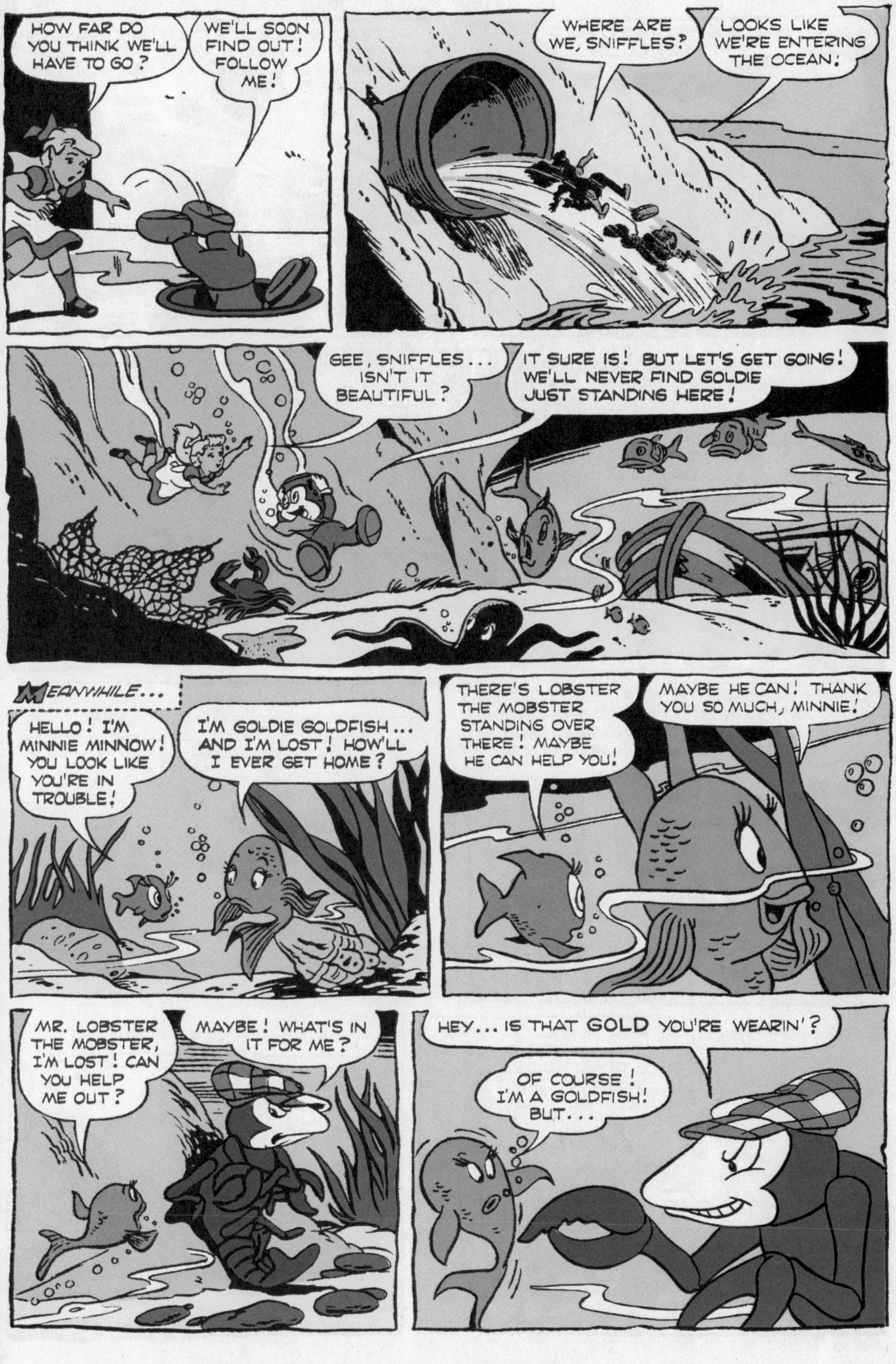
HOW FAR DO YOU THINK WE'LL HAVE TO GO?
WE'LL SOON FIND OUT! FOLLOW ME!
WHERE ARE WE, SNIFFLES?
LOOKS LIKE WE'RE ENTERING THE OCEAN!
GEE, SNIFFLES... ISN'T IT BEAUTIFUL?
IT SURE IS! BUT LET'S GET GOING! WE'LL NEVER FIND GOLDIE JUST STANDING HERE!
MEANWHILE...
HELLO! I'M MINNIE MINNOW! YOU LOOK LIKE YOU'RE IN TROUBLE!
I'M GOLDIE GOLDFISH... AND I'M LOST! HOW'LL I EVER GET HOME?
THERE'S LOBSTER THE MOBSTER STANDING OVER THERE! MAYBE HE CAN HELP YOU!
MAYBE HE CAN! THANK YOU SO MUCH, MINNIE!
MR. LOBSTER THE MOBSTER, I'M LOST! CAN YOU HELP ME OUT?
MAYBE! WHAT'S IN IT FOR ME?
HEY... IS THAT GOLD YOU'RE WEARIN'?
OF COURSE! I'M A GOLDFISH! BUT...

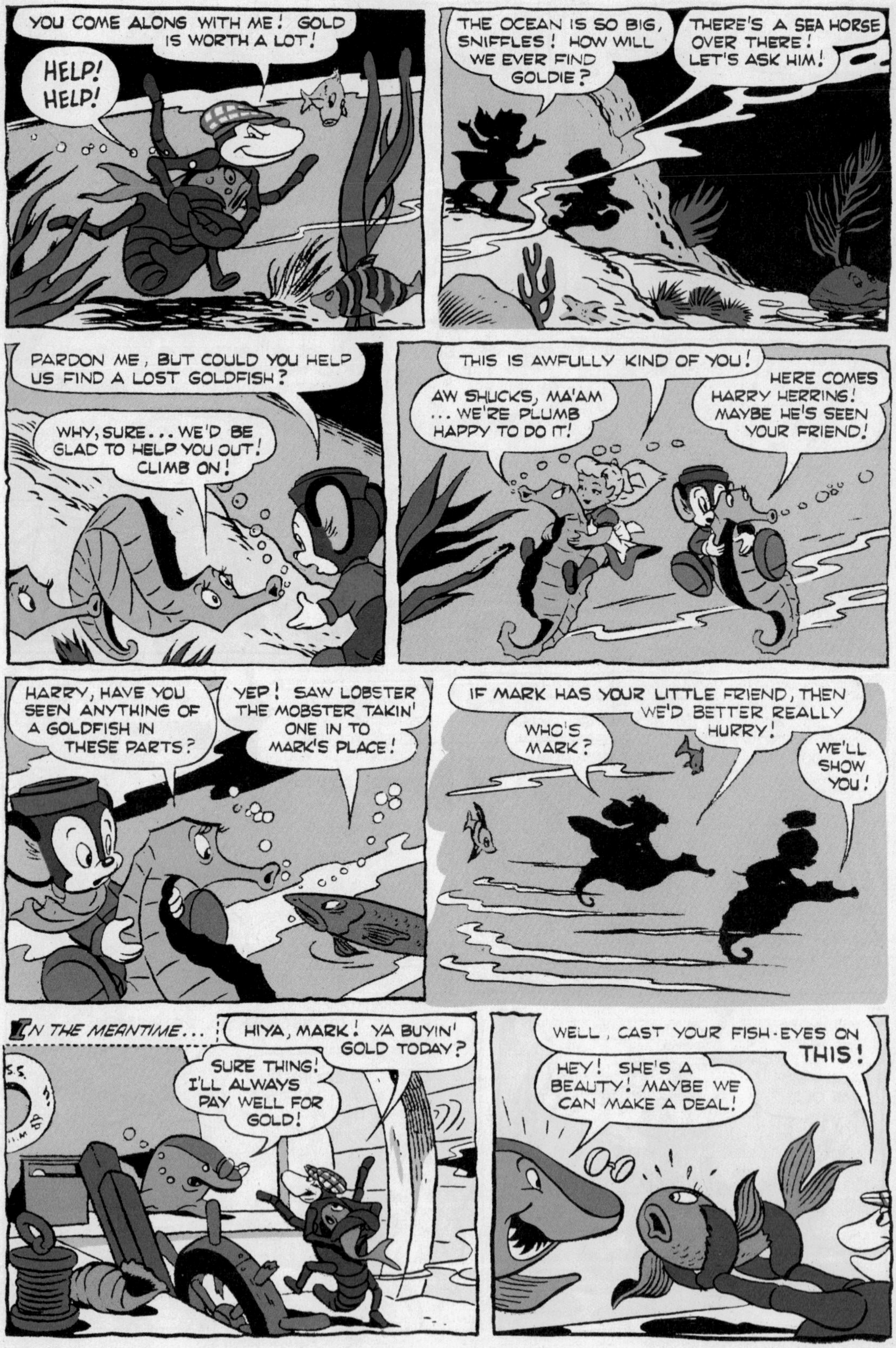
YOU COME ALONG WITH ME! GOLD IS WORTH A LOT!
HELP! HELP!
THE OCEAN IS SO BIG, SNIFFLES! HOW WILL WE EVER FIND GOLDIE?
THERE'S A SEA HORSE OVER THERE! LET'S ASK HIM!
PARDON ME, BUT COULD YOU HELP US FIND A LOST GOLDFISH?
WHY, SURE... WE'D BE GLAD TO HELP YOU OUT! CLIMB ON!
THIS IS AWFULLY KIND OF YOU!
AW SHUCKS, MA'AM ... WE'RE PLUMB HAPPY TO DO IT!
HERE COMES HARRY HERRING! MAYBE HE'S SEEN YOUR FRIEND!
HARRY, HAVE YOU SEEN ANYTHING OF A GOLDFISH IN THESE PARTS?
YEP! SAW LOBSTER THE MOBSTER TAKIN' ONE IN TO MARK'S PLACE!
IF MARK HAS YOUR LITTLE FRIEND, THEN WE'D BETTER REALLY HURRY!
WHO'S MARK?
WE'LL SHOW YOU!
IN THE MEANTIME...
HIYA, MARK! YA BUYIN' GOLD TODAY?
SURE THING! I'LL ALWAYS PAY WELL FOR GOLD!
WELL, CAST YOUR FISH-EYES ON THIS!
HEY! SHE'S A BEAUTY! MAYBE WE CAN MAKE A DEAL!

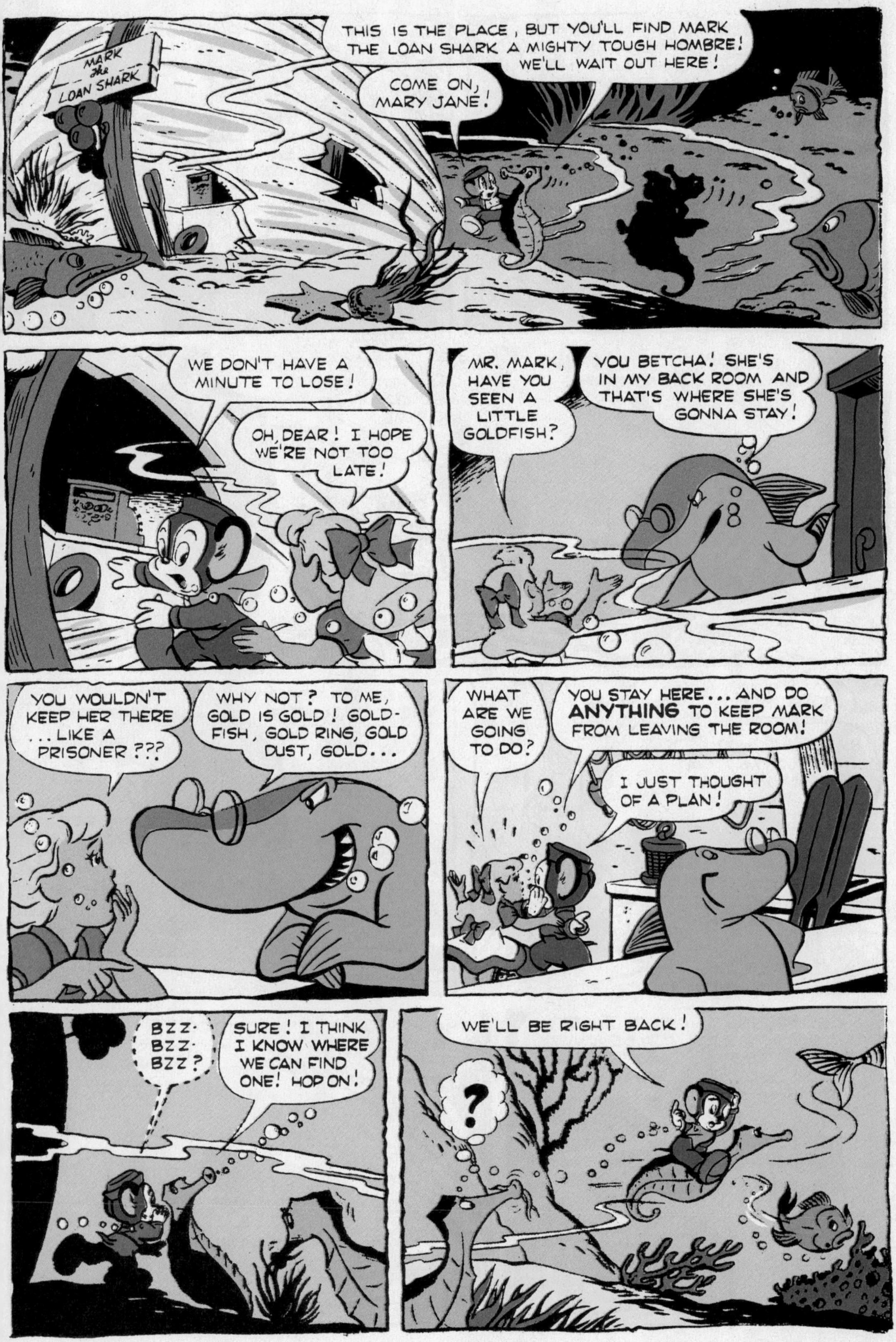
MARK the LOAN SHARK
THIS IS THE PLACE, BUT YOU'LL FIND MARK THE LOAN SHARK A MIGHTY TOUGH HOMBRE! WE'LL WAIT OUT HERE!
COME ON, MARY JANE!
WE DON'T HAVE A MINUTE TO LOSE!
OH, DEAR! I HOPE WE'RE NOT TOO LATE!
MR. MARK, HAVE YOU SEEN A LITTLE GOLDFISH?
YOU BETCHA! SHE'S IN MY BACK ROOM AND THAT'S WHERE SHE'S GONNA STAY!
YOU WOULDN'T KEEP HER THERE ...LIKE A PRISONER???
WHY NOT? TO ME, GOLD IS GOLD! GOLD-FISH, GOLD RING, GOLD DUST, GOLD...
WHAT ARE WE GOING TO DO?
YOU STAY HERE... AND DO **ANYTHING** TO KEEP MARK FROM LEAVING THE ROOM!
I JUST THOUGHT OF A PLAN!
BZZ-BZZ-BZZ?
SURE! I THINK I KNOW WHERE WE CAN FIND ONE! HOP ON!
WE'LL BE RIGHT BACK!
?

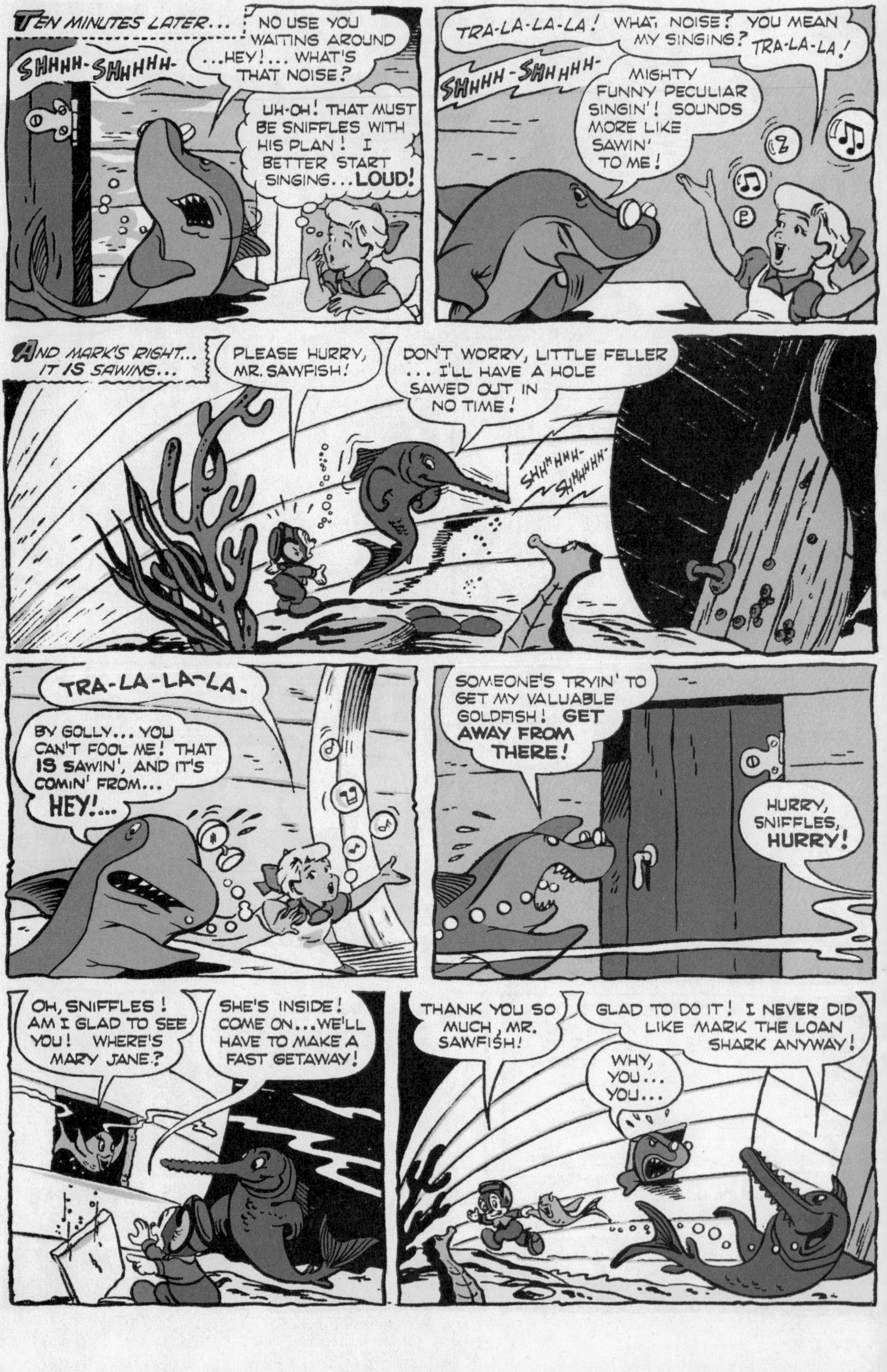
TEN MINUTES LATER...
SHHHH-SHHHHH-
NO USE YOU WAITING AROUND ...HEY! ... WHAT'S THAT NOISE?
UH-OH! THAT MUST BE SNIFFLES WITH HIS PLAN! I BETTER START SINGING... LOUD!
TRA-LA-LA-LA!
SHHHH-SHHHHH-
WHAT NOISE? YOU MEAN MY SINGING? TRA-LA-LA!
MIGHTY FUNNY PECULIAR SINGIN'! SOUNDS MORE LIKE SAWIN' TO ME!
AND MARK'S RIGHT... IT IS SAWING...
PLEASE HURRY, MR. SAWFISH!
DON'T WORRY, LITTLE FELLER ... I'LL HAVE A HOLE SAWED OUT IN NO TIME!
TRA-LA-LA-LA.
BY GOLLY... YOU CAN'T FOOL ME! THAT IS SAWIN', AND IT'S COMIN' FROM... HEY!...
SOMEONE'S TRYIN' TO GET MY VALUABLE GOLDFISH! GET AWAY FROM THERE!
HURRY, SNIFFLES, HURRY!
OH, SNIFFLES! AM I GLAD TO SEE YOU! WHERE'S MARY JANE?
SHE'S INSIDE! COME ON...WE'LL HAVE TO MAKE A FAST GETAWAY!
THANK YOU SO MUCH, MR. SAWFISH!
GLAD TO DO IT! I NEVER DID LIKE MARK THE LOAN SHARK ANYWAY!
WHY, YOU... YOU...

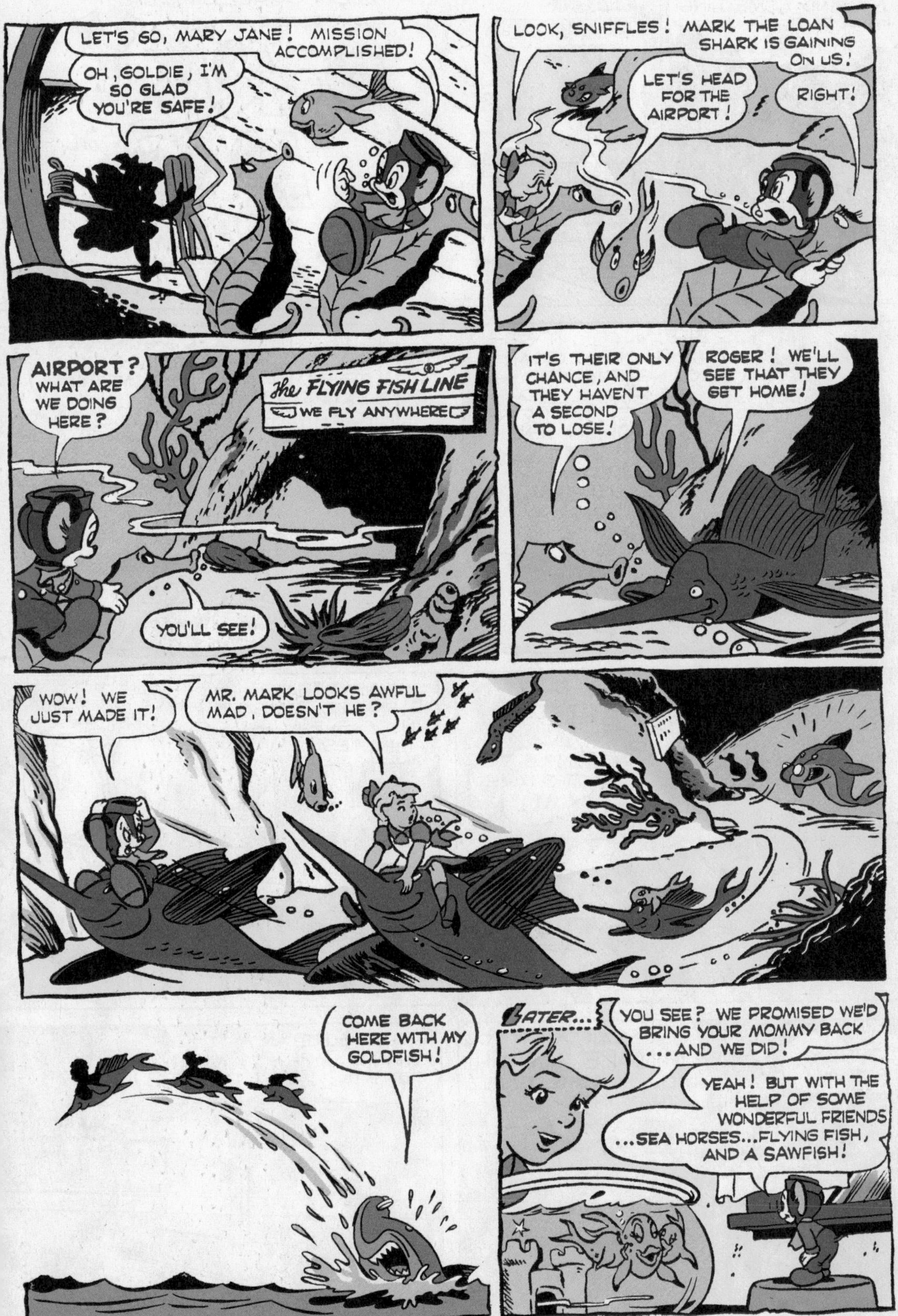
LET'S GO, MARY JANE! MISSION ACCOMPLISHED!
OH, GOLDIE, I'M SO GLAD YOU'RE SAFE!
LOOK, SNIFFLES! MARK THE LOAN SHARK IS GAINING ON US!
LET'S HEAD FOR THE AIRPORT!
RIGHT!
AIRPORT? WHAT ARE WE DOING HERE?
The FLYING FISH LINE
WE FLY ANYWHERE
YOU'LL SEE!
IT'S THEIR ONLY CHANCE, AND THEY HAVENT A SECOND TO LOSE!
ROGER! WE'LL SEE THAT THEY GET HOME!
WOW! WE JUST MADE IT!
MR. MARK LOOKS AWFUL MAD, DOESN'T HE?
COME BACK HERE WITH MY GOLDFISH!
LATER...
YOU SEE? WE PROMISED WE'D BRING YOUR MOMMY BACK ...AND WE DID!
YEAH! BUT WITH THE HELP OF SOME WONDERFUL FRIENDS ...SEA HORSES...FLYING FISH, AND A SAWFISH!

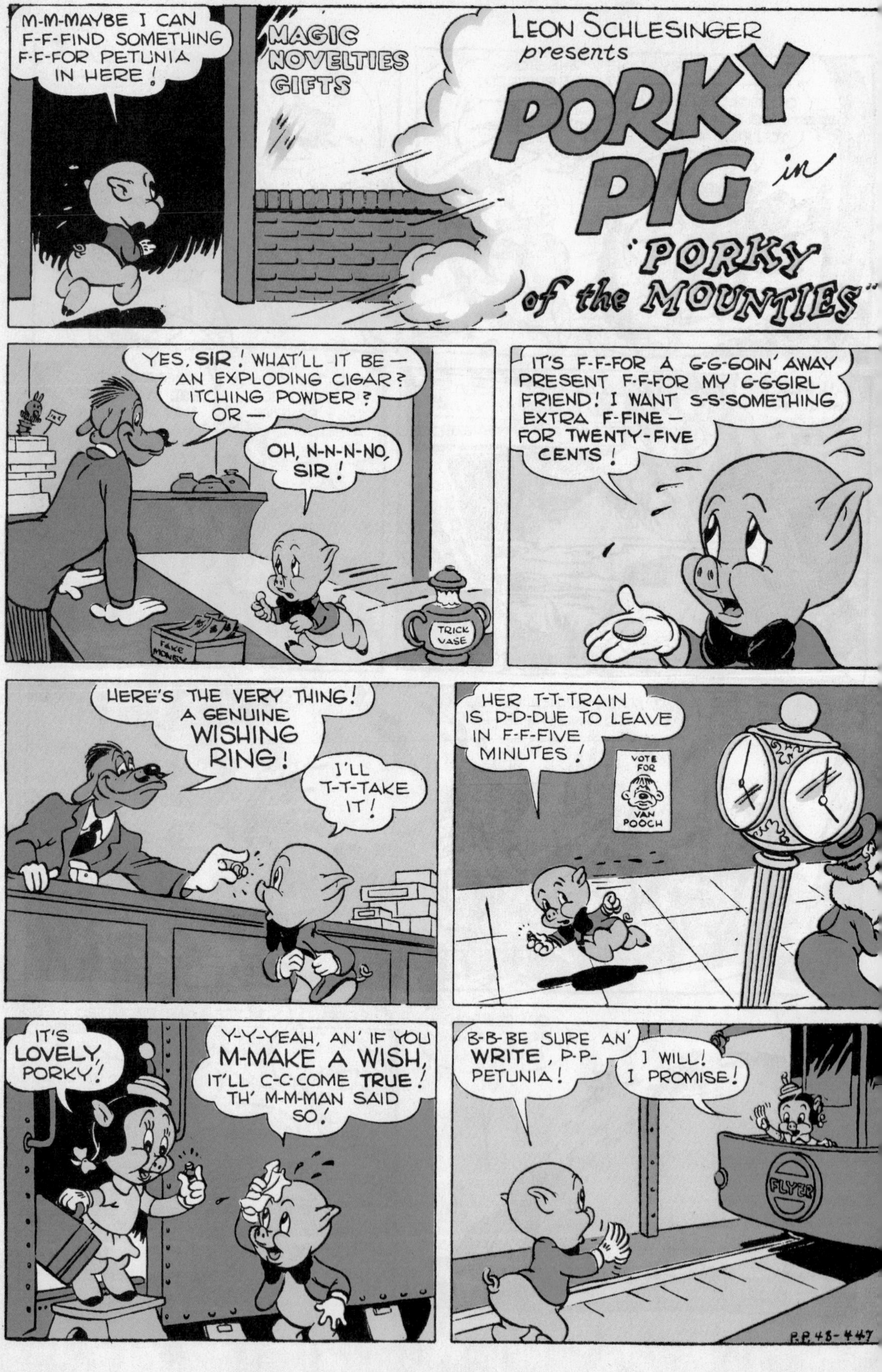
M-M-MAYBE I CAN F-F-FIND SOMETHING F-F-FOR PETUNIA IN HERE!
MAGIC NOVELTIES GIFTS
LEON SCHLESINGER presents
PORKY PIG in
"PORKY of the MOUNTIES"
YES, SIR! WHAT'LL IT BE — AN EXPLODING CIGAR? ITCHING POWDER? OR —
OH, N-N-N-NO, SIR!
FAKE MONEY
TRICK VASE
IT'S F-F-FOR A G-G-GOIN' AWAY PRESENT F-F-FOR MY G-G-GIRL FRIEND! I WANT S-S-SOMETHING EXTRA F-FINE — FOR TWENTY-FIVE CENTS!
HERE'S THE VERY THING! A GENUINE WISHING RING!
I'LL T-T-TAKE IT!
HER T-T-TRAIN IS D-D-DUE TO LEAVE IN F-F-FIVE MINUTES!
VOTE FOR VAN POOCH
IT'S LOVELY, PORKY!
Y-Y-YEAH, AN' IF YOU M-MAKE A WISH, IT'LL C-C-COME TRUE! TH' M-M-MAN SAID SO!
B-B-BE SURE AN' WRITE, P-P-PETUNIA!
I WILL! I PROMISE!
FLYER
P.P. 48-447

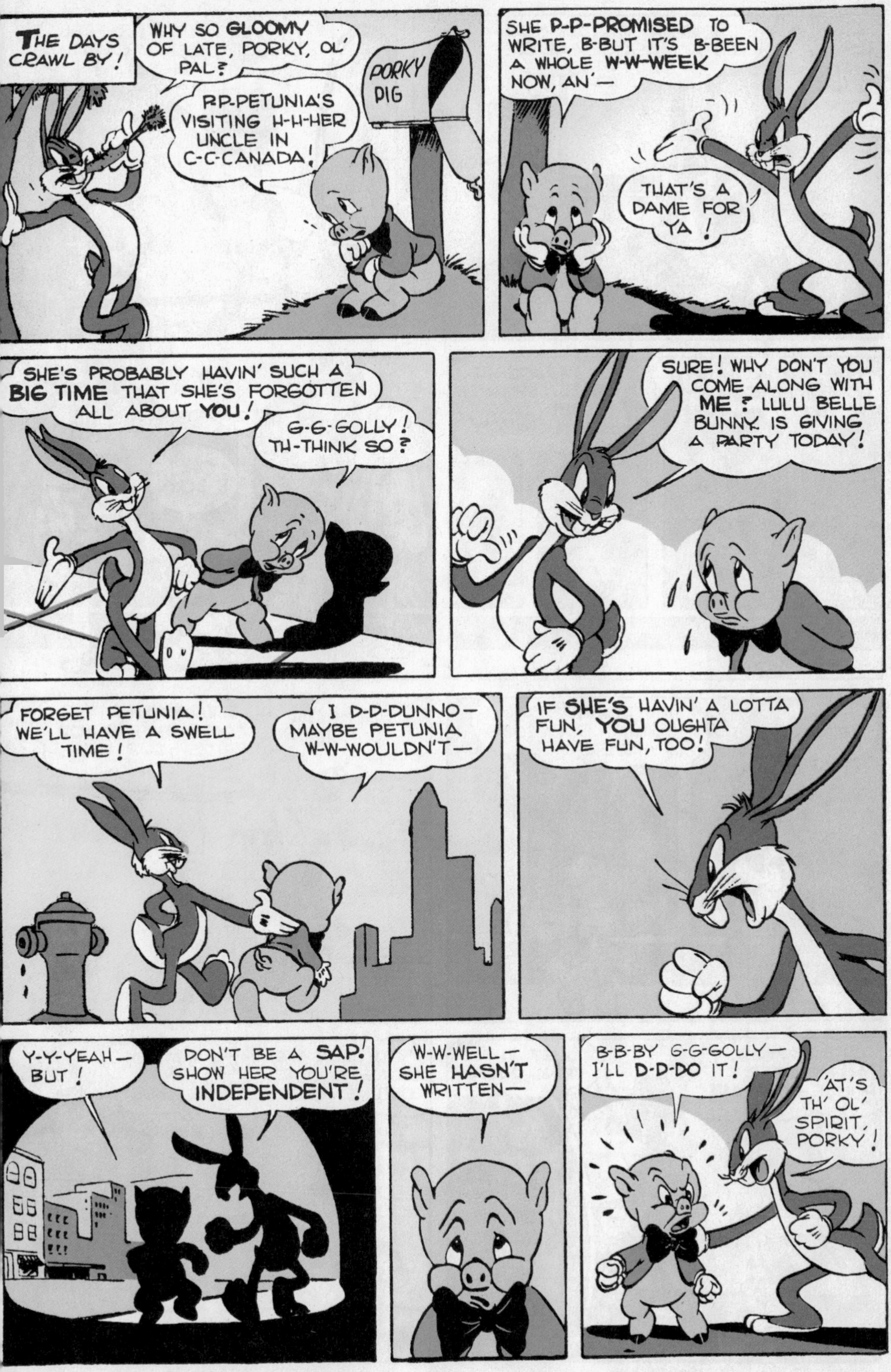
THE DAYS CRAWL BY!
WHY SO GLOOMY OF LATE, PORKY, OL' PAL?
PORKY PIG
P-P-PETUNIA'S VISITING H-H-HER UNCLE IN C-C-CANADA!
SHE P-P-PROMISED TO WRITE, B-BUT IT'S B-BEEN A WHOLE W-W-WEEK NOW, AN'—
THAT'S A DAME FOR YA!
SHE'S PROBABLY HAVIN' SUCH A BIG TIME THAT SHE'S FORGOTTEN ALL ABOUT YOU!
G-G-GOLLY! TH-THINK SO?
SURE! WHY DON'T YOU COME ALONG WITH ME? LULU BELLE BUNNY IS GIVING A PARTY TODAY!
FORGET PETUNIA! WE'LL HAVE A SWELL TIME!
I D-D-DUNNO— MAYBE PETUNIA W-W-WOULDN'T—
IF SHE'S HAVIN' A LOTTA FUN, YOU OUGHTA HAVE FUN, TOO!
Y-Y-YEAH— BUT!
DON'T BE A SAP! SHOW HER YOU'RE INDEPENDENT!
W-W-WELL— SHE HASN'T WRITTEN—
B-B-BY G-G-GOLLY— I'LL D-D-DO IT!
'AT'S TH' OL' SPIRIT, PORKY!

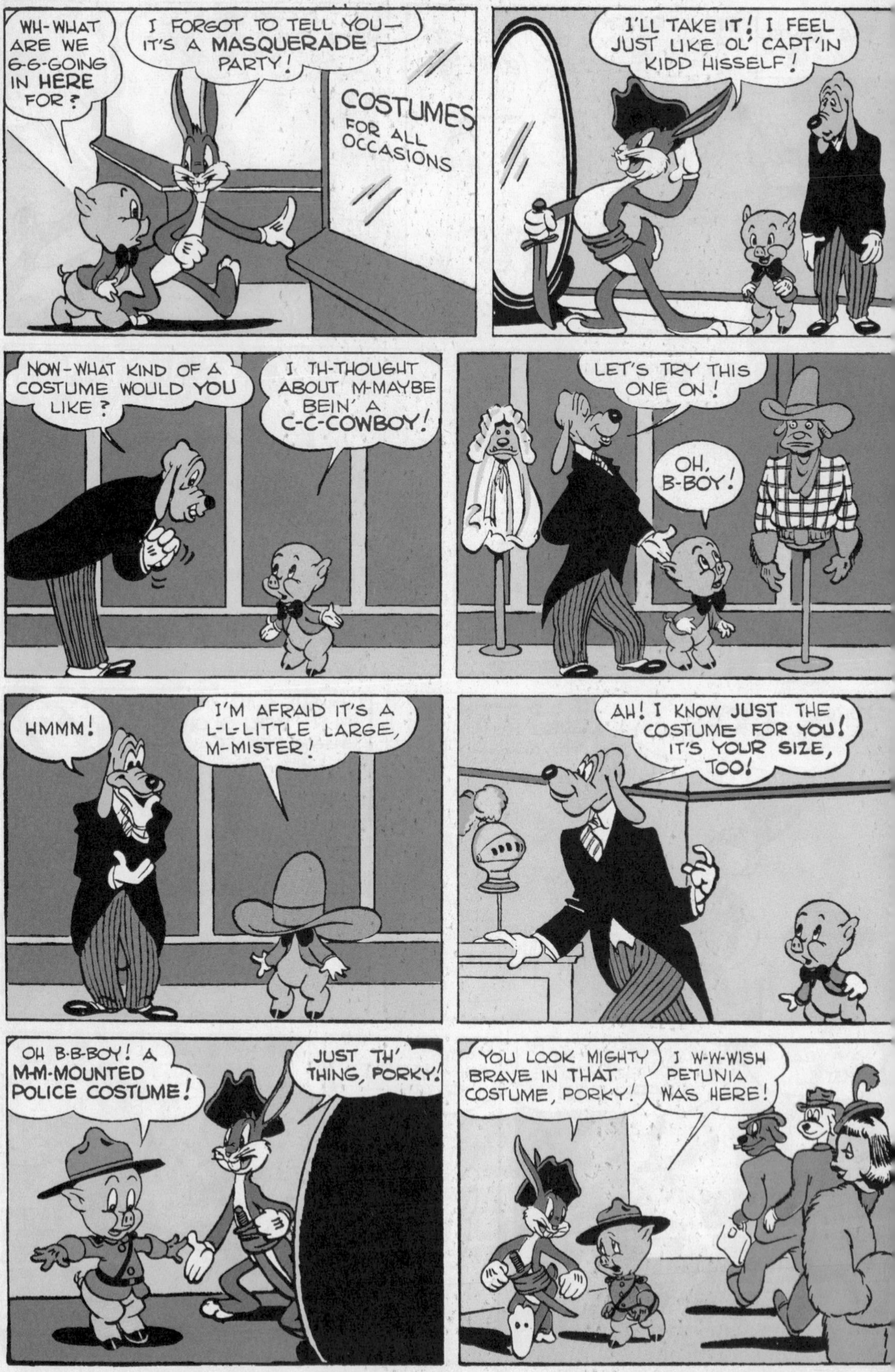

WH-WHAT ARE WE G-G-GOING IN HERE FOR?
I FORGOT TO TELL YOU— IT'S A MASQUERADE PARTY!
COSTUMES FOR ALL OCCASIONS
I'LL TAKE IT! I FEEL JUST LIKE OL' CAPT'IN KIDD HISSELF!
NOW-WHAT KIND OF A COSTUME WOULD YOU LIKE?
I TH-THOUGHT ABOUT M-MAYBE BEIN' A C-C-COWBOY!
LET'S TRY THIS ONE ON!
OH, B-BOY!
HMMM!
I'M AFRAID IT'S A L-L-LITTLE LARGE, M-MISTER!
AH! I KNOW JUST THE COSTUME FOR YOU! IT'S YOUR SIZE, TOO!
OH B-B-BOY! A M-M-MOUNTED POLICE COSTUME!
JUST TH' THING, PORKY!
YOU LOOK MIGHTY BRAVE IN THAT COSTUME, PORKY!
I W-W-WISH PETUNIA WAS HERE!

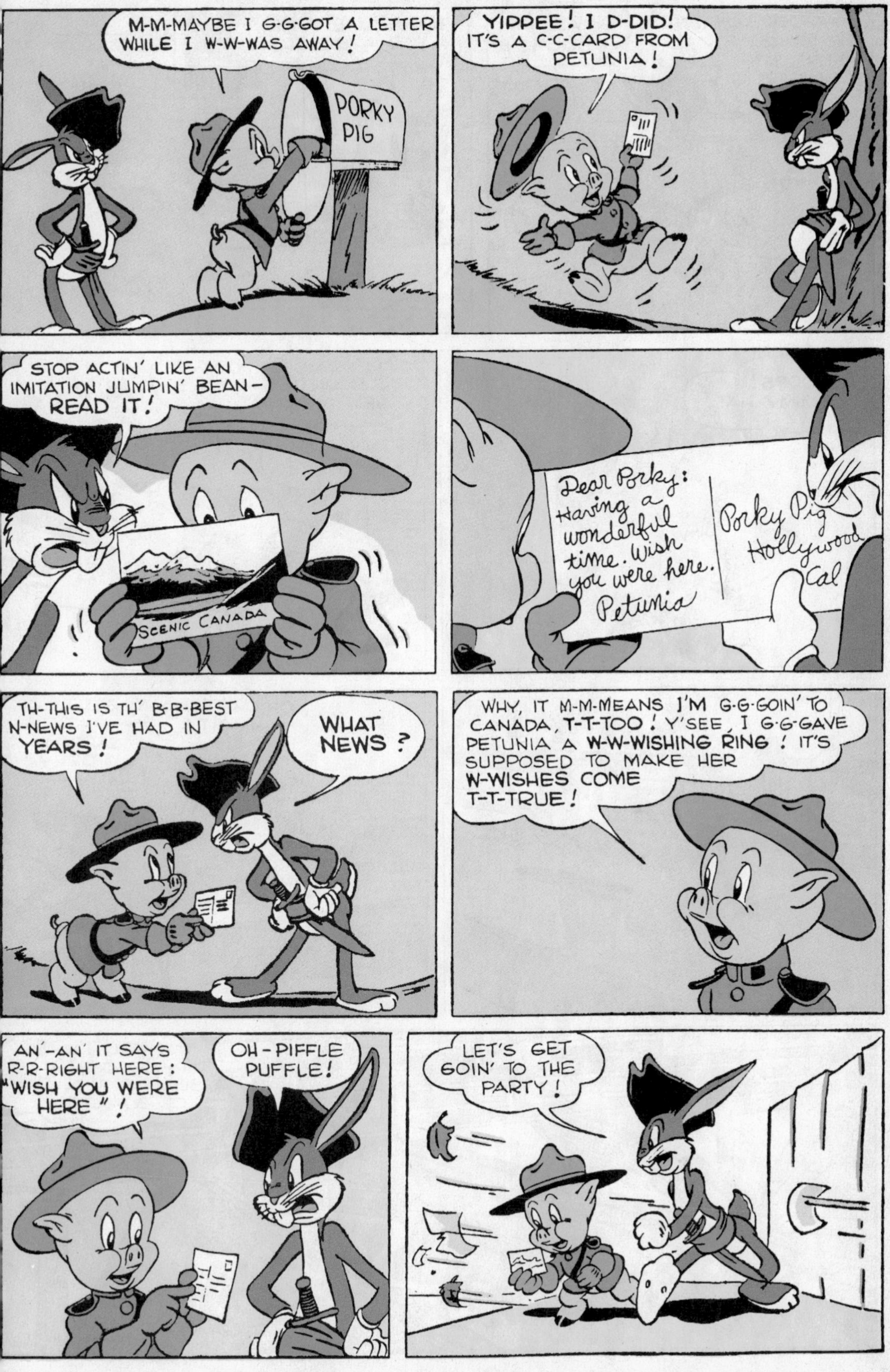
M-M-MAYBE I G-G-GOT A LETTER WHILE I W-W-WAS AWAY!
PORKY PIG
YIPPEE! I D-DID! IT'S A C-C-CARD FROM PETUNIA!
STOP ACTIN' LIKE AN IMITATION JUMPIN' BEAN— READ IT!
SCENIC CANADA
Dear Porky: Having a wonderful time. Wish you were here. Petunia
Porky Pig Hollywood Cal
TH-THIS IS TH' B-B-BEST N-NEWS I'VE HAD IN YEARS!
WHAT NEWS?
WHY, IT M-M-MEANS I'M G-G-GOIN' TO CANADA, T-T-TOO! Y'SEE, I G-G-GAVE PETUNIA A W-W-WISHING RING! IT'S SUPPOSED TO MAKE HER W-WISHES COME T-T-TRUE!
AN'-AN' IT SAYS R-R-RIGHT HERE: "WISH YOU WERE HERE"!
OH-PIFFLE PUFFLE!
LET'S GET GOIN' TO THE PARTY!

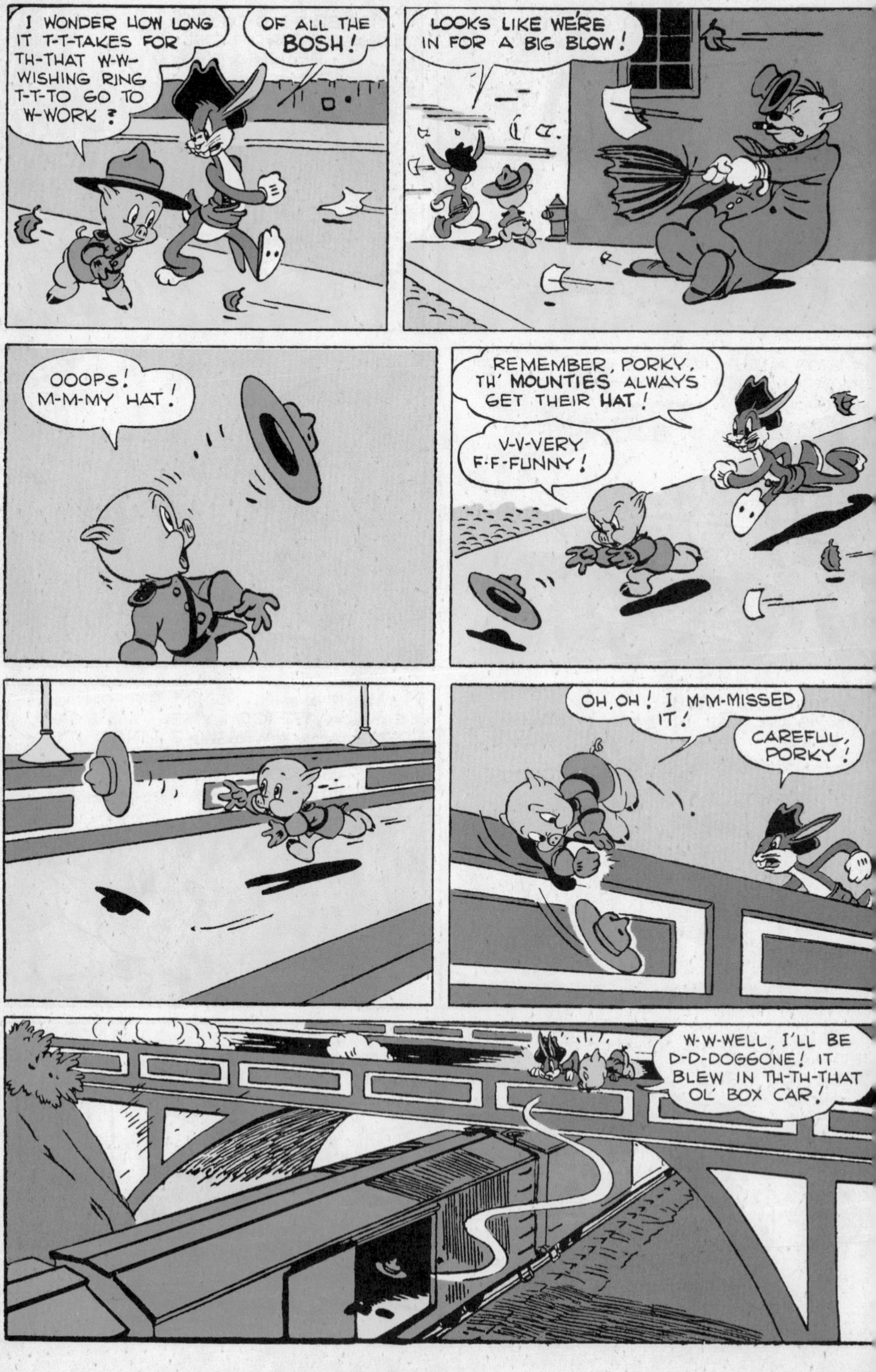
I WONDER HOW LONG IT T-T-TAKES FOR TH-THAT W-W-WISHING RING T-T-TO GO TO W-WORK ?
OF ALL THE BOSH!
LOOKS LIKE WE'RE IN FOR A BIG BLOW!
OOOPS! M-M-MY HAT!
REMEMBER, PORKY, TH' MOUNTIES ALWAYS GET THEIR HAT!
V-V-VERY F-F-FUNNY!
OH, OH! I M-M-MISSED IT!
CAREFUL, PORKY!
W-W-WELL, I'LL BE D-D-DOGGONE! IT BLEW IN TH-TH-THAT OL' BOX CAR!

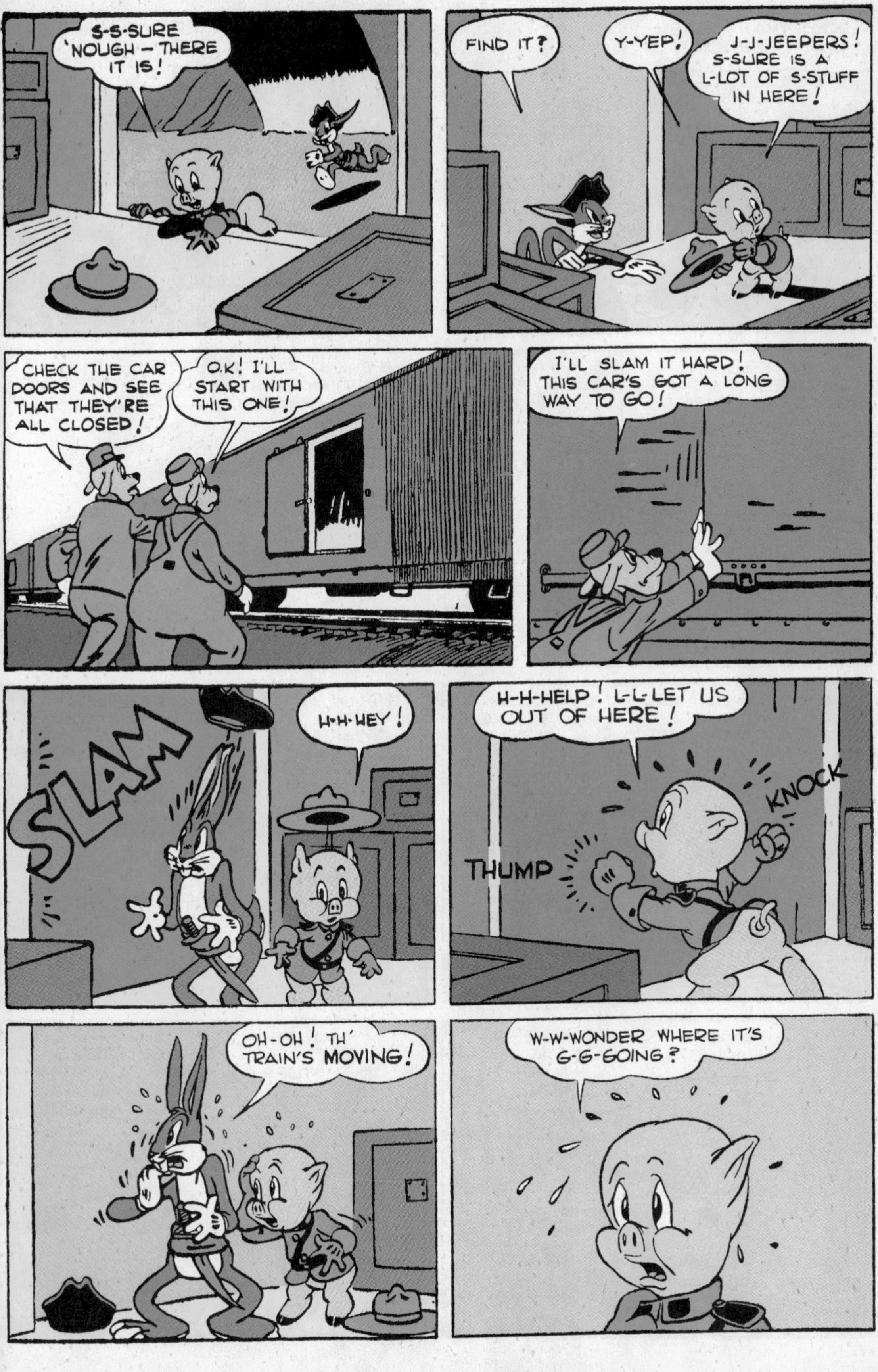
S-S-SURE 'NOUGH – THERE IT IS!
FIND IT?
Y-YEP!
J-J-JEEPERS! S-SURE IS A L-LOT OF S-STUFF IN HERE!
CHECK THE CAR DOORS AND SEE THAT THEY'RE ALL CLOSED!
O.K! I'LL START WITH THIS ONE!
I'LL SLAM IT HARD! THIS CAR'S GOT A LONG WAY TO GO!
SLAM
H-H-HEY!
H-H-HELP! L-L-LET US OUT OF HERE!
KNOCK
THUMP
OH-OH! TH' TRAIN'S MOVING!
W-W-WONDER WHERE IT'S G-G-GOING?

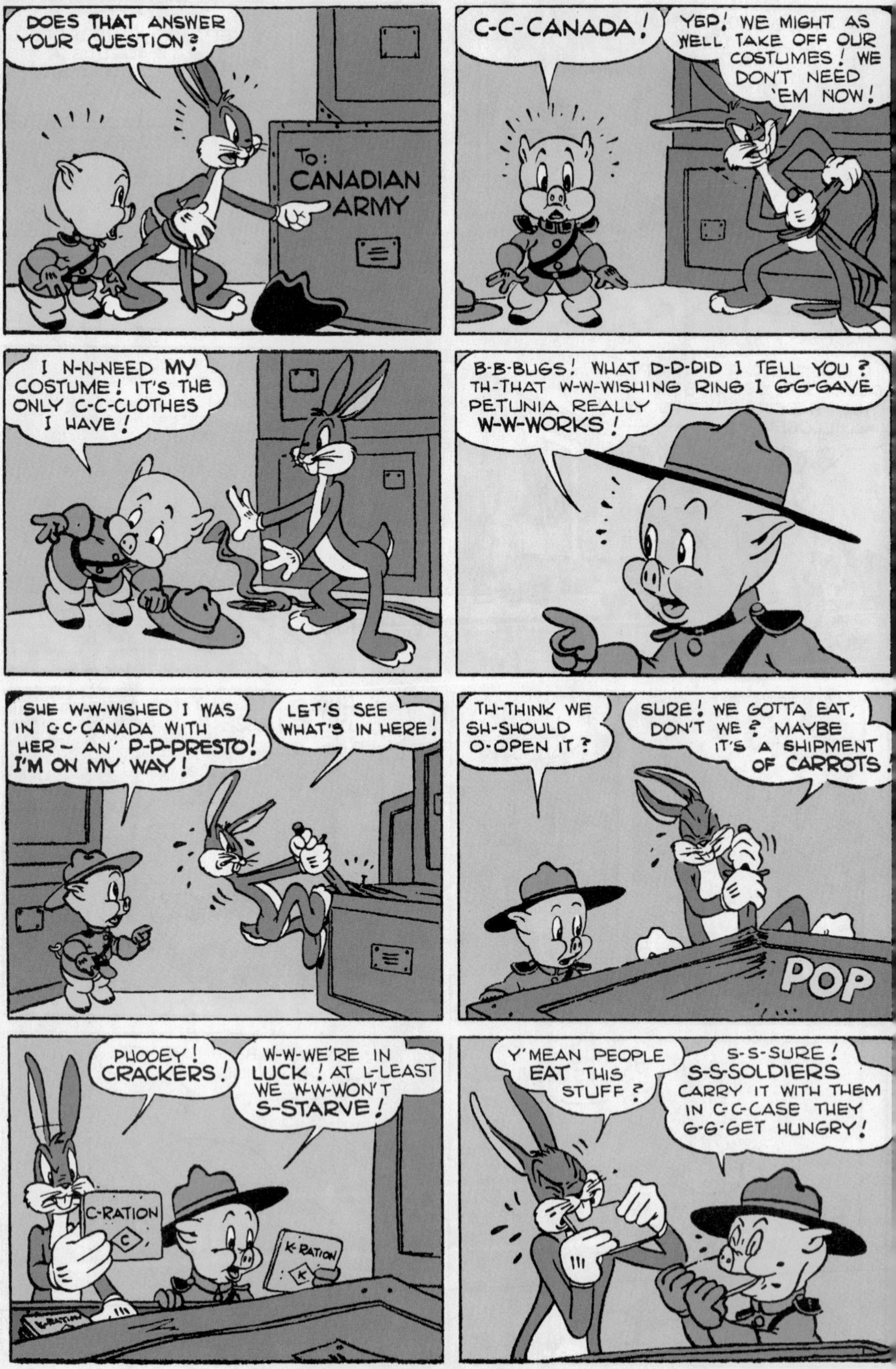

DOES THAT ANSWER YOUR QUESTION?
TO: CANADIAN ARMY
C-C-CANADA!
YEP! WE MIGHT AS WELL TAKE OFF OUR COSTUMES! WE DON'T NEED 'EM NOW!
I N-N-NEED MY COSTUME! IT'S THE ONLY C-C-CLOTHES I HAVE!
B-B-BUGS! WHAT D-D-DID I TELL YOU? TH-THAT W-W-WISHING RING I G-G-GAVE PETUNIA REALLY W-W-WORKS!
SHE W-W-WISHED I WAS IN C-C-CANADA WITH HER— AN' P-P-PRESTO! I'M ON MY WAY!
LET'S SEE WHAT'S IN HERE!
TH-THINK WE SH-SHOULD O-OPEN IT?
SURE! WE GOTTA EAT, DON'T WE? MAYBE IT'S A SHIPMENT OF CARROTS!
POP
PHOOEY! CRACKERS!
W-W-WE'RE IN LUCK! AT L-LEAST WE W-W-WON'T S-STARVE!
C-RATION
K-RATION
Y'MEAN PEOPLE EAT THIS STUFF?
S-S-SURE! S-S-SOLDIERS CARRY IT WITH THEM IN C-C-CASE THEY G-G-GET HUNGRY!

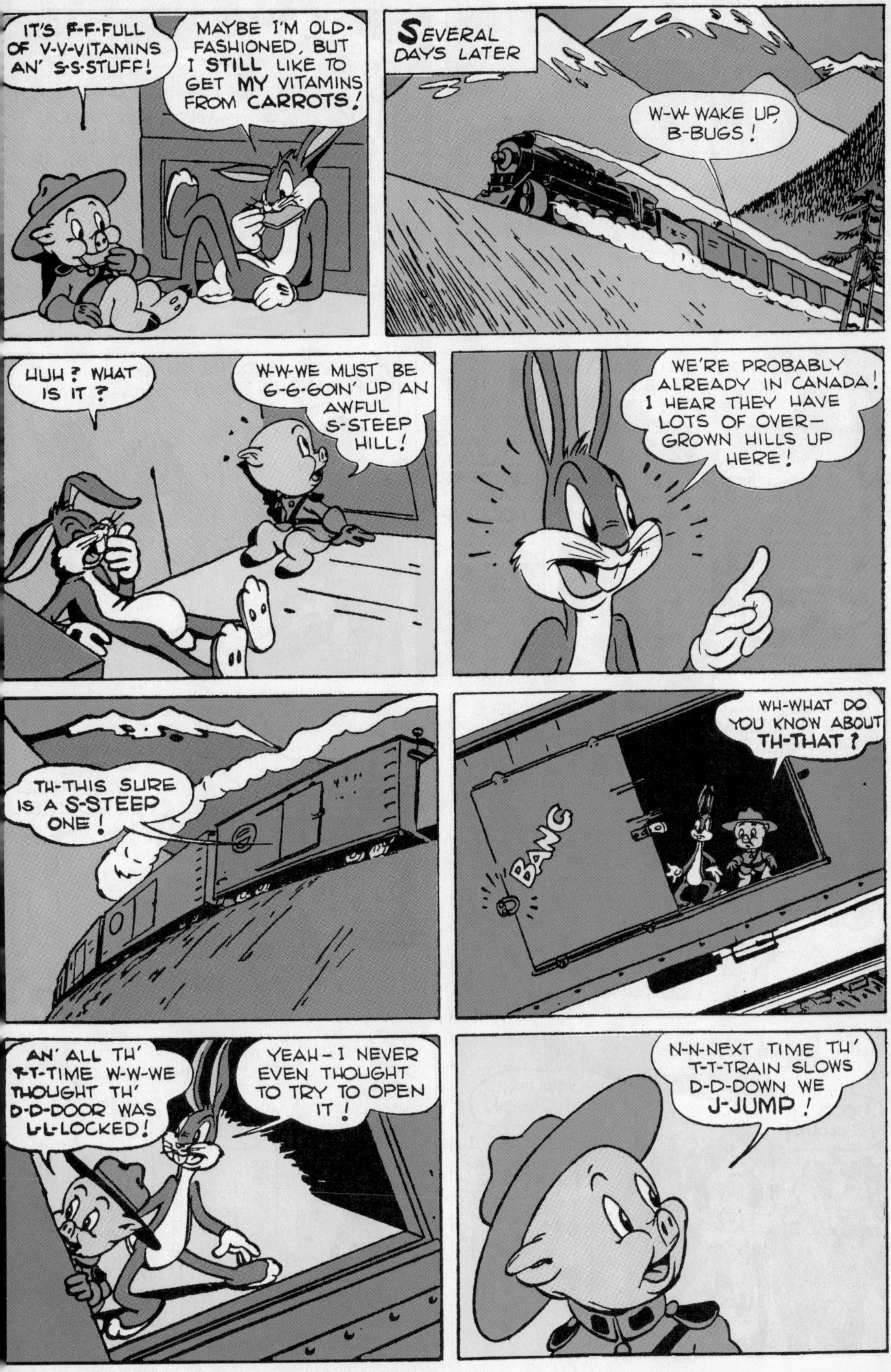
IT'S F-F-FULL OF V-V-VITAMINS AN' S-S-STUFF!
MAYBE I'M OLD-FASHIONED, BUT I STILL LIKE TO GET MY VITAMINS FROM CARROTS!
SEVERAL DAYS LATER
W-W-WAKE UP, B-BUGS!
HUH? WHAT IS IT?
W-W-WE MUST BE G-G-GOIN' UP AN AWFUL S-STEEP HILL!
WE'RE PROBABLY ALREADY IN CANADA! I HEAR THEY HAVE LOTS OF OVER-GROWN HILLS UP HERE!
TH-THIS SURE IS A S-STEEP ONE!
WH-WHAT DO YOU KNOW ABOUT TH-THAT?
BANG
AN' ALL TH' T-T-TIME W-W-WE THOUGHT TH' D-D-DOOR WAS L-L-LOCKED!
YEAH - I NEVER EVEN THOUGHT TO TRY TO OPEN IT!
N-N-NEXT TIME TH' T-T-TRAIN SLOWS D-D-DOWN WE J-JUMP!

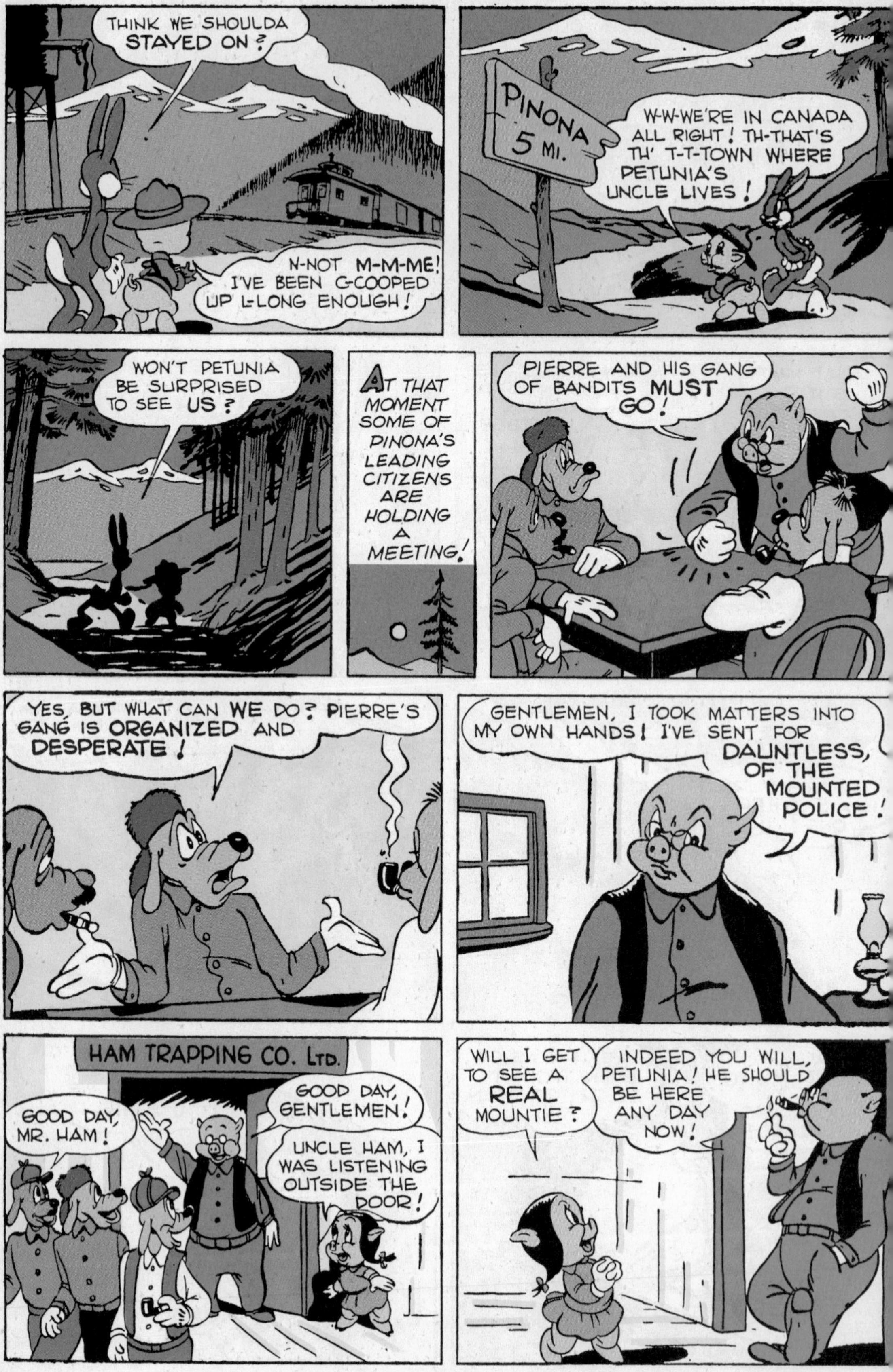
THINK WE SHOULDA STAYED ON ?
N-NOT M-M-ME! I'VE BEEN C-COOPED UP L-LONG ENOUGH!
PINONA 5 MI.
W-W-WE'RE IN CANADA ALL RIGHT! TH-THAT'S TH' T-T-TOWN WHERE PETUNIA'S UNCLE LIVES!
WON'T PETUNIA BE SURPRISED TO SEE US ?
AT THAT MOMENT SOME OF PINONA'S LEADING CITIZENS ARE HOLDING A MEETING!
PIERRE AND HIS GANG OF BANDITS MUST GO!
YES, BUT WHAT CAN WE DO? PIERRE'S GANG IS ORGANIZED AND DESPERATE!
GENTLEMEN, I TOOK MATTERS INTO MY OWN HANDS! I'VE SENT FOR DAUNTLESS, OF THE MOUNTED POLICE!
HAM TRAPPING CO. LTD.
GOOD DAY, MR. HAM!
GOOD DAY, GENTLEMEN!
UNCLE HAM, I WAS LISTENING OUTSIDE THE DOOR!
WILL I GET TO SEE A REAL MOUNTIE ?
INDEED YOU WILL, PETUNIA! HE SHOULD BE HERE ANY DAY NOW!

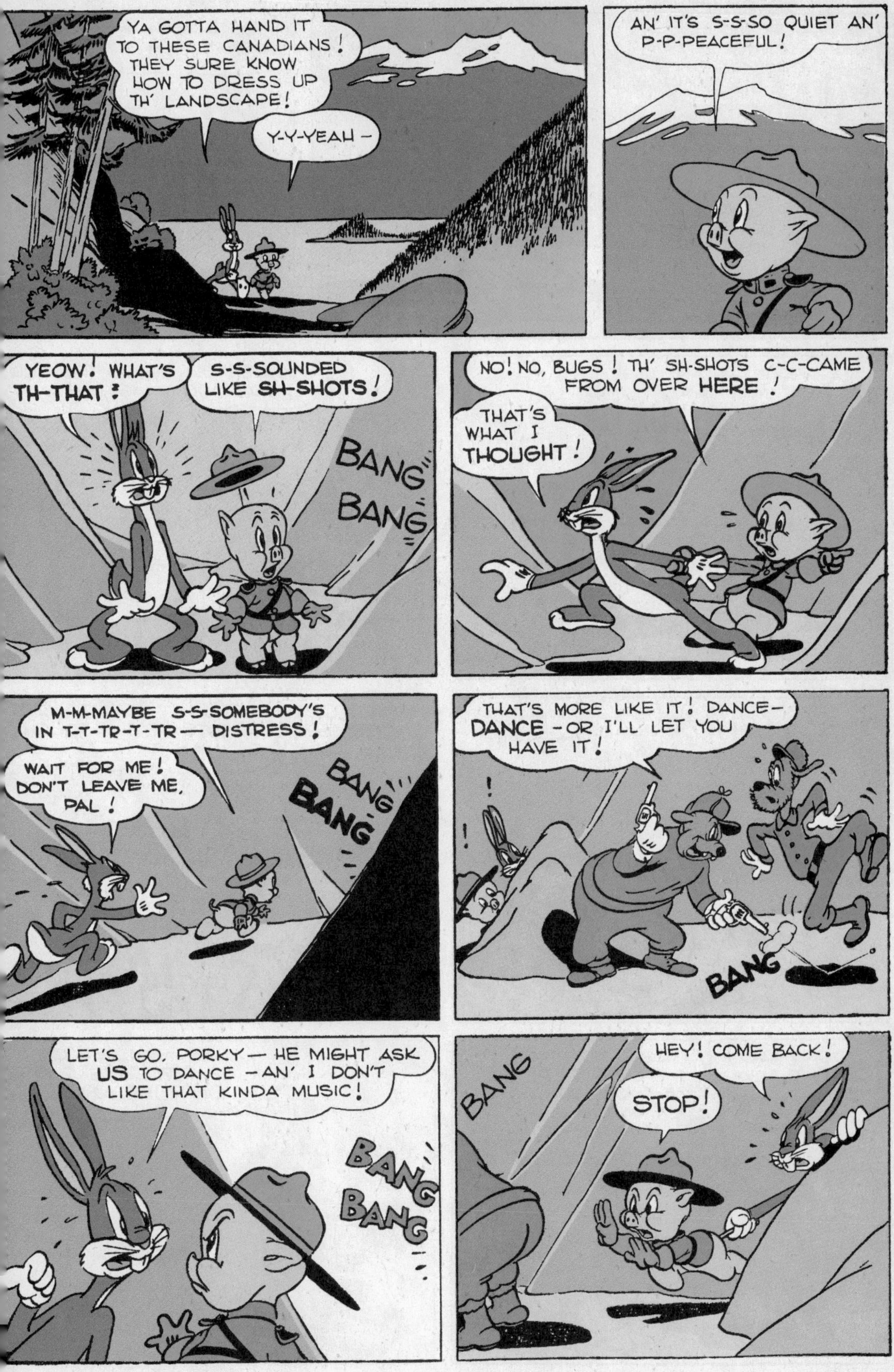

YA GOTTA HAND IT TO THESE CANADIANS! THEY SURE KNOW HOW TO DRESS UP TH' LANDSCAPE!
Y-Y-YEAH -
AN' IT'S S-S-SO QUIET AN' P-P-PEACEFUL!
YEOW! WHAT'S TH-THAT?
S-S-SOUNDED LIKE SH-SHOTS!
BANG
BANG
NO! NO, BUGS! TH' SH-SHOTS C-C-CAME FROM OVER HERE!
THAT'S WHAT I THOUGHT!
M-M-MAYBE S-S-SOMEBODY'S IN T-T-TR-T-TR— DISTRESS!
WAIT FOR ME! DON'T LEAVE ME, PAL!
BANG
BANG
THAT'S MORE LIKE IT! DANCE-DANCE -OR I'LL LET YOU HAVE IT!
BANG
LET'S GO, PORKY— HE MIGHT ASK US TO DANCE -AN' I DON'T LIKE THAT KINDA MUSIC!
BANG
BANG
BANG
HEY! COME BACK!
STOP!

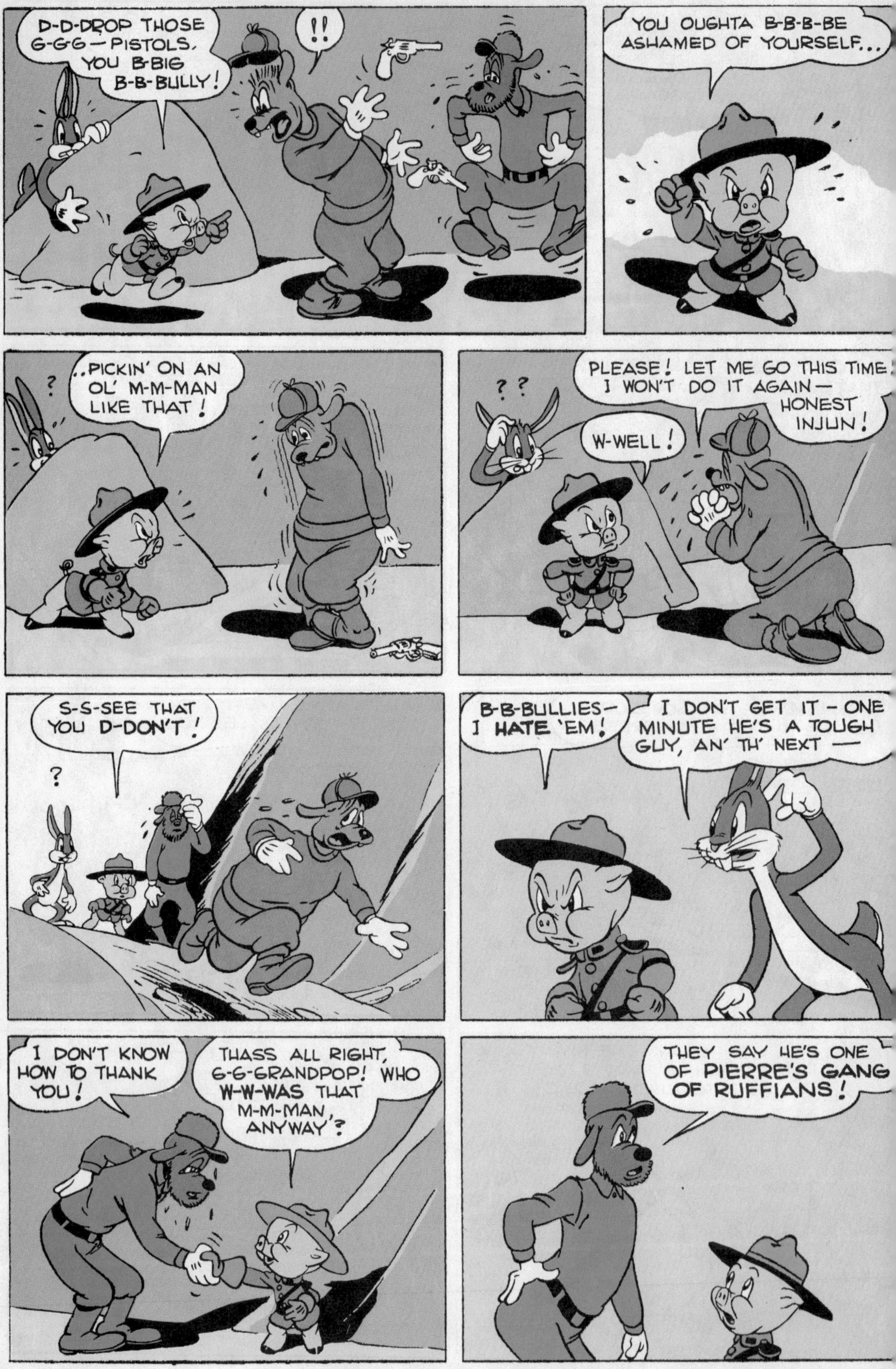
D-D-DROP THOSE G-G-G—PISTOLS, YOU B-BIG B-B-BULLY!
!!
YOU OUGHTA B-B-B-BE ASHAMED OF YOURSELF...
..PICKIN' ON AN OL' M-M-MAN LIKE THAT!
?
? ?
PLEASE! LET ME GO THIS TIME I WON'T DO IT AGAIN— HONEST INJUN!
W-WELL!
S-S-SEE THAT YOU D-DON'T!
?
B-B-BULLIES— I HATE 'EM!
I DON'T GET IT - ONE MINUTE HE'S A TOUGH GUY, AN' TH' NEXT —
I DON'T KNOW HOW TO THANK YOU!
THASS ALL RIGHT, G-G-GRANDPOP! WHO W-W-WAS THAT M-M-MAN, ANYWAY?
THEY SAY HE'S ONE OF PIERRE'S GANG OF RUFFIANS!

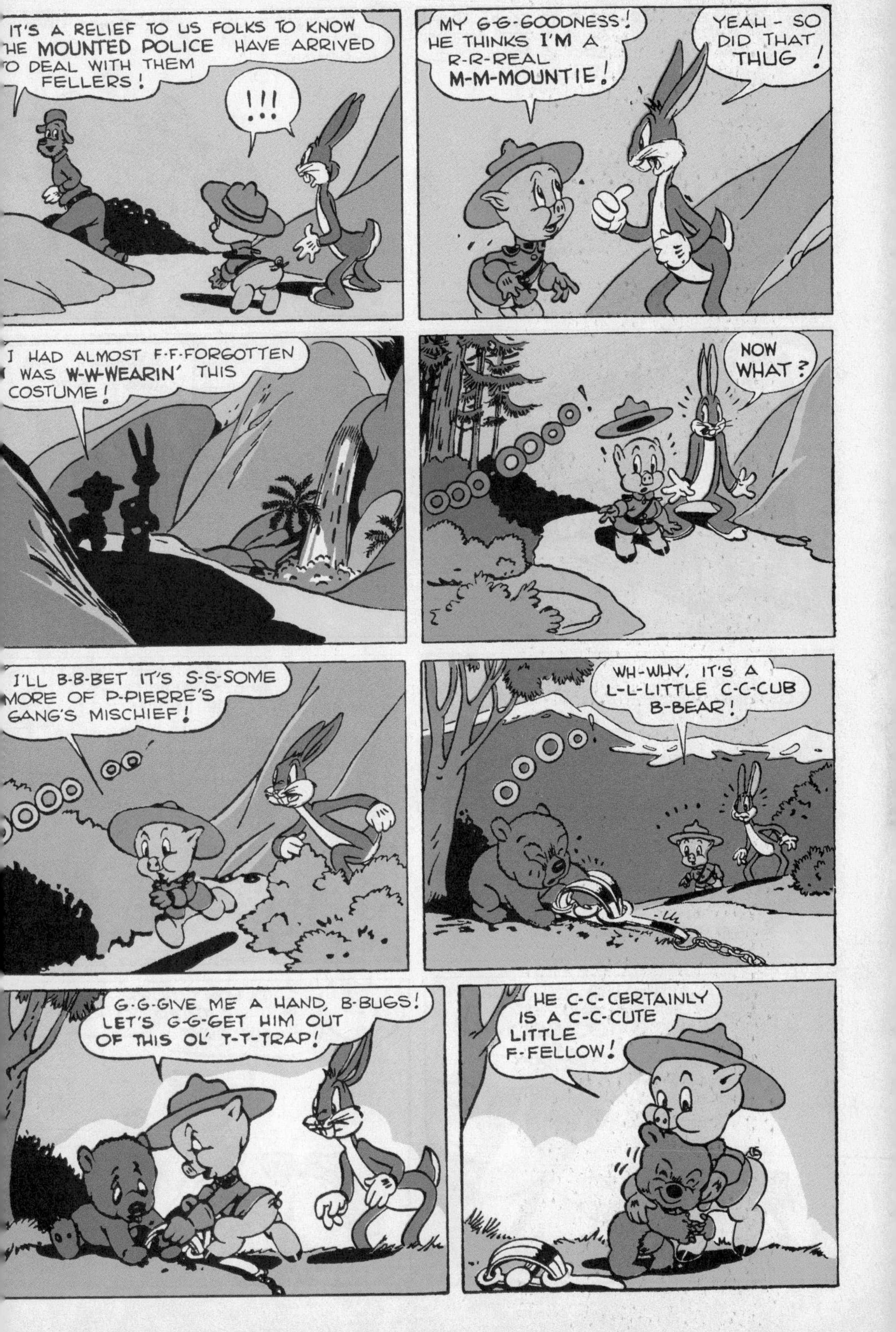
IT'S A RELIEF TO US FOLKS TO KNOW THE MOUNTED POLICE HAVE ARRIVED TO DEAL WITH THEM FELLERS!
!!!
MY G-G-GOODNESS! HE THINKS I'M A R-R-REAL M-M-MOUNTIE!
YEAH - SO DID THAT THUG!
I HAD ALMOST F-F-FORGOTTEN I WAS W-W-WEARIN' THIS COSTUME!
NOW WHAT?
I'LL B-B-BET IT'S S-S-SOME MORE OF P-PIERRE'S GANG'S MISCHIEF!
WH-WHY, IT'S A L-L-LITTLE C-C-CUB B-BEAR!
G-G-GIVE ME A HAND, B-BUGS! LET'S G-G-GET HIM OUT OF THIS OL' T-T-TRAP!
HE C-C-CERTAINLY IS A C-C-CUTE LITTLE F-FELLOW!

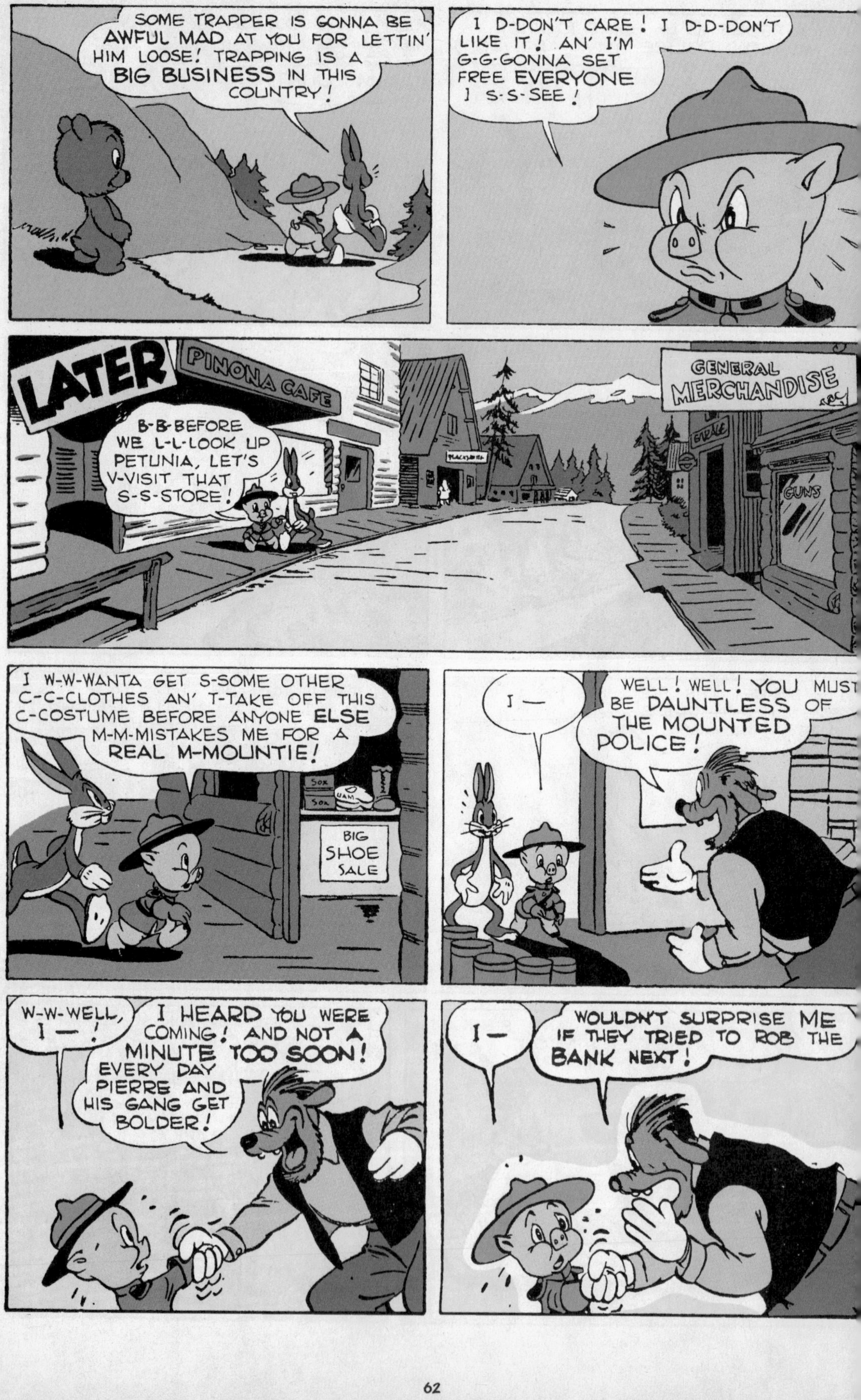
SOME TRAPPER IS GONNA BE AWFUL MAD AT YOU FOR LETTIN' HIM LOOSE! TRAPPING IS A BIG BUSINESS IN THIS COUNTRY!
I D-DON'T CARE! I D-D-DON'T LIKE IT! AN' I'M G-G-GONNA SET FREE EVERYONE I S-S-SEE!
LATER
PINONA CAFE
GENERAL MERCHANDISE
GUNS
B-B-BEFORE WE L-L-LOOK UP PETUNIA, LET'S V-VISIT THAT S-S-STORE!
I W-W-WANTA GET S-SOME OTHER C-C-CLOTHES AN' T-TAKE OFF THIS C-COSTUME BEFORE ANYONE ELSE M-M-MISTAKES ME FOR A REAL M-MOUNTIE!
SOX
SOX
BIG SHOE SALE
I —
WELL! WELL! YOU MUST BE DAUNTLESS OF THE MOUNTED POLICE!
W-W-WELL, I —!
I HEARD YOU WERE COMING! AND NOT A MINUTE TOO SOON!
EVERY DAY PIERRE AND HIS GANG GET BOLDER!
I —
WOULDN'T SURPRISE ME IF THEY TRIED TO ROB THE BANK NEXT!

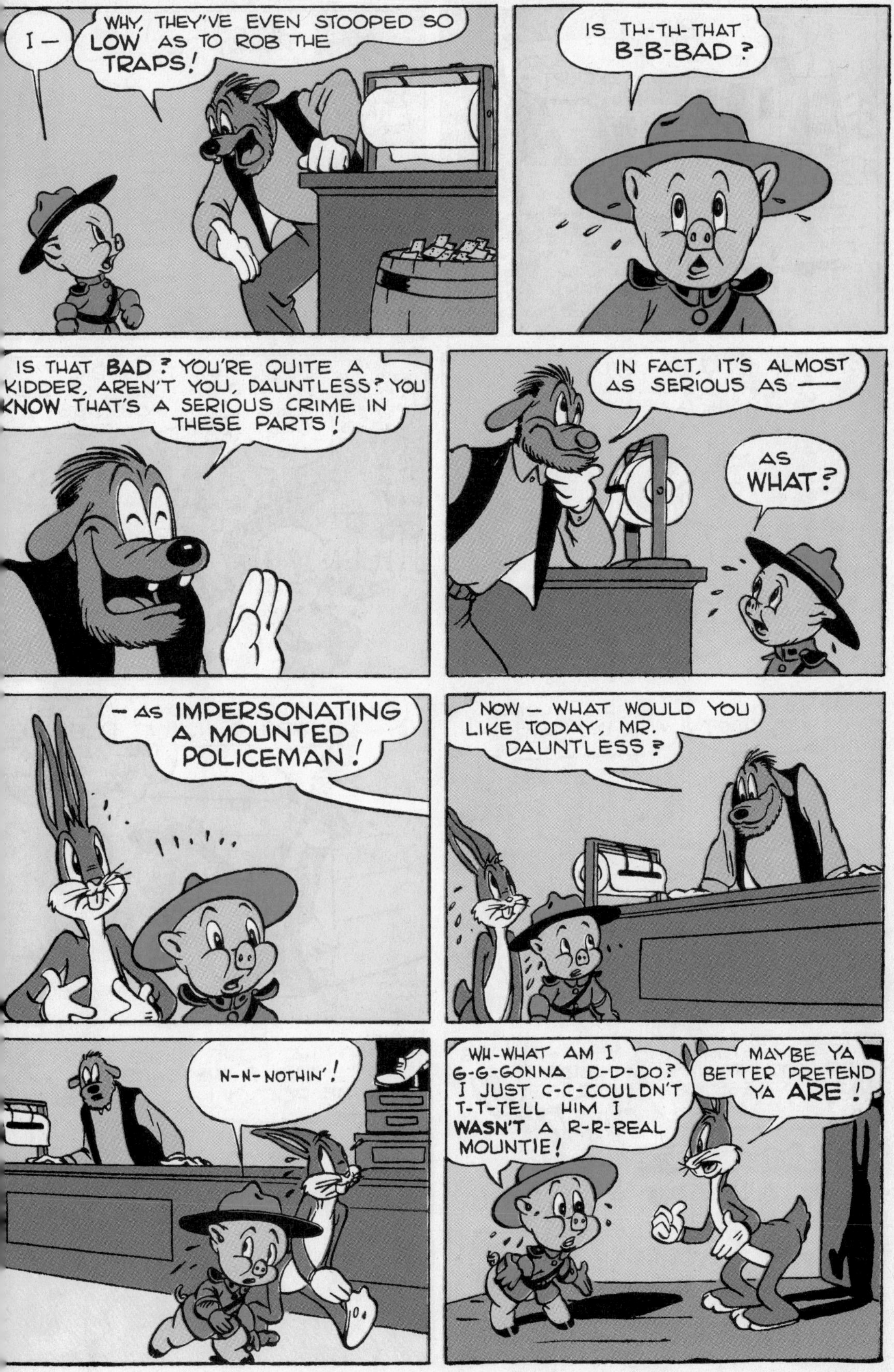
I —
WHY, THEY'VE EVEN STOOPED SO LOW AS TO ROB THE TRAPS!
IS TH-TH-THAT B-B-BAD?
IS THAT BAD? YOU'RE QUITE A KIDDER, AREN'T YOU, DAUNTLESS? YOU KNOW THAT'S A SERIOUS CRIME IN THESE PARTS!
IN FACT, IT'S ALMOST AS SERIOUS AS —
AS WHAT?
— AS IMPERSONATING A MOUNTED POLICEMAN!
NOW — WHAT WOULD YOU LIKE TODAY, MR. DAUNTLESS?
N-N-NOTHIN'!
WH-WHAT AM I G-G-GONNA D-D-DO? I JUST C-C-COULDN'T T-T-TELL HIM I WASN'T A R-R-REAL MOUNTIE!
MAYBE YA BETTER PRETEND YA ARE!

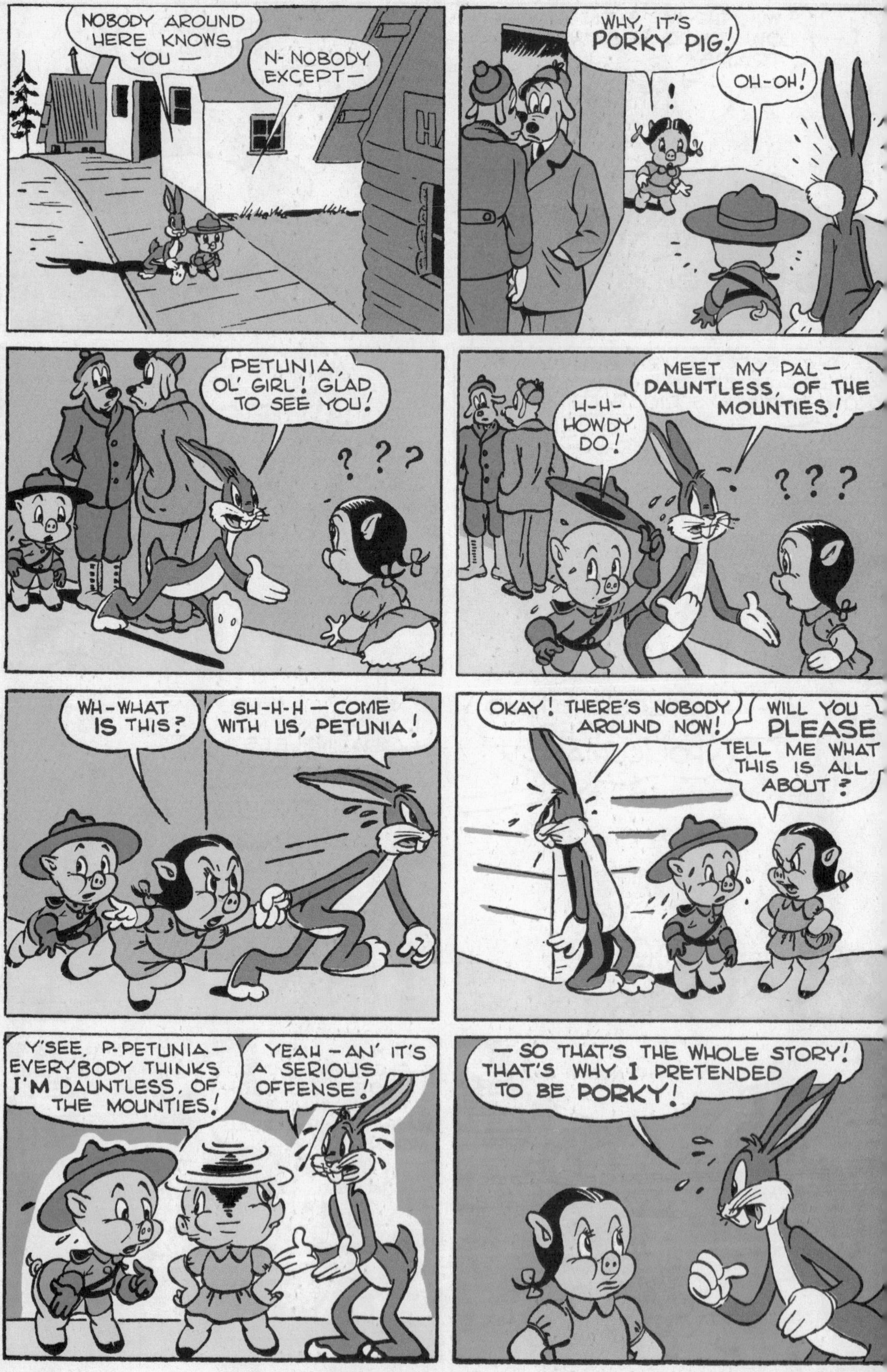
NOBODY AROUND HERE KNOWS YOU —
N- NOBODY EXCEPT—
WHY, IT'S PORKY PIG!
!
OH-OH!
PETUNIA, OL' GIRL! GLAD TO SEE YOU!
? ? ?
MEET MY PAL— DAUNTLESS, OF THE MOUNTIES!
H-H-HOWDY DO!
? ? ?
WH-WHAT IS THIS?
SH-H-H —COME WITH US, PETUNIA!
OKAY! THERE'S NOBODY AROUND NOW!
WILL YOU PLEASE TELL ME WHAT THIS IS ALL ABOUT?
Y'SEE, P-PETUNIA— EVERYBODY THINKS I'M DAUNTLESS, OF THE MOUNTIES!
YEAH —AN' IT'S A SERIOUS OFFENSE!
—SO THAT'S THE WHOLE STORY! THAT'S WHY I PRETENDED TO BE PORKY!

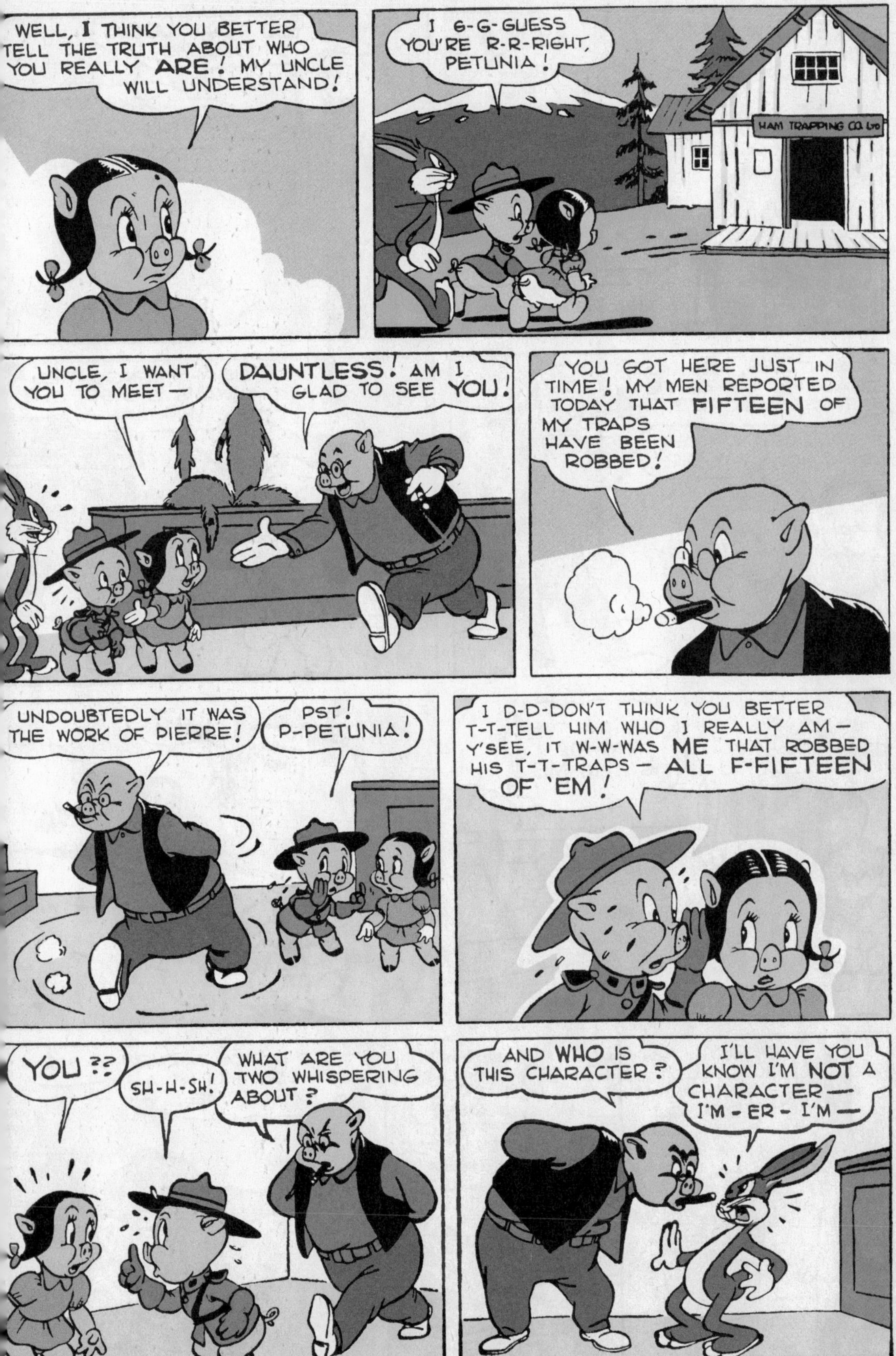
WELL, I THINK YOU BETTER TELL THE TRUTH ABOUT WHO YOU REALLY ARE! MY UNCLE WILL UNDERSTAND!
I G-G-GUESS YOU'RE R-R-RIGHT, PETUNIA!
HAM TRAPPING CO. LTD
UNCLE, I WANT YOU TO MEET—
DAUNTLESS! AM I GLAD TO SEE YOU!
YOU GOT HERE JUST IN TIME! MY MEN REPORTED TODAY THAT FIFTEEN OF MY TRAPS HAVE BEEN ROBBED!
UNDOUBTEDLY IT WAS THE WORK OF PIERRE!
PST! P-PETUNIA!
I D-D-DON'T THINK YOU BETTER T-T-TELL HIM WHO I REALLY AM— Y'SEE, IT W-W-WAS ME THAT ROBBED HIS T-T-TRAPS— ALL F-FIFTEEN OF 'EM!
YOU ??
SH-H-SH!
WHAT ARE YOU TWO WHISPERING ABOUT ?
AND WHO IS THIS CHARACTER ?
I'LL HAVE YOU KNOW I'M NOT A CHARACTER— I'M - ER - I'M —

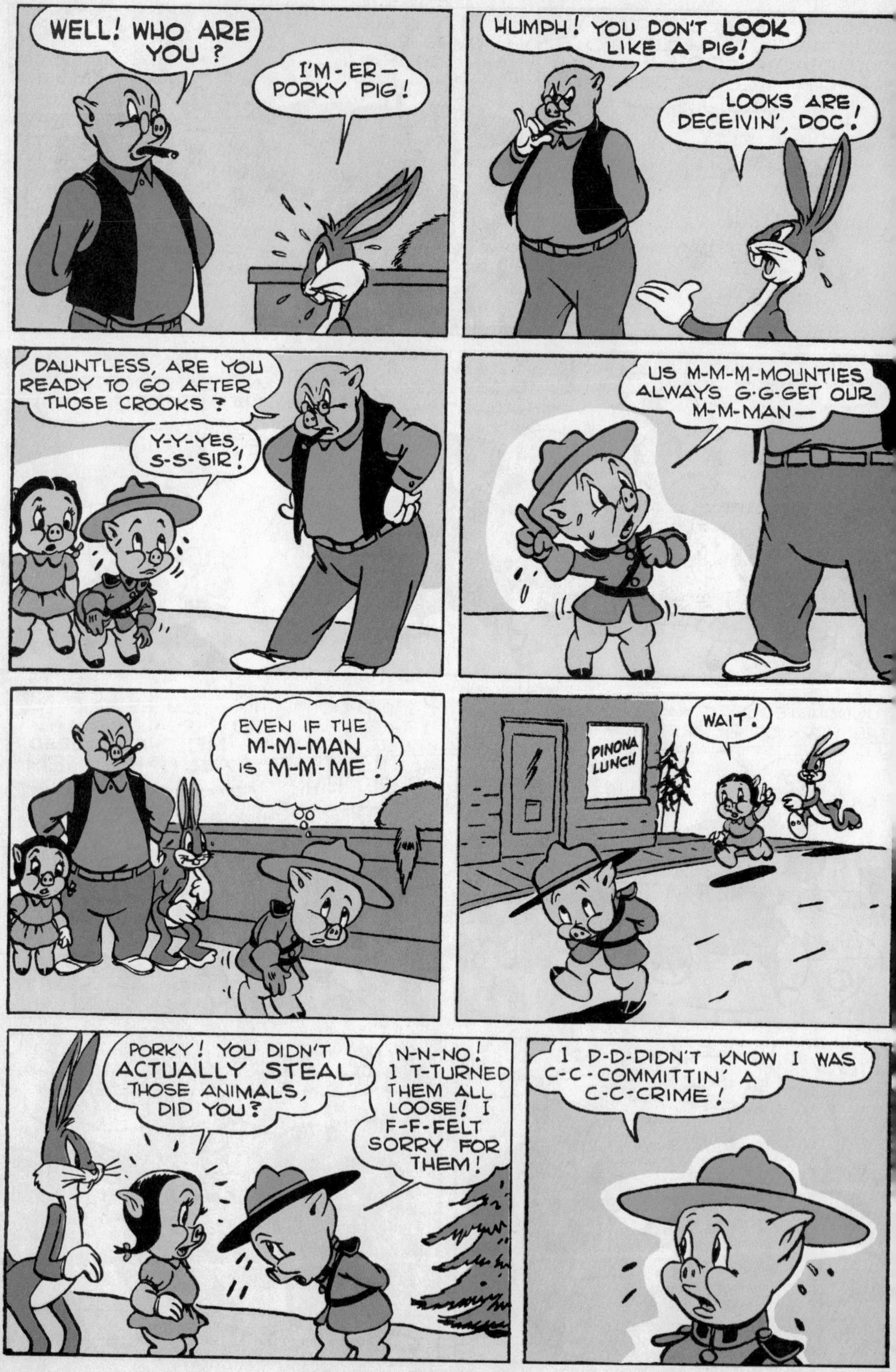
WELL! WHO ARE YOU ?
I'M - ER - PORKY PIG!
HUMPH! YOU DON'T LOOK LIKE A PIG!
LOOKS ARE DECEIVIN', DOC!
DAUNTLESS, ARE YOU READY TO GO AFTER THOSE CROOKS ?
Y-Y-YES, S-S-SIR!
US M-M-M-MOUNTIES ALWAYS G-G-GET OUR M-M-MAN—
EVEN IF THE M-M-MAN IS M-M-ME!
PINONA LUNCH
WAIT!
PORKY! YOU DIDN'T ACTUALLY STEAL THOSE ANIMALS, DID YOU?
N-N-NO! I T-TURNED THEM ALL LOOSE! I F-F-FELT SORRY FOR THEM!
I D-D-DIDN'T KNOW I WAS C-C-COMMITTIN' A C-C-CRIME!

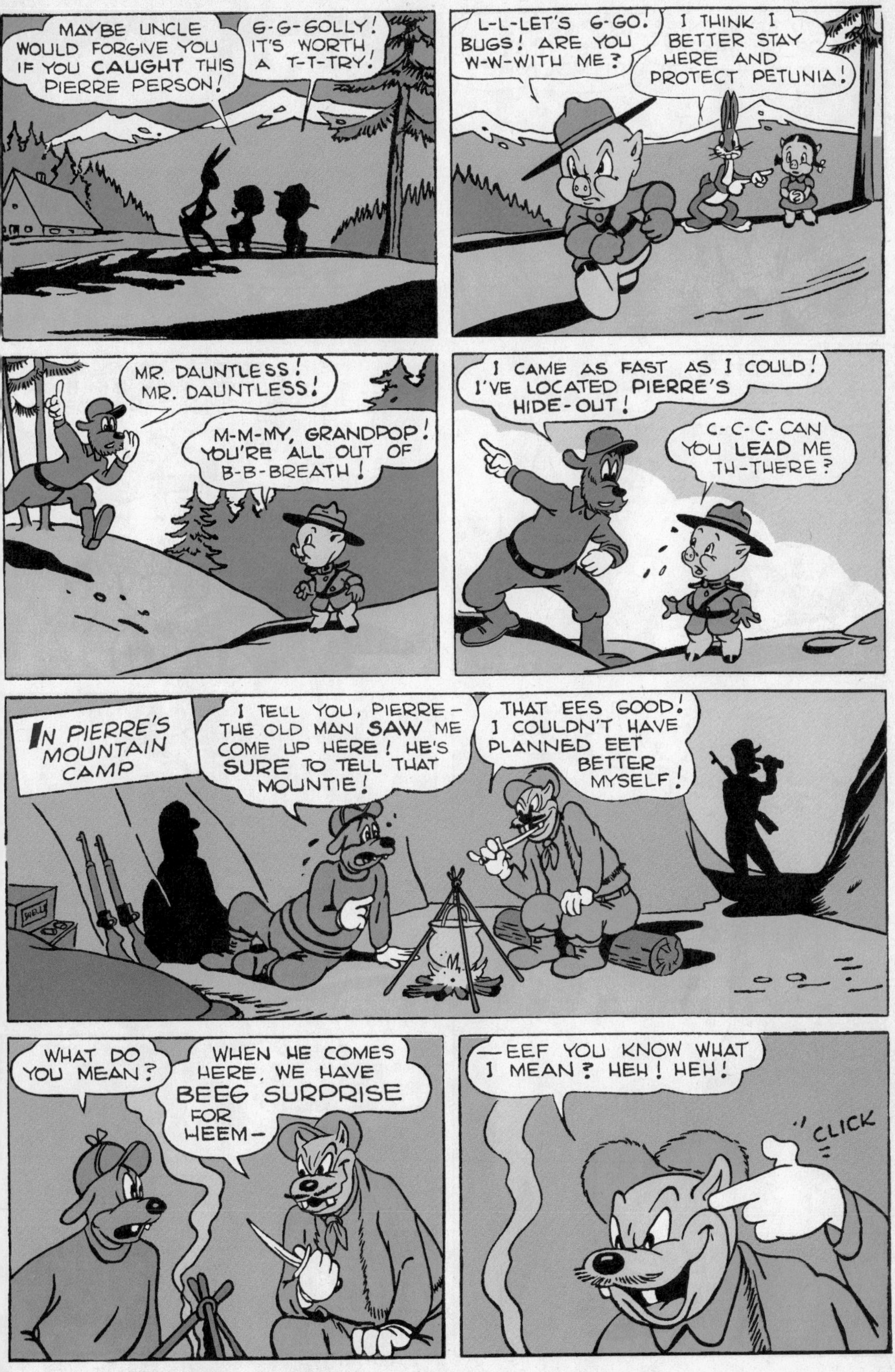
MAYBE UNCLE WOULD FORGIVE YOU IF YOU CAUGHT THIS PIERRE PERSON!
G-G-GOLLY! IT'S WORTH A T-T-TRY!
L-L-LET'S G-GO! BUGS! ARE YOU W-W-WITH ME?
I THINK I BETTER STAY HERE AND PROTECT PETUNIA!
MR. DAUNTLESS! MR. DAUNTLESS!
M-M-MY, GRANDPOP! YOU'RE ALL OUT OF B-B-BREATH!
I CAME AS FAST AS I COULD! I'VE LOCATED PIERRE'S HIDE-OUT!
C-C-C- CAN YOU LEAD ME TH-THERE?
IN PIERRE'S MOUNTAIN CAMP
I TELL YOU, PIERRE— THE OLD MAN SAW ME COME UP HERE! HE'S SURE TO TELL THAT MOUNTIE!
THAT EES GOOD! I COULDN'T HAVE PLANNED EET BETTER MYSELF!
WHAT DO YOU MEAN?
WHEN HE COMES HERE, WE HAVE BEEG SURPRISE FOR HEEM—
—EEF YOU KNOW WHAT I MEAN? HEH! HEH!
CLICK

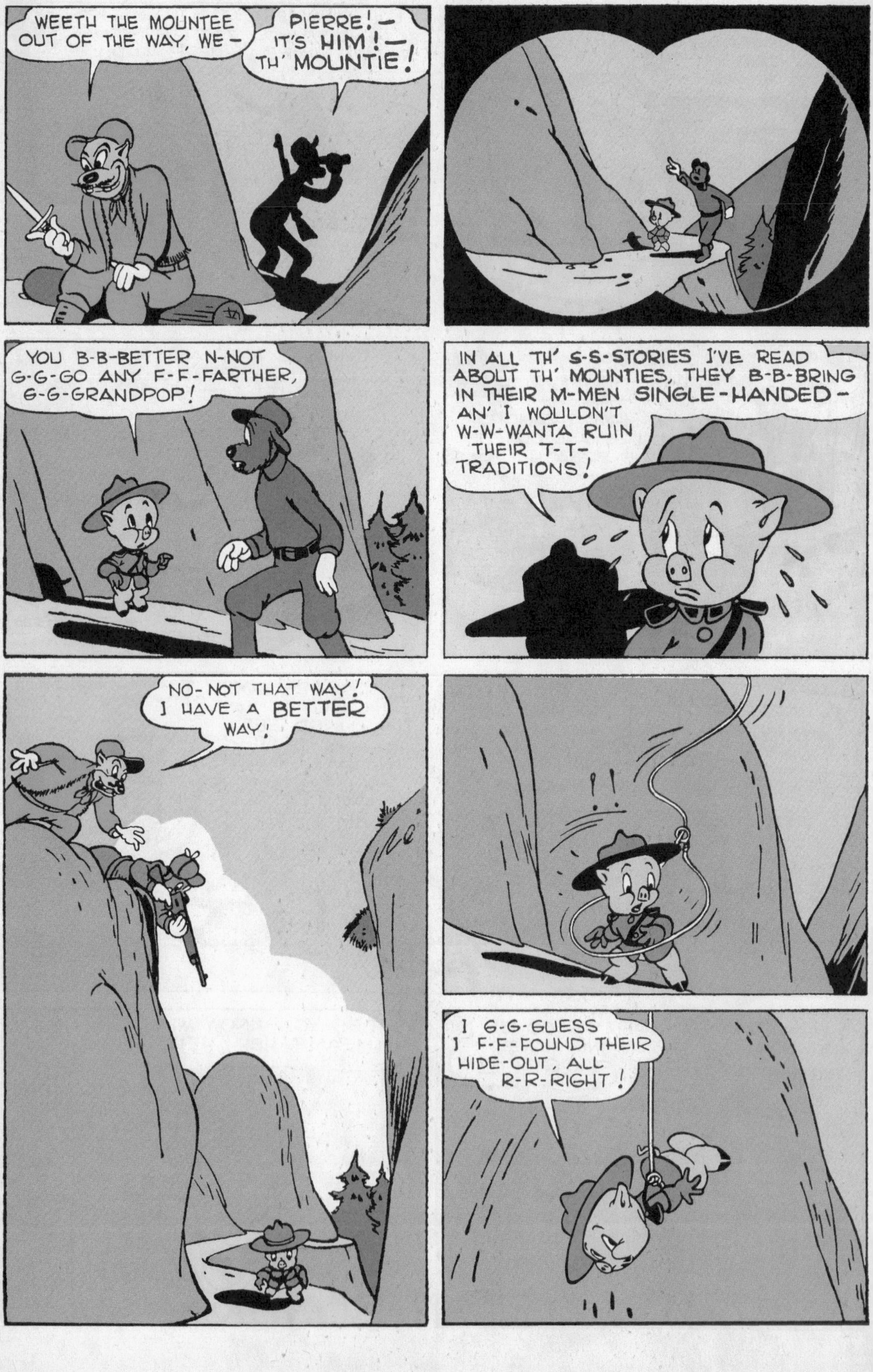
WEETH THE MOUNTEE OUT OF THE WAY, WE –
PIERRE! – IT'S HIM! – TH' MOUNTIE!
YOU B-B-BETTER N-NOT G-G-GO ANY F-F-FARTHER, G-G-GRANDPOP!
IN ALL TH' S-S-STORIES I'VE READ ABOUT TH' MOUNTIES, THEY B-B-BRING IN THEIR M-MEN SINGLE-HANDED – AN' I WOULDN'T W-W-WANTA RUIN THEIR T-T-TRADITIONS!
NO- NOT THAT WAY! I HAVE A BETTER WAY!
! !
I G-G-GUESS I F-F-FOUND THEIR HIDE-OUT, ALL R-R-RIGHT!

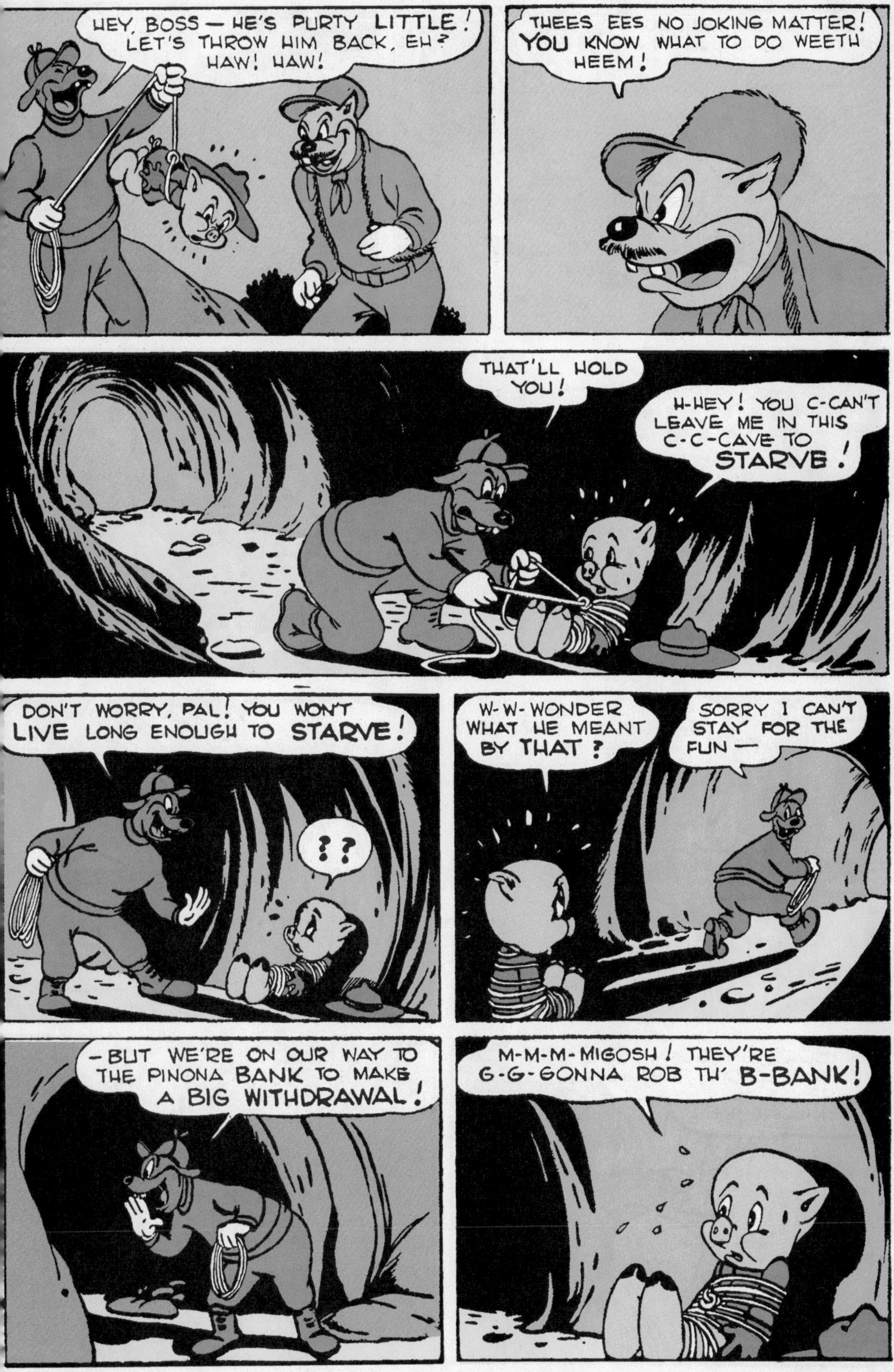
HEY, BOSS — HE'S PURTY LITTLE! LET'S THROW HIM BACK, EH? HAW! HAW!
THEES EES NO JOKING MATTER! YOU KNOW WHAT TO DO WEETH HEEM!
THAT'LL HOLD YOU!
H-HEY! YOU C-CAN'T LEAVE ME IN THIS C-C-CAVE TO STARVE!
DON'T WORRY, PAL! YOU WON'T LIVE LONG ENOUGH TO STARVE!
??
W-W-WONDER WHAT HE MEANT BY THAT?
SORRY I CAN'T STAY FOR THE FUN —
— BUT WE'RE ON OUR WAY TO THE PINONA BANK TO MAKE A BIG WITHDRAWAL!
M-M-M-MIGOSH! THEY'RE G-G-GONNA ROB TH' B-BANK!

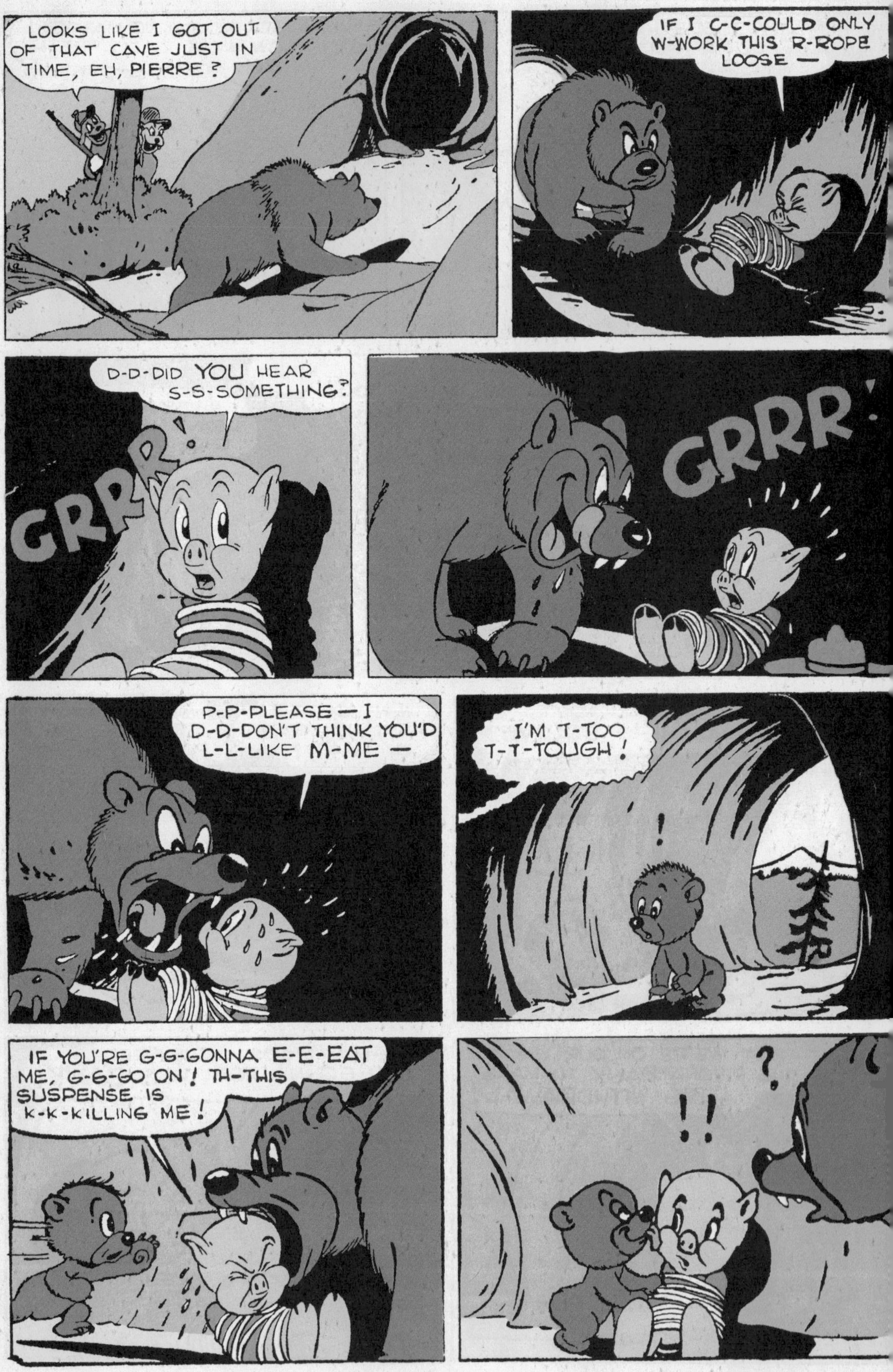
LOOKS LIKE I GOT OUT OF THAT CAVE JUST IN TIME, EH, PIERRE?
IF I C-C-COULD ONLY W-WORK THIS R-ROPE LOOSE —
D-D-DID YOU HEAR S-S-SOMETHING?
GRRR!
GRRR!
P-P-PLEASE — I D-D-DON'T THINK YOU'D L-L-LIKE M-ME —
I'M T-TOO T-T-TOUGH!
!
IF YOU'RE G-G-GONNA E-E-EAT ME, G-G-GO ON! TH-THIS SUSPENSE IS K-K-KILLING ME!
?
!!

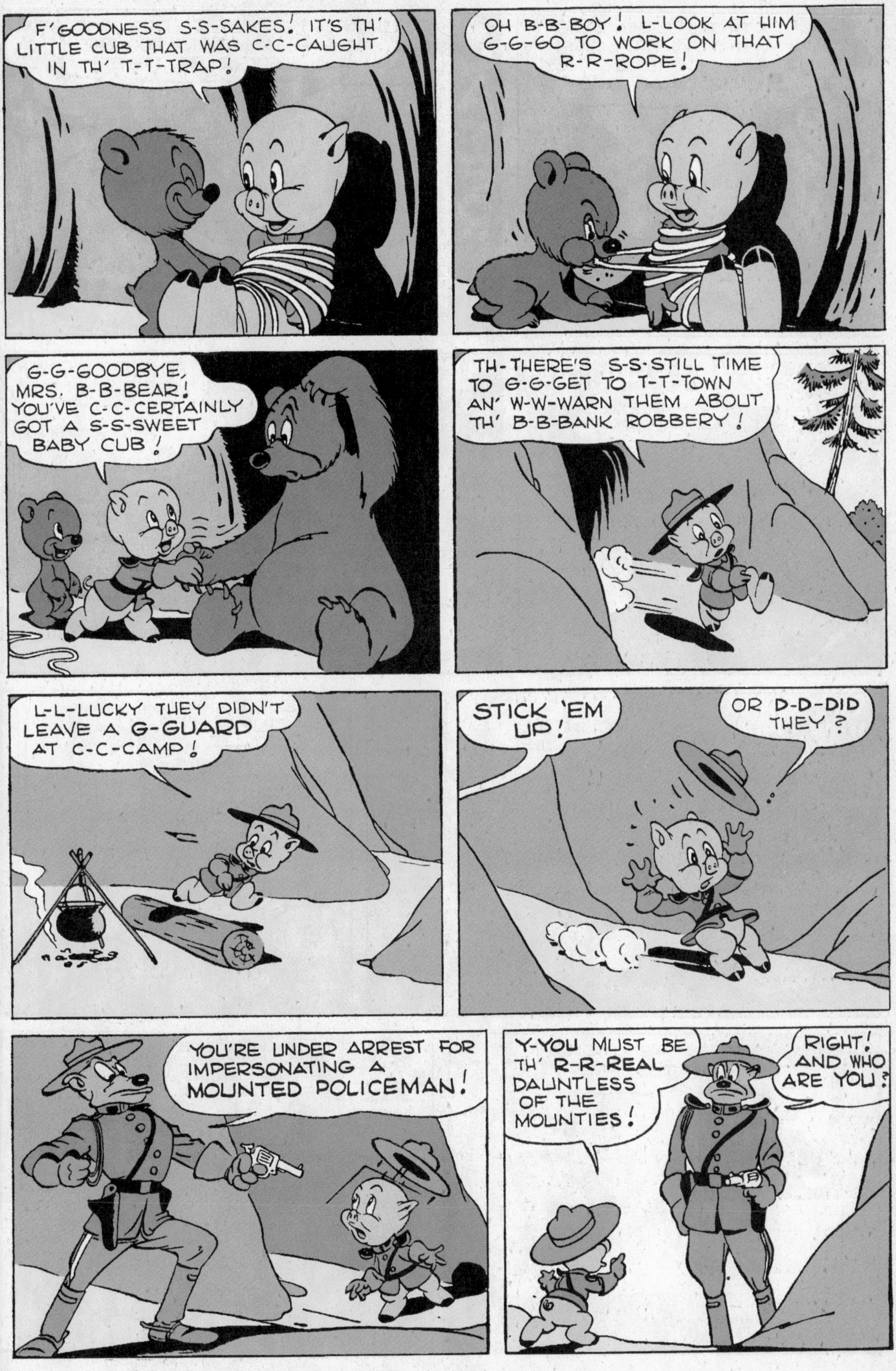
F'GOODNESS S-S-SAKES! IT'S TH' LITTLE CUB THAT WAS C-C-CAUGHT IN TH' T-T-TRAP!
OH B-B-BOY! L-LOOK AT HIM G-G-GO TO WORK ON THAT R-R-ROPE!
G-G-GOODBYE, MRS. B-B-BEAR! YOU'VE C-C-CERTAINLY GOT A S-S-SWEET BABY CUB!
TH-THERE'S S-S-STILL TIME TO G-G-GET TO T-T-TOWN AN' W-W-WARN THEM ABOUT TH' B-B-BANK ROBBERY!
L-L-LUCKY THEY DIDN'T LEAVE A G-GUARD AT C-C-CAMP!
OR D-D-DID THEY?
STICK 'EM UP!
YOU'RE UNDER ARREST FOR IMPERSONATING A MOUNTED POLICEMAN!
Y-YOU MUST BE TH' R-R-REAL DAUNTLESS OF THE MOUNTIES!
RIGHT! AND WHO ARE YOU?

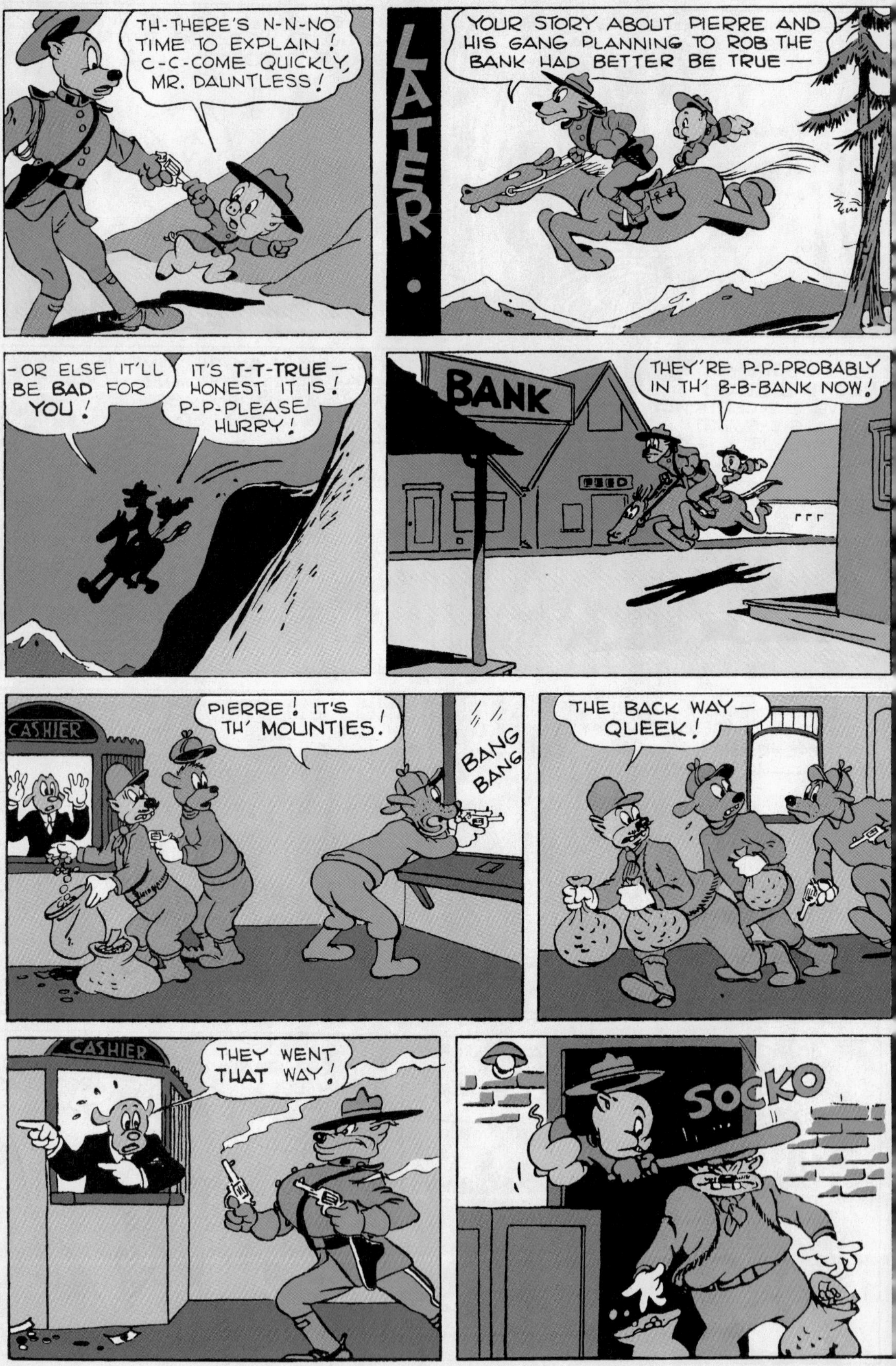
TH-THERE'S N-N-NO TIME TO EXPLAIN! C-C-COME QUICKLY, MR. DAUNTLESS!
LATER.
YOUR STORY ABOUT PIERRE AND HIS GANG PLANNING TO ROB THE BANK HAD BETTER BE TRUE—
-OR ELSE IT'LL BE BAD FOR YOU!
IT'S T-T-TRUE— HONEST IT IS! P-P-PLEASE HURRY!
BANK
FEED
THEY'RE P-P-PROBABLY IN TH' B-B-BANK NOW!
CASHIER
PIERRE! IT'S TH' MOUNTIES!
BANG BANG
THE BACK WAY— QUEEK!
CASHIER
THEY WENT THAT WAY!
SOCKO

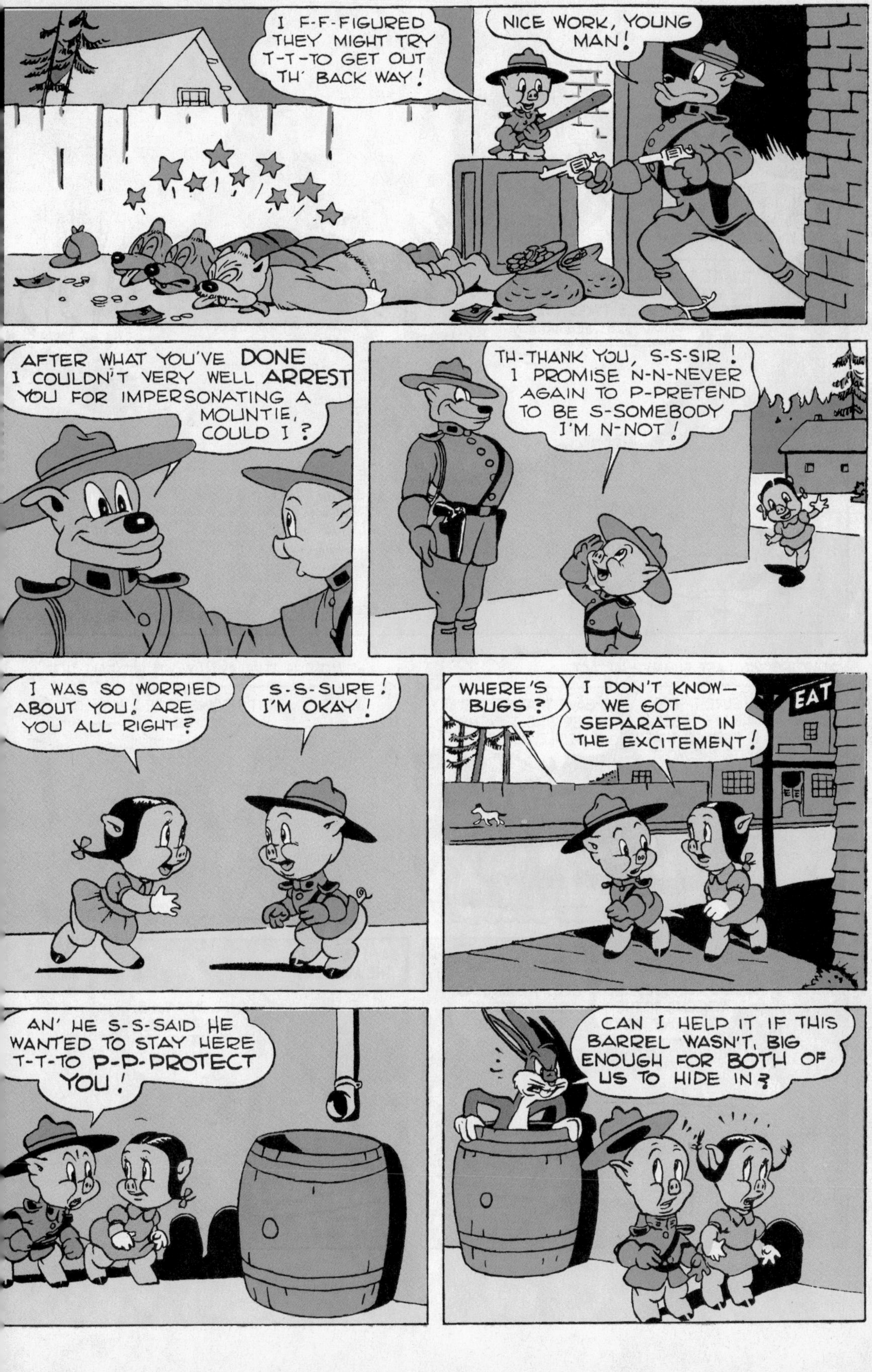

I F-F-FIGURED THEY MIGHT TRY T-T-TO GET OUT TH' BACK WAY!
NICE WORK, YOUNG MAN!
AFTER WHAT YOU'VE DONE I COULDN'T VERY WELL ARREST YOU FOR IMPERSONATING A MOUNTIE, COULD I?
TH-THANK YOU, S-S-SIR! I PROMISE N-N-NEVER AGAIN TO P-PRETEND TO BE S-SOMEBODY I'M N-NOT!
I WAS SO WORRIED ABOUT YOU! ARE YOU ALL RIGHT?
S-S-SURE! I'M OKAY!
WHERE'S BUGS?
I DON'T KNOW— WE GOT SEPARATED IN THE EXCITEMENT!
EAT
AN' HE S-S-SAID HE WANTED TO STAY HERE T-T-TO P-P-PROTECT YOU!
CAN I HELP IT IF THIS BARREL WASN'T BIG ENOUGH FOR BOTH OF US TO HIDE IN?

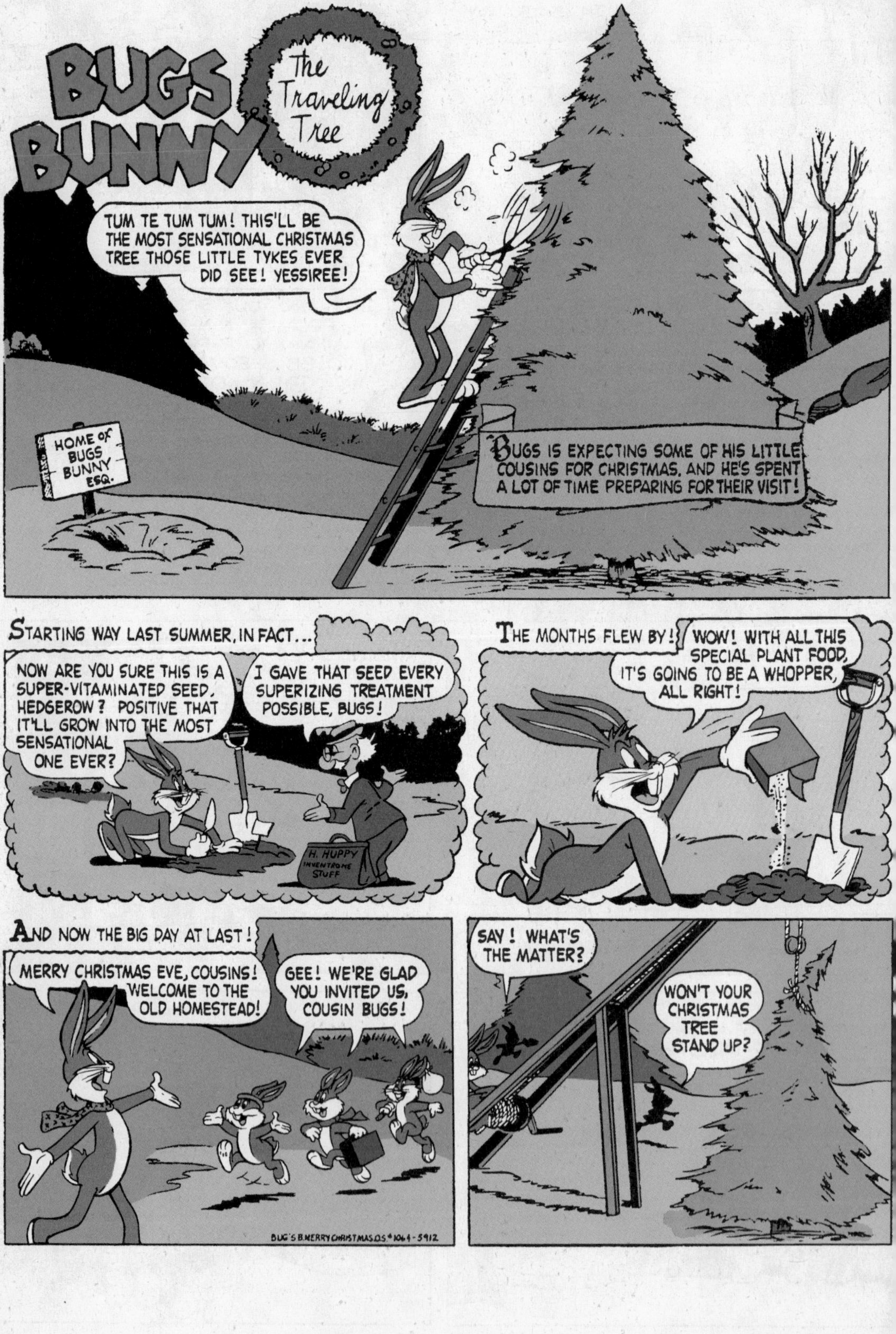

BUGS BUNNY
The Traveling Tree
TUM TE TUM TUM! THIS'LL BE THE MOST SENSATIONAL CHRISTMAS TREE THOSE LITTLE TYKES EVER DID SEE! YESSIREE!
HOME OF BUGS BUNNY ESQ.
BUGS IS EXPECTING SOME OF HIS LITTLE COUSINS FOR CHRISTMAS, AND HE'S SPENT A LOT OF TIME PREPARING FOR THEIR VISIT!
STARTING WAY LAST SUMMER, IN FACT...
NOW ARE YOU SURE THIS IS A SUPER-VITAMINATED SEED, HEDGEROW? POSITIVE THAT IT'LL GROW INTO THE MOST SENSATIONAL ONE EVER?
I GAVE THAT SEED EVERY SUPERIZING TREATMENT POSSIBLE, BUGS!
H. HUPPY INVENTRONS STUFF
THE MONTHS FLEW BY!
WOW! WITH ALL THIS SPECIAL PLANT FOOD, IT'S GOING TO BE A WHOPPER, ALL RIGHT!
AND NOW THE BIG DAY AT LAST!
MERRY CHRISTMAS EVE, COUSINS! WELCOME TO THE OLD HOMESTEAD!
GEE! WE'RE GLAD YOU INVITED US, COUSIN BUGS!
BUG'S B.MERRY CHRISTMAS D.S.# 1064-5912
SAY! WHAT'S THE MATTER?
WON'T YOUR CHRISTMAS TREE STAND UP?

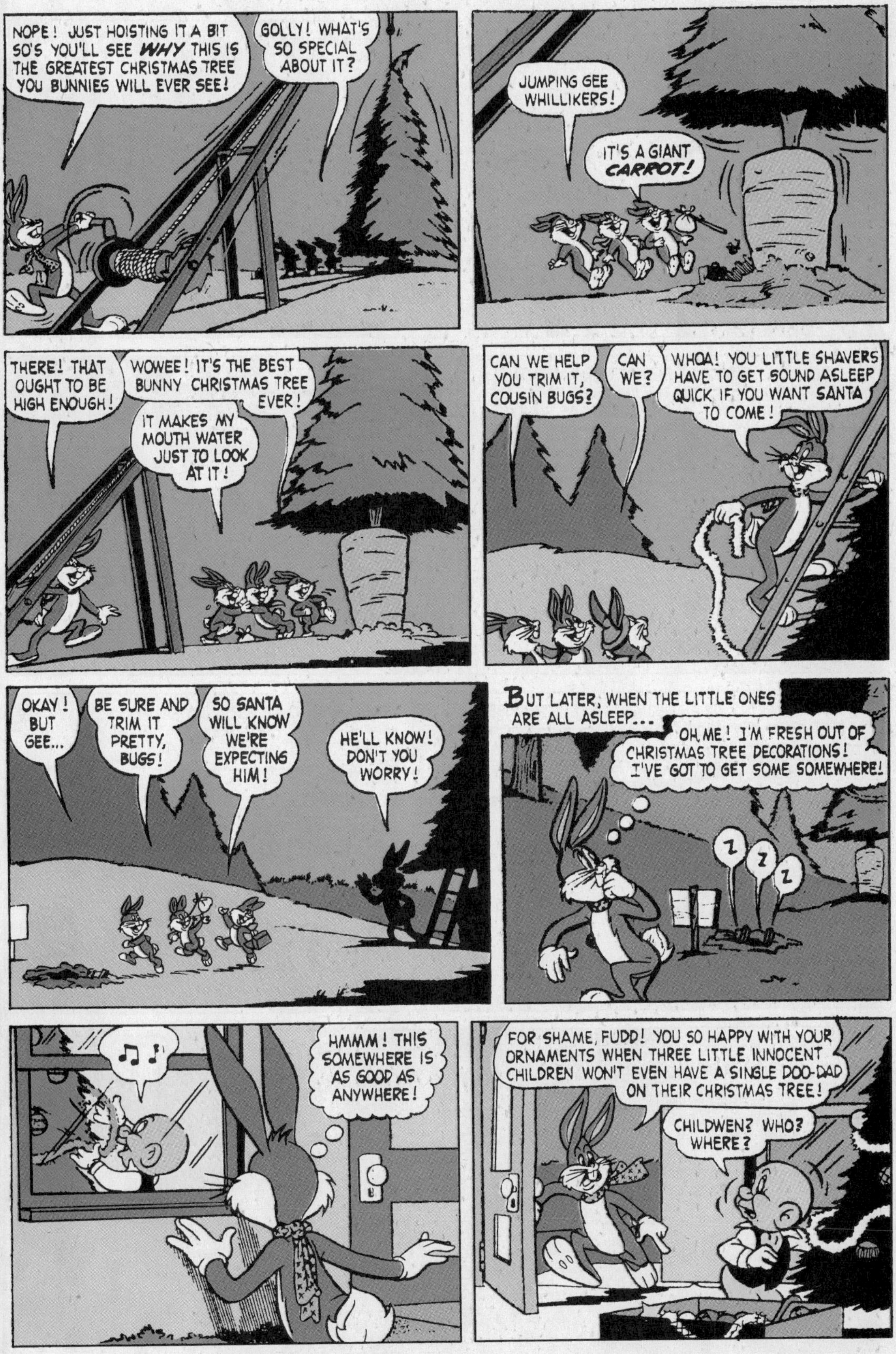
NOPE! JUST HOISTING IT A BIT SO'S YOU'LL SEE *WHY* THIS IS THE GREATEST CHRISTMAS TREE YOU BUNNIES WILL EVER SEE!
GOLLY! WHAT'S SO SPECIAL ABOUT IT?
JUMPING GEE WHILLIKERS!
IT'S A GIANT *CARROT!*
THERE! THAT OUGHT TO BE HIGH ENOUGH!
WOWEE! IT'S THE BEST BUNNY CHRISTMAS TREE EVER!
IT MAKES MY MOUTH WATER JUST TO LOOK AT IT!
CAN WE HELP YOU TRIM IT, COUSIN BUGS?
CAN WE?
WHOA! YOU LITTLE SHAVERS HAVE TO GET SOUND ASLEEP QUICK IF YOU WANT SANTA TO COME!
OKAY! BUT GEE...
BE SURE AND TRIM IT PRETTY, BUGS!
SO SANTA WILL KNOW WE'RE EXPECTING HIM!
HE'LL KNOW! DON'T YOU WORRY!
BUT LATER, WHEN THE LITTLE ONES ARE ALL ASLEEP...
OH, ME! I'M FRESH OUT OF CHRISTMAS TREE DECORATIONS! I'VE GOT TO GET SOME SOMEWHERE!
Z Z Z
HMMM! THIS SOMEWHERE IS AS GOOD AS ANYWHERE!
FOR SHAME, FUDD! YOU SO HAPPY WITH YOUR ORNAMENTS WHEN THREE LITTLE INNOCENT CHILDREN WON'T EVEN HAVE A SINGLE DOO-DAD ON THEIR CHRISTMAS TREE!
CHILDWEN? WHO? WHERE?

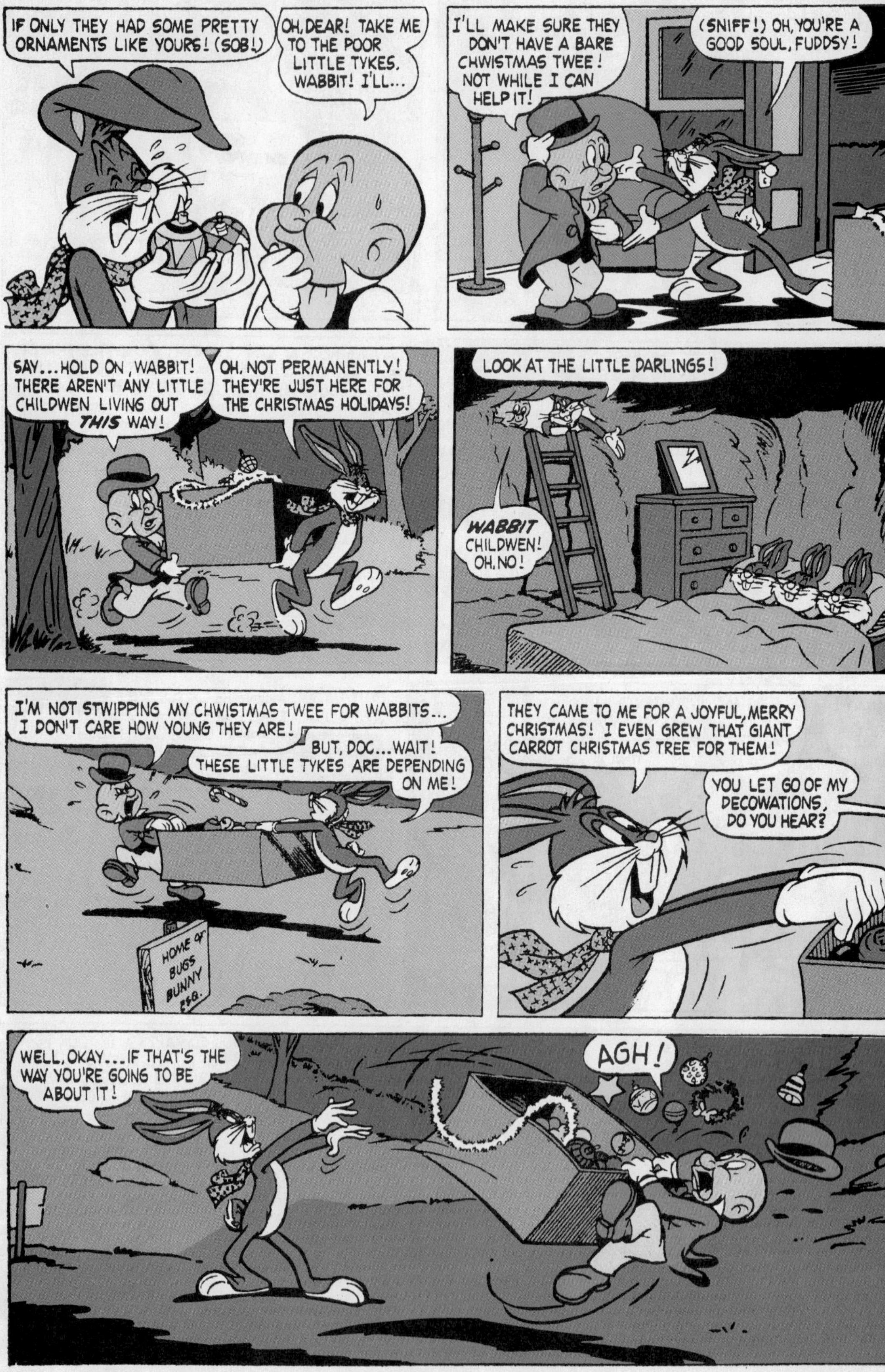
IF ONLY THEY HAD SOME PRETTY ORNAMENTS LIKE YOURS! (SOB!)
OH, DEAR! TAKE ME TO THE POOR LITTLE TYKES, WABBIT! I'LL...
I'LL MAKE SURE THEY DON'T HAVE A BARE CHWISTMAS TWEE! NOT WHILE I CAN HELP IT!
(SNIFF!) OH, YOU'RE A GOOD SOUL, FUDDSY!
SAY...HOLD ON, WABBIT! THERE AREN'T ANY LITTLE CHILDWEN LIVING OUT THIS WAY!
OH, NOT PERMANENTLY! THEY'RE JUST HERE FOR THE CHRISTMAS HOLIDAYS!
LOOK AT THE LITTLE DARLINGS!
WABBIT CHILDWEN! OH, NO!
I'M NOT STWIPPING MY CHWISTMAS TWEE FOR WABBITS... I DON'T CARE HOW YOUNG THEY ARE!
BUT, DOC...WAIT! THESE LITTLE TYKES ARE DEPENDING ON ME!
HOME OF BUGS BUNNY
THEY CAME TO ME FOR A JOYFUL, MERRY CHRISTMAS! I EVEN GREW THAT GIANT CARROT CHRISTMAS TREE FOR THEM!
YOU LET GO OF MY DECOWATIONS, DO YOU HEAR?
WELL, OKAY...IF THAT'S THE WAY YOU'RE GOING TO BE ABOUT IT!
AGH!

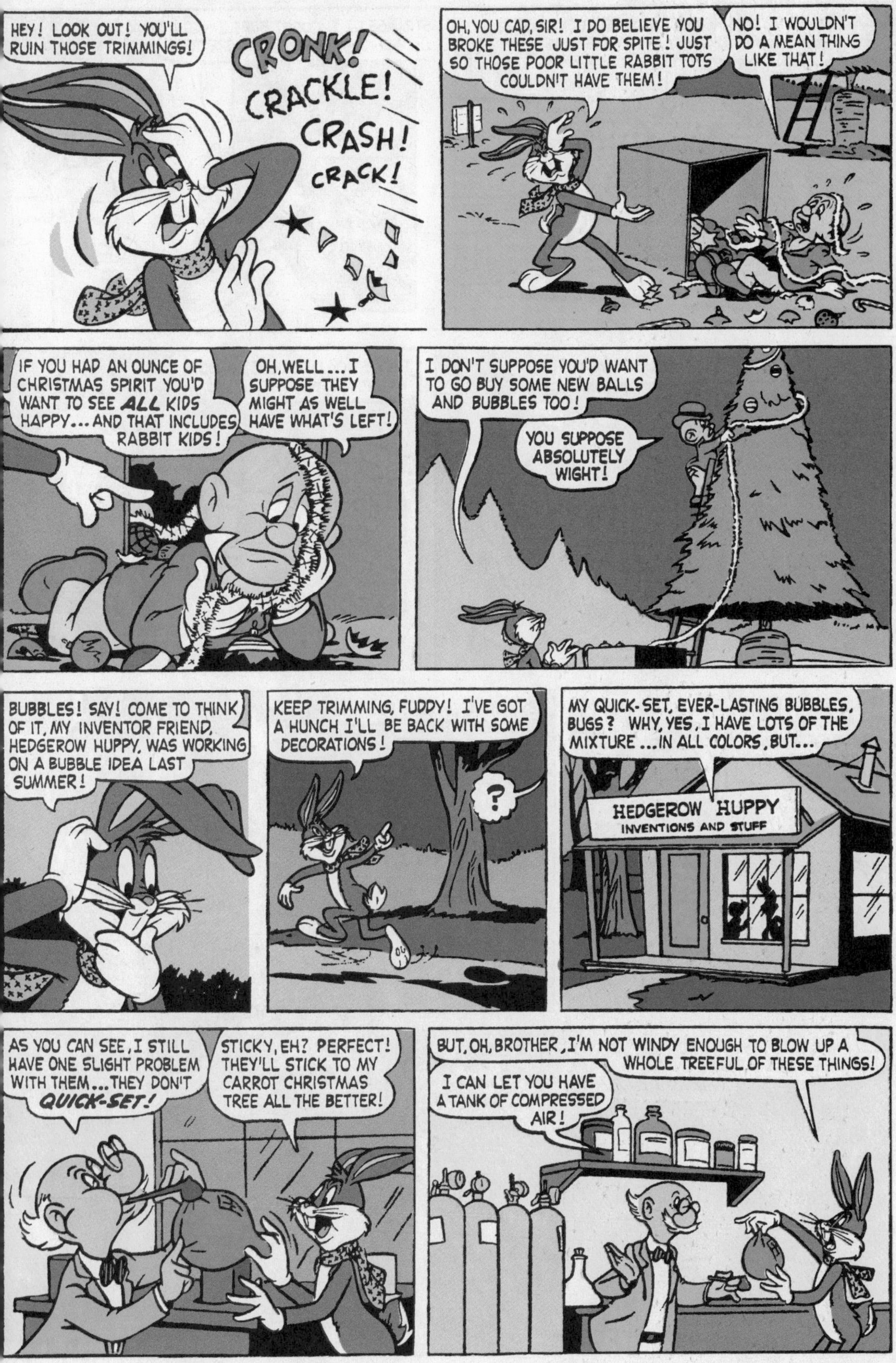
HEY! LOOK OUT! YOU'LL RUIN THOSE TRIMMINGS!
CRONK! CRACKLE! CRASH! CRACK!
OH, YOU CAD, SIR! I DO BELIEVE YOU BROKE THESE JUST FOR SPITE! JUST SO THOSE POOR LITTLE RABBIT TOTS COULDN'T HAVE THEM!
NO! I WOULDN'T DO A MEAN THING LIKE THAT!
IF YOU HAD AN OUNCE OF CHRISTMAS SPIRIT YOU'D WANT TO SEE ALL KIDS HAPPY... AND THAT INCLUDES RABBIT KIDS!
OH, WELL... I SUPPOSE THEY MIGHT AS WELL HAVE WHAT'S LEFT!
I DON'T SUPPOSE YOU'D WANT TO GO BUY SOME NEW BALLS AND BUBBLES TOO!
YOU SUPPOSE ABSOLUTELY WIGHT!
BUBBLES! SAY! COME TO THINK OF IT, MY INVENTOR FRIEND, HEDGEROW HUPPY, WAS WORKING ON A BUBBLE IDEA LAST SUMMER!
KEEP TRIMMING, FUDDY! I'VE GOT A HUNCH I'LL BE BACK WITH SOME DECORATIONS!
?
MY QUICK-SET, EVER-LASTING BUBBLES, BUGS? WHY, YES, I HAVE LOTS OF THE MIXTURE ... IN ALL COLORS, BUT...
HEDGEROW HUPPY
INVENTIONS AND STUFF
AS YOU CAN SEE, I STILL HAVE ONE SLIGHT PROBLEM WITH THEM... THEY DON'T QUICK-SET!
STICKY, EH? PERFECT! THEY'LL STICK TO MY CARROT CHRISTMAS TREE ALL THE BETTER!
BUT, OH, BROTHER, I'M NOT WINDY ENOUGH TO BLOW UP A WHOLE TREEFUL OF THESE THINGS!
I CAN LET YOU HAVE A TANK OF COMPRESSED AIR!

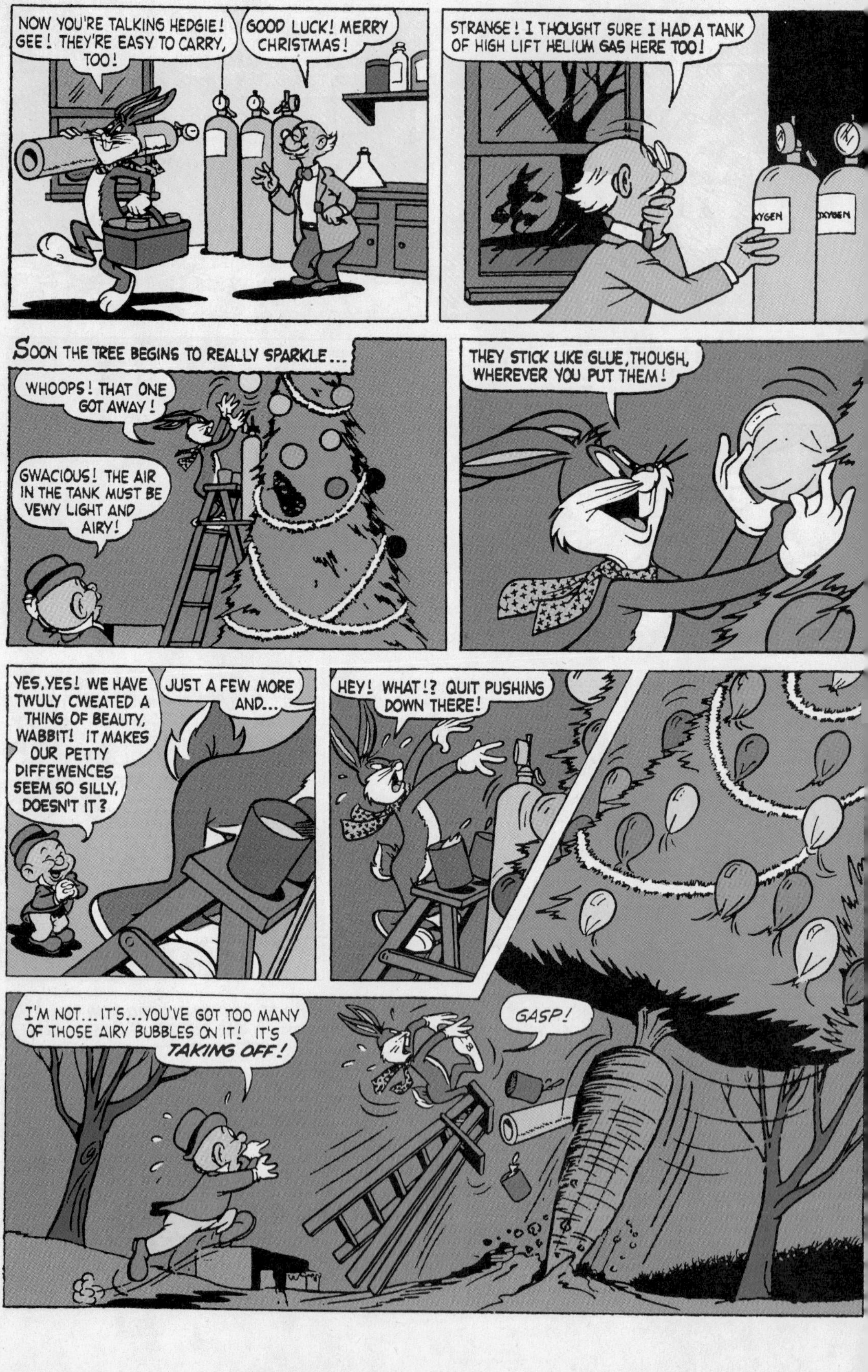
NOW YOU'RE TALKING HEDGIE! GEE! THEY'RE EASY TO CARRY, TOO!
GOOD LUCK! MERRY CHRISTMAS!
STRANGE! I THOUGHT SURE I HAD A TANK OF HIGH LIFT HELIUM GAS HERE TOO!
SOON THE TREE BEGINS TO REALLY SPARKLE...
WHOOPS! THAT ONE GOT AWAY!
GWACIOUS! THE AIR IN THE TANK MUST BE VEWY LIGHT AND AIRY!
THEY STICK LIKE GLUE, THOUGH, WHEREVER YOU PUT THEM!
YES, YES! WE HAVE TWULY CWEATED A THING OF BEAUTY, WABBIT! IT MAKES OUR PETTY DIFFEWENCES SEEM SO SILLY, DOESN'T IT?
JUST A FEW MORE AND...
HEY! WHAT!? QUIT PUSHING DOWN THERE!
I'M NOT... IT'S... YOU'VE GOT TOO MANY OF THOSE AIRY BUBBLES ON IT! IT'S TAKING OFF!
GASP!

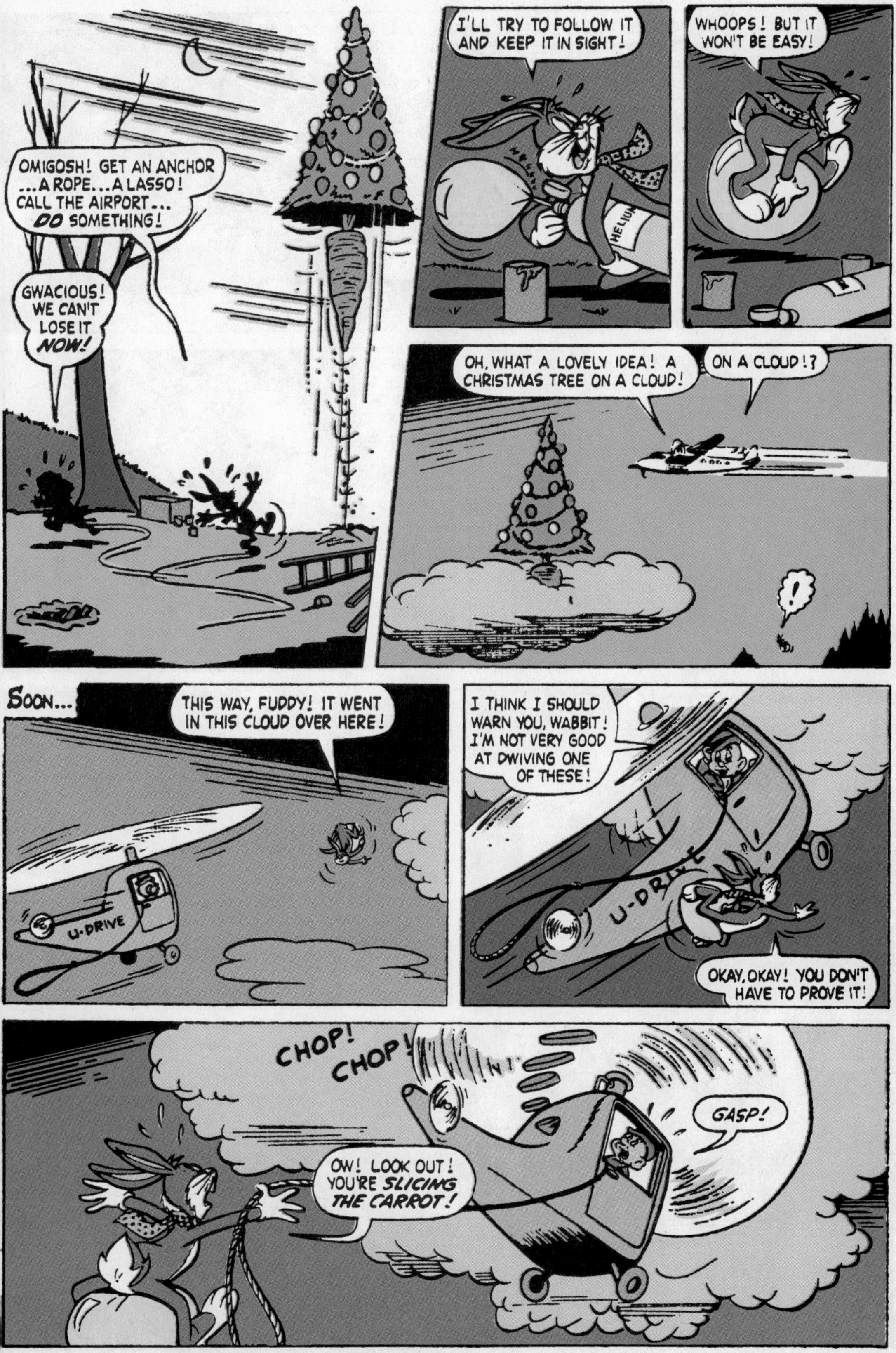
OMIGOSH! GET AN ANCHOR ...A ROPE...A LASSO! CALL THE AIRPORT... DO SOMETHING!
GWACIOUS! WE CAN'T LOSE IT NOW!
I'LL TRY TO FOLLOW IT AND KEEP IT IN SIGHT!
WHOOPS! BUT IT WON'T BE EASY!
OH, WHAT A LOVELY IDEA! A CHRISTMAS TREE ON A CLOUD!
ON A CLOUD!?
!
SOON...
THIS WAY, FUDDY! IT WENT IN THIS CLOUD OVER HERE!
U-DRIVE
I THINK I SHOULD WARN YOU, WABBIT! I'M NOT VERY GOOD AT DWIVING ONE OF THESE!
U-DRIVE
OKAY, OKAY! YOU DON'T HAVE TO PROVE IT!
CHOP! CHOP!
GASP!
OW! LOOK OUT! YOU'RE SLICING THE CARROT!

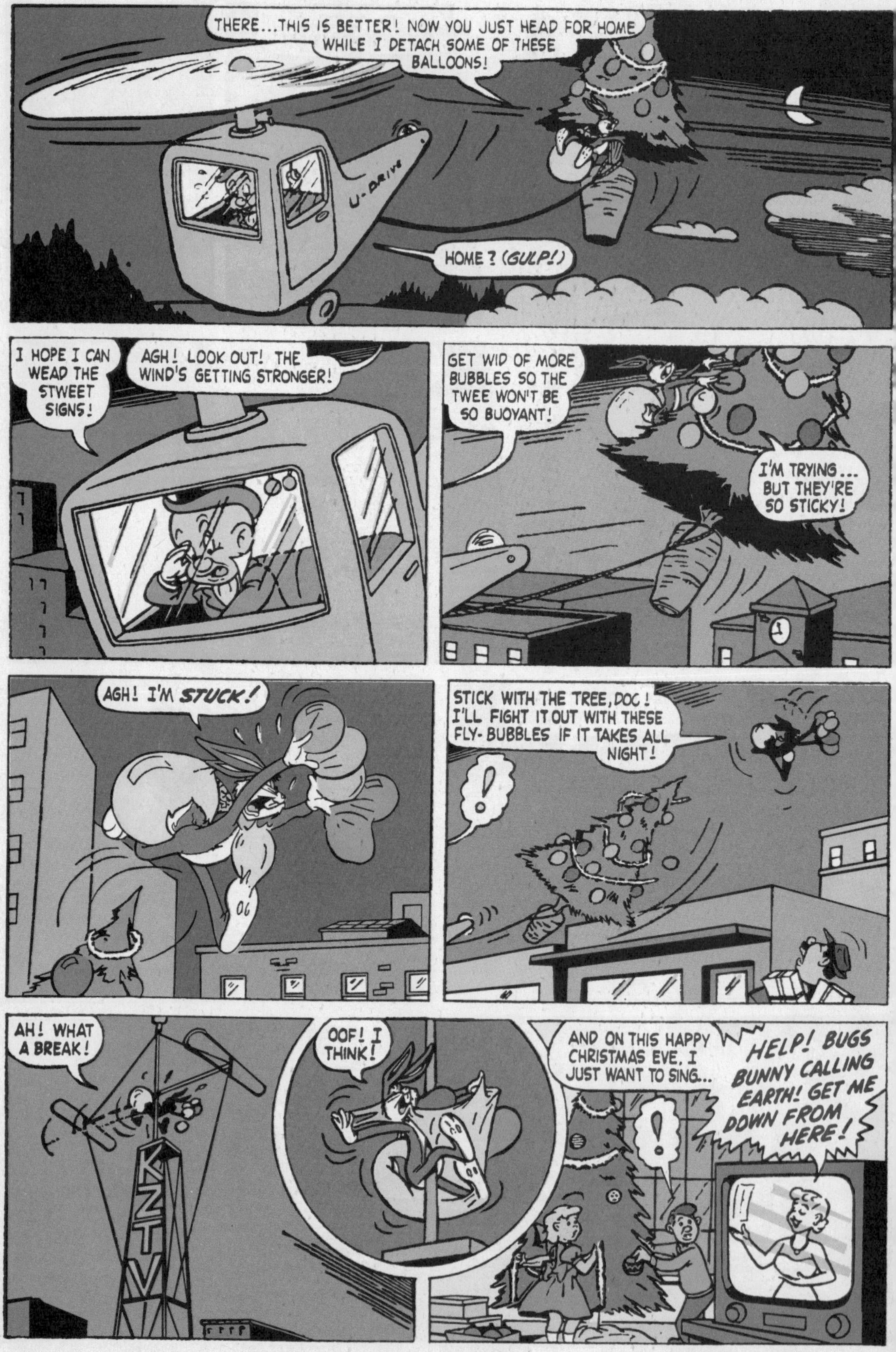
THERE...THIS IS BETTER! NOW YOU JUST HEAD FOR HOME WHILE I DETACH SOME OF THESE BALLOONS!
U-DRIVE
HOME? (GULP!)
I HOPE I CAN WEAD THE STWEET SIGNS!
AGH! LOOK OUT! THE WIND'S GETTING STRONGER!
GET WID OF MORE BUBBLES SO THE TWEE WON'T BE SO BUOYANT!
I'M TRYING... BUT THEY'RE SO STICKY!
AGH! I'M STUCK!
STICK WITH THE TREE, DOC! I'LL FIGHT IT OUT WITH THESE FLY-BUBBLES IF IT TAKES ALL NIGHT!
!
AH! WHAT A BREAK!
KZTV
OOF! I THINK!
AND ON THIS HAPPY CHRISTMAS EVE, I JUST WANT TO SING...
HELP! BUGS BUNNY CALLING EARTH! GET ME DOWN FROM HERE!
!

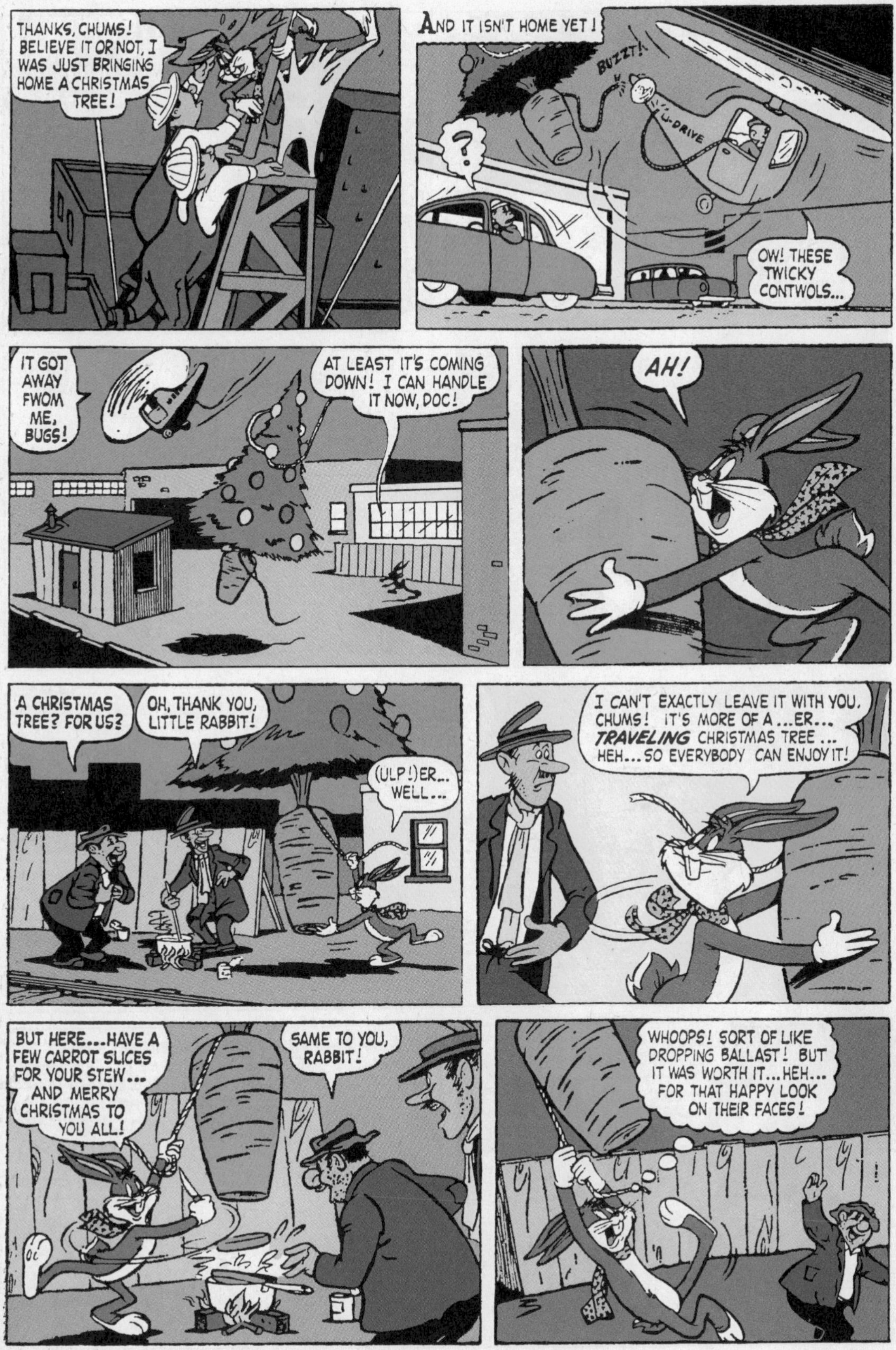
THANKS, CHUMS! BELIEVE IT OR NOT, I WAS JUST BRINGING HOME A CHRISTMAS TREE!
AND IT ISN'T HOME YET!
BUZZT!
?
U-DRIVE
OW! THESE TWICKY CONTWOLS...
IT GOT AWAY FWOM ME, BUGS!
AT LEAST IT'S COMING DOWN! I CAN HANDLE IT NOW, DOC!
AH!
A CHRISTMAS TREE? FOR US?
OH, THANK YOU, LITTLE RABBIT!
(ULP!) ER... WELL...
I CAN'T EXACTLY LEAVE IT WITH YOU, CHUMS! IT'S MORE OF A ...ER... *TRAVELING* CHRISTMAS TREE ... HEH... SO EVERYBODY CAN ENJOY IT!
BUT HERE...HAVE A FEW CARROT SLICES FOR YOUR STEW... AND MERRY CHRISTMAS TO YOU ALL!
SAME TO YOU, RABBIT!
WHOOPS! SORT OF LIKE DROPPING BALLAST! BUT IT WAS WORTH IT... HEH... FOR THAT HAPPY LOOK ON THEIR FACES!

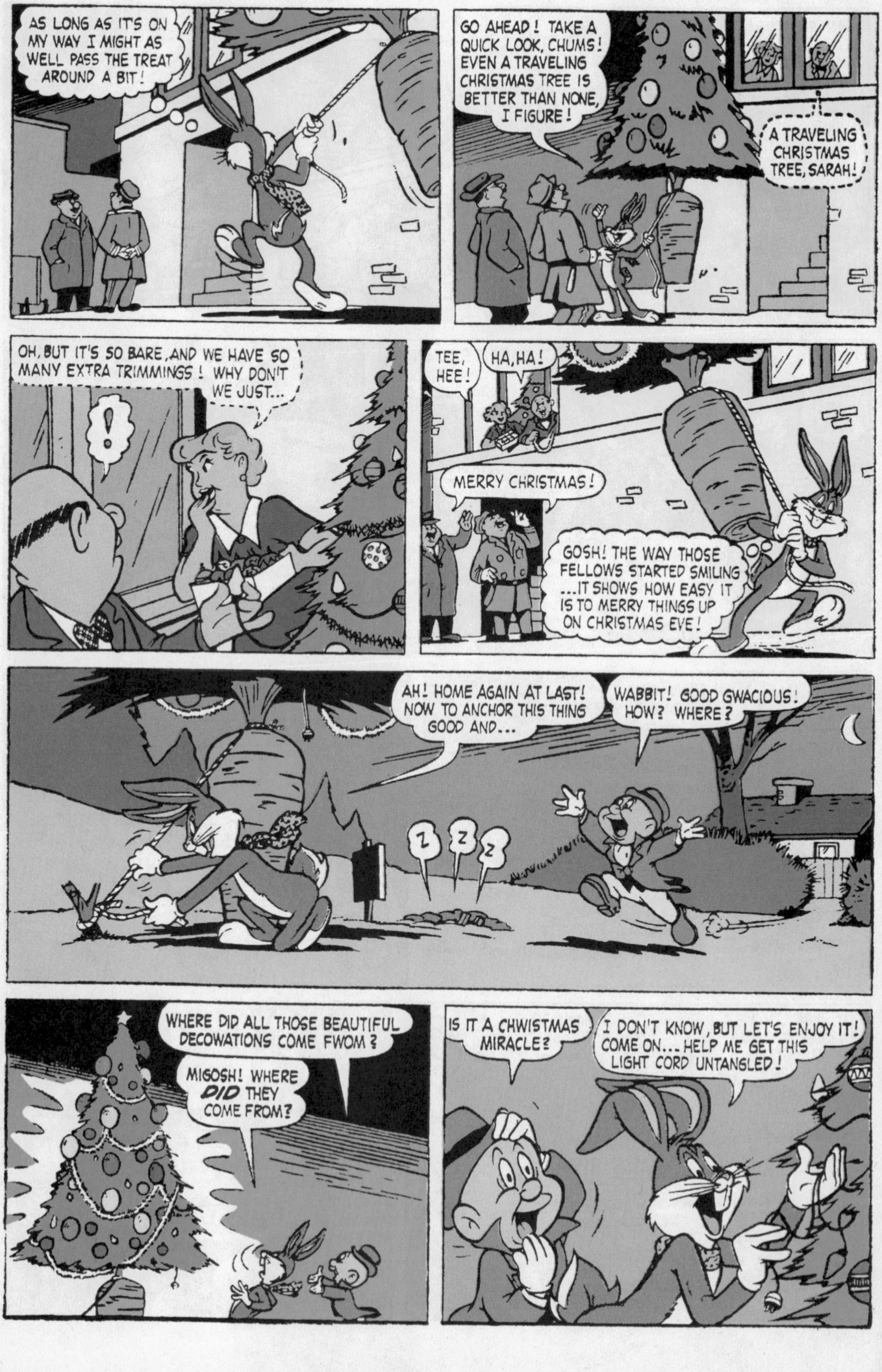
AS LONG AS IT'S ON MY WAY I MIGHT AS WELL PASS THE TREAT AROUND A BIT!
GO AHEAD! TAKE A QUICK LOOK, CHUMS! EVEN A TRAVELING CHRISTMAS TREE IS BETTER THAN NONE, I FIGURE!
A TRAVELING CHRISTMAS TREE, SARAH!
OH, BUT IT'S SO BARE, AND WE HAVE SO MANY EXTRA TRIMMINGS! WHY DON'T WE JUST...
!
TEE, HEE!
HA, HA!
MERRY CHRISTMAS!
GOSH! THE WAY THOSE FELLOWS STARTED SMILING ...IT SHOWS HOW EASY IT IS TO MERRY THINGS UP ON CHRISTMAS EVE!
AH! HOME AGAIN AT LAST! NOW TO ANCHOR THIS THING GOOD AND...
WABBIT! GOOD GWACIOUS! HOW? WHERE?
Z Z Z
WHERE DID ALL THOSE BEAUTIFUL DECOWATIONS COME FWOM?
MIGOSH! WHERE DID THEY COME FROM?
IS IT A CHWISTMAS MIRACLE?
I DON'T KNOW, BUT LET'S ENJOY IT! COME ON... HELP ME GET THIS LIGHT CORD UNTANGLED!

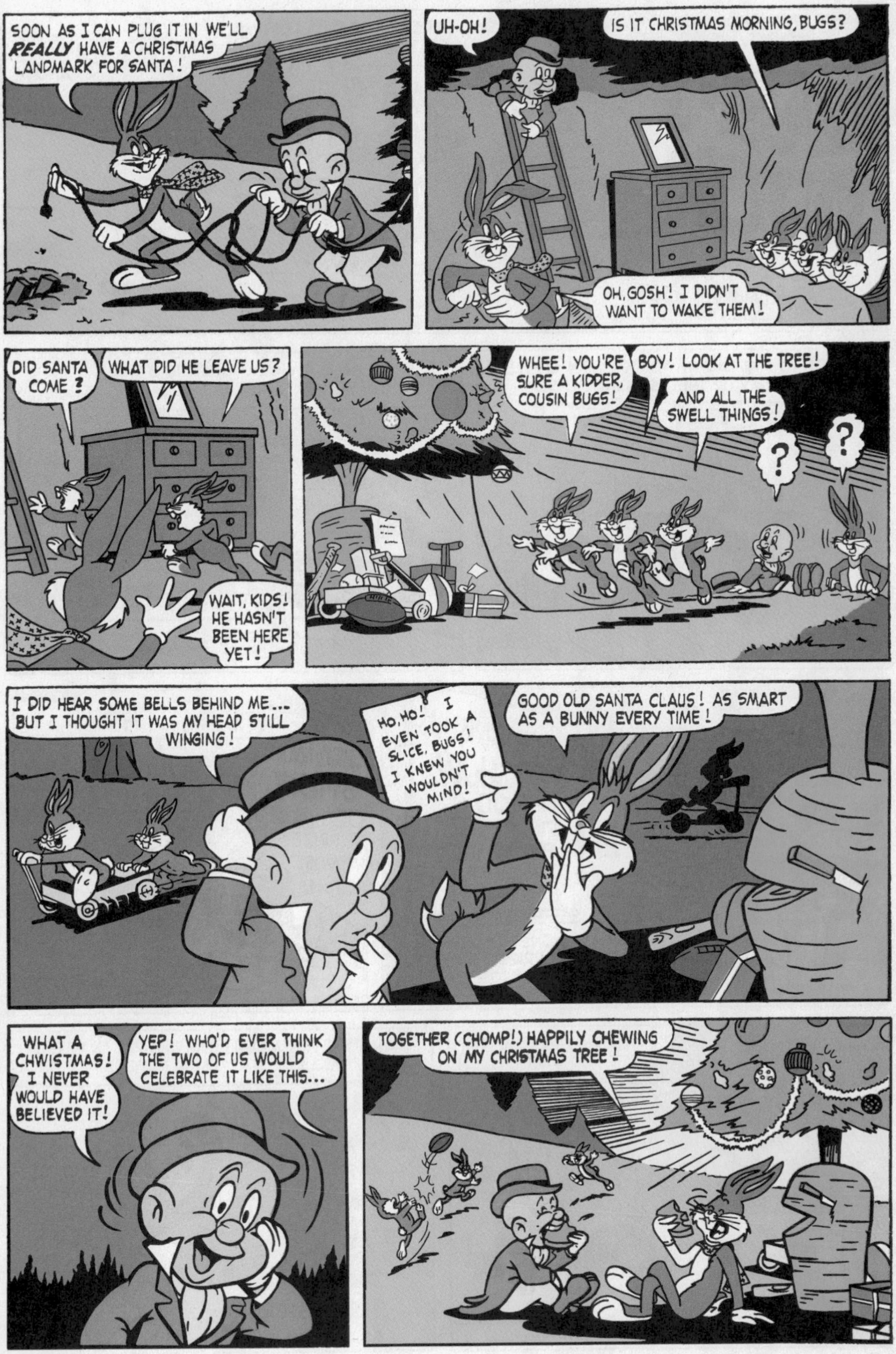
SOON AS I CAN PLUG IT IN WE'LL *REALLY* HAVE A CHRISTMAS LANDMARK FOR SANTA!
UH-OH!
IS IT CHRISTMAS MORNING, BUGS?
OH, GOSH! I DIDN'T WANT TO WAKE THEM!
DID SANTA COME?
WHAT DID HE LEAVE US?
WAIT, KIDS! HE HASN'T BEEN HERE YET!
WHEE! YOU'RE SURE A KIDDER, COUSIN BUGS!
BOY! LOOK AT THE TREE!
AND ALL THE SWELL THINGS!
?
?
I DID HEAR SOME BELLS BEHIND ME... BUT I THOUGHT IT WAS MY HEAD STILL WINGING!
HO, HO! I EVEN TOOK A SLICE, BUGS! I KNEW YOU WOULDN'T MIND!
GOOD OLD SANTA CLAUS! AS SMART AS A BUNNY EVERY TIME!
WHAT A CHWISTMAS! I NEVER WOULD HAVE BELIEVED IT!
YEP! WHO'D EVER THINK THE TWO OF US WOULD CELEBRATE IT LIKE THIS...
TOGETHER (CHOMP!) HAPPILY CHEWING ON MY CHRISTMAS TREE!

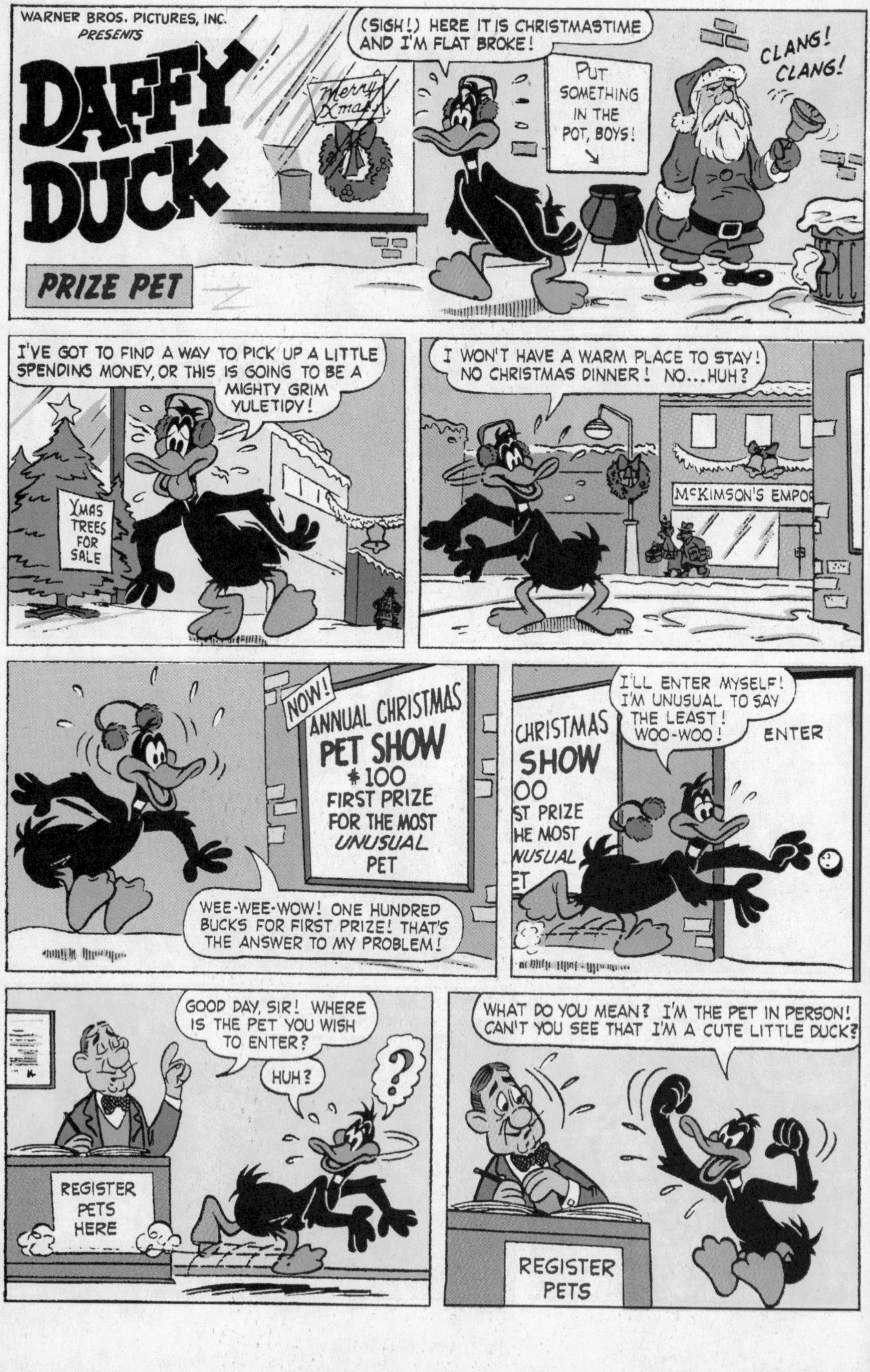
WARNER BROS. PICTURES, INC.
PRESENTS
DAFFY DUCK
PRIZE PET
(SIGH!) HERE IT IS CHRISTMASTIME AND I'M FLAT BROKE!
Merry Xmas
PUT SOMETHING IN THE POT, BOYS!
CLANG! CLANG!
I'VE GOT TO FIND A WAY TO PICK UP A LITTLE SPENDING MONEY, OR THIS IS GOING TO BE A MIGHTY GRIM YULETIDY!
XMAS TREES FOR SALE
I WON'T HAVE A WARM PLACE TO STAY! NO CHRISTMAS DINNER! NO...HUH?
McKIMSON'S EMPOR
NOW!
ANNUAL CHRISTMAS PET SHOW $100 FIRST PRIZE FOR THE MOST UNUSUAL PET
WEE-WEE-WOW! ONE HUNDRED BUCKS FOR FIRST PRIZE! THAT'S THE ANSWER TO MY PROBLEM!
I'LL ENTER MYSELF! I'M UNUSUAL TO SAY THE LEAST! WOO-WOO!
ENTER
GOOD DAY, SIR! WHERE IS THE PET YOU WISH TO ENTER?
HUH?
?
REGISTER PETS HERE
WHAT DO YOU MEAN? I'M THE PET IN PERSON! CAN'T YOU SEE THAT I'M A CUTE LITTLE DUCK?
REGISTER PETS

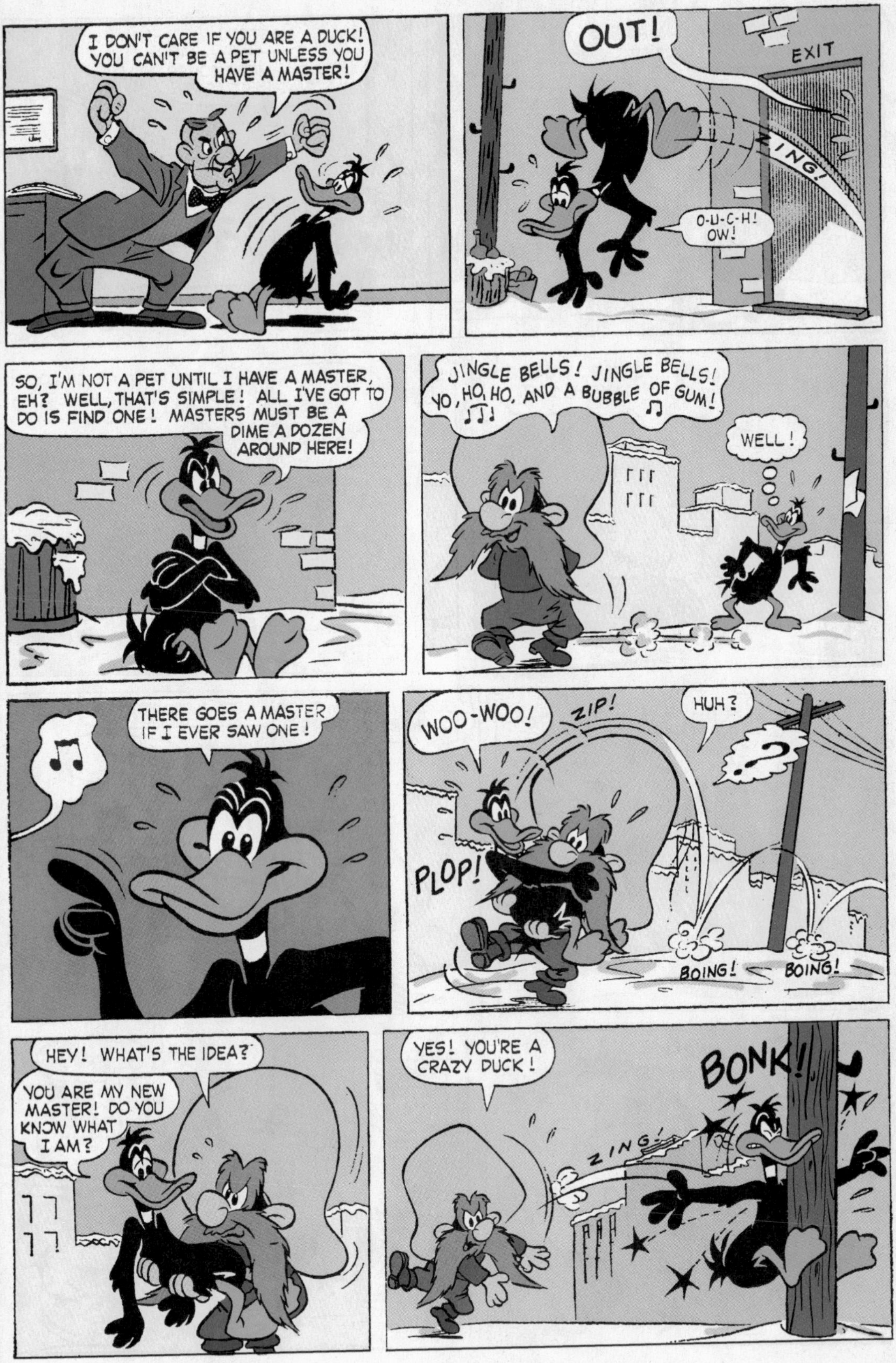
I DON'T CARE IF YOU ARE A DUCK! YOU CAN'T BE A PET UNLESS YOU HAVE A MASTER!
OUT!
EXIT
ZING!
O-U-C-H! OW!
SO, I'M NOT A PET UNTIL I HAVE A MASTER, EH? WELL, THAT'S SIMPLE! ALL I'VE GOT TO DO IS FIND ONE! MASTERS MUST BE A DIME A DOZEN AROUND HERE!
JINGLE BELLS! JINGLE BELLS! YO, HO, HO, AND A BUBBLE OF GUM!
WELL!
THERE GOES A MASTER IF I EVER SAW ONE!
WOO-WOO!
ZIP!
HUH?
?
PLOP!
BOING!
BOING!
HEY! WHAT'S THE IDEA?
YOU ARE MY NEW MASTER! DO YOU KNOW WHAT I AM?
YES! YOU'RE A CRAZY DUCK!
BONK!
ZING!

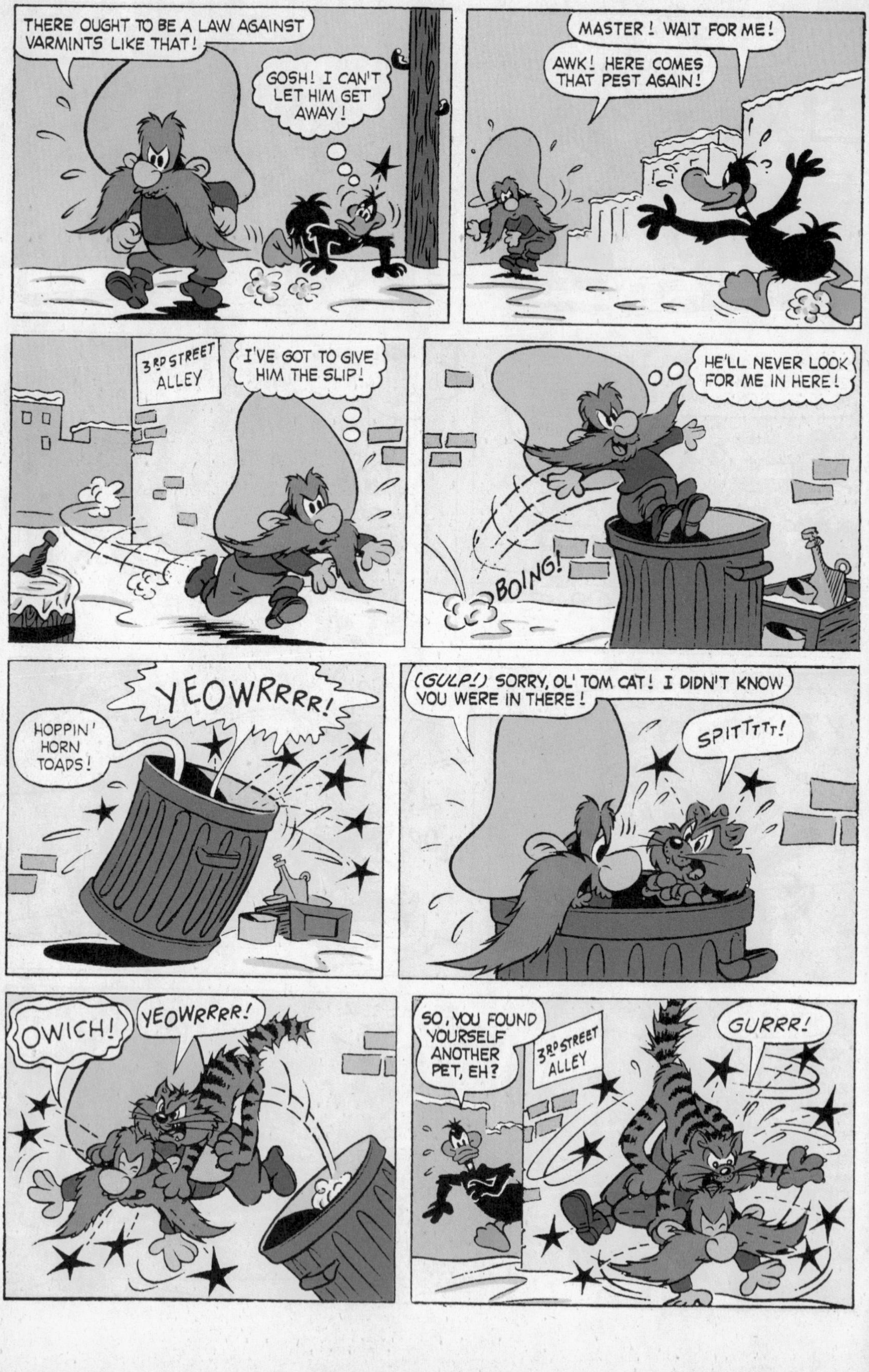
THERE OUGHT TO BE A LAW AGAINST VARMINTS LIKE THAT!
GOSH! I CAN'T LET HIM GET AWAY!
MASTER! WAIT FOR ME!
AWK! HERE COMES THAT PEST AGAIN!
3RD STREET ALLEY
I'VE GOT TO GIVE HIM THE SLIP!
HE'LL NEVER LOOK FOR ME IN HERE!
BOING!
YEOWRRRR!
HOPPIN' HORN TOADS!
(GULP!) SORRY, OL' TOM CAT! I DIDN'T KNOW YOU WERE IN THERE!
SPITTTTT!
OWICH!
YEOWRRRR!
SO, YOU FOUND YOURSELF ANOTHER PET, EH?
3RD STREET ALLEY
GURRR!

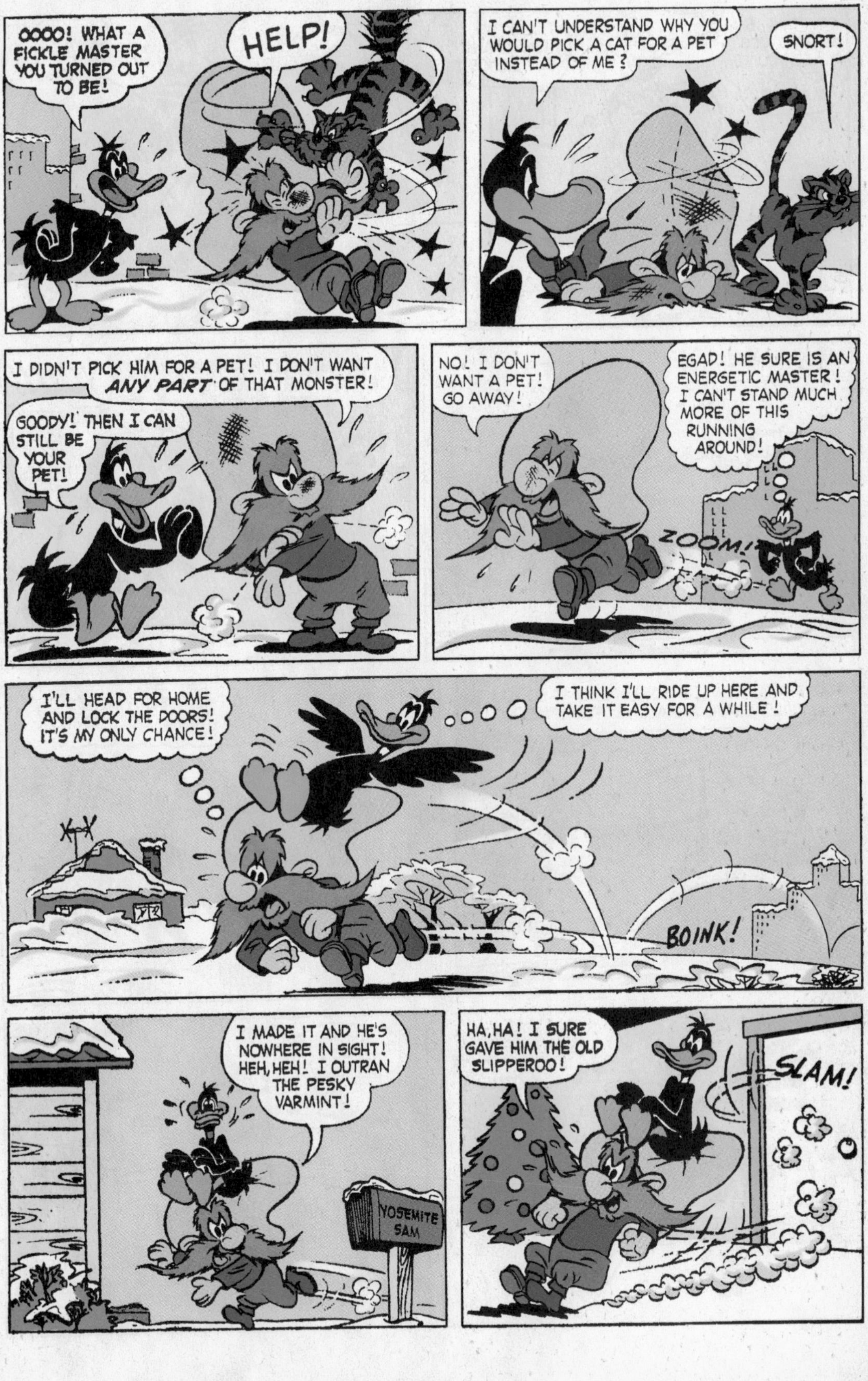
OOOO! WHAT A FICKLE MASTER YOU TURNED OUT TO BE!
HELP!
I CAN'T UNDERSTAND WHY YOU WOULD PICK A CAT FOR A PET INSTEAD OF ME?
SNORT!
I DIDN'T PICK HIM FOR A PET! I DON'T WANT ANY PART OF THAT MONSTER!
GOODY! THEN I CAN STILL BE YOUR PET!
NO! I DON'T WANT A PET! GO AWAY!
EGAD! HE SURE IS AN ENERGETIC MASTER! I CAN'T STAND MUCH MORE OF THIS RUNNING AROUND!
ZOOM!
I'LL HEAD FOR HOME AND LOCK THE DOORS! IT'S MY ONLY CHANCE!
I THINK I'LL RIDE UP HERE AND TAKE IT EASY FOR A WHILE!
BOINK!
I MADE IT AND HE'S NOWHERE IN SIGHT! HEH, HEH! I OUTRAN THE PESKY VARMINT!
YOSEMITE SAM
HA, HA! I SURE GAVE HIM THE OLD SLIPPEROO!
SLAM!

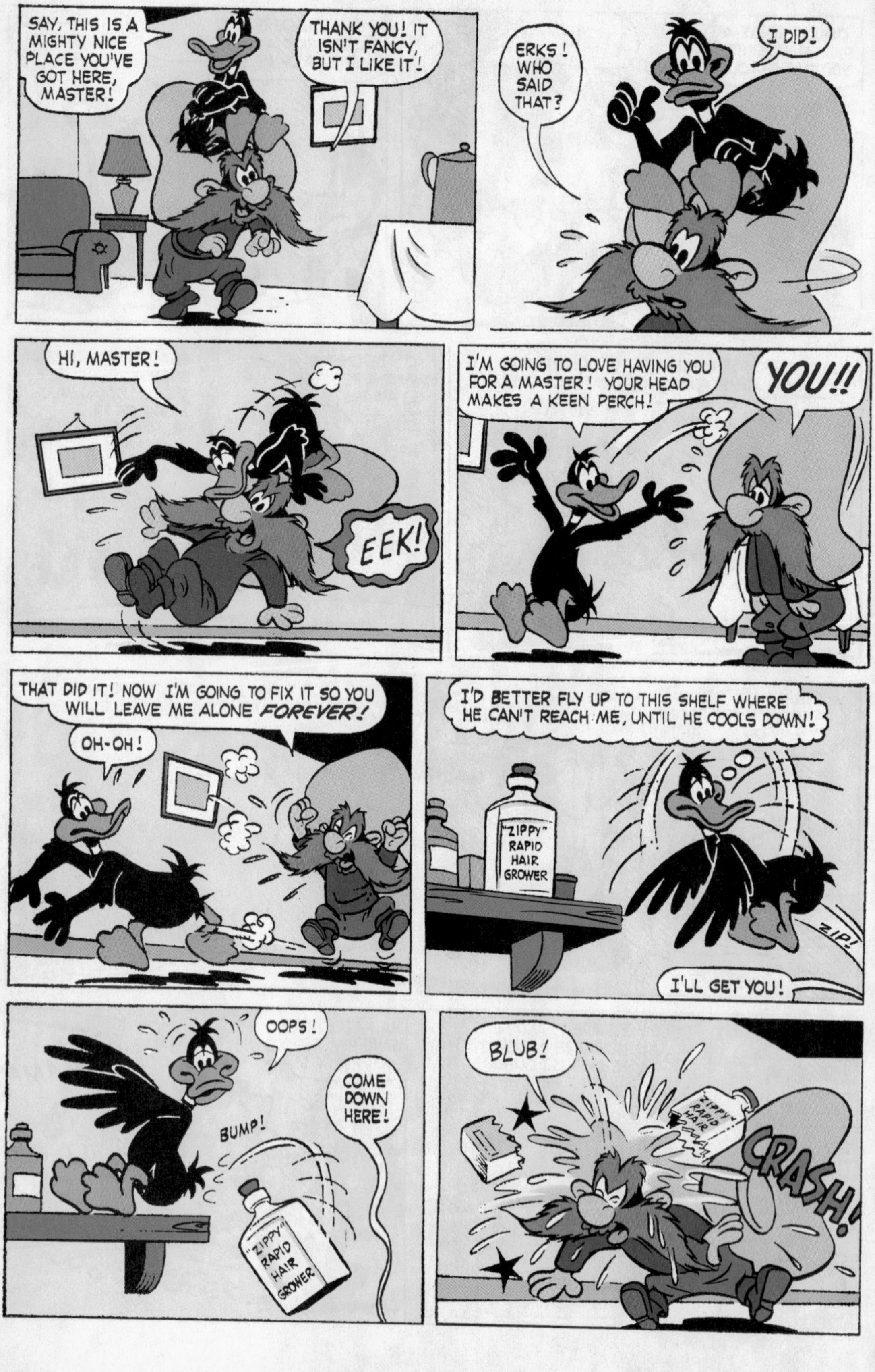

SAY, THIS IS A MIGHTY NICE PLACE YOU'VE GOT HERE, MASTER!
THANK YOU! IT ISN'T FANCY, BUT I LIKE IT!
ERKS! WHO SAID THAT?
I DID!
HI, MASTER!
EEK!
I'M GOING TO LOVE HAVING YOU FOR A MASTER! YOUR HEAD MAKES A KEEN PERCH!
YOU!!
THAT DID IT! NOW I'M GOING TO FIX IT SO YOU WILL LEAVE ME ALONE FOREVER!
OH-OH!
I'D BETTER FLY UP TO THIS SHELF WHERE HE CAN'T REACH ME, UNTIL HE COOLS DOWN!
"ZIPPY" RAPID HAIR GROWER
ZIP!
I'LL GET YOU!
OOPS!
COME DOWN HERE!
BUMP!
"ZIPPY" RAPID HAIR GROWER
BLUB!
"ZIPPY" RAPID HAIR
CRASH!

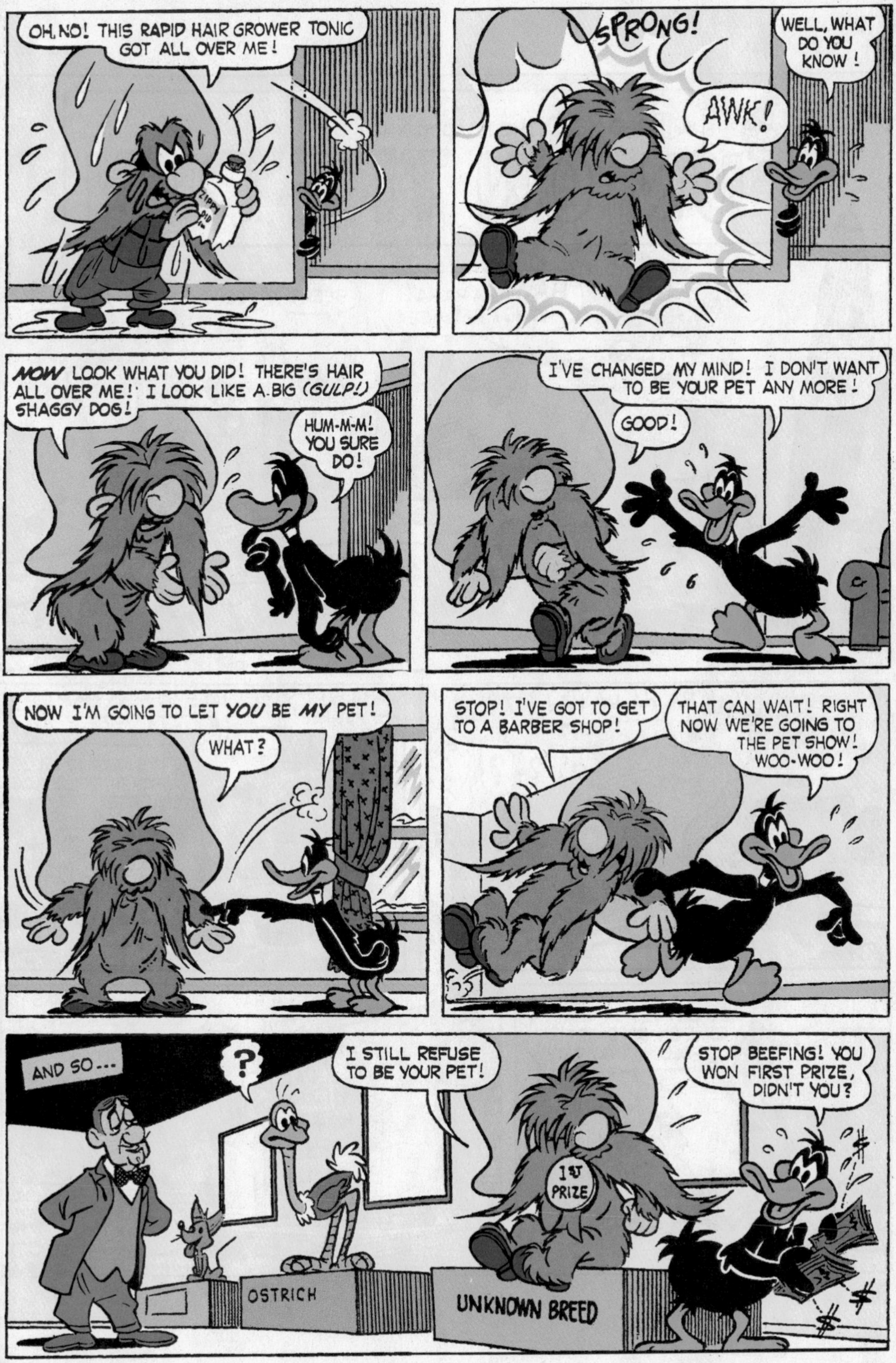
OH, NO! THIS RAPID HAIR GROWER TONIC GOT ALL OVER ME!
SPRONG!
WELL, WHAT DO YOU KNOW!
AWK!
NOW LOOK WHAT YOU DID! THERE'S HAIR ALL OVER ME! I LOOK LIKE A BIG (GULP!) SHAGGY DOG!
HUM-M-M! YOU SURE DO!
I'VE CHANGED MY MIND! I DON'T WANT TO BE YOUR PET ANY MORE!
GOOD!
NOW I'M GOING TO LET YOU BE MY PET!
WHAT?
STOP! I'VE GOT TO GET TO A BARBER SHOP!
THAT CAN WAIT! RIGHT NOW WE'RE GOING TO THE PET SHOW! WOO-WOO!
AND SO...
?
I STILL REFUSE TO BE YOUR PET!
STOP BEEFING! YOU WON FIRST PRIZE, DIDN'T YOU?
1ST PRIZE
OSTRICH
UNKNOWN BREED

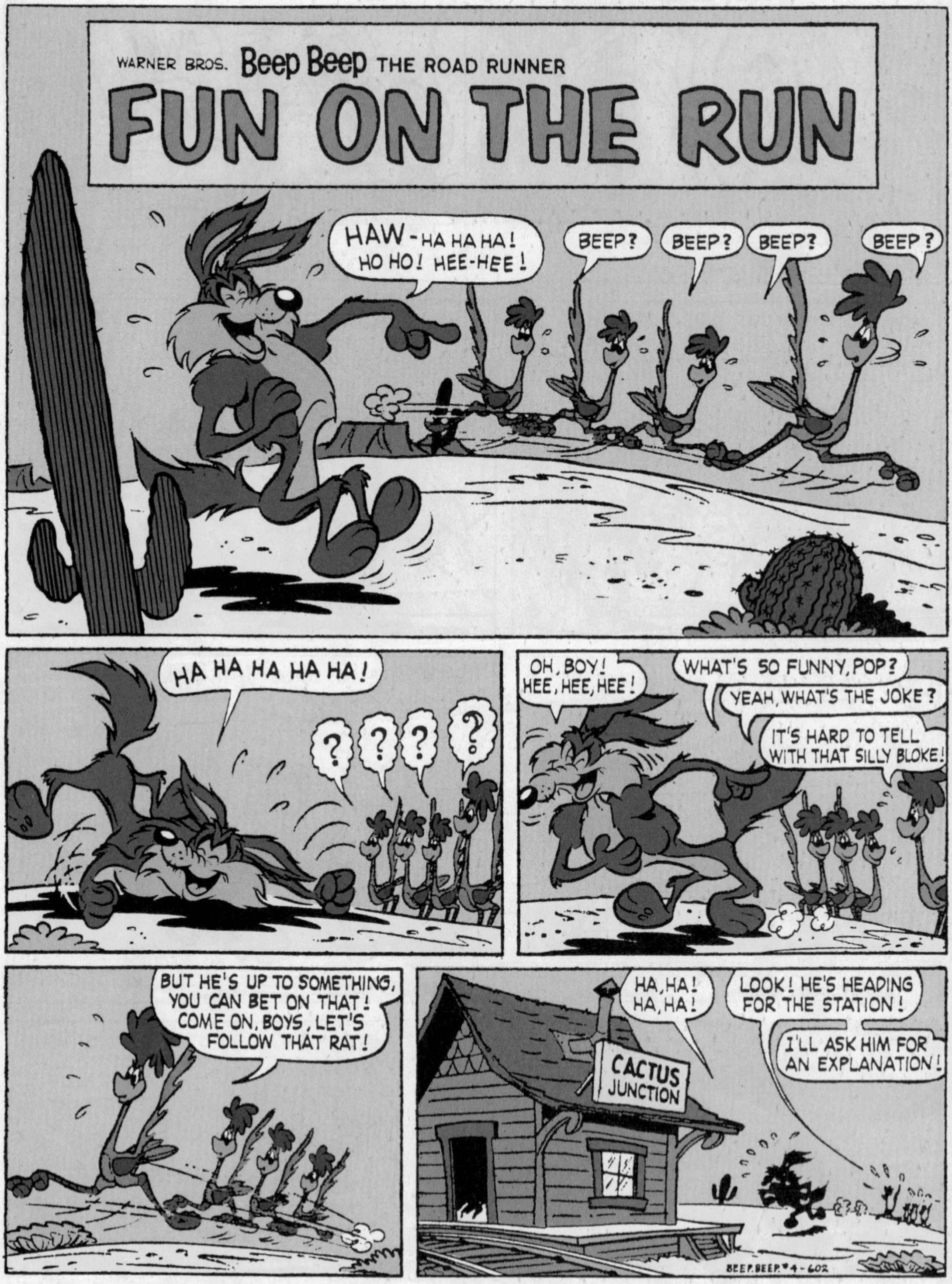
WARNER BROS. Beep Beep THE ROAD RUNNER
FUN ON THE RUN
HAW-HA HA HA! HO HO! HEE-HEE!
BEEP?
BEEP?
BEEP?
BEEP?
HA HA HA HA HA!
?
?
?
?
OH, BOY! HEE, HEE, HEE!
WHAT'S SO FUNNY, POP?
YEAH, WHAT'S THE JOKE?
IT'S HARD TO TELL WITH THAT SILLY BLOKE!
BUT HE'S UP TO SOMETHING, YOU CAN BET ON THAT! COME ON, BOYS, LET'S FOLLOW THAT RAT!
HA, HA! HA, HA!
CACTUS JUNCTION
LOOK! HE'S HEADING FOR THE STATION!
I'LL ASK HIM FOR AN EXPLANATION!

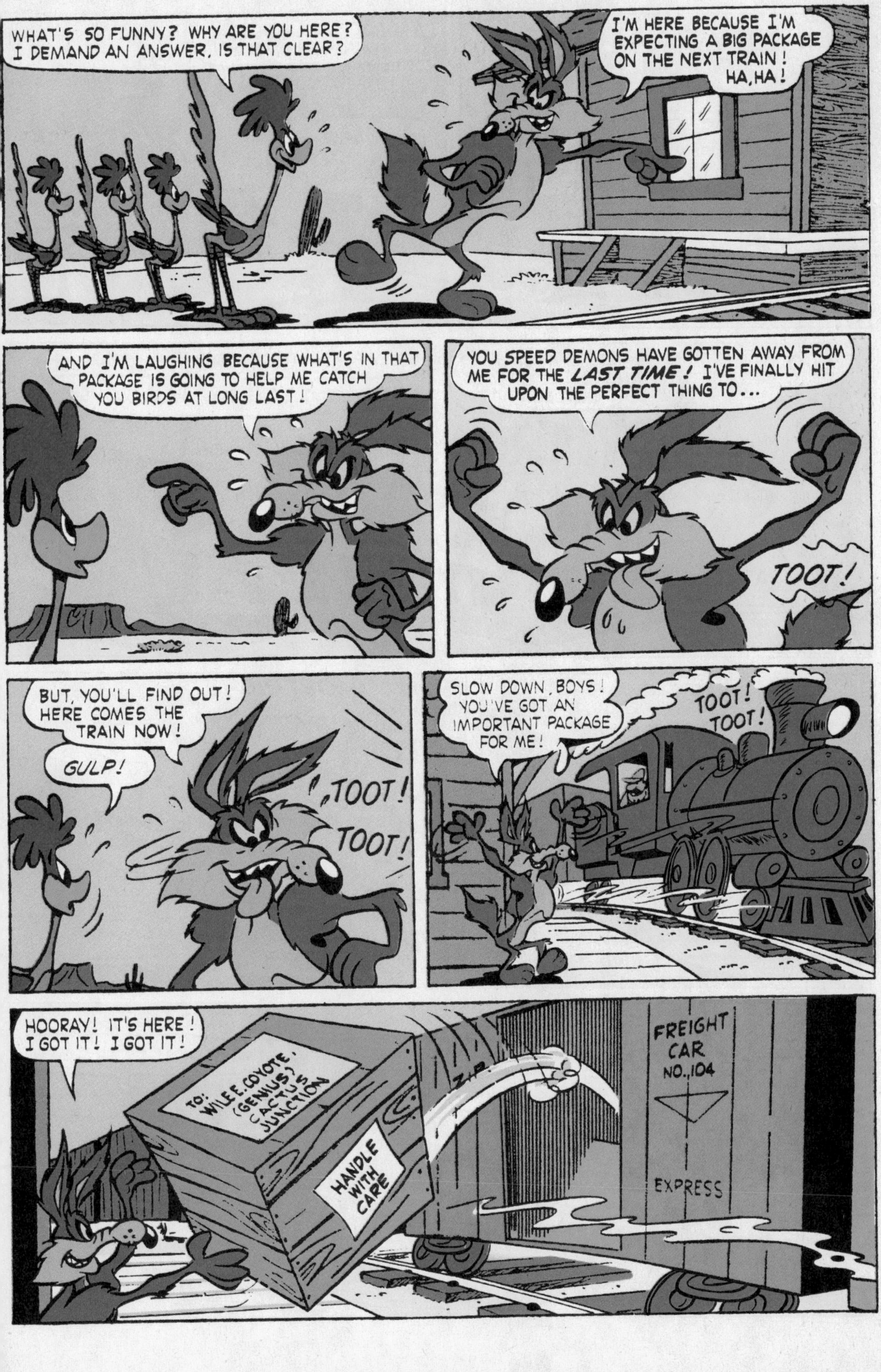
WHAT'S SO FUNNY? WHY ARE YOU HERE? I DEMAND AN ANSWER. IS THAT CLEAR?
I'M HERE BECAUSE I'M EXPECTING A BIG PACKAGE ON THE NEXT TRAIN! HA, HA!
AND I'M LAUGHING BECAUSE WHAT'S IN THAT PACKAGE IS GOING TO HELP ME CATCH YOU BIRDS AT LONG LAST!
YOU SPEED DEMONS HAVE GOTTEN AWAY FROM ME FOR THE *LAST TIME!* I'VE FINALLY HIT UPON THE PERFECT THING TO...
TOOT!
BUT, YOU'LL FIND OUT! HERE COMES THE TRAIN NOW!
GULP!
TOOT!
TOOT!
SLOW DOWN, BOYS! YOU'VE GOT AN IMPORTANT PACKAGE FOR ME!
TOOT!
TOOT!
HOORAY! IT'S HERE! I GOT IT! I GOT IT!
TO: WILE E. COYOTE (GENIUS) CACTUS JUNCTION
HANDLE WITH CARE
FREIGHT CAR NO. 104
EXPRESS

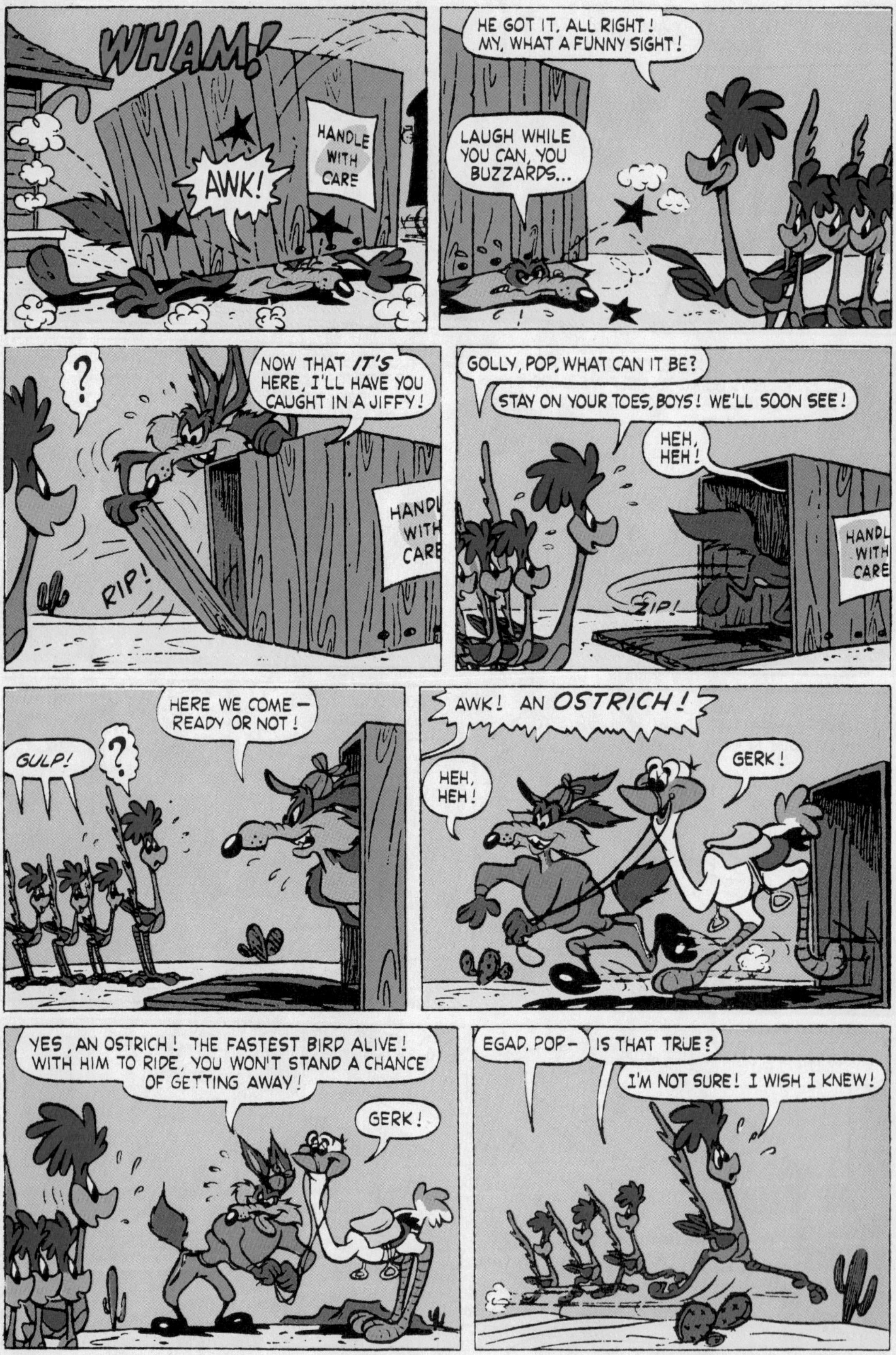
WHAM!
AWK!
HANDLE WITH CARE
HE GOT IT, ALL RIGHT! MY, WHAT A FUNNY SIGHT!
LAUGH WHILE YOU CAN, YOU BUZZARDS...
?
NOW THAT IT'S HERE, I'LL HAVE YOU CAUGHT IN A JIFFY!
RIP!
GOLLY, POP, WHAT CAN IT BE?
STAY ON YOUR TOES, BOYS! WE'LL SOON SEE!
HEH, HEH!
ZIP!
HERE WE COME — READY OR NOT!
GULP!
?
AWK! AN OSTRICH!
HEH, HEH!
GERK!
YES, AN OSTRICH! THE FASTEST BIRD ALIVE! WITH HIM TO RIDE, YOU WON'T STAND A CHANCE OF GETTING AWAY!
GERK!
EGAD, POP—
IS THAT TRUE?
I'M NOT SURE! I WISH I KNEW!

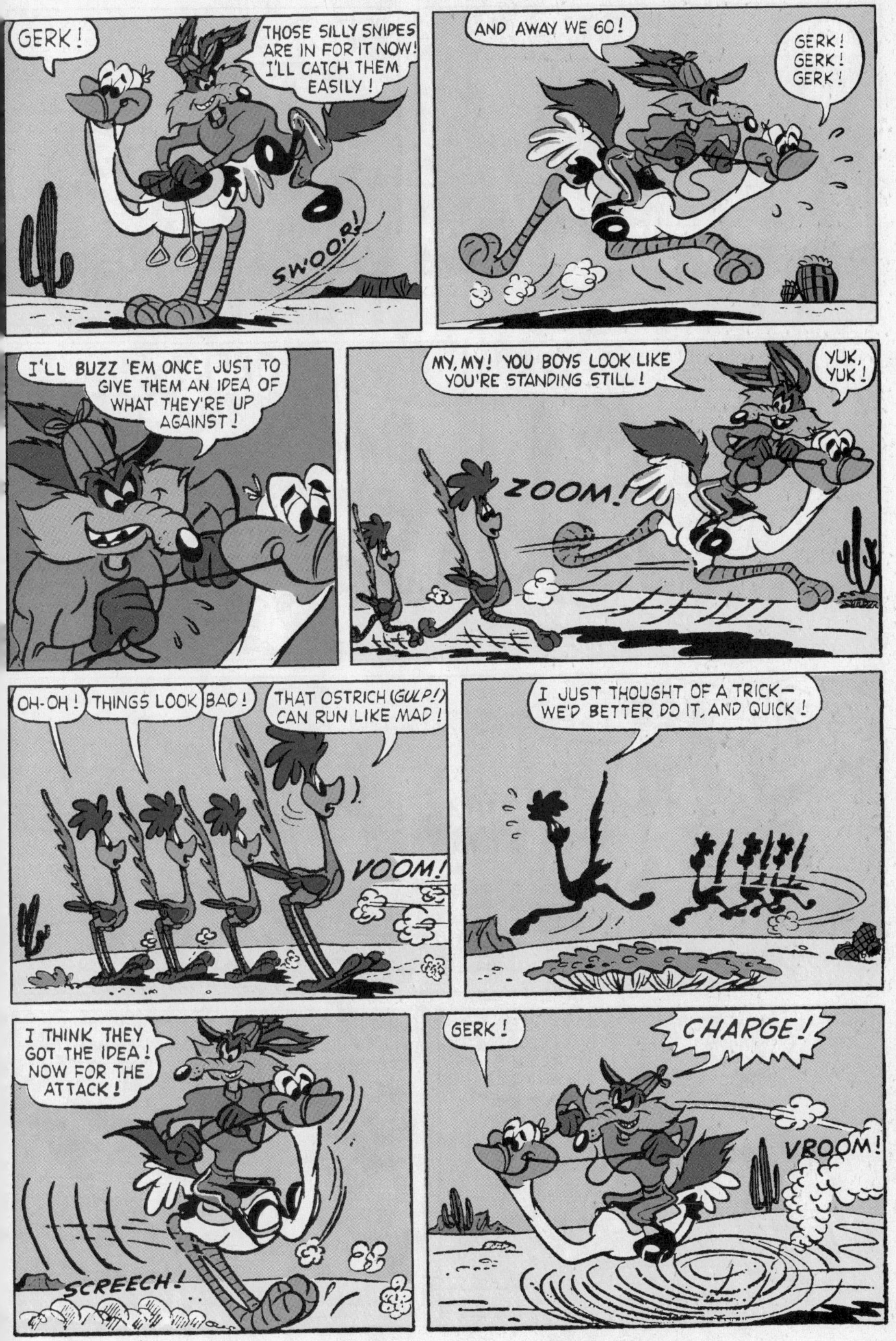
GERK!
THOSE SILLY SNIPES ARE IN FOR IT NOW! I'LL CATCH THEM EASILY!
SWOOR!
AND AWAY WE GO!
GERK! GERK! GERK!
I'LL BUZZ 'EM ONCE JUST TO GIVE THEM AN IDEA OF WHAT THEY'RE UP AGAINST!
MY, MY! YOU BOYS LOOK LIKE YOU'RE STANDING STILL!
YUK, YUK!
ZOOM!
OH-OH!
THINGS LOOK
BAD!
THAT OSTRICH (GULP!) CAN RUN LIKE MAD!
VOOM!
I JUST THOUGHT OF A TRICK— WE'D BETTER DO IT, AND QUICK!
I THINK THEY GOT THE IDEA! NOW FOR THE ATTACK!
SCREECH!
GERK!
CHARGE!
VROOM!

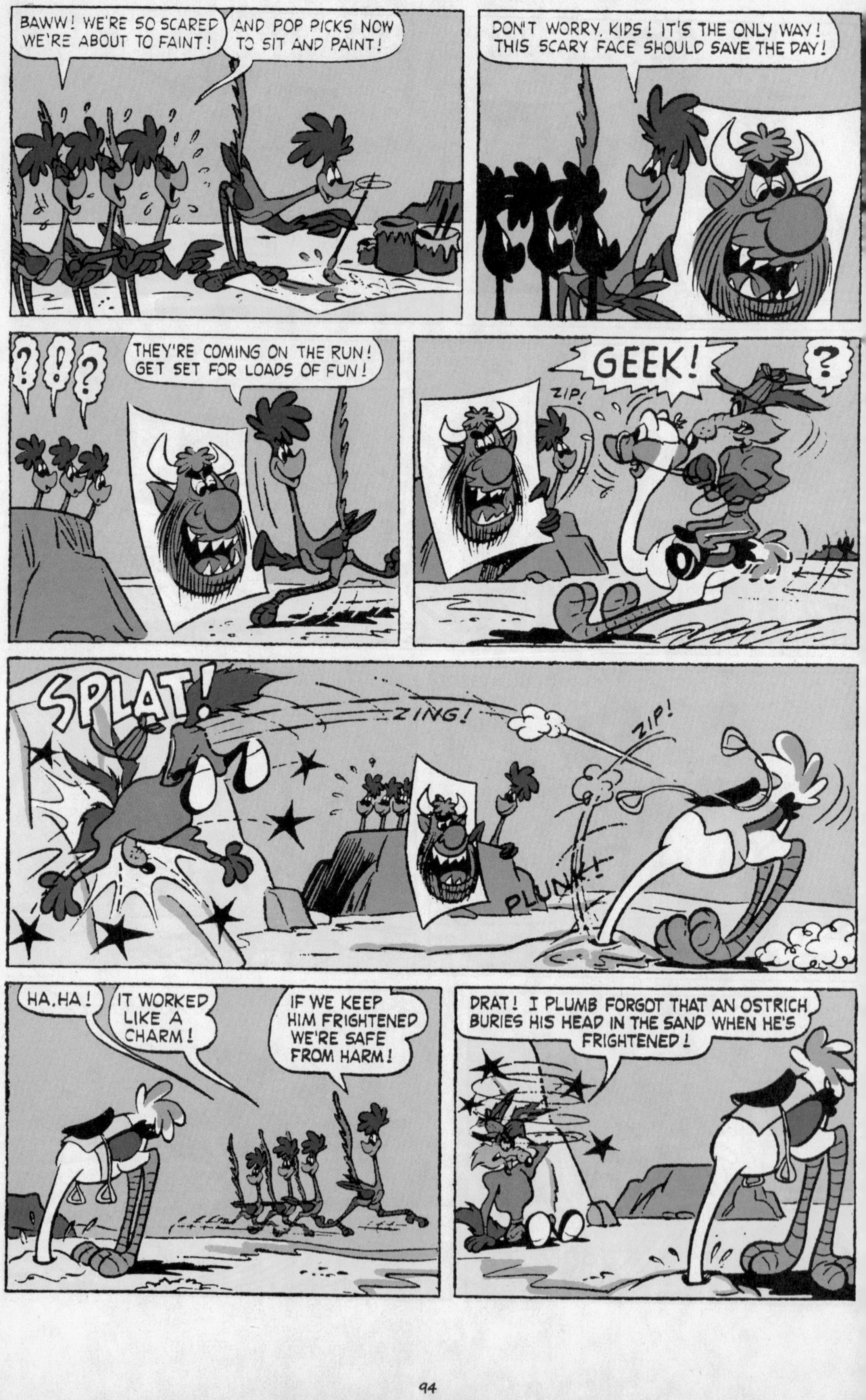
BAWW! WE'RE SO SCARED WE'RE ABOUT TO FAINT!
AND POP PICKS NOW TO SIT AND PAINT!
DON'T WORRY, KIDS! IT'S THE ONLY WAY! THIS SCARY FACE SHOULD SAVE THE DAY!
?!?
THEY'RE COMING ON THE RUN! GET SET FOR LOADS OF FUN!
GEEK!
ZIP!
?
SPLAT!
ZING!
ZIP!
PLUNK!
HA.HA!
IT WORKED LIKE A CHARM!
IF WE KEEP HIM FRIGHTENED WE'RE SAFE FROM HARM!
DRAT! I PLUMB FORGOT THAT AN OSTRICH BURIES HIS HEAD IN THE SAND WHEN HE'S FRIGHTENED!

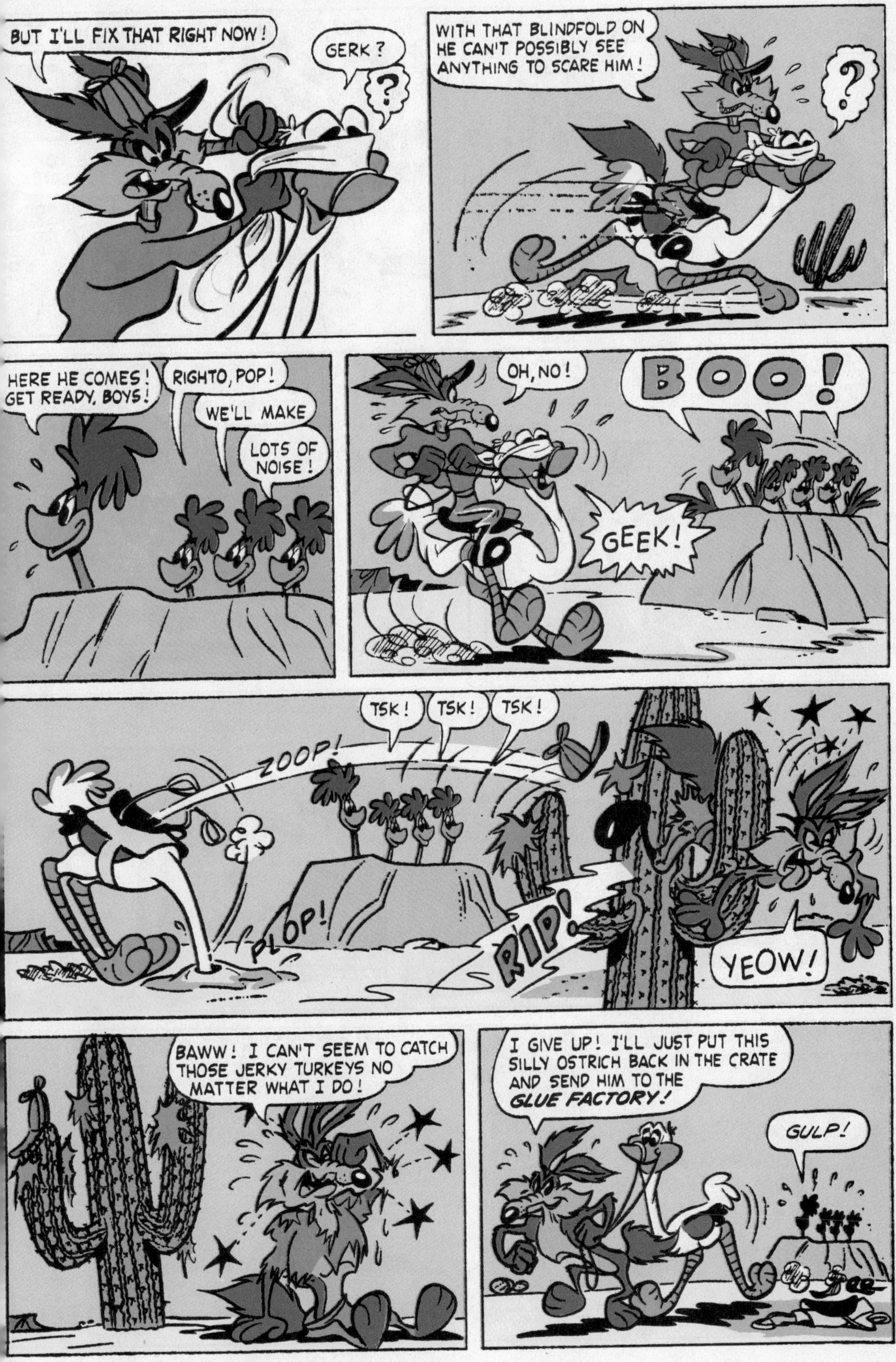
BUT I'LL FIX THAT RIGHT NOW!
GERK?
?
WITH THAT BLINDFOLD ON HE CAN'T POSSIBLY SEE ANYTHING TO SCARE HIM!
?
HERE HE COMES! GET READY, BOYS!
RIGHTO, POP!
WE'LL MAKE
LOTS OF NOISE!
OH, NO!
BOO!
GEEK!
TSK!
TSK!
TSK!
ZOOP!
PLOP!
RIP!
YEOW!
BAWW! I CAN'T SEEM TO CATCH THOSE JERKY TURKEYS NO MATTER WHAT I DO!
I GIVE UP! I'LL JUST PUT THIS SILLY OSTRICH BACK IN THE CRATE AND SEND HIM TO THE GLUE FACTORY!
GULP!

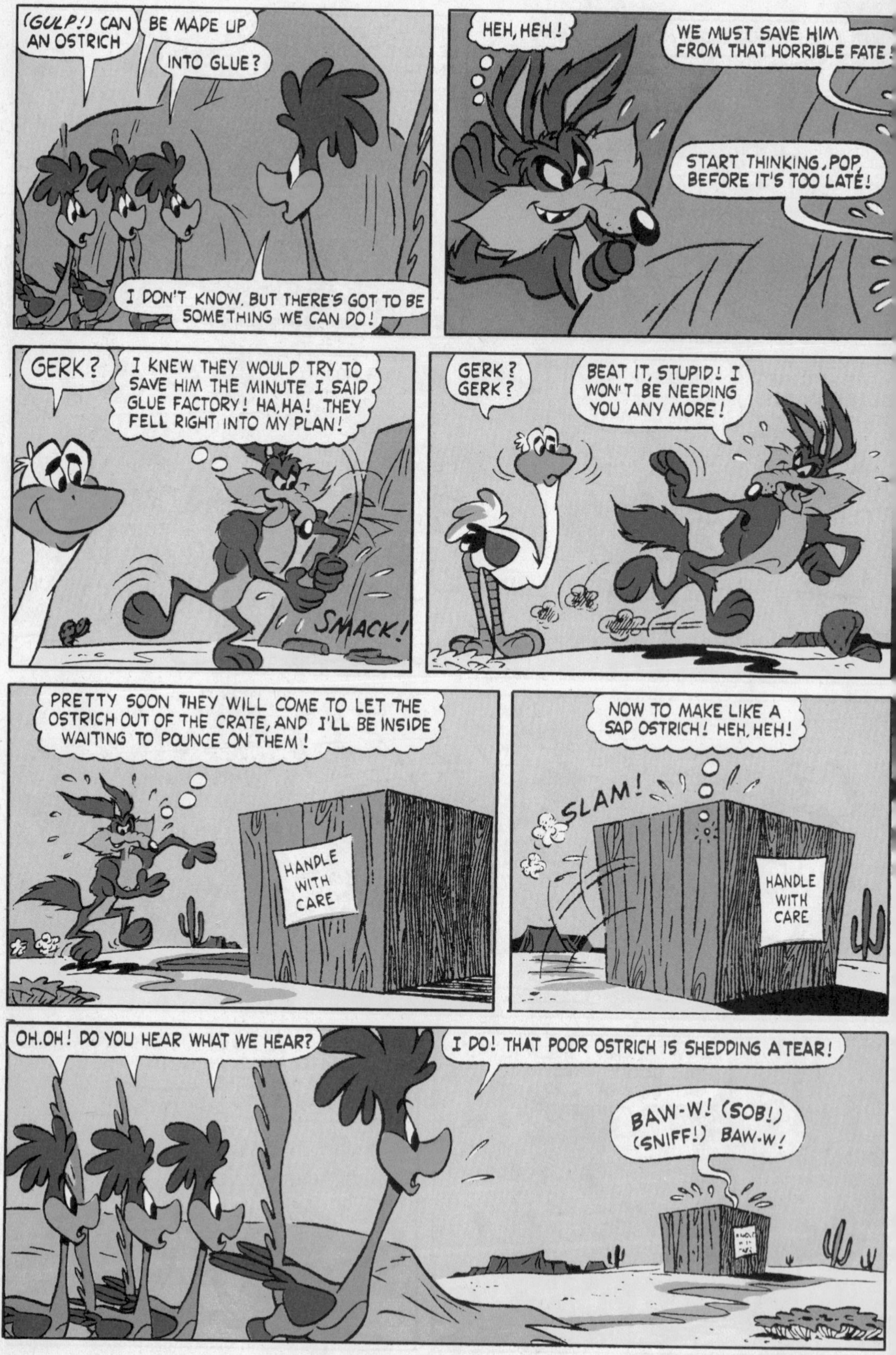
(GULP!) CAN AN OSTRICH
BE MADE UP
INTO GLUE?
I DON'T KNOW. BUT THERE'S GOT TO BE SOMETHING WE CAN DO!
HEH, HEH!
WE MUST SAVE HIM FROM THAT HORRIBLE FATE!
START THINKING, POP, BEFORE IT'S TOO LATE!
GERK?
I KNEW THEY WOULD TRY TO SAVE HIM THE MINUTE I SAID GLUE FACTORY! HA, HA! THEY FELL RIGHT INTO MY PLAN!
SMACK!
GERK? GERK?
BEAT IT, STUPID! I WON'T BE NEEDING YOU ANY MORE!
PRETTY SOON THEY WILL COME TO LET THE OSTRICH OUT OF THE CRATE, AND I'LL BE INSIDE WAITING TO POUNCE ON THEM!
HANDLE WITH CARE
NOW TO MAKE LIKE A SAD OSTRICH! HEH, HEH!
SLAM!
HANDLE WITH CARE
OH.OH! DO YOU HEAR WHAT WE HEAR?
I DO! THAT POOR OSTRICH IS SHEDDING A TEAR!
BAW-W! (SOB!) (SNIFF!) BAW-W!

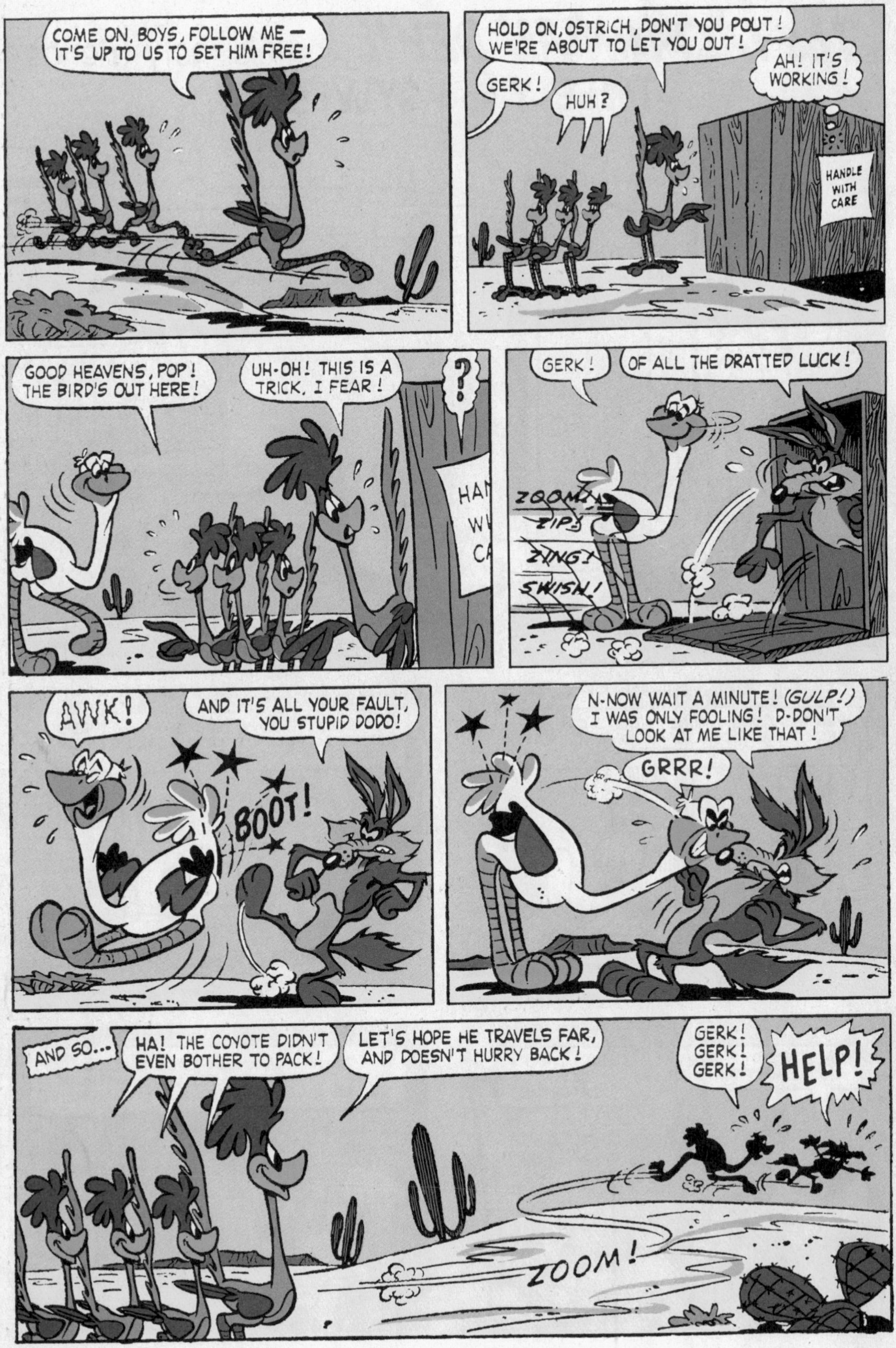
COME ON, BOYS, FOLLOW ME — IT'S UP TO US TO SET HIM FREE!
HOLD ON, OSTRICH, DON'T YOU POUT! WE'RE ABOUT TO LET YOU OUT!
GERK!
HUH?
AH! IT'S WORKING!
HANDLE WITH CARE
GOOD HEAVENS, POP! THE BIRD'S OUT HERE!
UH-OH! THIS IS A TRICK, I FEAR!
?
GERK!
OF ALL THE DRATTED LUCK!
ZOOM!
ZIP!
ZING!
SWISH!
AWK!
AND IT'S ALL YOUR FAULT, YOU STUPID DODO!
BOOT!
N-NOW WAIT A MINUTE! (GULP!) I WAS ONLY FOOLING! D-DON'T LOOK AT ME LIKE THAT!
GRRR!
AND SO...
HA! THE COYOTE DIDN'T EVEN BOTHER TO PACK!
LET'S HOPE HE TRAVELS FAR, AND DOESN'T HURRY BACK!
GERK! GERK! GERK!
HELP!
ZOOM!

The TASMANIAN DEVIL and his tasty friends
TWEETY and SYLVESTER

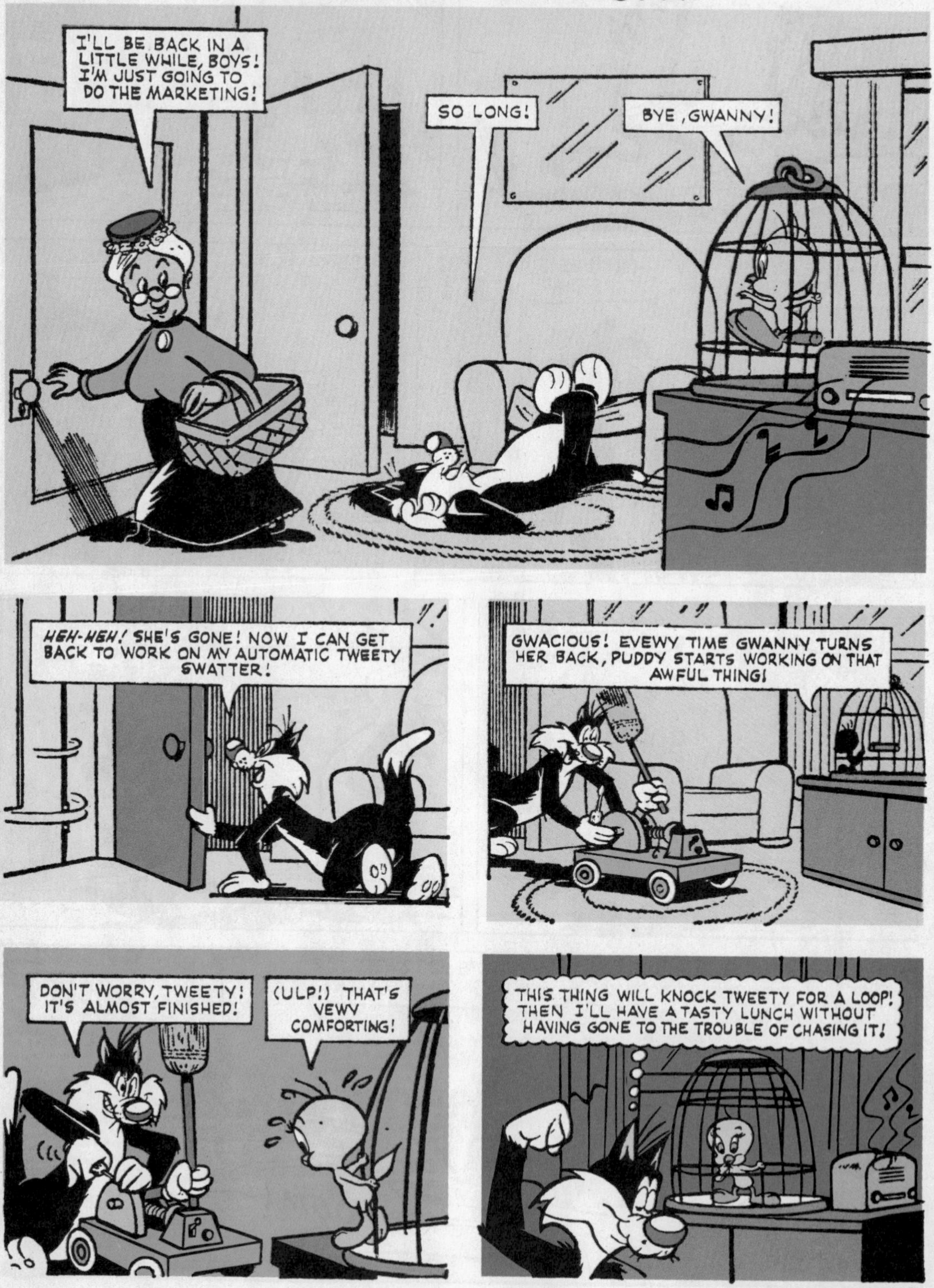

I'LL BE BACK IN A LITTLE WHILE, BOYS! I'M JUST GOING TO DO THE MARKETING!
SO LONG!
BYE, GWANNY!
HEH-HEH! SHE'S GONE! NOW I CAN GET BACK TO WORK ON MY AUTOMATIC TWEETY SWATTER!
GWACIOUS! EVEWY TIME GWANNY TURNS HER BACK, PUDDY STARTS WORKING ON THAT AWFUL THING!
DON'T WORRY, TWEETY! IT'S ALMOST FINISHED!
(ULP!) THAT'S VEWY COMFORTING!
THIS THING WILL KNOCK TWEETY FOR A LOOP! THEN I'LL HAVE A TASTY LUNCH WITHOUT HAVING GONE TO THE TROUBLE OF CHASING IT!

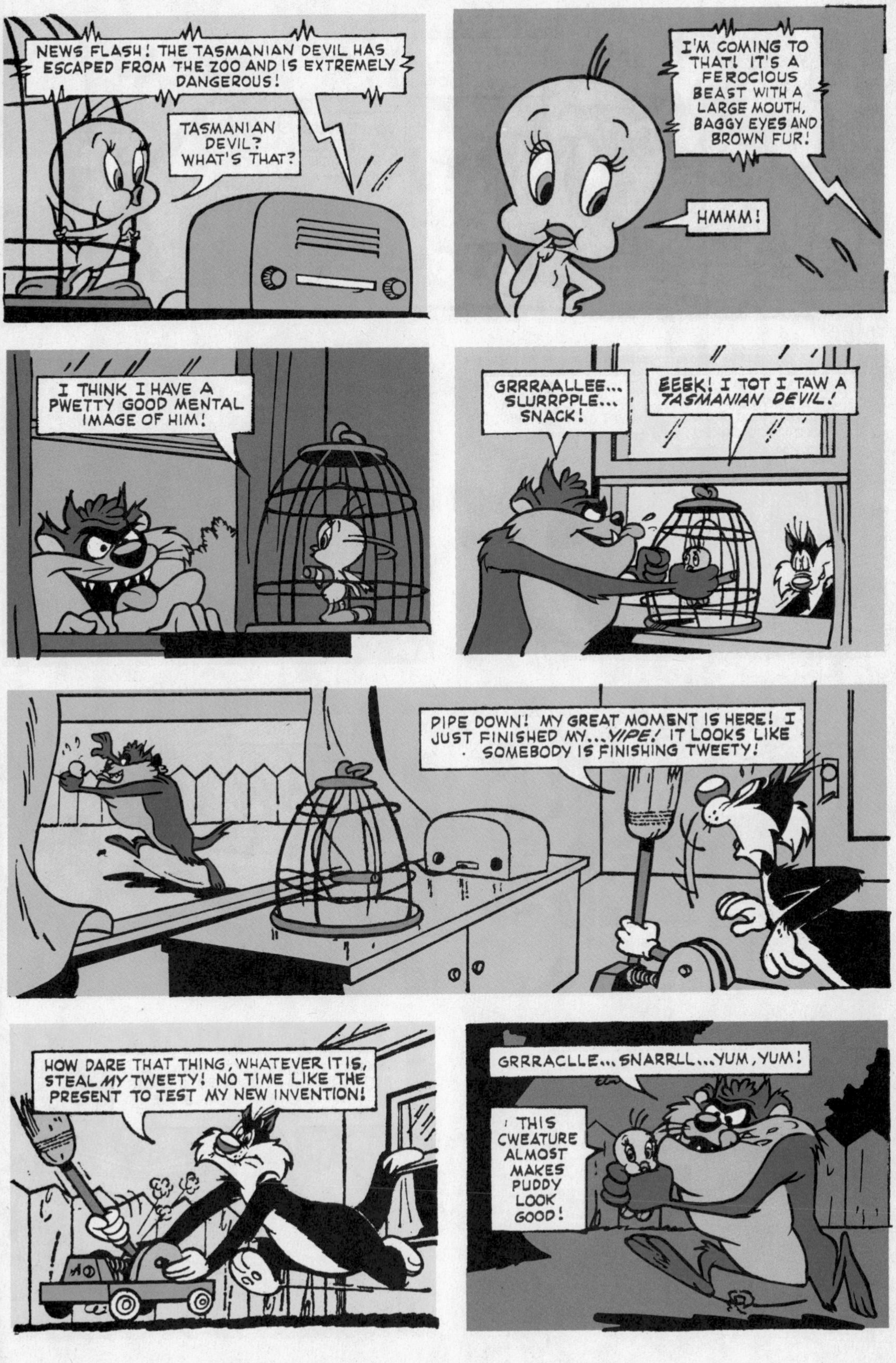
NEWS FLASH! THE TASMANIAN DEVIL HAS ESCAPED FROM THE ZOO AND IS EXTREMELY DANGEROUS!
TASMANIAN DEVIL? WHAT'S THAT?
I'M COMING TO THAT! IT'S A FEROCIOUS BEAST WITH A LARGE MOUTH, BAGGY EYES AND BROWN FUR!
HMMM!
I THINK I HAVE A PWETTY GOOD MENTAL IMAGE OF HIM!
GRRRAALLEE... SLURRPPLE... SNACK!
EEEK! I TOT I TAW A *TASMANIAN DEVIL!*
PIPE DOWN! MY GREAT MOMENT IS HERE! I JUST FINISHED MY... *YIPE!* IT LOOKS LIKE SOMEBODY IS FINISHING TWEETY!
HOW DARE THAT THING, WHATEVER IT IS, STEAL *MY* TWEETY! NO TIME LIKE THE PRESENT TO TEST MY NEW INVENTION!
GRRRACLLE... SNARRLL... YUM, YUM!
THIS CWEATURE ALMOST MAKES PUDDY LOOK GOOD!

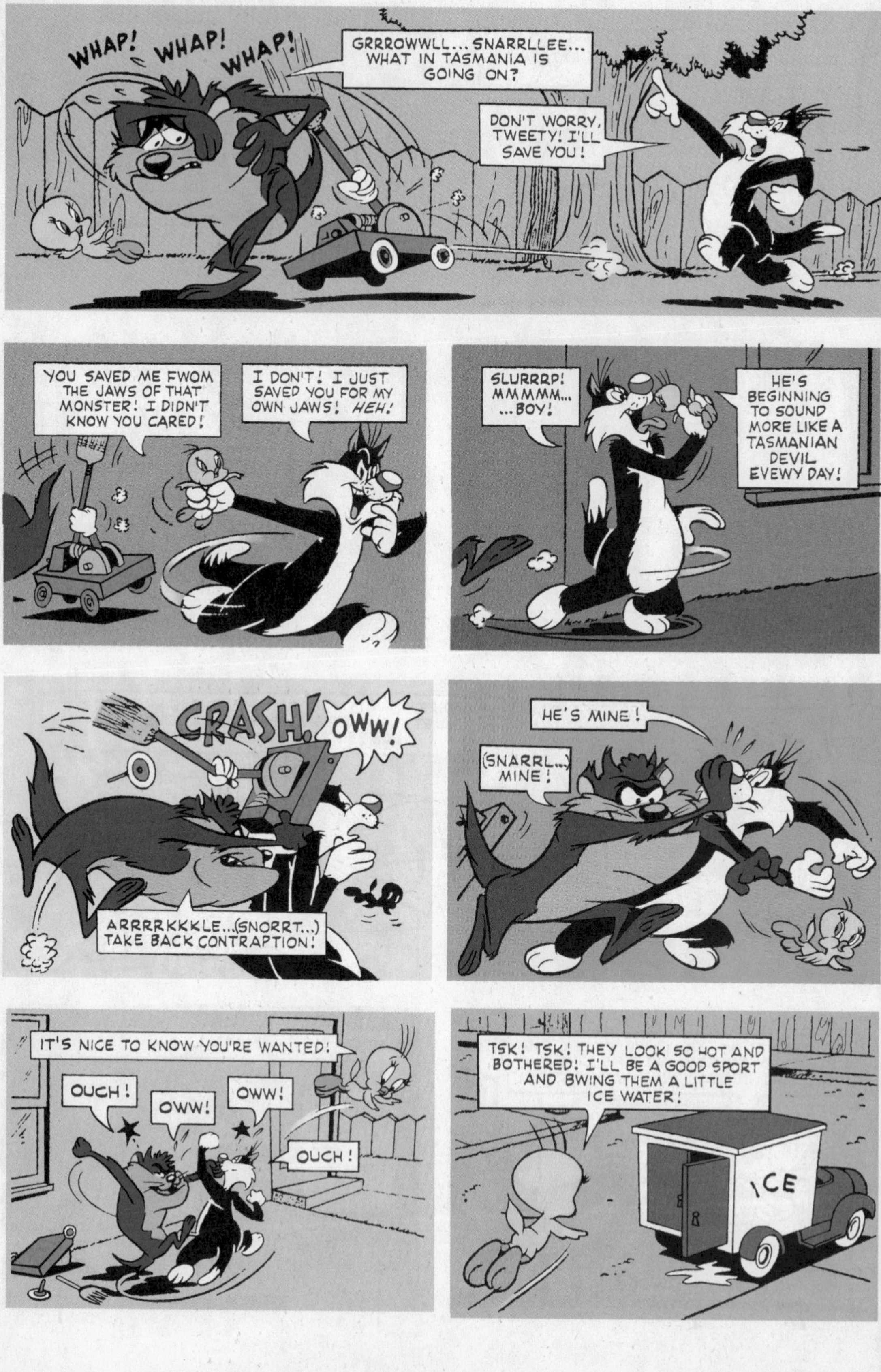
WHAP! WHAP! WHAP!
GRRROWLL... SNARRLLEE... WHAT IN TASMANIA IS GOING ON?
DON'T WORRY, TWEETY! I'LL SAVE YOU!
YOU SAVED ME FWOM THE JAWS OF THAT MONSTER! I DIDN'T KNOW YOU CARED!
I DON'T! I JUST SAVED YOU FOR MY OWN JAWS! HEH!
SLURRRP! MMMMM... ...BOY!
HE'S BEGINNING TO SOUND MORE LIKE A TASMANIAN DEVIL EVEWY DAY!
CRASH!
OWW!
ARRRRKKKLE...(SNORRT...) TAKE BACK CONTRAPTION!
HE'S MINE!
(SNARRL...) MINE!
IT'S NICE TO KNOW YOU'RE WANTED!
OUCH!
OWW!
OWW!
OUCH!
TSK! TSK! THEY LOOK SO HOT AND BOTHERED! I'LL BE A GOOD SPORT AND BWING THEM A LITTLE ICE WATER!
ICE

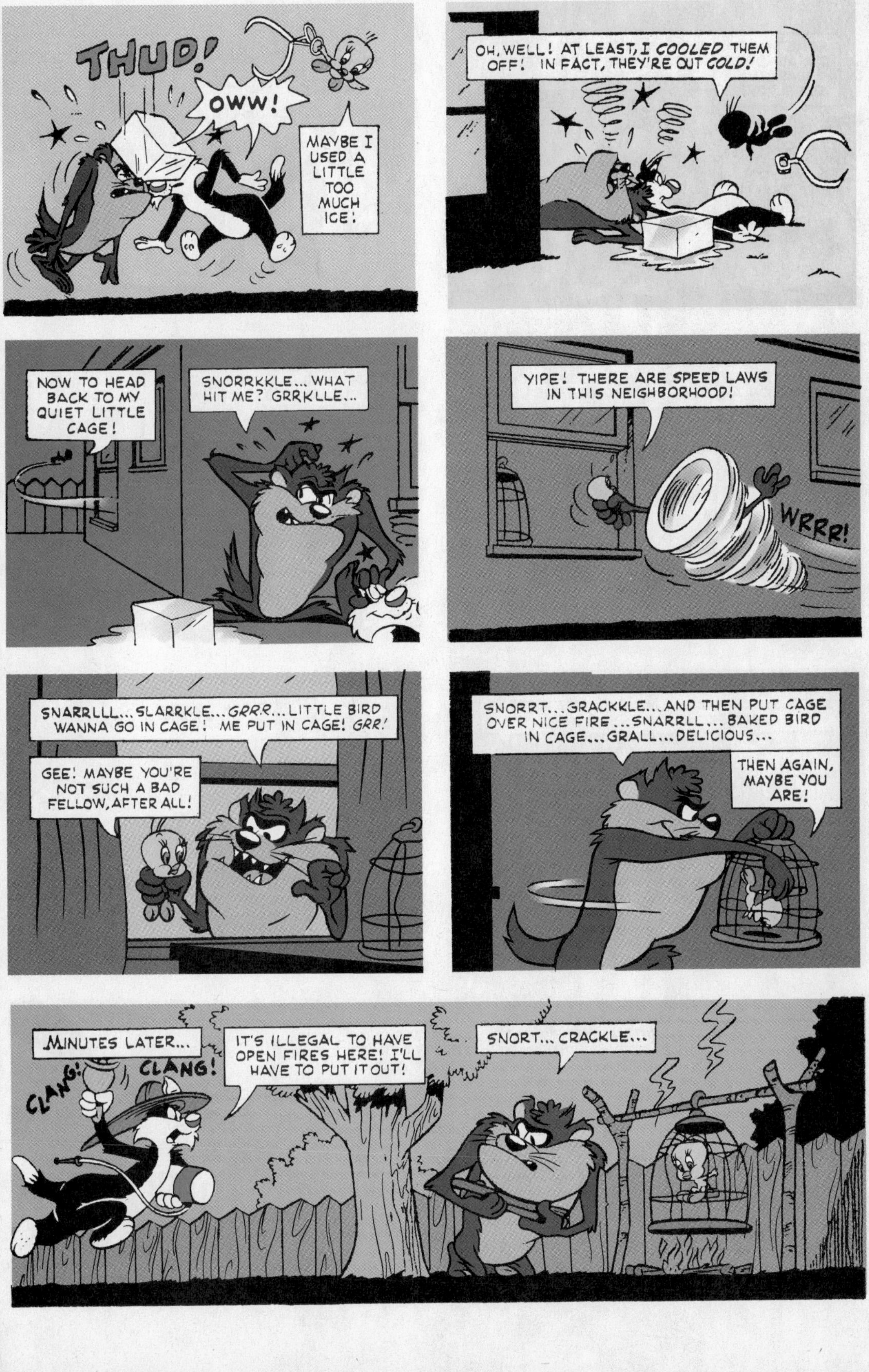
THUD!
OWW!
MAYBE I USED A LITTLE TOO MUCH ICE!
OH, WELL! AT LEAST, I COOLED THEM OFF! IN FACT, THEY'RE OUT COLD!
NOW TO HEAD BACK TO MY QUIET LITTLE CAGE!
SNORRKKLE... WHAT HIT ME? GRRKLLE...
YIPE! THERE ARE SPEED LAWS IN THIS NEIGHBORHOOD!
WRRR!
SNARRLLL... SLARRKLE... GRR.R... LITTLE BIRD WANNA GO IN CAGE! ME PUT IN CAGE! GRR!
GEE! MAYBE YOU'RE NOT SUCH A BAD FELLOW, AFTER ALL!
SNORRT... GRACKKLE... AND THEN PUT CAGE OVER NICE FIRE... SNARRLL... BAKED BIRD IN CAGE... GRALL... DELICIOUS...
THEN AGAIN, MAYBE YOU ARE!
MINUTES LATER...
CLANG!
CLANG!
IT'S ILLEGAL TO HAVE OPEN FIRES HERE! I'LL HAVE TO PUT IT OUT!
SNORT... CRACKLE...

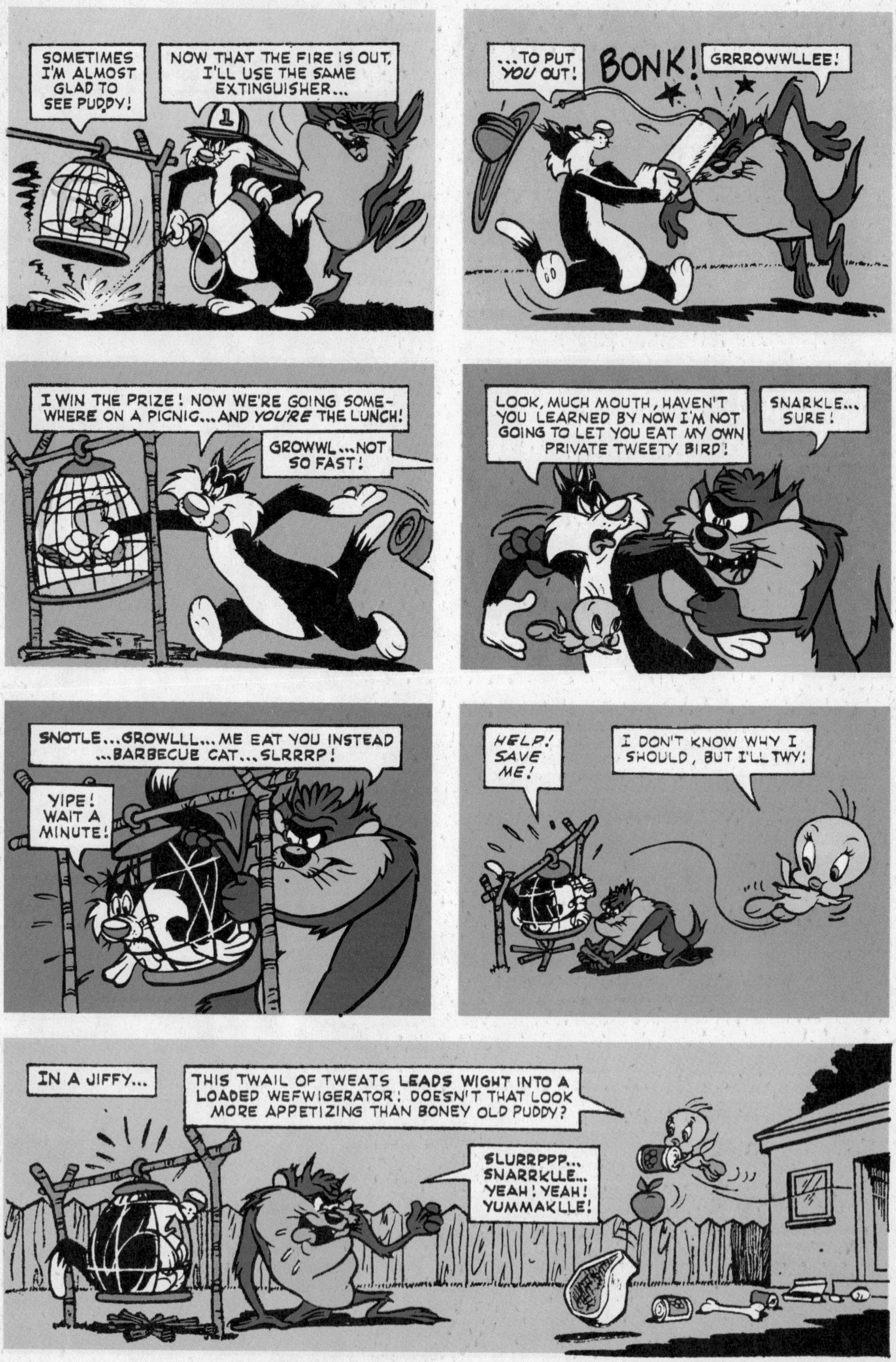
SOMETIMES I'M ALMOST GLAD TO SEE PUDDY!
NOW THAT THE FIRE IS OUT, I'LL USE THE SAME EXTINGUISHER...
...TO PUT YOU OUT!
BONK!
GRRROWWLLEE!
I WIN THE PRIZE! NOW WE'RE GOING SOMEWHERE ON A PICNIC...AND YOU'RE THE LUNCH!
GROWWL...NOT SO FAST!
LOOK, MUCH MOUTH, HAVEN'T YOU LEARNED BY NOW I'M NOT GOING TO LET YOU EAT MY OWN PRIVATE TWEETY BIRD!
SNARKLE... SURE!
SNOTLE...GROWLLL...ME EAT YOU INSTEAD ...BARBECUE CAT...SLRRRP!
YIPE! WAIT A MINUTE!
HELP! SAVE ME!
I DON'T KNOW WHY I SHOULD, BUT I'LL TWY!
IN A JIFFY...
THIS TWAIL OF TWEATS LEADS WIGHT INTO A LOADED WEFWIGERATOR! DOESN'T THAT LOOK MORE APPETIZING THAN BONEY OLD PUDDY?
SLURRPPP... SNARRKLLE... YEAH! YEAH! YUMMAKLLE!

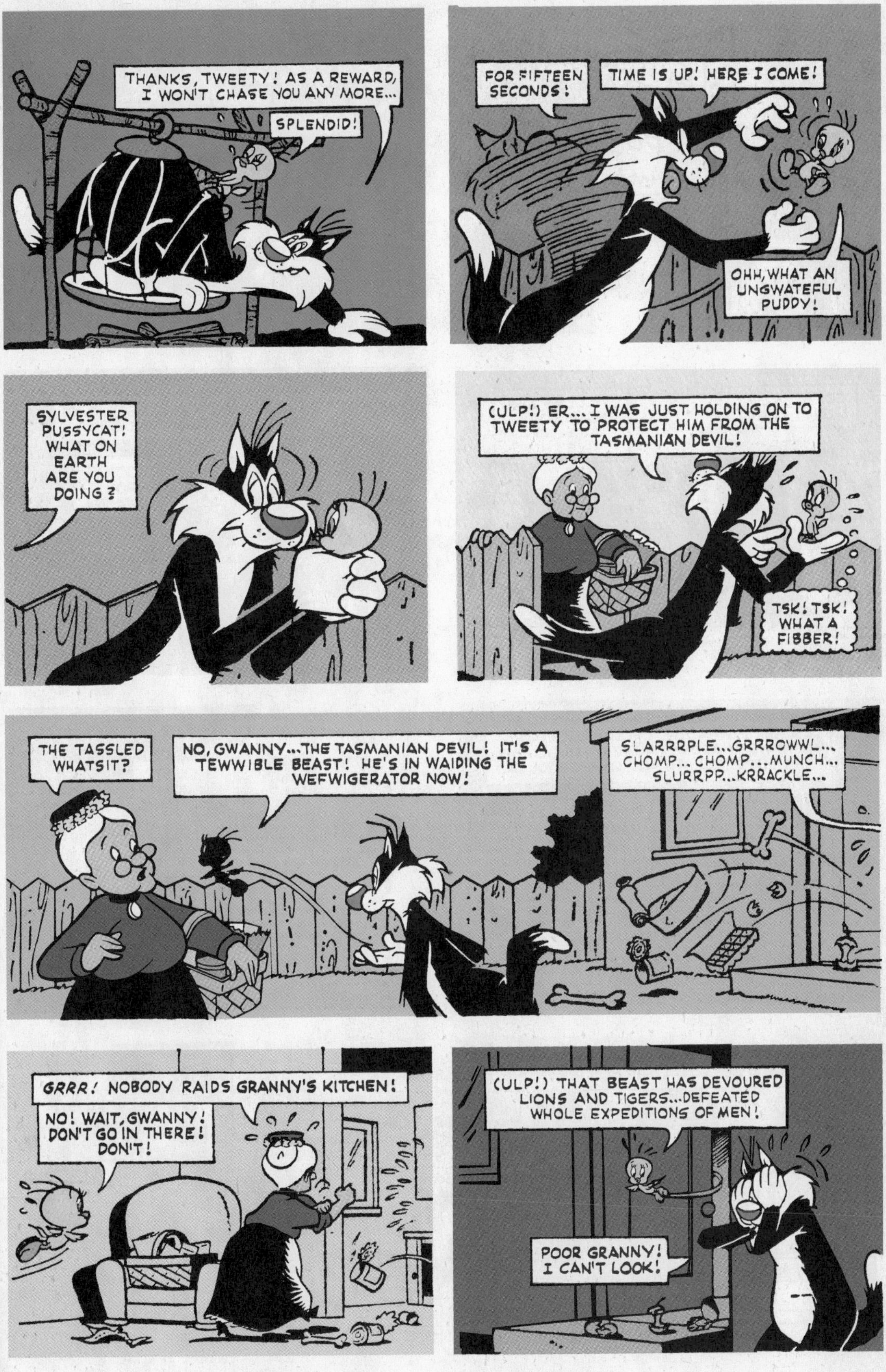
THANKS, TWEETY! AS A REWARD, I WON'T CHASE YOU ANY MORE...
SPLENDID!
FOR FIFTEEN SECONDS!
TIME IS UP! HERE I COME!
OHH, WHAT AN UNGWATEFUL PUDDY!
SYLVESTER PUSSYCAT! WHAT ON EARTH ARE YOU DOING?
(ULP!) ER... I WAS JUST HOLDING ON TO TWEETY TO PROTECT HIM FROM THE TASMANIAN DEVIL!
TSK! TSK! WHAT A FIBBER!
THE TASSLED WHATSIT?
NO, GWANNY...THE TASMANIAN DEVIL! IT'S A TEWWIBLE BEAST! HE'S IN WAIDING THE WEFWIGERATOR NOW!
SLARRRPLE...GRRROWWL... CHOMP... CHOMP...MUNCH... SLURRPP...KRRACKLE...
GRRR! NOBODY RAIDS GRANNY'S KITCHEN!
NO! WAIT, GWANNY! DON'T GO IN THERE! DON'T!
(ULP!) THAT BEAST HAS DEVOURED LIONS AND TIGERS...DEFEATED WHOLE EXPEDITIONS OF MEN!
POOR GRANNY! I CAN'T LOOK!

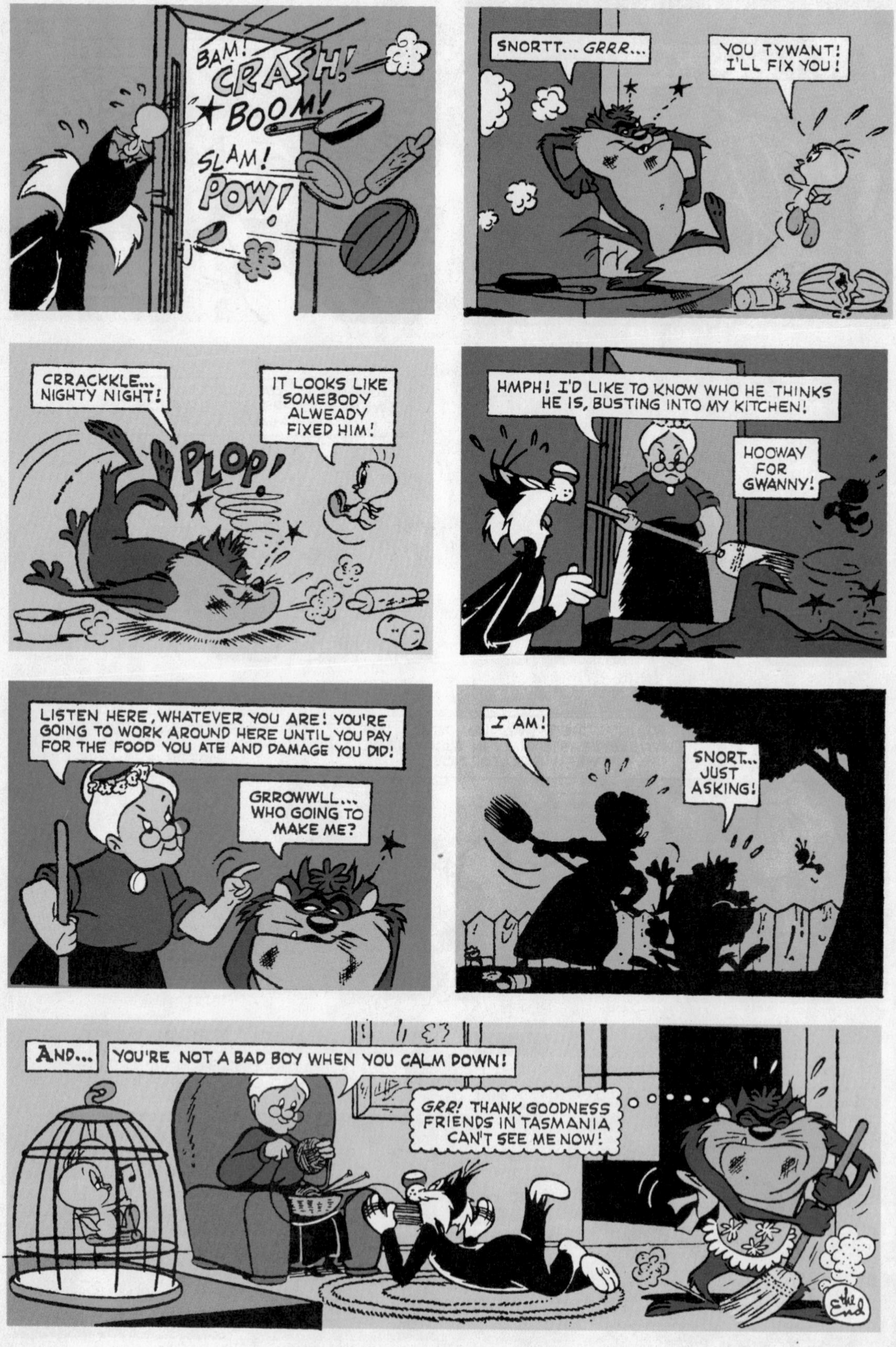
BAM!
CRASH!
BOOM!
SLAM!
POW!
SNORTT... GRRR...
YOU TYWANT! I'LL FIX YOU!
CRRACKKLE... NIGHTY NIGHT!
PLOP!
IT LOOKS LIKE SOMEBODY ALWEADY FIXED HIM!
HMPH! I'D LIKE TO KNOW WHO HE THINKS HE IS, BUSTING INTO MY KITCHEN!
HOOWAY FOR GWANNY!
LISTEN HERE, WHATEVER YOU ARE! YOU'RE GOING TO WORK AROUND HERE UNTIL YOU PAY FOR THE FOOD YOU ATE AND DAMAGE YOU DID!
GRROWWLL... WHO GOING TO MAKE ME?
I AM!
SNORT... JUST ASKING!
AND...
YOU'RE NOT A BAD BOY WHEN YOU CALM DOWN!
GRR! THANK GOODNESS FRIENDS IN TASMANIA CAN'T SEE ME NOW!
the End

DAFFY DUCK
SNOOPER IN A STUPOR

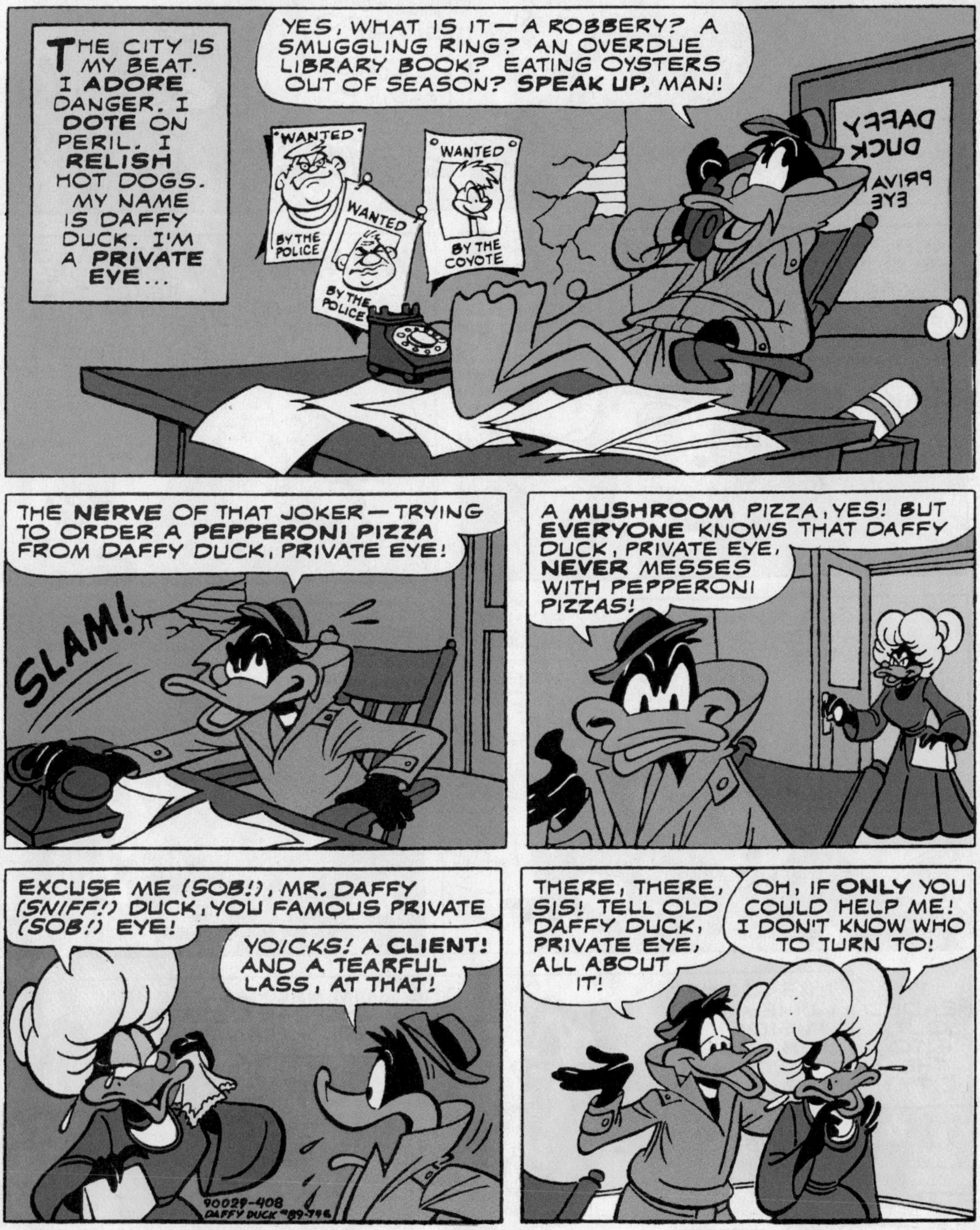
THE CITY IS MY BEAT. I **ADORE** DANGER. I **DOTE** ON PERIL. I **RELISH** HOT DOGS. MY NAME IS DAFFY DUCK. I'M A **PRIVATE** EYE...
YES, WHAT IS IT—A ROBBERY? A SMUGGLING RING? AN OVERDUE LIBRARY BOOK? EATING OYSTERS OUT OF SEASON? **SPEAK UP,** MAN!
WANTED BY THE POLICE
WANTED BY THE POLICE
WANTED BY THE COYOTE
THE **NERVE** OF THAT JOKER—TRYING TO ORDER A **PEPPERONI PIZZA** FROM DAFFY DUCK, PRIVATE EYE!
SLAM!
A **MUSHROOM** PIZZA, YES! BUT **EVERYONE** KNOWS THAT DAFFY DUCK, PRIVATE EYE, **NEVER** MESSES WITH PEPPERONI PIZZAS!
EXCUSE ME *(SOB!)*, MR. DAFFY *(SNIFF!)* DUCK, YOU FAMOUS PRIVATE *(SOB!)* EYE!
YOICKS! A **CLIENT!** AND A TEARFUL LASS, AT THAT!
THERE, THERE, SIS! TELL OLD DAFFY DUCK, PRIVATE EYE, ALL ABOUT IT!
OH, IF **ONLY** YOU COULD HELP ME! I DON'T KNOW WHO TO TURN TO!

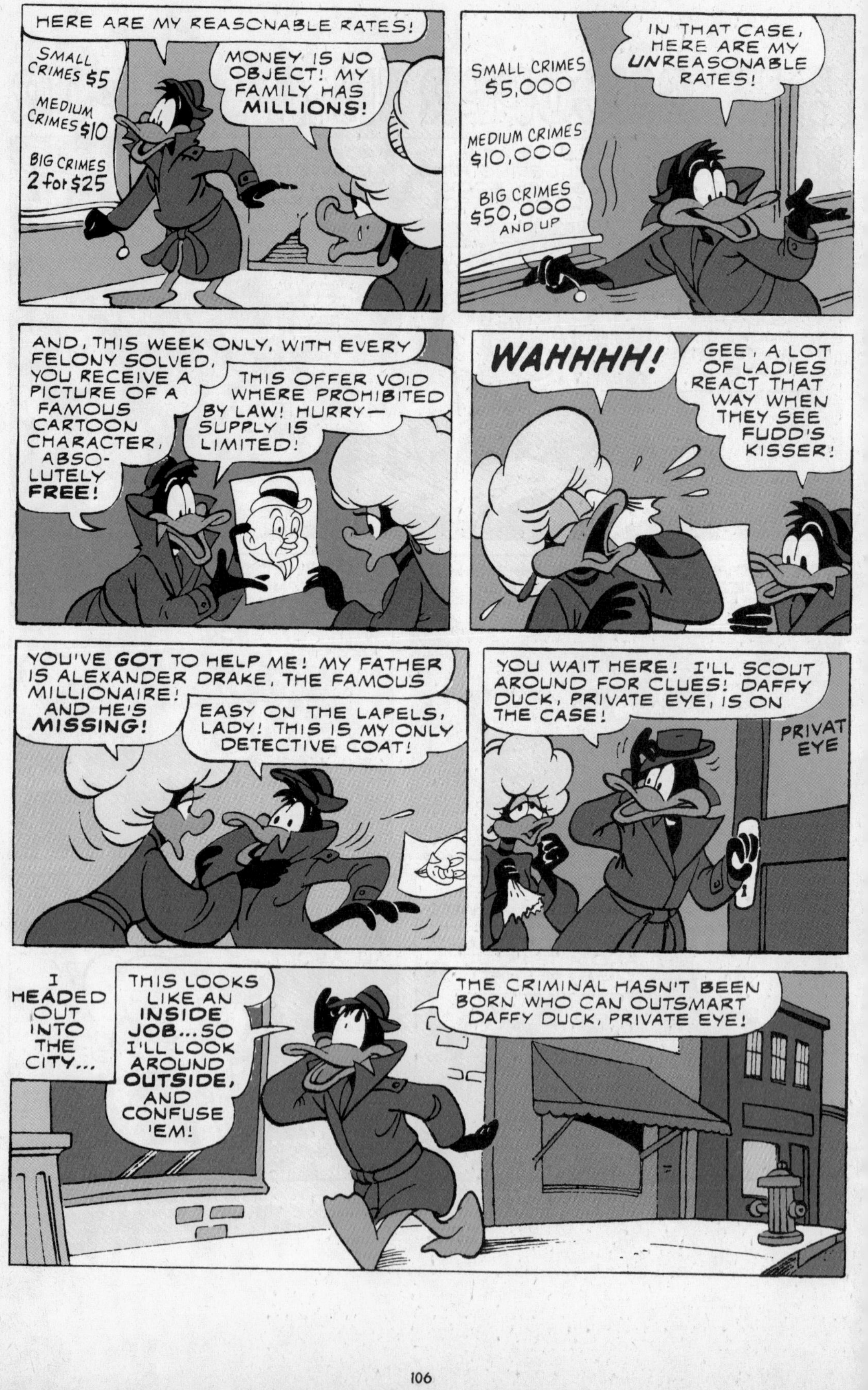
HERE ARE MY REASONABLE RATES!
SMALL CRIMES $5
MEDIUM CRIMES $10
BIG CRIMES 2 for $25
MONEY IS NO OBJECT! MY FAMILY HAS MILLIONS!
SMALL CRIMES $5,000
MEDIUM CRIMES $10,000
BIG CRIMES $50,000 AND UP
IN THAT CASE, HERE ARE MY UNREASONABLE RATES!
AND, THIS WEEK ONLY, WITH EVERY FELONY SOLVED, YOU RECEIVE A PICTURE OF A FAMOUS CARTOON CHARACTER, ABSOLUTELY FREE!
THIS OFFER VOID WHERE PROHIBITED BY LAW! HURRY— SUPPLY IS LIMITED!
WAHHHH!
GEE, A LOT OF LADIES REACT THAT WAY WHEN THEY SEE FUDD'S KISSER!
YOU'VE GOT TO HELP ME! MY FATHER IS ALEXANDER DRAKE, THE FAMOUS MILLIONAIRE!
AND HE'S MISSING!
EASY ON THE LAPELS, LADY! THIS IS MY ONLY DETECTIVE COAT!
YOU WAIT HERE! I'LL SCOUT AROUND FOR CLUES! DAFFY DUCK, PRIVATE EYE, IS ON THE CASE!
PRIVAT EYE
I HEADED OUT INTO THE CITY...
THIS LOOKS LIKE AN INSIDE JOB...SO I'LL LOOK AROUND OUTSIDE, AND CONFUSE 'EM!
THE CRIMINAL HASN'T BEEN BORN WHO CAN OUTSMART DAFFY DUCK, PRIVATE EYE!

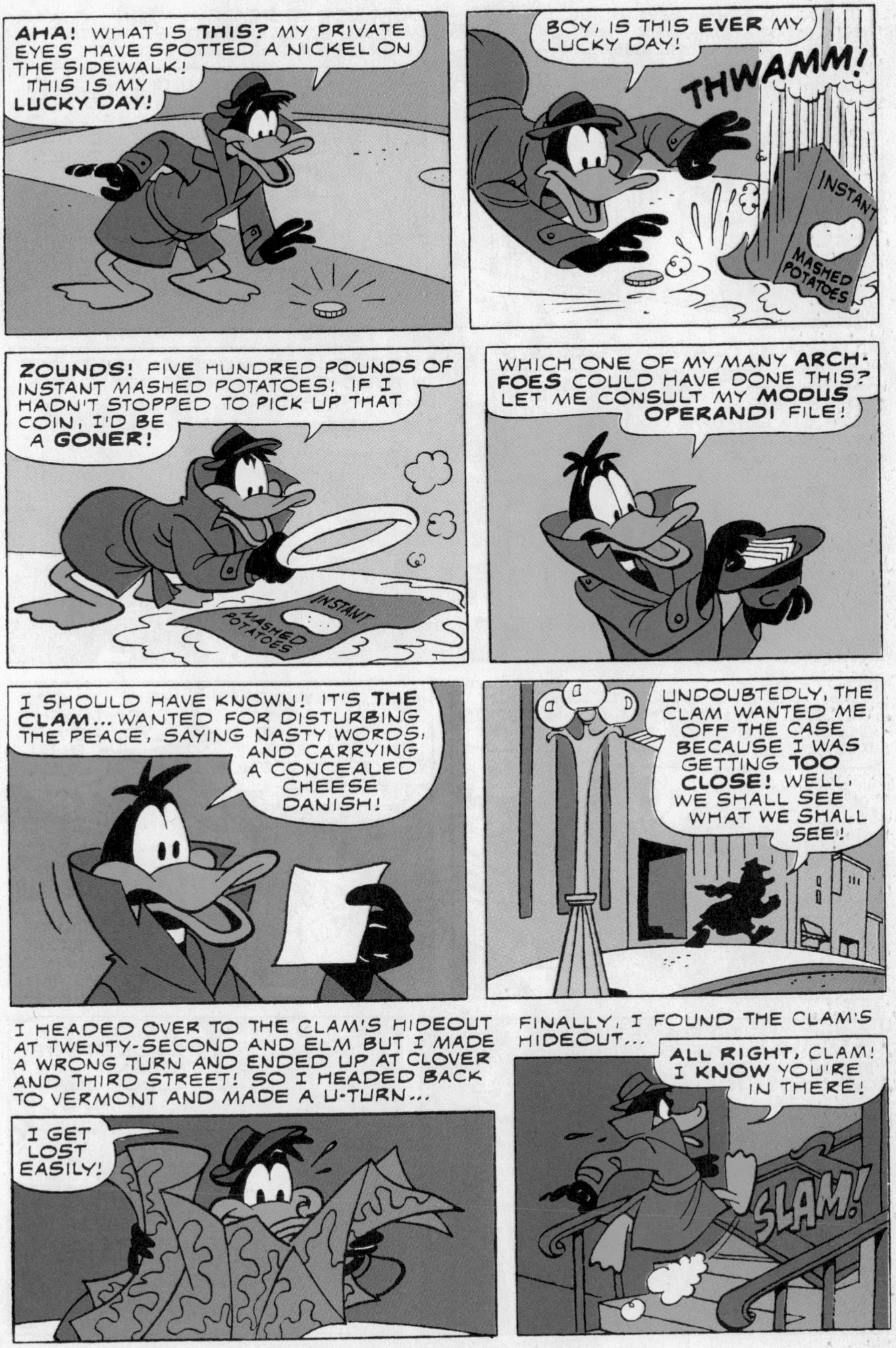
AHA! WHAT IS THIS? MY PRIVATE EYES HAVE SPOTTED A NICKEL ON THE SIDEWALK! THIS IS MY LUCKY DAY!
BOY, IS THIS EVER MY LUCKY DAY!
THWAMM!
INSTANT MASHED POTATOES
ZOUNDS! FIVE HUNDRED POUNDS OF INSTANT MASHED POTATOES! IF I HADN'T STOPPED TO PICK UP THAT COIN, I'D BE A GONER!
INSTANT MASHED POTATOES
WHICH ONE OF MY MANY ARCH-FOES COULD HAVE DONE THIS? LET ME CONSULT MY MODUS OPERANDI FILE!
I SHOULD HAVE KNOWN! IT'S THE CLAM... WANTED FOR DISTURBING THE PEACE, SAYING NASTY WORDS, AND CARRYING A CONCEALED CHEESE DANISH!
UNDOUBTEDLY, THE CLAM WANTED ME OFF THE CASE BECAUSE I WAS GETTING TOO CLOSE! WELL, WE SHALL SEE WHAT WE SHALL SEE!
I HEADED OVER TO THE CLAM'S HIDEOUT AT TWENTY-SECOND AND ELM BUT I MADE A WRONG TURN AND ENDED UP AT CLOVER AND THIRD STREET! SO I HEADED BACK TO VERMONT AND MADE A U-TURN...
I GET LOST EASILY!
FINALLY, I FOUND THE CLAM'S HIDEOUT...
ALL RIGHT, CLAM! I KNOW YOU'RE IN THERE!
SLAM!

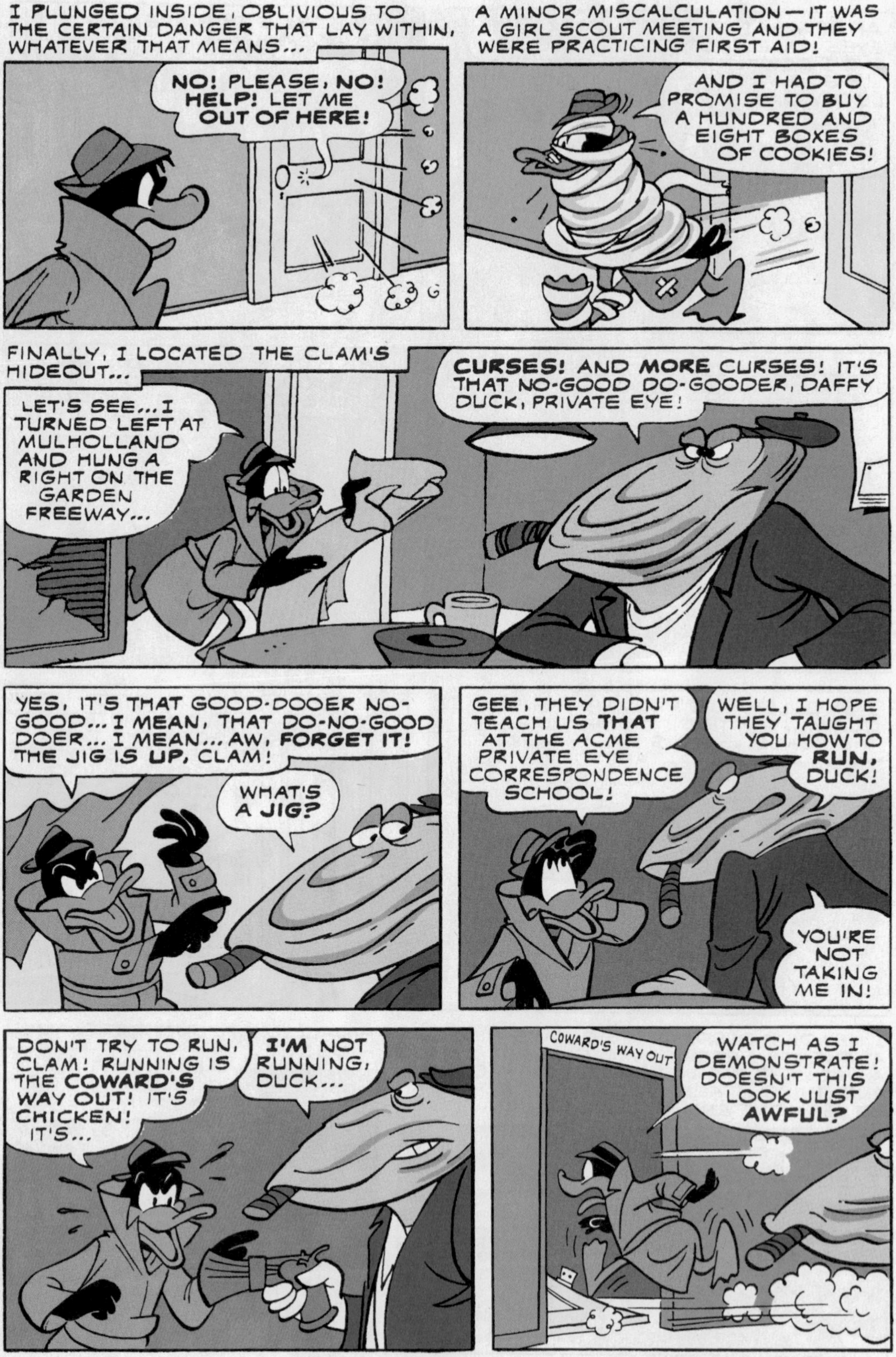

I PLUNGED INSIDE, OBLIVIOUS TO THE CERTAIN DANGER THAT LAY WITHIN, WHATEVER THAT MEANS...
NO! PLEASE, NO! HELP! LET ME OUT OF HERE!
A MINOR MISCALCULATION — IT WAS A GIRL SCOUT MEETING AND THEY WERE PRACTICING FIRST AID!
AND I HAD TO PROMISE TO BUY A HUNDRED AND EIGHT BOXES OF COOKIES!
FINALLY, I LOCATED THE CLAM'S HIDEOUT...
LET'S SEE... I TURNED LEFT AT MULHOLLAND AND HUNG A RIGHT ON THE GARDEN FREEWAY...
CURSES! AND MORE CURSES! IT'S THAT NO-GOOD DO-GOODER, DAFFY DUCK, PRIVATE EYE!
YES, IT'S THAT GOOD-DOOER NO-GOOD... I MEAN, THAT DO-NO-GOOD DOER... I MEAN... AW, FORGET IT! THE JIG IS UP, CLAM!
WHAT'S A JIG?
GEE, THEY DIDN'T TEACH US THAT AT THE ACME PRIVATE EYE CORRESPONDENCE SCHOOL!
WELL, I HOPE THEY TAUGHT YOU HOW TO RUN, DUCK!
YOU'RE NOT TAKING ME IN!
DON'T TRY TO RUN, CLAM! RUNNING IS THE COWARD'S WAY OUT! IT'S CHICKEN! IT'S...
I'M NOT RUNNING, DUCK...
COWARD'S WAY OUT
WATCH AS I DEMONSTRATE! DOESN'T THIS LOOK JUST AWFUL?

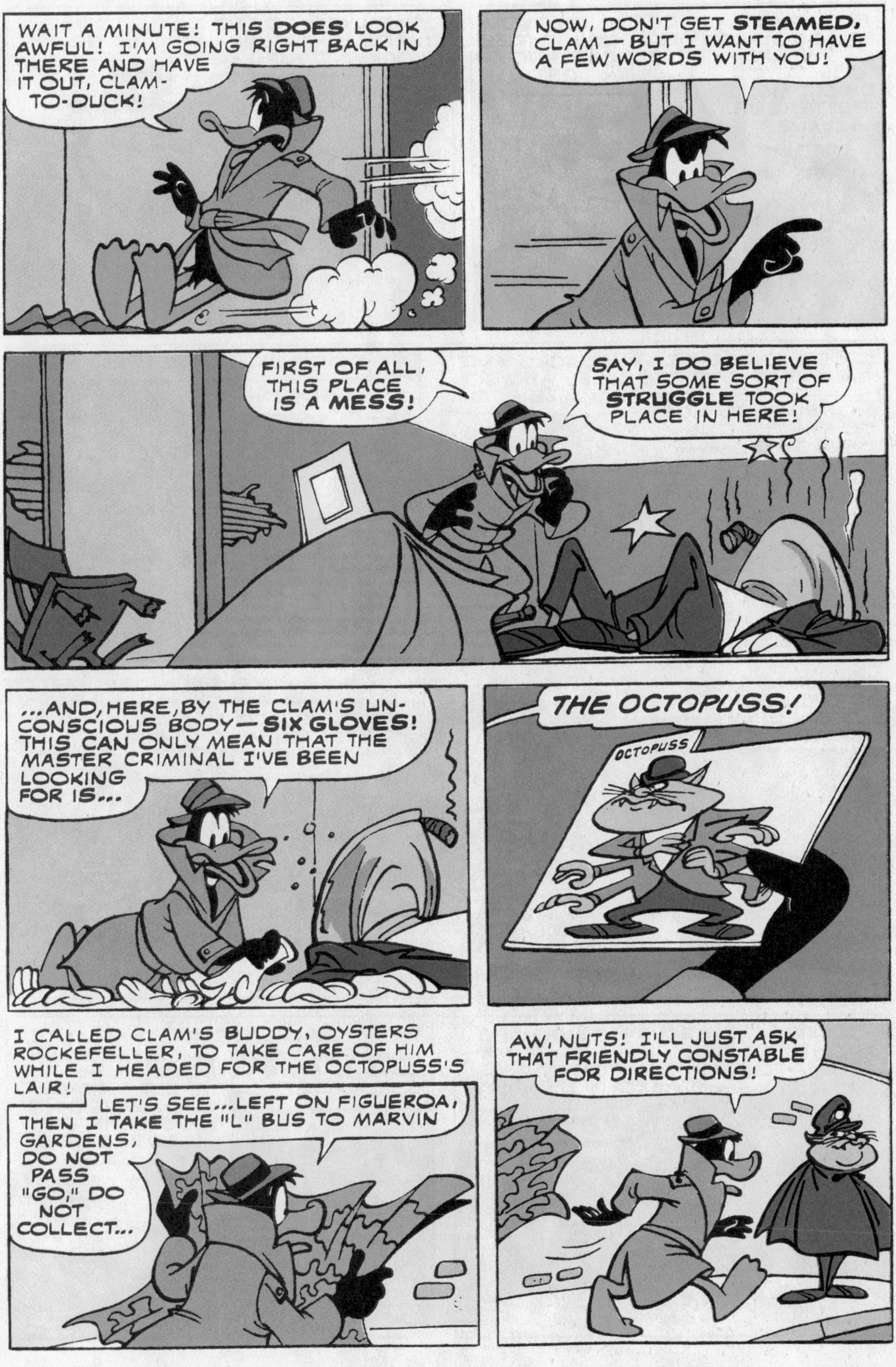
WAIT A MINUTE! THIS DOES LOOK AWFUL! I'M GOING RIGHT BACK IN THERE AND HAVE IT OUT, CLAM-TO-DUCK!
NOW, DON'T GET STEAMED, CLAM — BUT I WANT TO HAVE A FEW WORDS WITH YOU!
FIRST OF ALL, THIS PLACE IS A MESS!
SAY, I DO BELIEVE THAT SOME SORT OF STRUGGLE TOOK PLACE IN HERE!
...AND, HERE, BY THE CLAM'S UNCONSCIOUS BODY — SIX GLOVES! THIS CAN ONLY MEAN THAT THE MASTER CRIMINAL I'VE BEEN LOOKING FOR IS...
THE OCTOPUSS!
OCTOPUSS
I CALLED CLAM'S BUDDY, OYSTERS ROCKEFELLER, TO TAKE CARE OF HIM WHILE I HEADED FOR THE OCTOPUSS'S LAIR!
LET'S SEE...LEFT ON FIGUEROA, THEN I TAKE THE "L" BUS TO MARVIN GARDENS, DO NOT PASS "GO," DO NOT COLLECT...
AW, NUTS! I'LL JUST ASK THAT FRIENDLY CONSTABLE FOR DIRECTIONS!

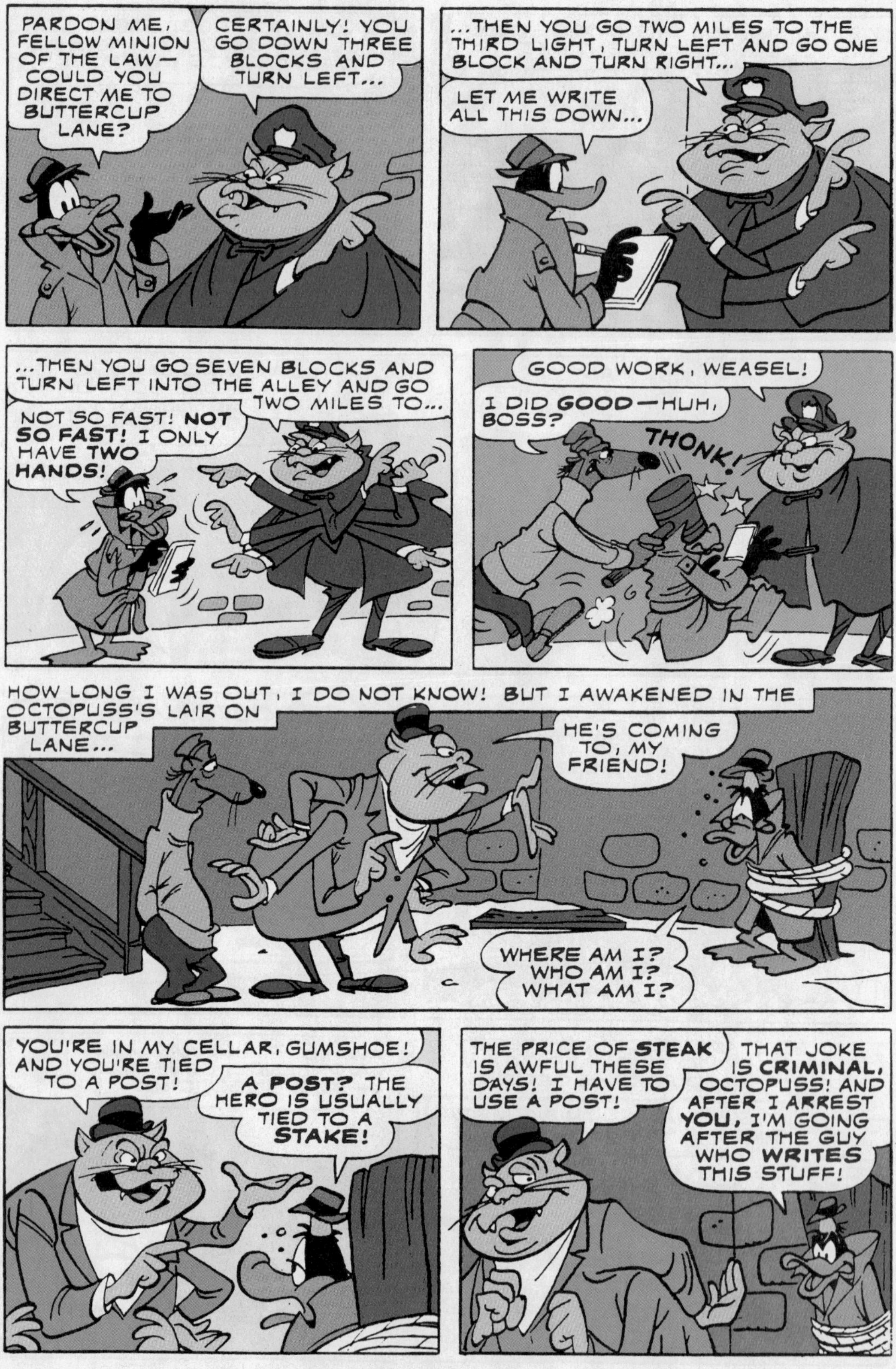
PARDON ME, FELLOW MINION OF THE LAW—COULD YOU DIRECT ME TO BUTTERCUP LANE?
CERTAINLY! YOU GO DOWN THREE BLOCKS AND TURN LEFT...
...THEN YOU GO TWO MILES TO THE THIRD LIGHT, TURN LEFT AND GO ONE BLOCK AND TURN RIGHT...
LET ME WRITE ALL THIS DOWN...
...THEN YOU GO SEVEN BLOCKS AND TURN LEFT INTO THE ALLEY AND GO TWO MILES TO...
NOT SO FAST! **NOT SO FAST!** I ONLY HAVE **TWO HANDS!**
GOOD WORK, WEASEL!
I DID **GOOD**—HUH, BOSS?
THONK!
HOW LONG I WAS OUT, I DO NOT KNOW! BUT I AWAKENED IN THE OCTOPUSS'S LAIR ON BUTTERCUP LANE...
HE'S COMING TO, MY FRIEND!
WHERE AM I? WHO AM I? WHAT AM I?
YOU'RE IN MY CELLAR, GUMSHOE! AND YOU'RE TIED TO A POST!
A **POST?** THE HERO IS USUALLY TIED TO A **STAKE!**
THE PRICE OF **STEAK** IS AWFUL THESE DAYS! I HAVE TO USE A POST!
THAT JOKE IS **CRIMINAL,** OCTOPUSS! AND AFTER I ARREST **YOU,** I'M GOING AFTER THE GUY WHO **WRITES** THIS STUFF!

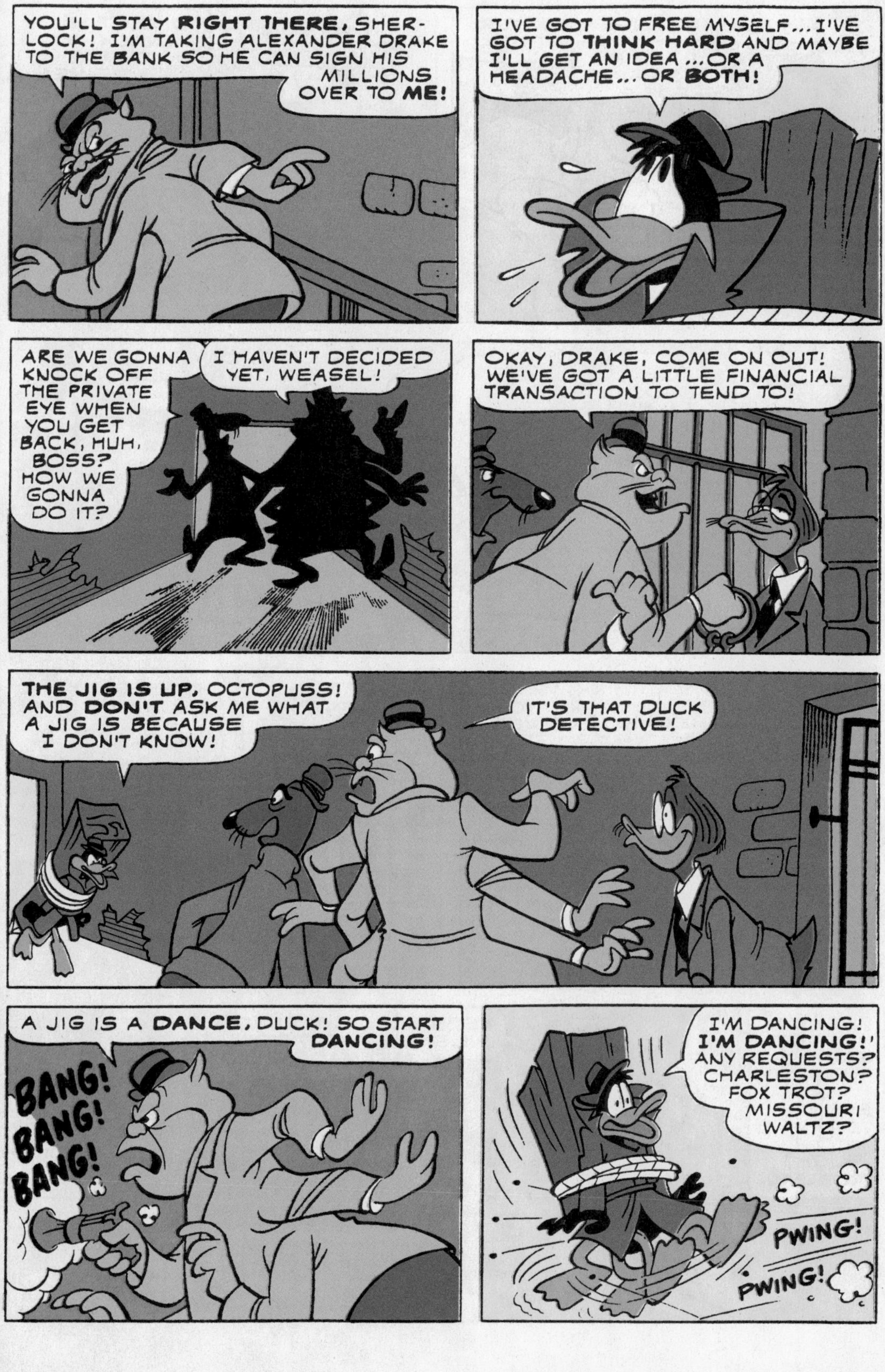
YOU'LL STAY RIGHT THERE, SHERLOCK! I'M TAKING ALEXANDER DRAKE TO THE BANK SO HE CAN SIGN HIS MILLIONS OVER TO ME!
I'VE GOT TO FREE MYSELF... I'VE GOT TO THINK HARD AND MAYBE I'LL GET AN IDEA ...OR A HEADACHE... OR BOTH!
ARE WE GONNA KNOCK OFF THE PRIVATE EYE WHEN YOU GET BACK, HUH, BOSS? HOW WE GONNA DO IT?
I HAVEN'T DECIDED YET, WEASEL!
OKAY, DRAKE, COME ON OUT! WE'VE GOT A LITTLE FINANCIAL TRANSACTION TO TEND TO!
THE JIG IS UP, OCTOPUSS! AND DON'T ASK ME WHAT A JIG IS BECAUSE I DON'T KNOW!
IT'S THAT DUCK DETECTIVE!
A JIG IS A DANCE, DUCK! SO START DANCING!
BANG! BANG! BANG!
I'M DANCING! I'M DANCING! ANY REQUESTS? CHARLESTON? FOX TROT? MISSOURI WALTZ?
PWING!
PWING!

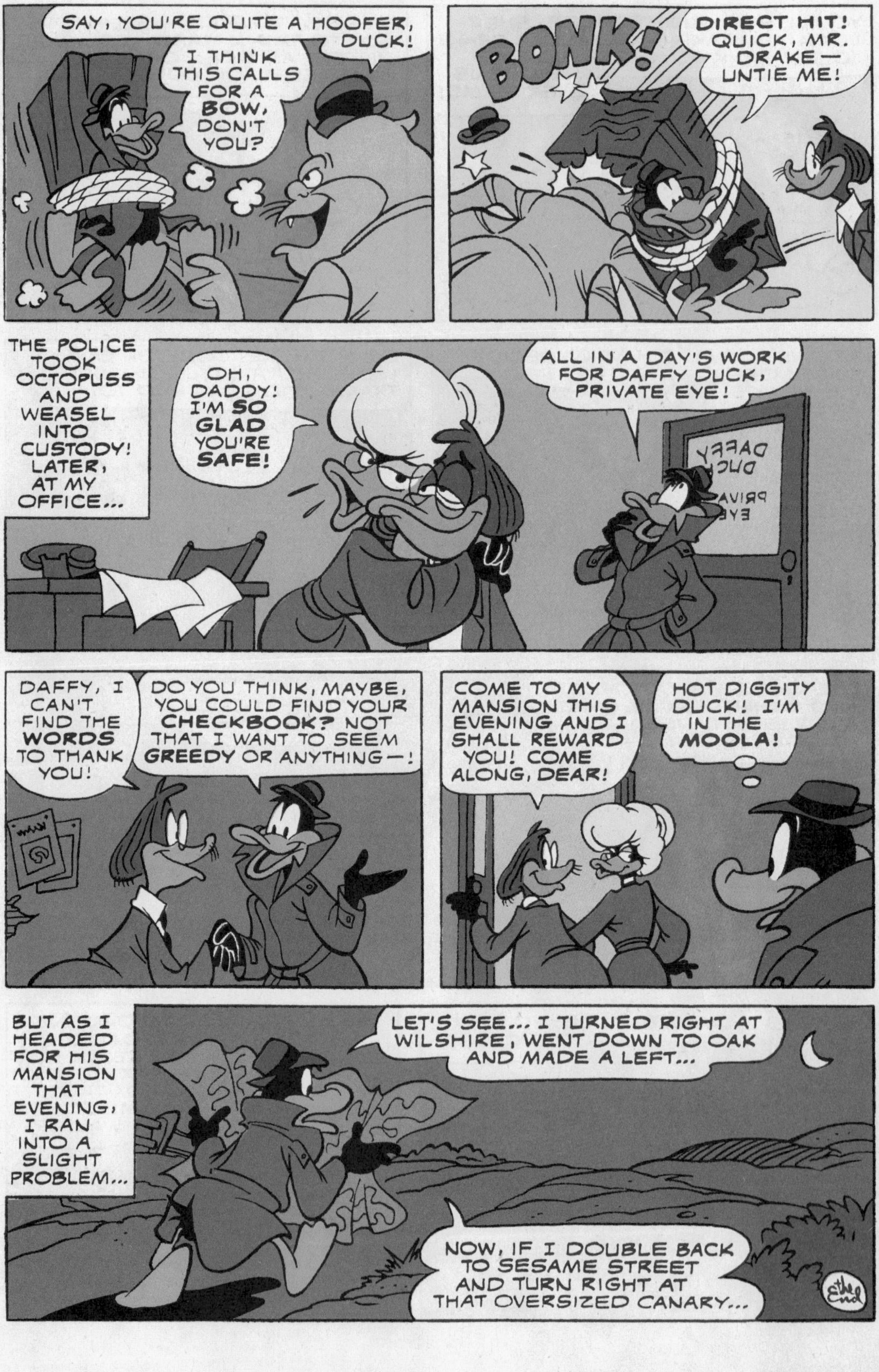
SAY, YOU'RE QUITE A HOOFER, DUCK!
I THINK THIS CALLS FOR A BOW, DON'T YOU?
BONK!
DIRECT HIT! QUICK, MR. DRAKE— UNTIE ME!
THE POLICE TOOK OCTOPUSS AND WEASEL INTO CUSTODY! LATER, AT MY OFFICE...
OH, DADDY! I'M SO GLAD YOU'RE SAFE!
ALL IN A DAY'S WORK FOR DAFFY DUCK, PRIVATE EYE!
DAFFY, I CAN'T FIND THE WORDS TO THANK YOU!
DO YOU THINK, MAYBE, YOU COULD FIND YOUR CHECKBOOK? NOT THAT I WANT TO SEEM GREEDY OR ANYTHING—!
COME TO MY MANSION THIS EVENING AND I SHALL REWARD YOU! COME ALONG, DEAR!
HOT DIGGITY DUCK! I'M IN THE MOOLA!
BUT AS I HEADED FOR HIS MANSION THAT EVENING, I RAN INTO A SLIGHT PROBLEM...
LET'S SEE... I TURNED RIGHT AT WILSHIRE, WENT DOWN TO OAK AND MADE A LEFT...
NOW, IF I DOUBLE BACK TO SESAME STREET AND TURN RIGHT AT THAT OVERSIZED CANARY...
the End

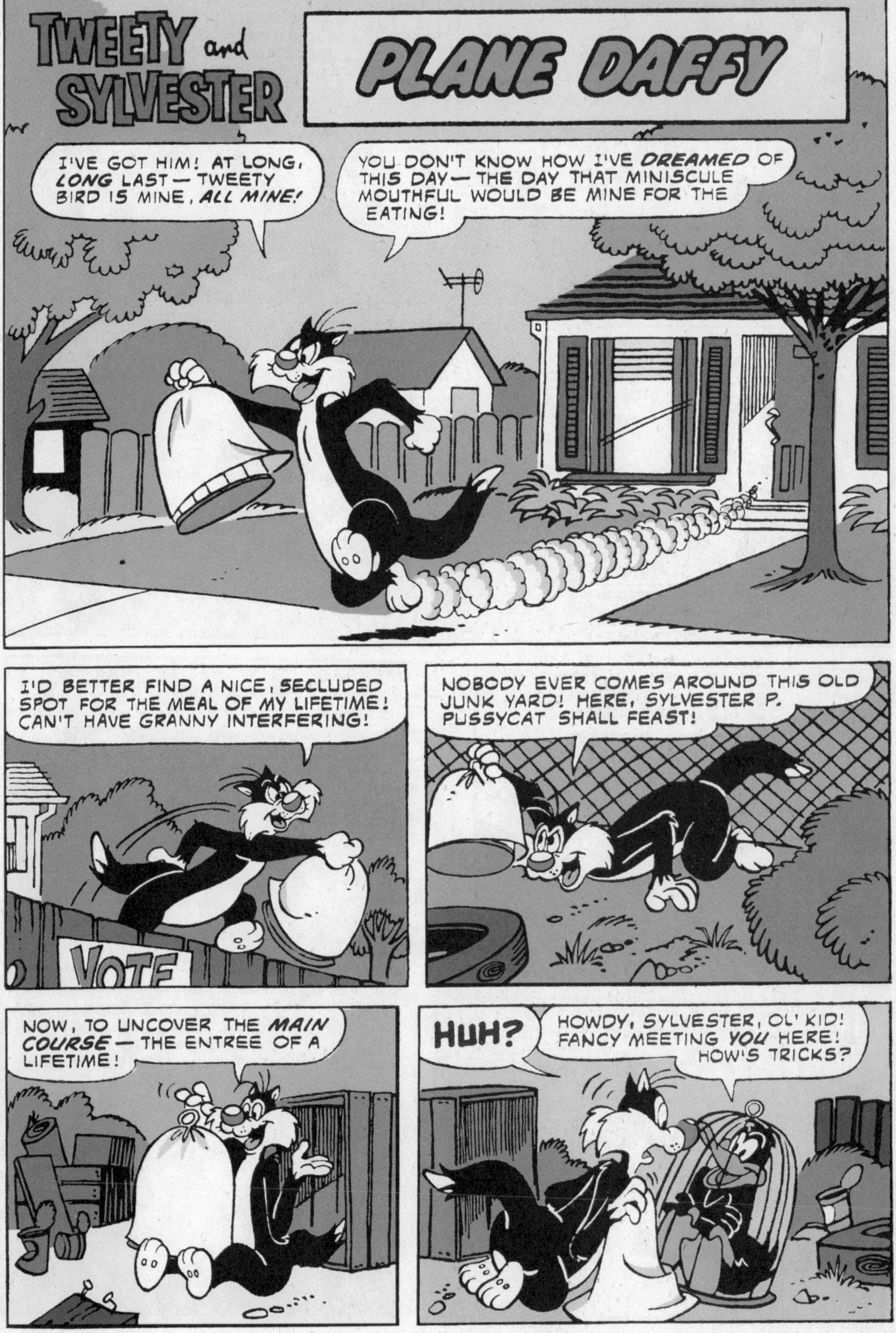
TWEETY and SYLVESTER
PLANE DAFFY
I'VE GOT HIM! AT LONG, LONG LAST — TWEETY BIRD IS MINE, ALL MINE!
YOU DON'T KNOW HOW I'VE DREAMED OF THIS DAY — THE DAY THAT MINISCULE MOUTHFUL WOULD BE MINE FOR THE EATING!
I'D BETTER FIND A NICE, SECLUDED SPOT FOR THE MEAL OF MY LIFETIME! CAN'T HAVE GRANNY INTERFERING!
VOTE
NOBODY EVER COMES AROUND THIS OLD JUNK YARD! HERE, SYLVESTER P. PUSSYCAT SHALL FEAST!
NOW, TO UNCOVER THE MAIN COURSE — THE ENTREE OF A LIFETIME!
HUH?
HOWDY, SYLVESTER, OL' KID! FANCY MEETING YOU HERE! HOW'S TRICKS?

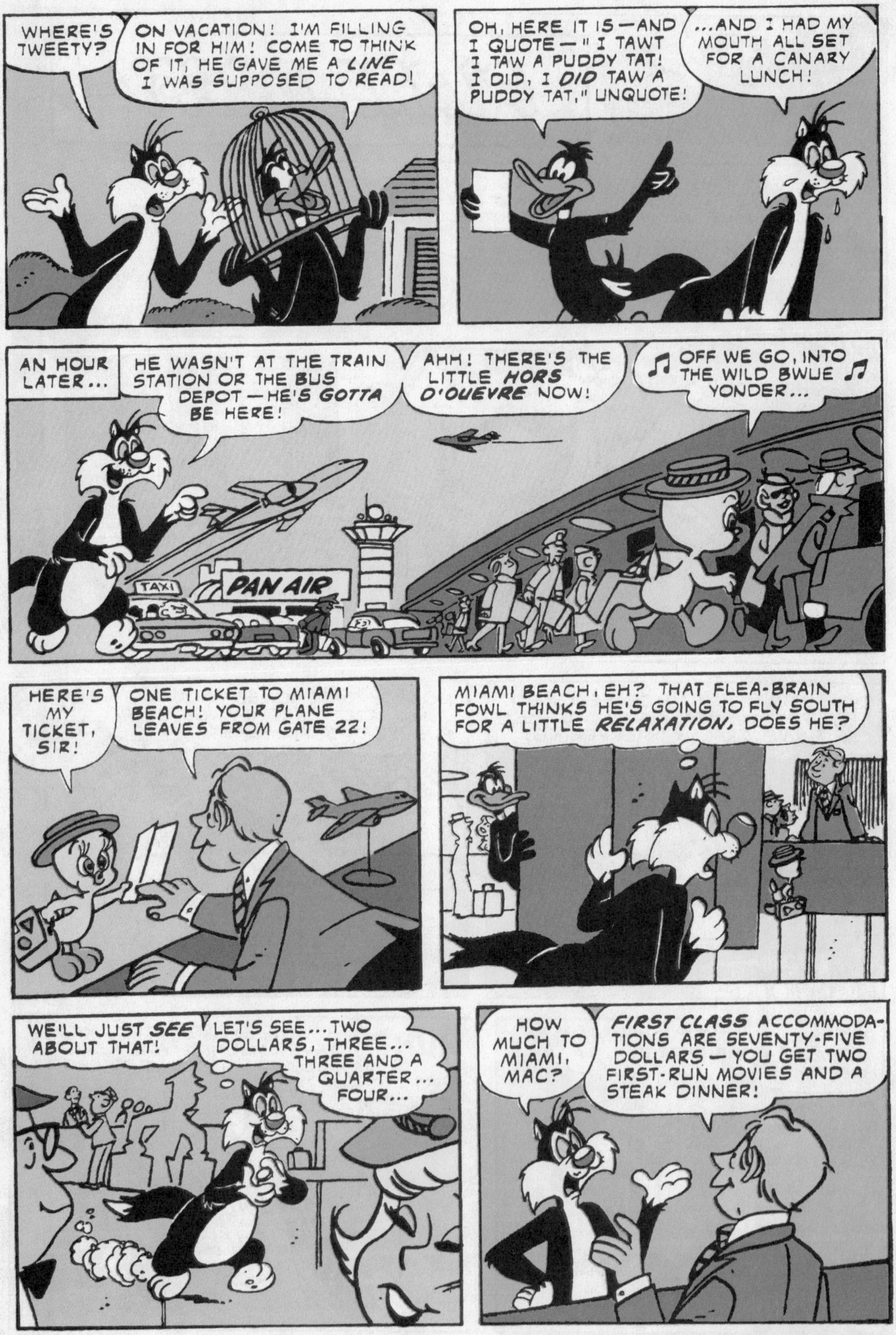

WHERE'S TWEETY?
ON VACATION! I'M FILLING IN FOR HIM! COME TO THINK OF IT, HE GAVE ME A *LINE* I WAS SUPPOSED TO READ!
OH, HERE IT IS—AND I QUOTE—"I TAWT I TAW A PUDDY TAT! I DID, I *DID* TAW A PUDDY TAT," UNQUOTE!
...AND I HAD MY MOUTH ALL SET FOR A CANARY LUNCH!
AN HOUR LATER...
HE WASN'T AT THE TRAIN STATION OR THE BUS DEPOT—HE'S *GOTTA* BE HERE!
AHH! THERE'S THE LITTLE *HORS D'OUEVRE* NOW!
♫ OFF WE GO, INTO THE WILD BWUE YONDER... ♫
TAXI
PAN AIR
HERE'S MY TICKET, SIR!
ONE TICKET TO MIAMI BEACH! YOUR PLANE LEAVES FROM GATE 22!
MIAMI BEACH, EH? THAT FLEA-BRAIN FOWL THINKS HE'S GOING TO FLY SOUTH FOR A LITTLE *RELAXATION*, DOES HE?
WE'LL JUST *SEE* ABOUT THAT!
LET'S SEE...TWO DOLLARS, THREE... THREE AND A QUARTER... FOUR...
HOW MUCH TO MIAMI, MAC?
FIRST CLASS ACCOMMODATIONS ARE SEVENTY-FIVE DOLLARS—YOU GET TWO FIRST-RUN MOVIES AND A STEAK DINNER!

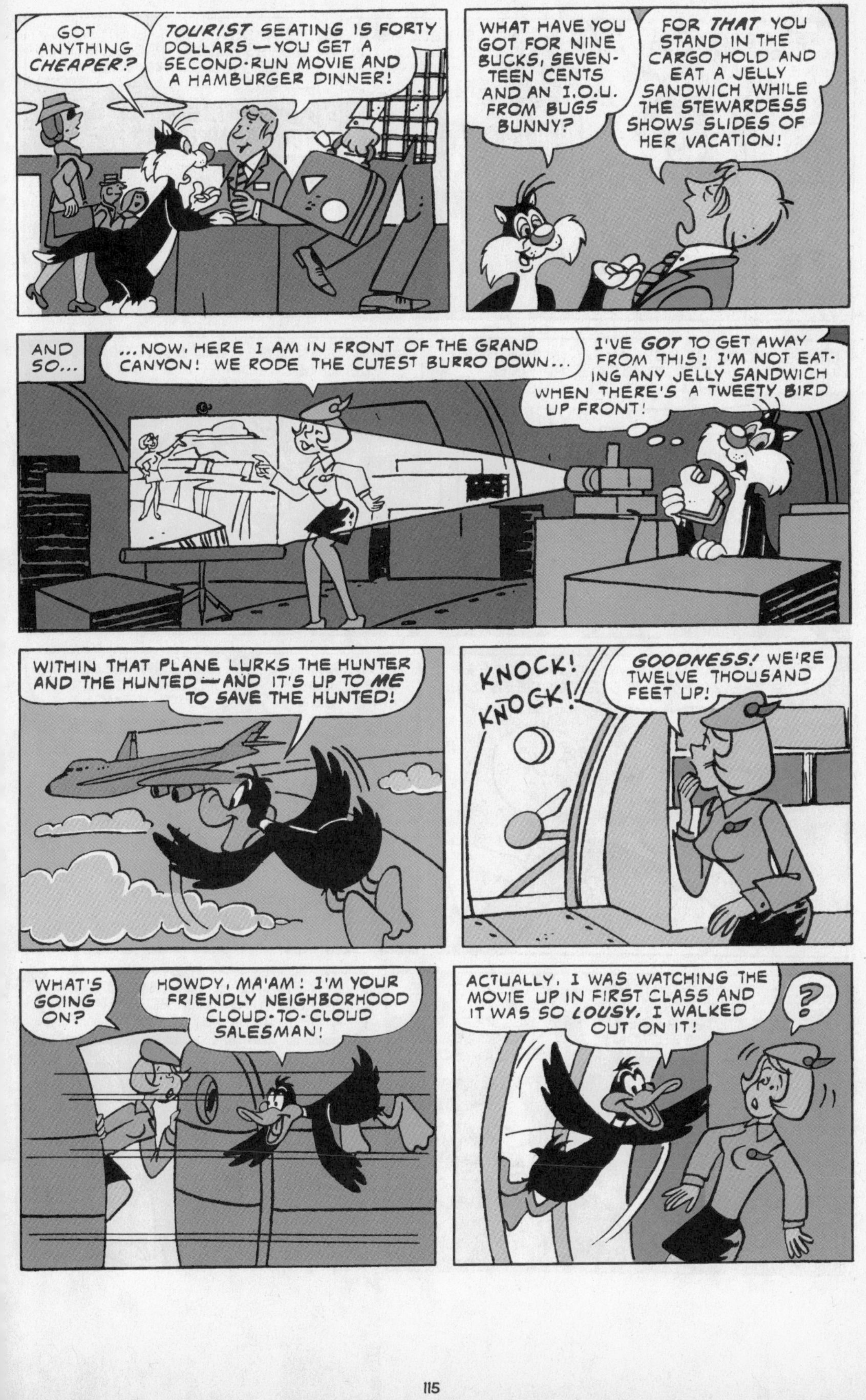
GOT ANYTHING CHEAPER?
TOURIST SEATING IS FORTY DOLLARS — YOU GET A SECOND-RUN MOVIE AND A HAMBURGER DINNER!
WHAT HAVE YOU GOT FOR NINE BUCKS, SEVENTEEN CENTS AND AN I.O.U. FROM BUGS BUNNY?
FOR THAT YOU STAND IN THE CARGO HOLD AND EAT A JELLY SANDWICH WHILE THE STEWARDESS SHOWS SLIDES OF HER VACATION!
AND SO...
...NOW, HERE I AM IN FRONT OF THE GRAND CANYON! WE RODE THE CUTEST BURRO DOWN...
I'VE GOT TO GET AWAY FROM THIS! I'M NOT EATING ANY JELLY SANDWICH WHEN THERE'S A TWEETY BIRD UP FRONT!
WITHIN THAT PLANE LURKS THE HUNTER AND THE HUNTED — AND IT'S UP TO ME TO SAVE THE HUNTED!
KNOCK! KNOCK!
GOODNESS! WE'RE TWELVE THOUSAND FEET UP!
WHAT'S GOING ON?
HOWDY, MA'AM! I'M YOUR FRIENDLY NEIGHBORHOOD CLOUD-TO-CLOUD SALESMAN!
ACTUALLY, I WAS WATCHING THE MOVIE UP IN FIRST CLASS AND IT WAS SO LOUSY, I WALKED OUT ON IT!
?

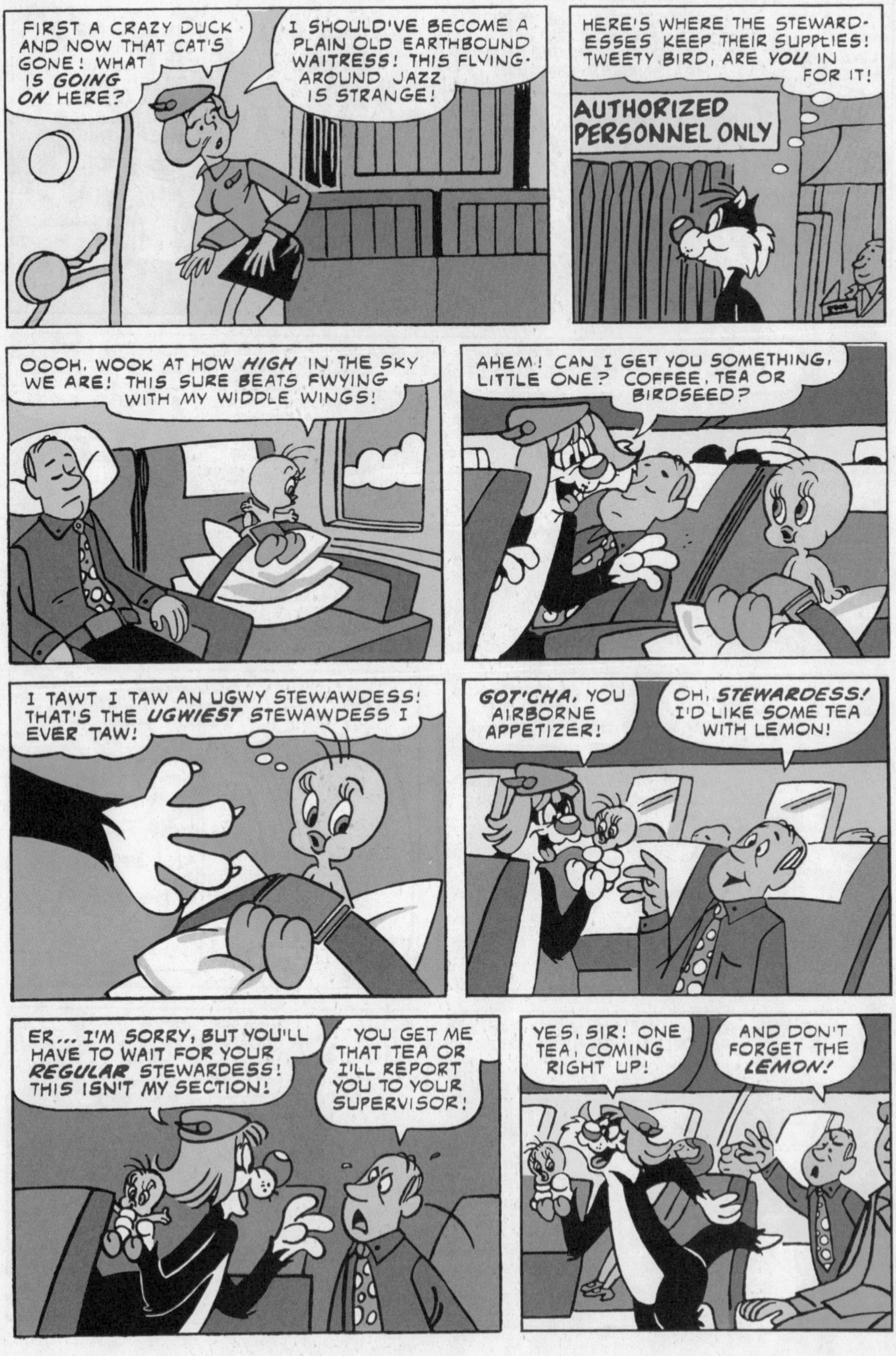

FIRST A CRAZY DUCK AND NOW THAT CAT'S GONE! WHAT IS GOING ON HERE?
I SHOULD'VE BECOME A PLAIN OLD EARTHBOUND WAITRESS! THIS FLYING-AROUND JAZZ IS STRANGE!
HERE'S WHERE THE STEWARDESSES KEEP THEIR SUPPLIES! TWEETY BIRD, ARE YOU IN FOR IT!
AUTHORIZED PERSONNEL ONLY
OOOH, WOOK AT HOW HIGH IN THE SKY WE ARE! THIS SURE BEATS FWYING WITH MY WIDDLE WINGS!
AHEM! CAN I GET YOU SOMETHING, LITTLE ONE? COFFEE, TEA OR BIRDSEED?
I TAWT I TAW AN UGWY STEWAWDESS! THAT'S THE UGWIEST STEWAWDESS I EVER TAW!
GOT'CHA, YOU AIRBORNE APPETIZER!
OH, STEWARDESS! I'D LIKE SOME TEA WITH LEMON!
ER... I'M SORRY, BUT YOU'LL HAVE TO WAIT FOR YOUR REGULAR STEWARDESS! THIS ISN'T MY SECTION!
YOU GET ME THAT TEA OR I'LL REPORT YOU TO YOUR SUPERVISOR!
YES, SIR! ONE TEA, COMING RIGHT UP!
AND DON'T FORGET THE LEMON!

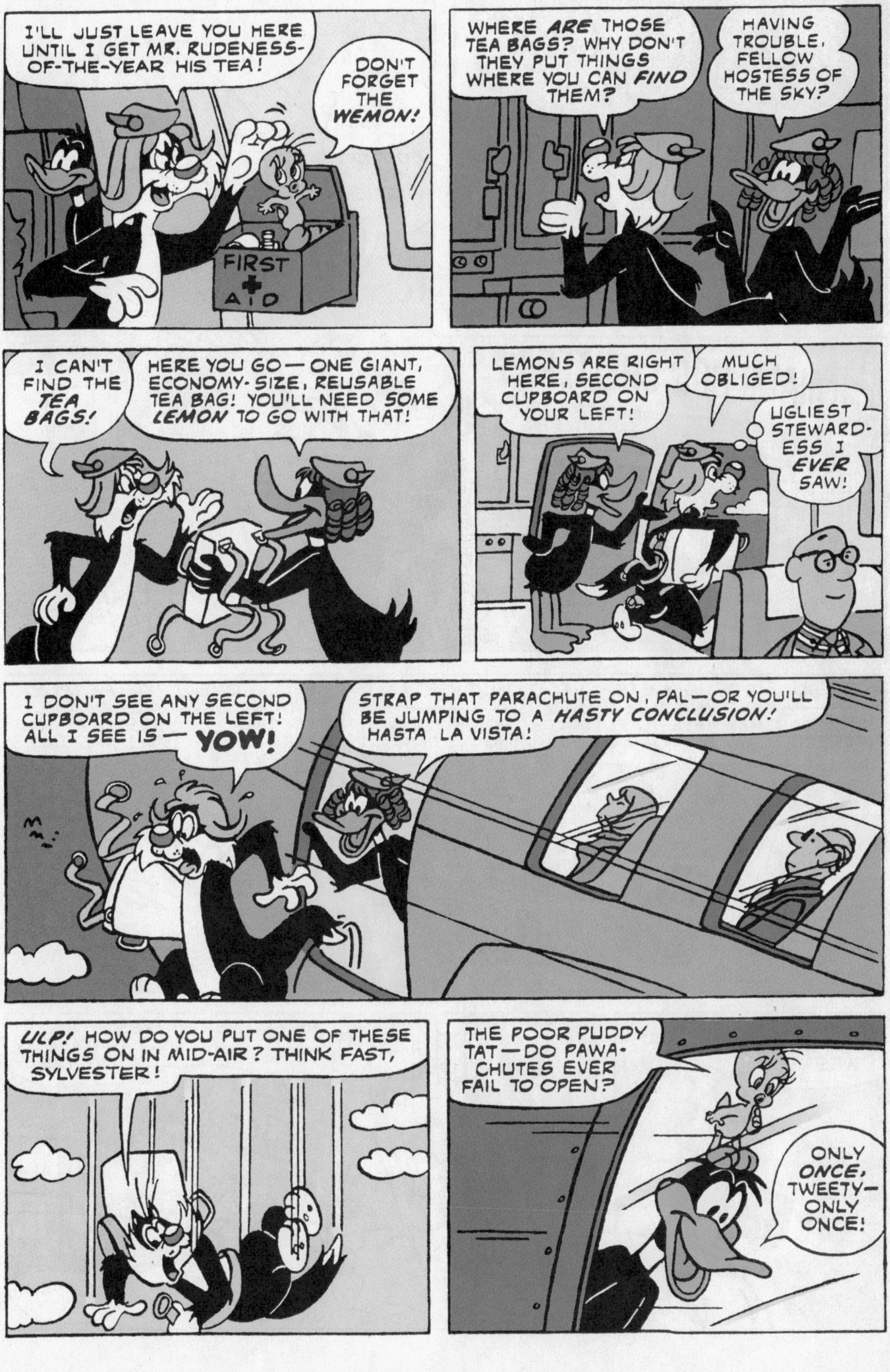
I'LL JUST LEAVE YOU HERE UNTIL I GET MR. RUDENESS-OF-THE-YEAR HIS TEA!
DON'T FORGET THE WEMON!
WHERE ARE THOSE TEA BAGS? WHY DON'T THEY PUT THINGS WHERE YOU CAN FIND THEM?
HAVING TROUBLE, FELLOW HOSTESS OF THE SKY?
FIRST AID
I CAN'T FIND THE TEA BAGS!
HERE YOU GO — ONE GIANT, ECONOMY-SIZE, REUSABLE TEA BAG! YOU'LL NEED SOME LEMON TO GO WITH THAT!
LEMONS ARE RIGHT HERE, SECOND CUPBOARD ON YOUR LEFT!
MUCH OBLIGED!
UGLIEST STEWARDESS I EVER SAW!
I DON'T SEE ANY SECOND CUPBOARD ON THE LEFT! ALL I SEE IS — YOW!
STRAP THAT PARACHUTE ON, PAL — OR YOU'LL BE JUMPING TO A HASTY CONCLUSION! HASTA LA VISTA!
ULP! HOW DO YOU PUT ONE OF THESE THINGS ON IN MID-AIR? THINK FAST, SYLVESTER!
THE POOR PUDDY TAT — DO PAWA-CHUTES EVER FAIL TO OPEN?
ONLY ONCE, TWEETY — ONLY ONCE!

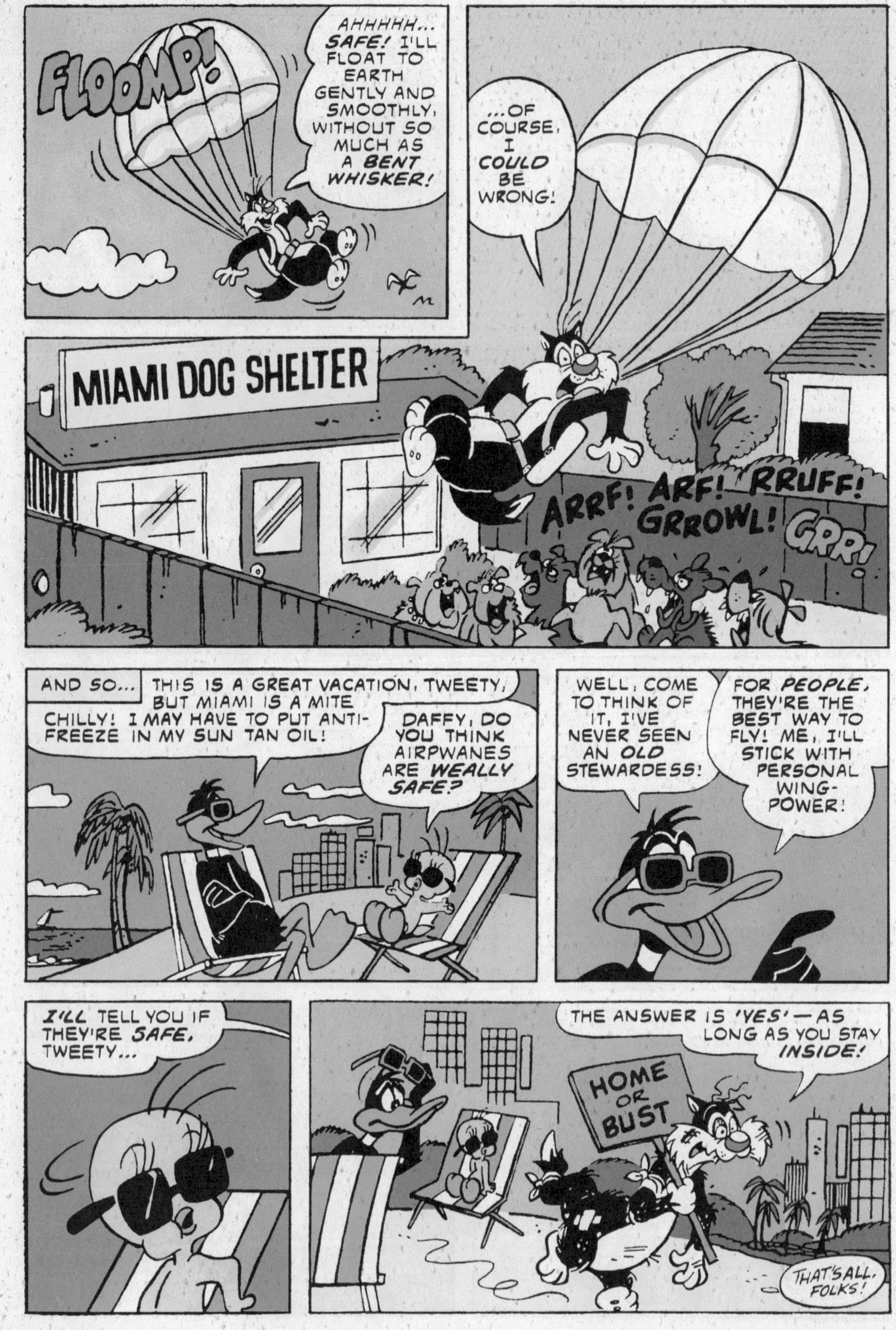
FLOOMP!
AHHHHH... SAFE! I'LL FLOAT TO EARTH GENTLY AND SMOOTHLY, WITHOUT SO MUCH AS A BENT WHISKER!
...OF COURSE, I COULD BE WRONG!
MIAMI DOG SHELTER
ARRF! ARF! RRUFF! GRROWL! GRR!
AND SO...
THIS IS A GREAT VACATION, TWEETY, BUT MIAMI IS A MITE CHILLY! I MAY HAVE TO PUT ANTI-FREEZE IN MY SUN TAN OIL!
DAFFY, DO YOU THINK AIRPWANES ARE WEALLY SAFE?
WELL, COME TO THINK OF IT, I'VE NEVER SEEN AN OLD STEWARDESS!
FOR PEOPLE, THEY'RE THE BEST WAY TO FLY! ME, I'LL STICK WITH PERSONAL WING-POWER!
I'LL TELL YOU IF THEY'RE SAFE, TWEETY...
THE ANSWER IS 'YES'—AS LONG AS YOU STAY INSIDE!
HOME OR BUST
THAT'S ALL, FOLKS!

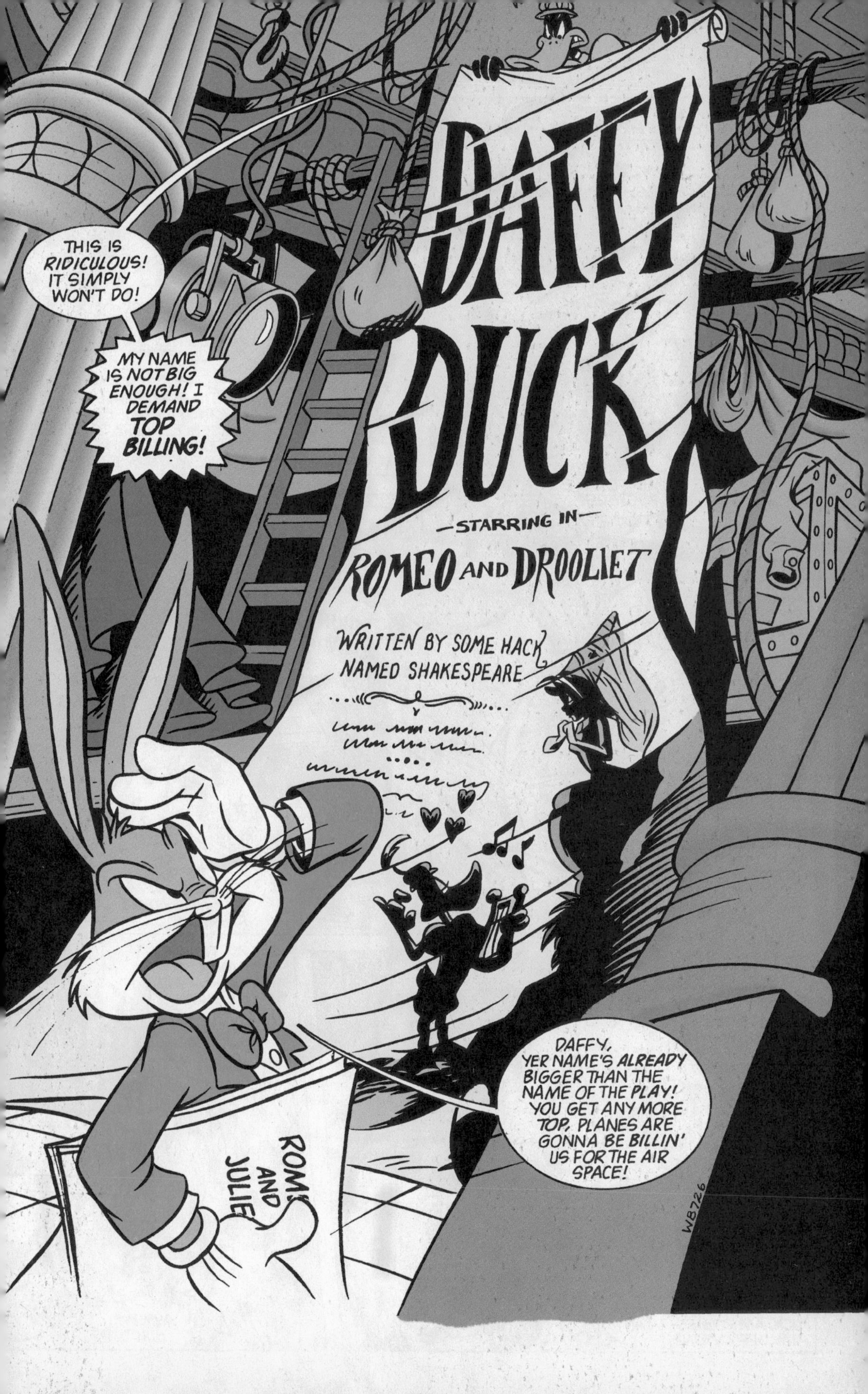
THIS IS RIDICULOUS! IT SIMPLY WON'T DO!
MY NAME IS NOT BIG ENOUGH! I DEMAND TOP BILLING!
DAFFY DUCK
—STARRING IN—
ROMEO AND DROOLIET
WRITTEN BY SOME HACK NAMED SHAKESPEARE
DAFFY, YER NAME'S ALREADY BIGGER THAN THE NAME OF THE PLAY! YOU GET ANY MORE TOP, PLANES ARE GONNA BE BILLIN' US FOR THE AIR SPACE!
WB726

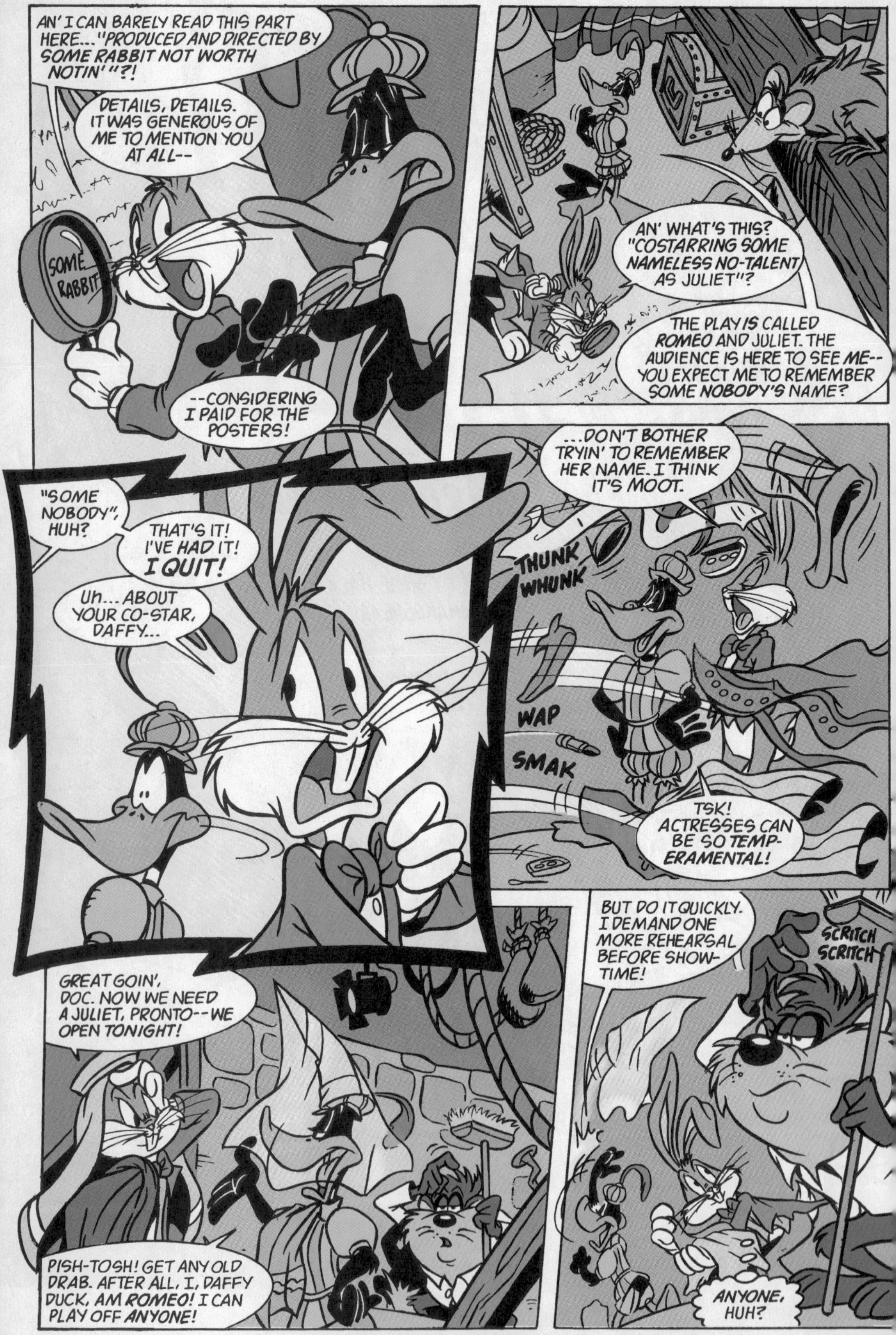
AN' I CAN BARELY READ THIS PART HERE... "PRODUCED AND DIRECTED BY SOME RABBIT NOT WORTH NOTIN' "?!
DETAILS, DETAILS. IT WAS GENEROUS OF ME TO MENTION YOU AT ALL--
SOME RABBIT
--CONSIDERING I PAID FOR THE POSTERS!
AN' WHAT'S THIS? "COSTARRING SOME NAMELESS NO-TALENT AS JULIET"?
THE PLAY IS CALLED ROMEO AND JULIET. THE AUDIENCE IS HERE TO SEE ME--YOU EXPECT ME TO REMEMBER SOME NOBODY'S NAME?
"SOME NOBODY", HUH?
THAT'S IT! I'VE HAD IT! I QUIT!
Uh... ABOUT YOUR CO-STAR, DAFFY...
...DON'T BOTHER TRYIN' TO REMEMBER HER NAME. I THINK IT'S MOOT.
THUNK
WHUNK
WAP
SMAK
TSK! ACTRESSES CAN BE SO TEMPERAMENTAL!
GREAT GOIN', DOC. NOW WE NEED A JULIET, PRONTO--WE OPEN TONIGHT!
PISH-TOSH! GET ANY OLD DRAB. AFTER ALL, I, DAFFY DUCK, AM ROMEO! I CAN PLAY OFF ANYONE!
BUT DO IT QUICKLY. I DEMAND ONE MORE REHEARSAL BEFORE SHOW-TIME!
SCRITCH
SCRITCH
ANYONE, HUH?

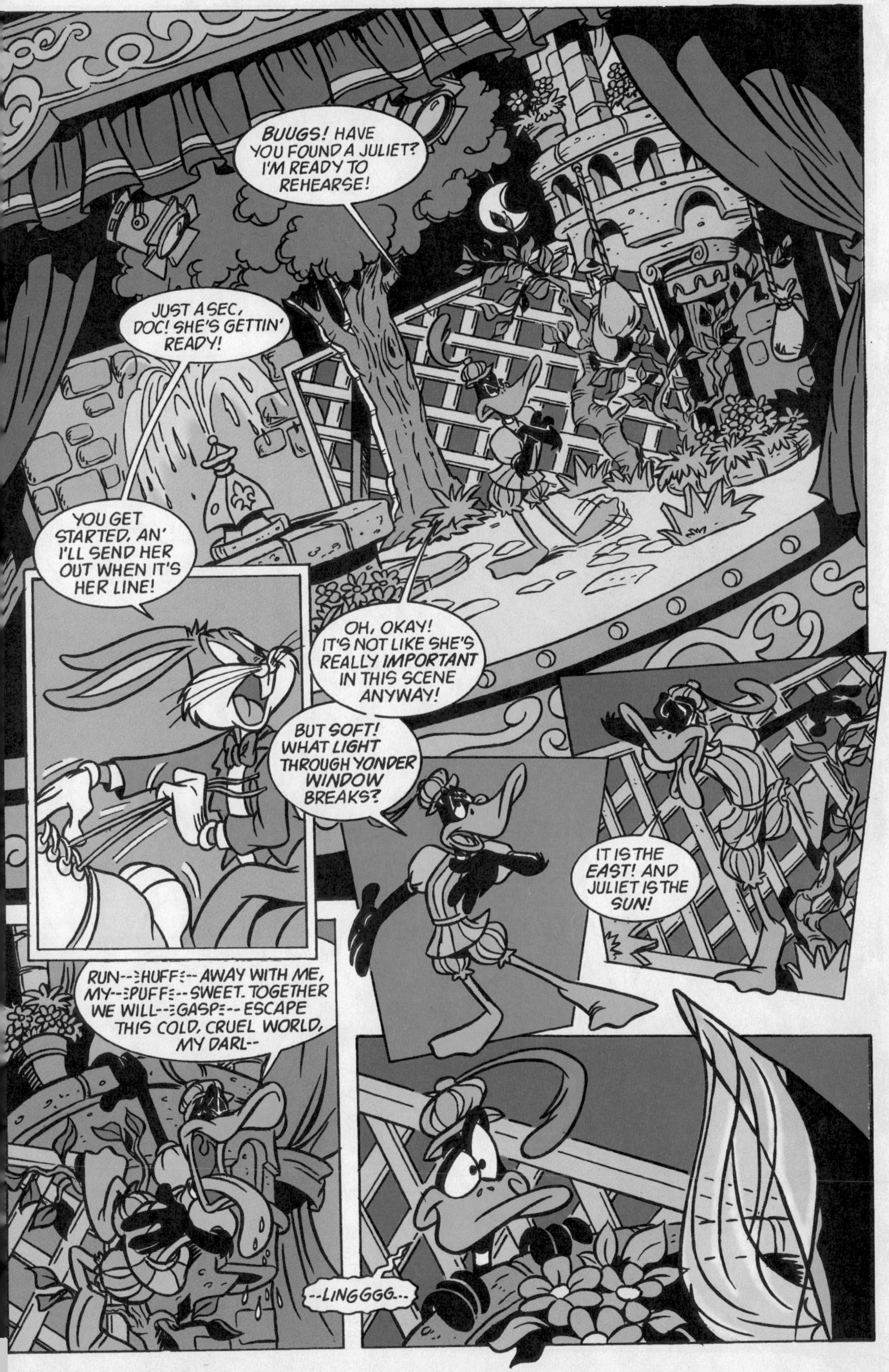
BUUGS! HAVE YOU FOUND A JULIET? I'M READY TO REHEARSE!
JUST A SEC, DOC! SHE'S GETTIN' READY!
YOU GET STARTED, AN' I'LL SEND HER OUT WHEN IT'S HER LINE!
OH, OKAY! IT'S NOT LIKE SHE'S REALLY IMPORTANT IN THIS SCENE ANYWAY!
BUT SOFT! WHAT LIGHT THROUGH YONDER WINDOW BREAKS?
IT IS THE EAST! AND JULIET IS THE SUN!
RUN--HUFF--AWAY WITH ME, MY--PUFF--SWEET. TOGETHER WE WILL--GASP--ESCAPE THIS COLD, CRUEL WORLD, MY DARL--
--LINGGGG...

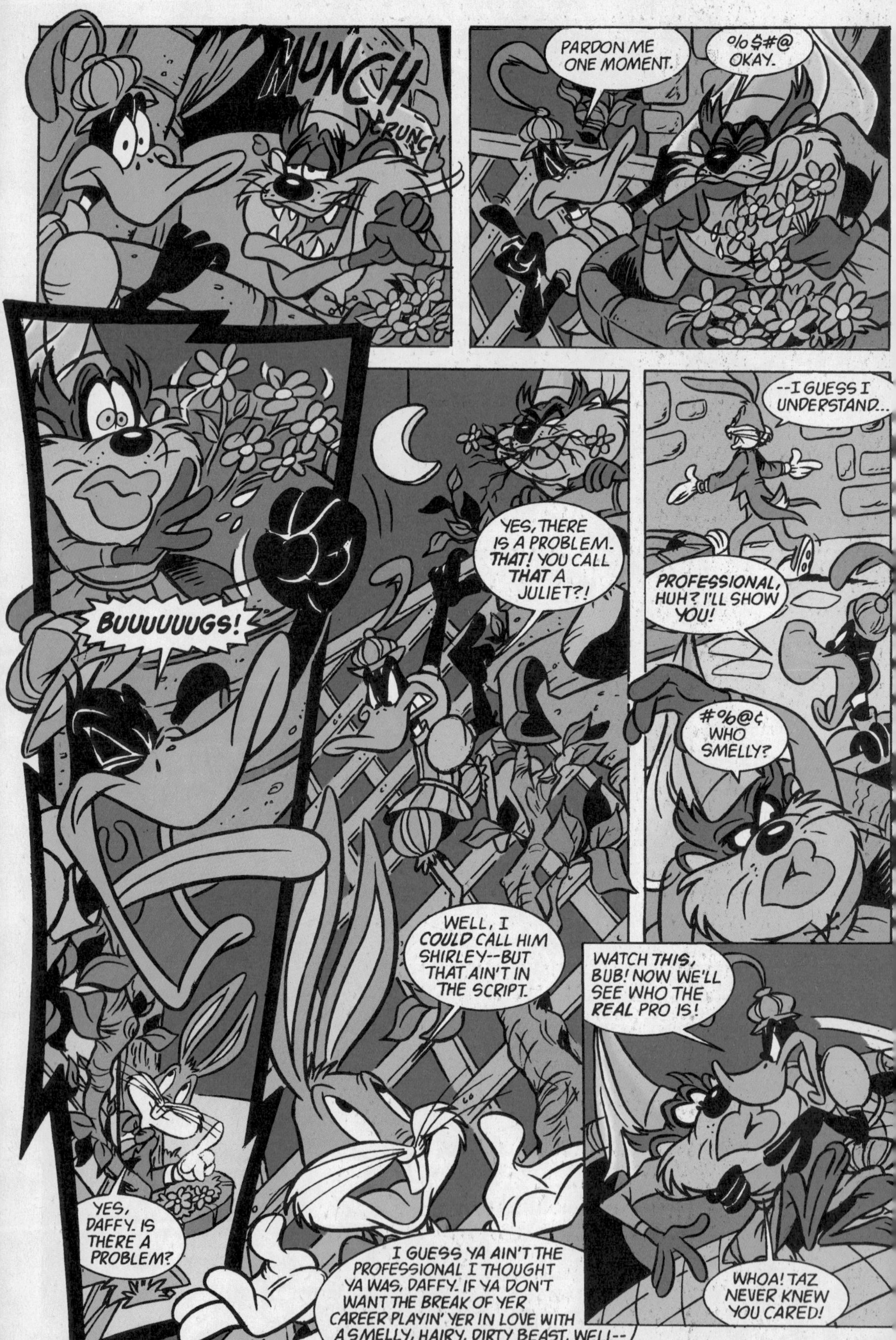
MUNCH
CRUNCH
PARDON ME ONE MOMENT.
%$#@ OKAY.
BUUUUUUGS!
YES, DAFFY. IS THERE A PROBLEM?
YES, THERE IS A PROBLEM. THAT! YOU CALL THAT A JULIET?!
WELL, I COULD CALL HIM SHIRLEY--BUT THAT AIN'T IN THE SCRIPT.
I GUESS YA AIN'T THE PROFESSIONAL I THOUGHT YA WAS, DAFFY. IF YA DON'T WANT THE BREAK OF YER CAREER PLAYIN' YER IN LOVE WITH A SMELLY, HAIRY, DIRTY BEAST, WELL--
--I GUESS I UNDERSTAND...
PROFESSIONAL, HUH? I'LL SHOW YOU!
#%@¢ WHO SMELLY?
WATCH THIS, BUB! NOW WE'LL SEE WHO THE REAL PRO IS!
WHOA! TAZ NEVER KNEW YOU CARED!

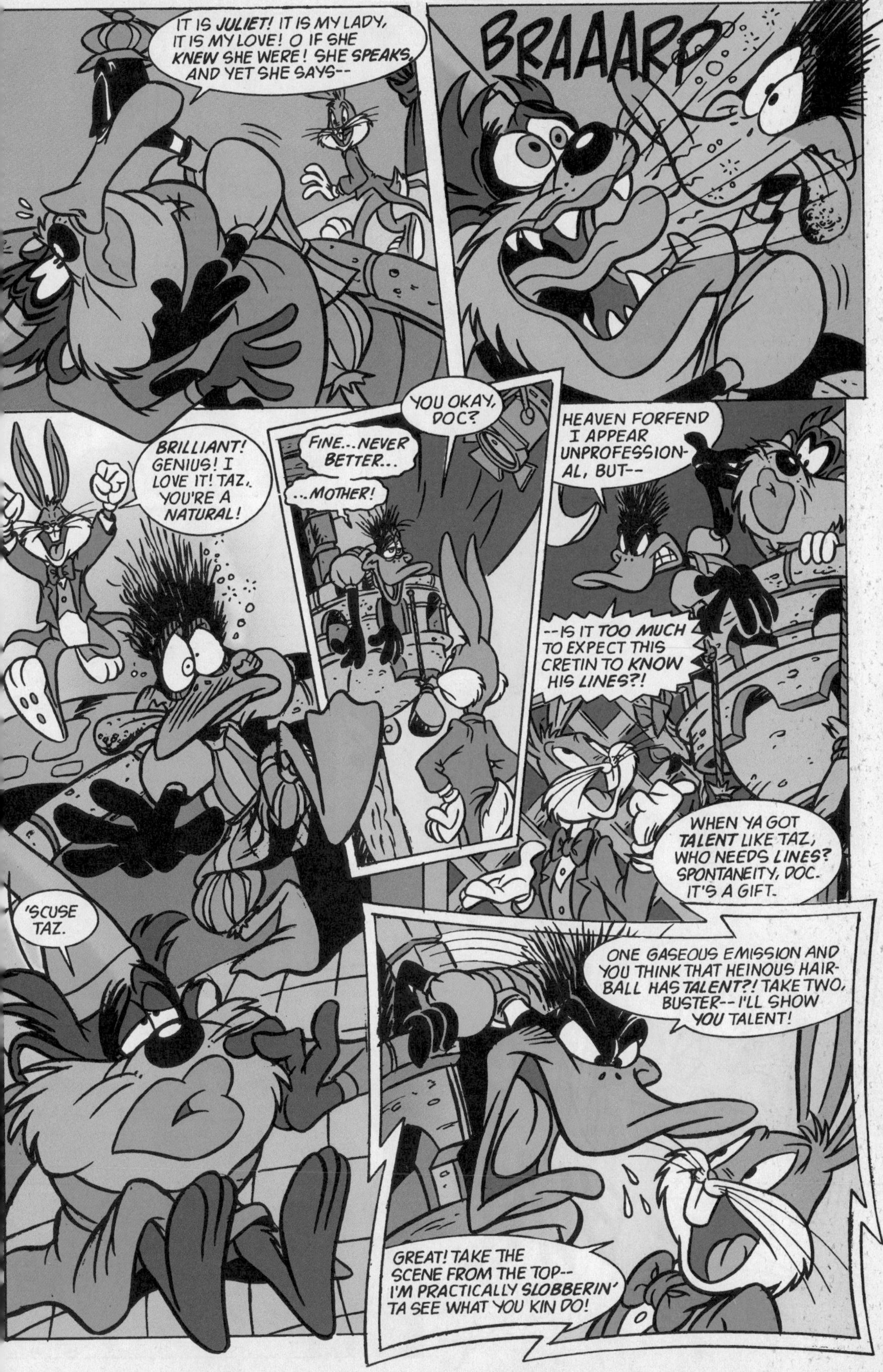
IT IS JULIET! IT IS MY LADY, IT IS MY LOVE! O IF SHE KNEW SHE WERE! SHE SPEAKS, AND YET SHE SAYS--
BRAAARP
BRILLIANT! GENIUS! I LOVE IT! TAZ, YOU'RE A NATURAL!
YOU OKAY, DOC?
FINE...NEVER BETTER...
...MOTHER!
HEAVEN FORFEND I APPEAR UNPROFESSION-AL, BUT--
--IS IT TOO MUCH TO EXPECT THIS CRETIN TO KNOW HIS LINES?!
WHEN YA GOT TALENT LIKE TAZ, WHO NEEDS LINES? SPONTANEITY, DOC. IT'S A GIFT.
'SCUSE TAZ.
ONE GASEOUS EMISSION AND YOU THINK THAT HEINOUS HAIR-BALL HAS TALENT?! TAKE TWO, BUSTER-- I'LL SHOW YOU TALENT!
GREAT! TAKE THE SCENE FROM THE TOP-- I'M PRACTICALLY SLOBBERIN' TA SEE WHAT YOU KIN DO!

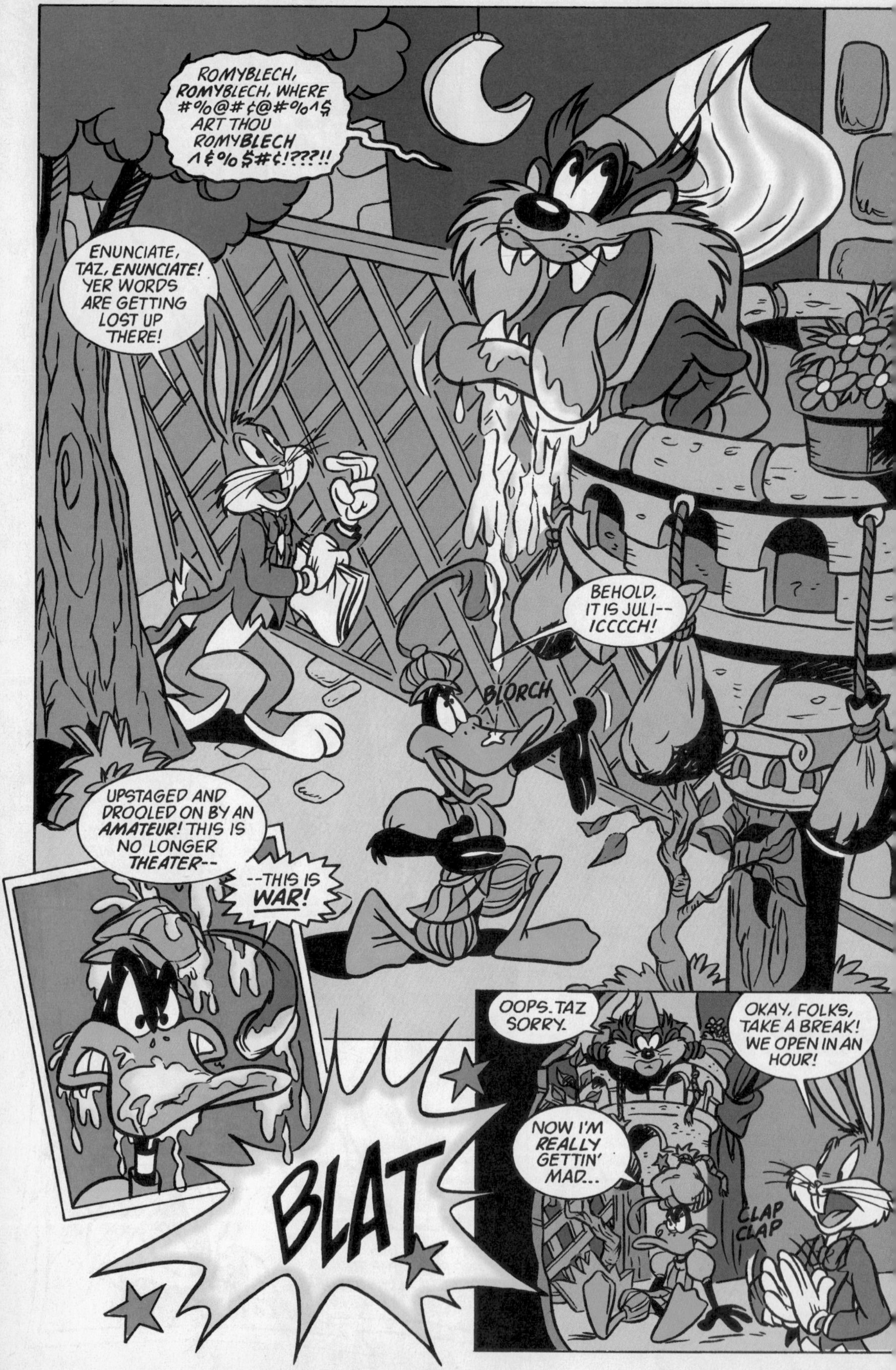
ROMYBLECH, ROMYBLECH, WHERE #%@#¢@#%^$ ART THOU ROMYBLECH ^&%$#¢!???!!
ENUNCIATE, TAZ, ENUNCIATE! YER WORDS ARE GETTING LOST UP THERE!
BEHOLD, IT IS JULI-- ICCCCH!
BLORCH
UPSTAGED AND DROOLED ON BY AN AMATEUR! THIS IS NO LONGER THEATER--
--THIS IS WAR!
BLAT
OOPS. TAZ SORRY.
OKAY, FOLKS, TAKE A BREAK! WE OPEN IN AN HOUR!
NOW I'M REALLY GETTIN' MAD...
CLAP CLAP

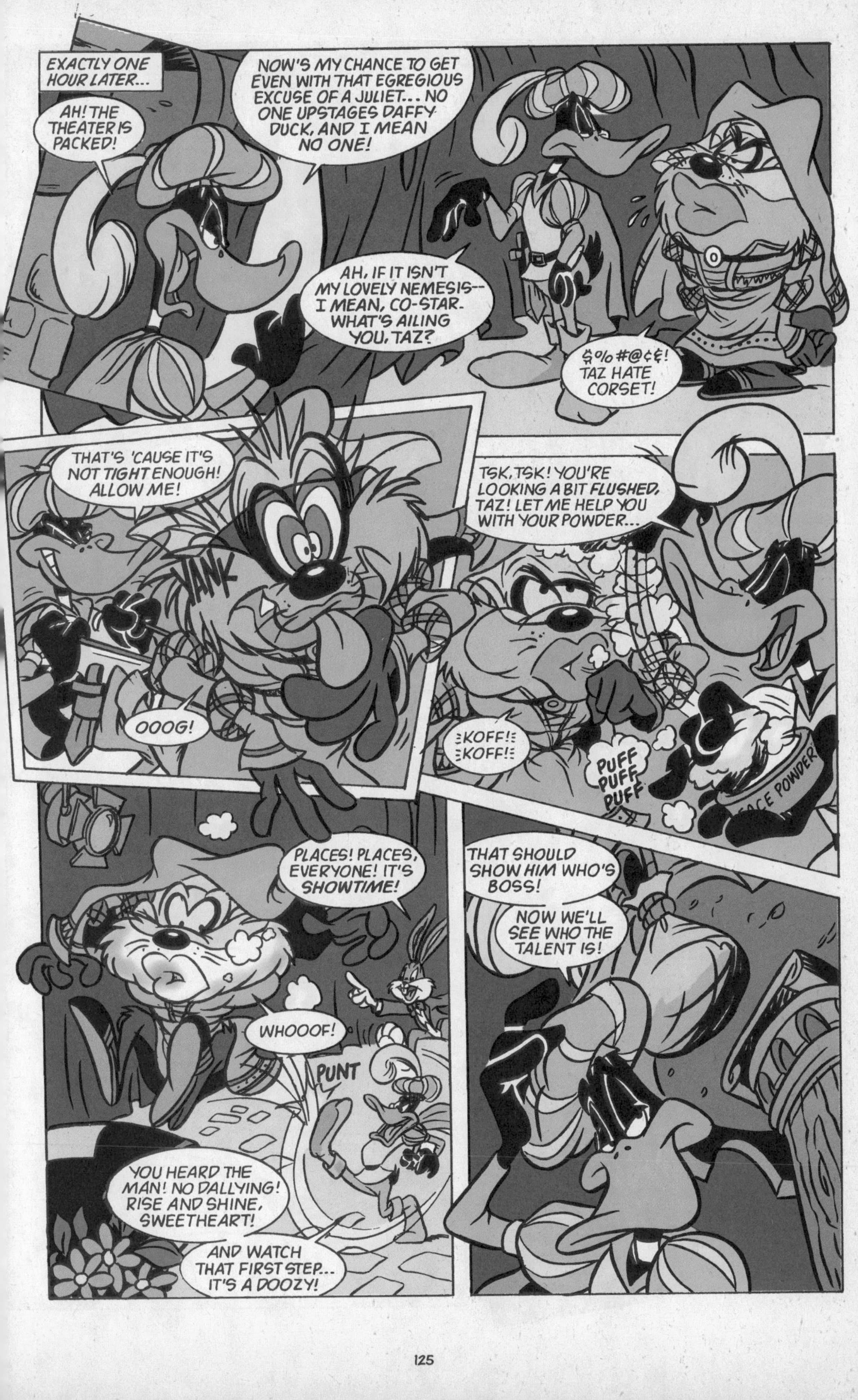

EXACTLY ONE HOUR LATER...
AH! THE THEATER IS PACKED!
NOW'S MY CHANCE TO GET EVEN WITH THAT EGREGIOUS EXCUSE OF A JULIET... NO ONE UPSTAGES DAFFY DUCK, AND I MEAN NO ONE!
AH, IF IT ISN'T MY LOVELY NEMESIS-- I MEAN, CO-STAR. WHAT'S AILING YOU, TAZ?
$%#@¢¢! TAZ HATE CORSET!
THAT'S 'CAUSE IT'S NOT TIGHT ENOUGH! ALLOW ME!
YANK
OOOG!
TSK, TSK! YOU'RE LOOKING A BIT FLUSHED, TAZ! LET ME HELP YOU WITH YOUR POWDER...
KOFF! KOFF!
PUFF PUFF PUFF
FACE POWDER
PLACES! PLACES, EVERYONE! IT'S SHOWTIME!
WHOOOF!
PUNT
YOU HEARD THE MAN! NO DALLYING! RISE AND SHINE, SWEETHEART!
AND WATCH THAT FIRST STEP... IT'S A DOOZY!
THAT SHOULD SHOW HIM WHO'S BOSS!
NOW WE'LL SEE WHO THE TALENT IS!

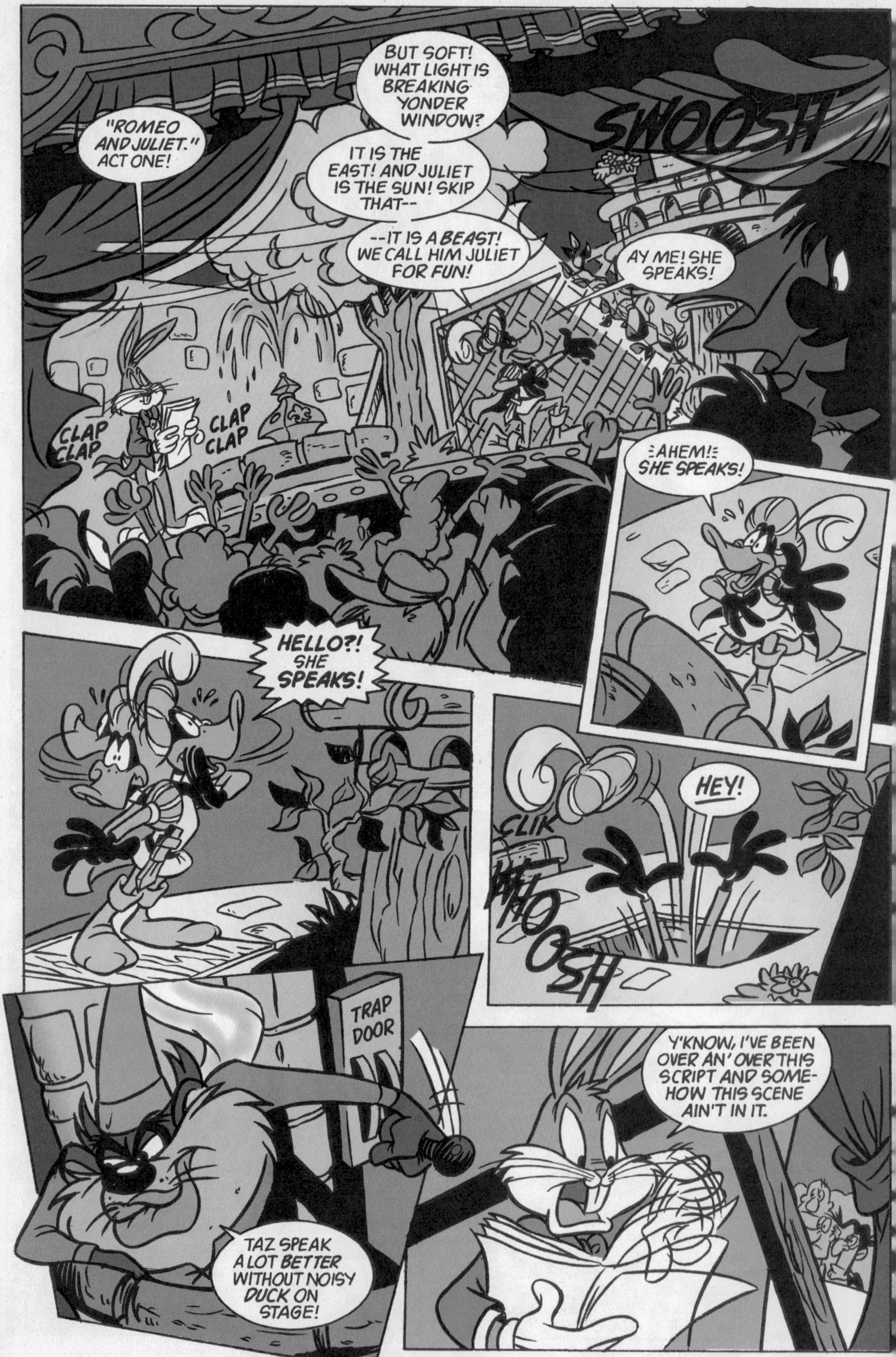
"ROMEO AND JULIET." ACT ONE!
BUT SOFT! WHAT LIGHT IS BREAKING YONDER WINDOW?
IT IS THE EAST! AND JULIET IS THE SUN! SKIP THAT--
--IT IS A BEAST! WE CALL HIM JULIET FOR FUN!
SWOOSH
AY ME! SHE SPEAKS!
CLAP CLAP
CLAP CLAP
AHEM! SHE SPEAKS!
HELLO?! SHE SPEAKS!
HEY!
CLIK
WHOOSH
TRAP DOOR
TAZ SPEAK A LOT BETTER WITHOUT NOISY DUCK ON STAGE!
Y'KNOW, I'VE BEEN OVER AN' OVER THIS SCRIPT AND SOMEHOW THIS SCENE AIN'T IN IT.

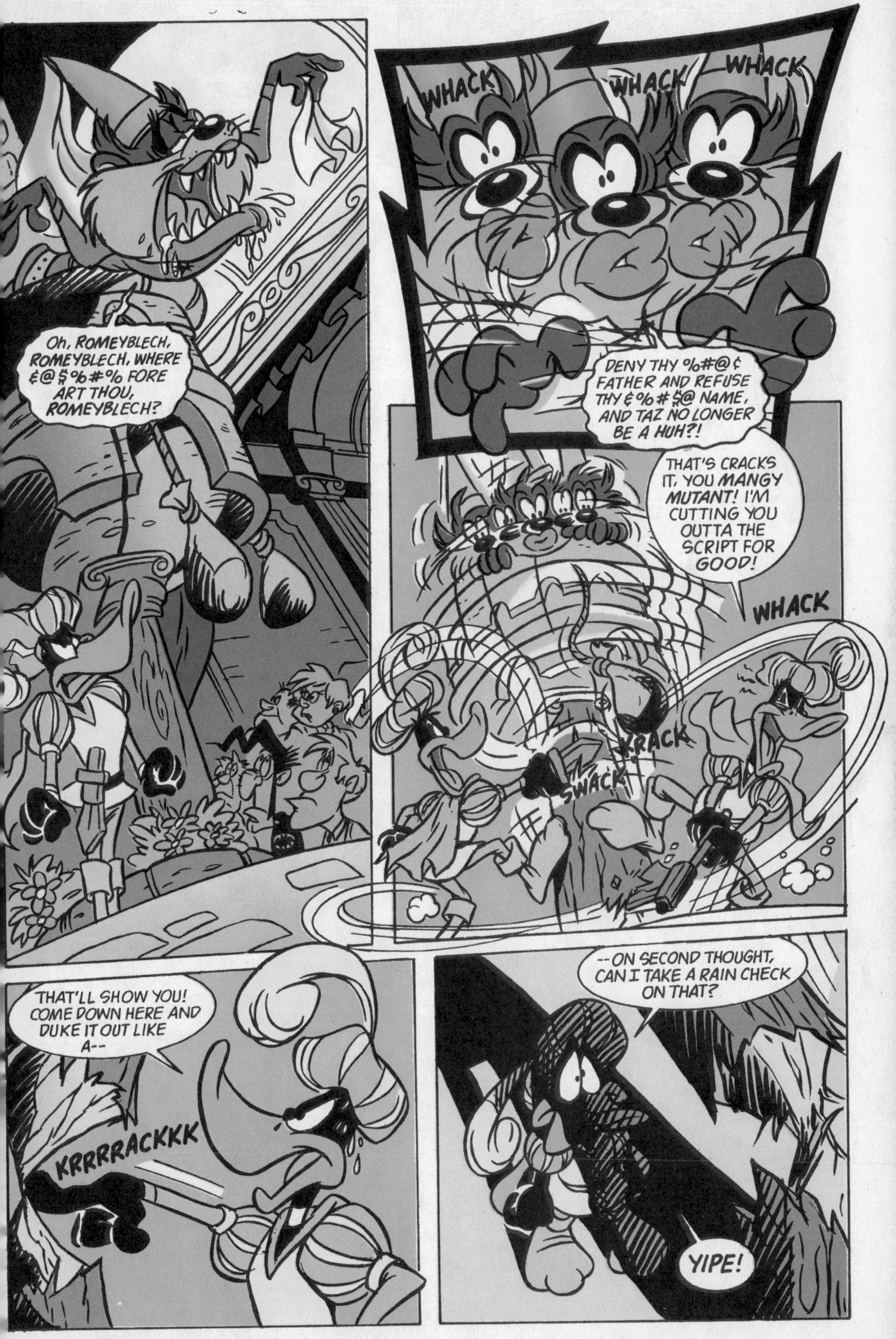
Oh, ROMEYBLECH, ROMEYBLECH, WHERE ¢@$%#% FORE ART THOU, ROMEYBLECH?
WHACK
WHACK
WHACK
DENY THY %#@¢ FATHER AND REFUSE THY ¢%#$@ NAME, AND TAZ NO LONGER BE A HUH?!
THAT'S CRACKS IT, YOU MANGY MUTANT! I'M CUTTING YOU OUTTA THE SCRIPT FOR GOOD!
WHACK
KRACK
SWACK
THAT'LL SHOW YOU! COME DOWN HERE AND DUKE IT OUT LIKE A--
KRRRRACKKK
--ON SECOND THOUGHT, CAN I TAKE A RAIN CHECK ON THAT?
YIPE!

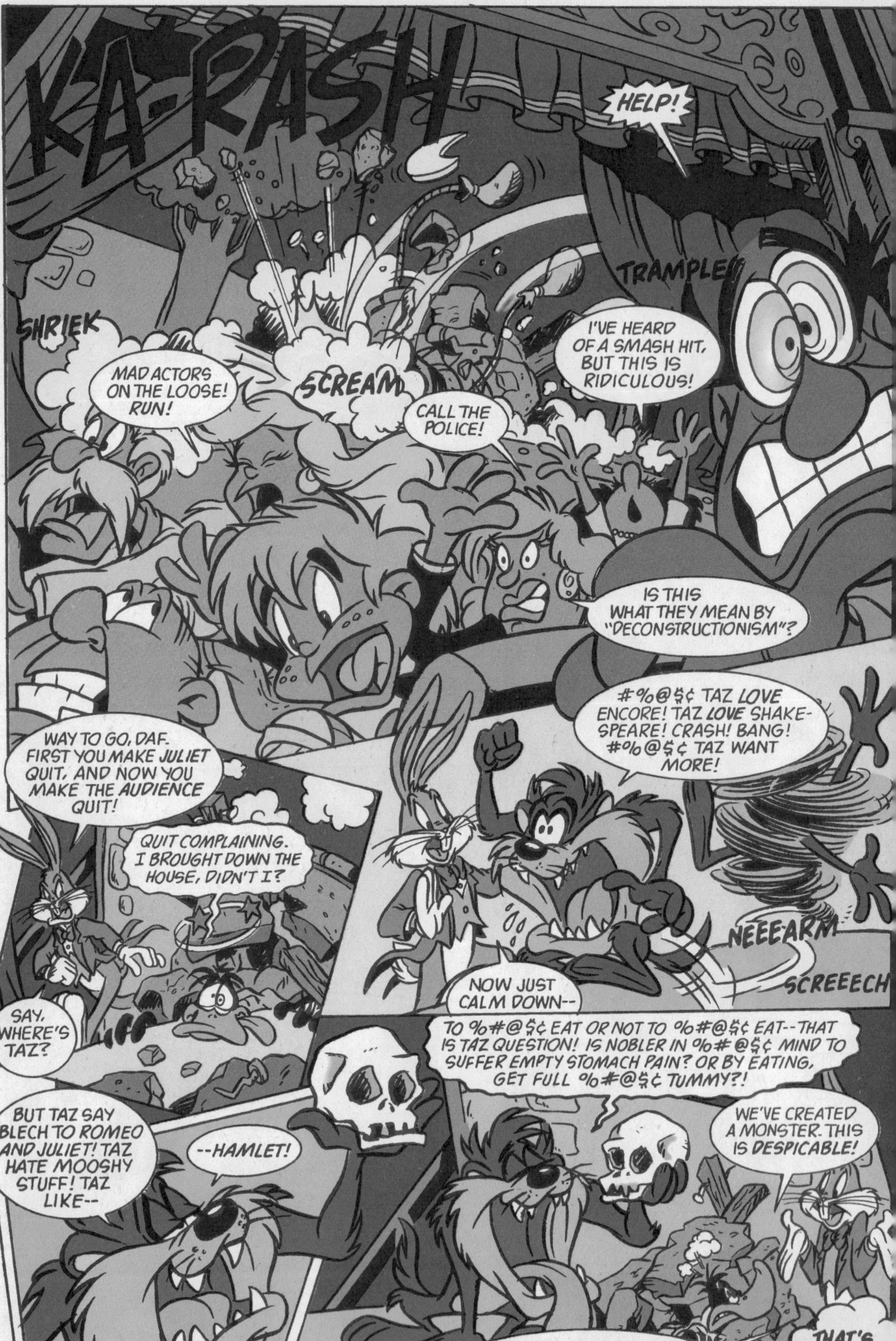
KA-RASH
HELP!
TRAMPLE
SHRIEK
MAD ACTORS ON THE LOOSE! RUN!
SCREAM
I'VE HEARD OF A SMASH HIT, BUT THIS IS RIDICULOUS!
CALL THE POLICE!
IS THIS WHAT THEY MEAN BY "DECONSTRUCTIONISM"?
#%@$¢ TAZ LOVE ENCORE! TAZ LOVE SHAKE-SPEARE! CRASH! BANG! #%@$¢ TAZ WANT MORE!
WAY TO GO, DAF. FIRST YOU MAKE JULIET QUIT, AND NOW YOU MAKE THE AUDIENCE QUIT!
QUIT COMPLAINING. I BROUGHT DOWN THE HOUSE, DIDN'T I?
NEEE-ARM
SCREEECH
NOW JUST CALM DOWN--
SAY, WHERE'S TAZ?
TO %#@$¢ EAT OR NOT TO %#@$¢ EAT--THAT IS TAZ QUESTION! IS NOBLER IN %#@$¢ MIND TO SUFFER EMPTY STOMACH PAIN? OR BY EATING, GET FULL %#@$¢ TUMMY?!
BUT TAZ SAY BLECH TO ROMEO AND JULIET! TAZ HATE MOOSHY STUFF! TAZ LIKE--
--HAMLET!
WE'VE CREATED A MONSTER. THIS IS DESPICABLE!
I HATE TA SAY IT, DOC--BUT THAT'S SHOW BIZ!
THAT'S ALL, FOLKS!

Writer: Dana Kurtin Penciller: Walter Carzon Inker: Scott McRae
Letterer: Bob Pinaha Colorist: Jo Meugniot

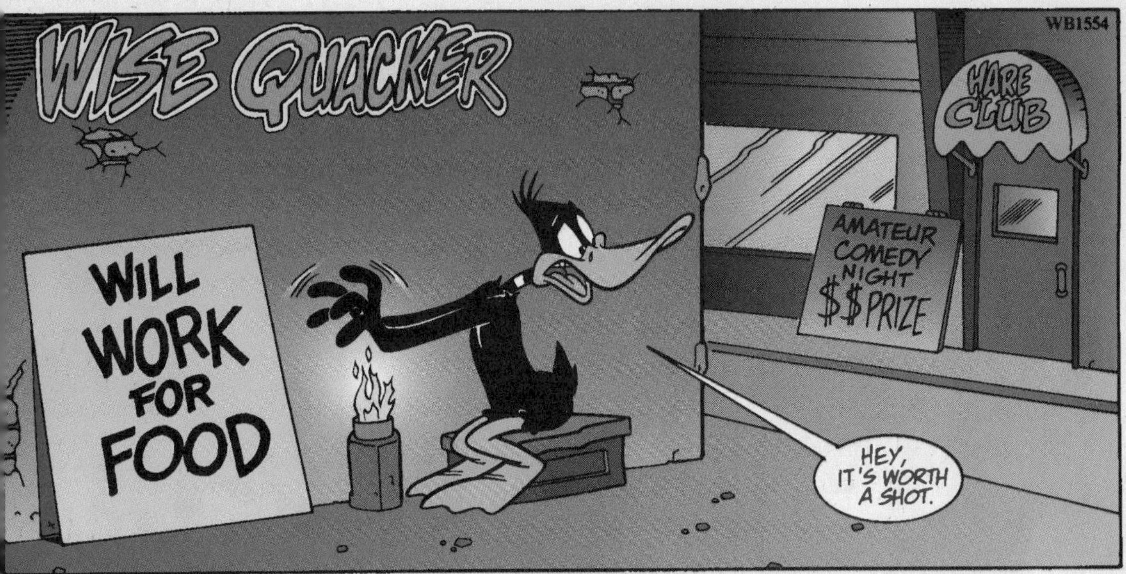
WB1554
WISE QUACKER
HARE CLUB
AMATEUR COMEDY NIGHT $$ PRIZE
WILL WORK FOR FOOD
HEY, IT'S WORTH A SHOT.

Writer: David Cody Weiss Penciller: David Alvarez Inker: Mike DeCarlo Letterer: John Costanza Colors: Prismacolor

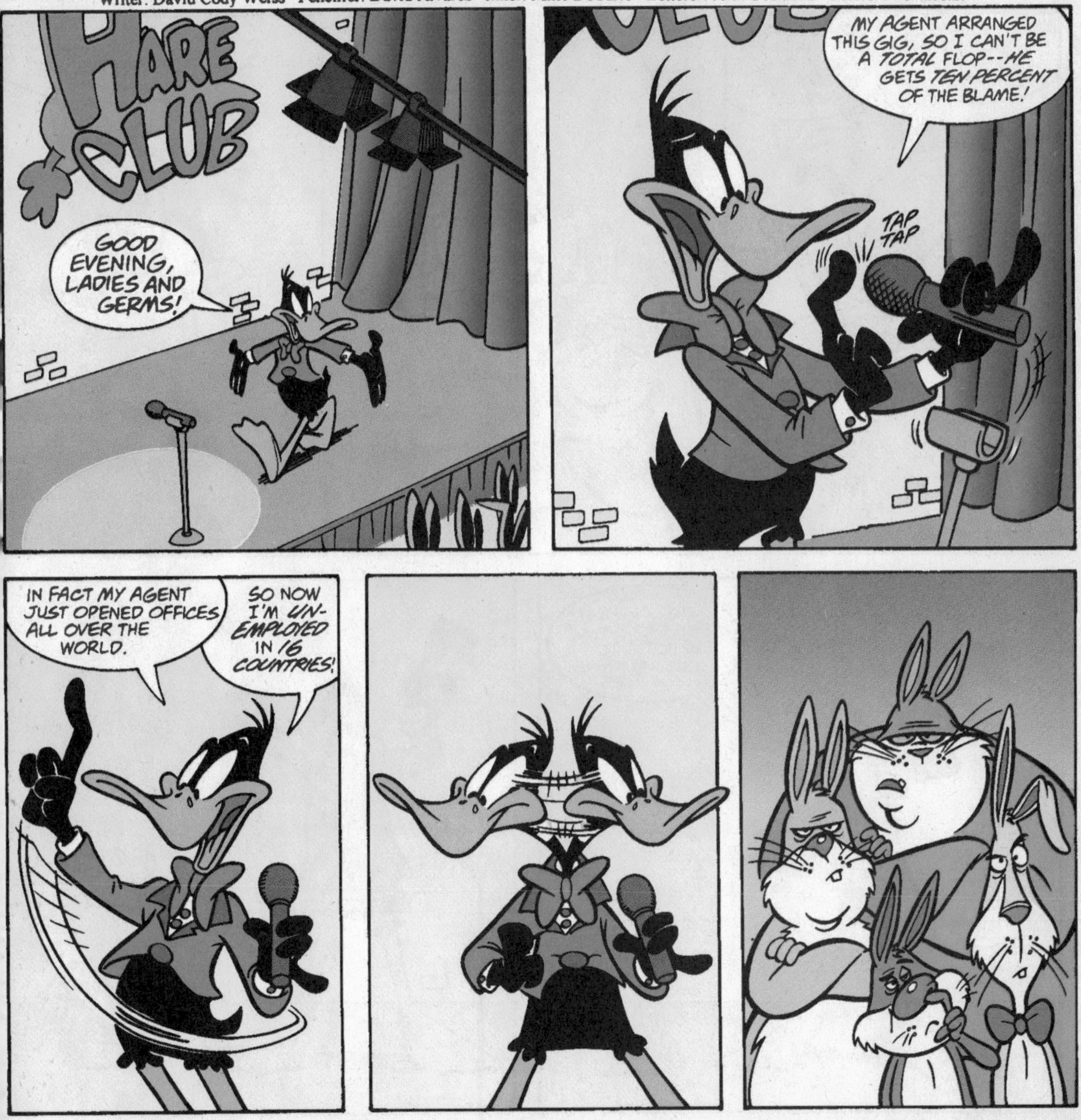
HARE CLUB
GOOD EVENING, LADIES AND GERMS!
MY AGENT ARRANGED THIS GIG, SO I CAN'T BE A *TOTAL* FLOP--*HE* GETS *TEN PERCENT* OF THE BLAME!
TAP TAP
IN FACT MY AGENT JUST OPENED OFFICES ALL OVER THE WORLD.
SO NOW I'M *UN-EMPLOYED* IN *16 COUNTRIES!*

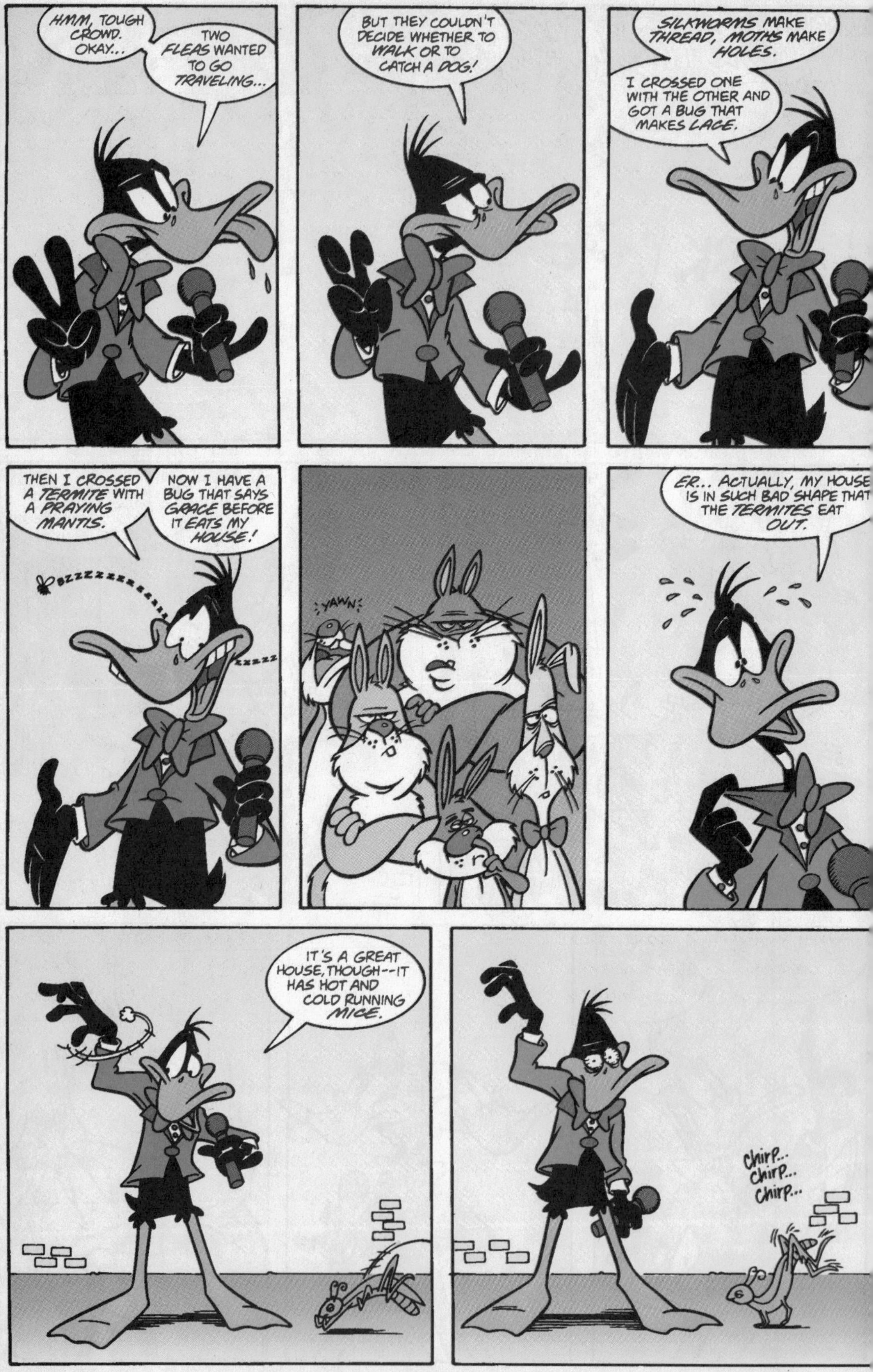
HMM, TOUGH CROWD. OKAY...
TWO FLEAS WANTED TO GO TRAVELING...
BUT THEY COULDN'T DECIDE WHETHER TO WALK OR TO CATCH A DOG!
SILKWORMS MAKE THREAD, MOTHS MAKE HOLES.
I CROSSED ONE WITH THE OTHER AND GOT A BUG THAT MAKES LACE.
THEN I CROSSED A TERMITE WITH A PRAYING MANTIS.
NOW I HAVE A BUG THAT SAYS GRACE BEFORE IT EATS MY HOUSE!
BZZZZZZZ
ZZZZZ
YAWN
ER... ACTUALLY, MY HOUSE IS IN SUCH BAD SHAPE THAT THE TERMITES EAT OUT.
IT'S A GREAT HOUSE, THOUGH--IT HAS HOT AND COLD RUNNING MICE.
Chirp... Chirp... Chirp...

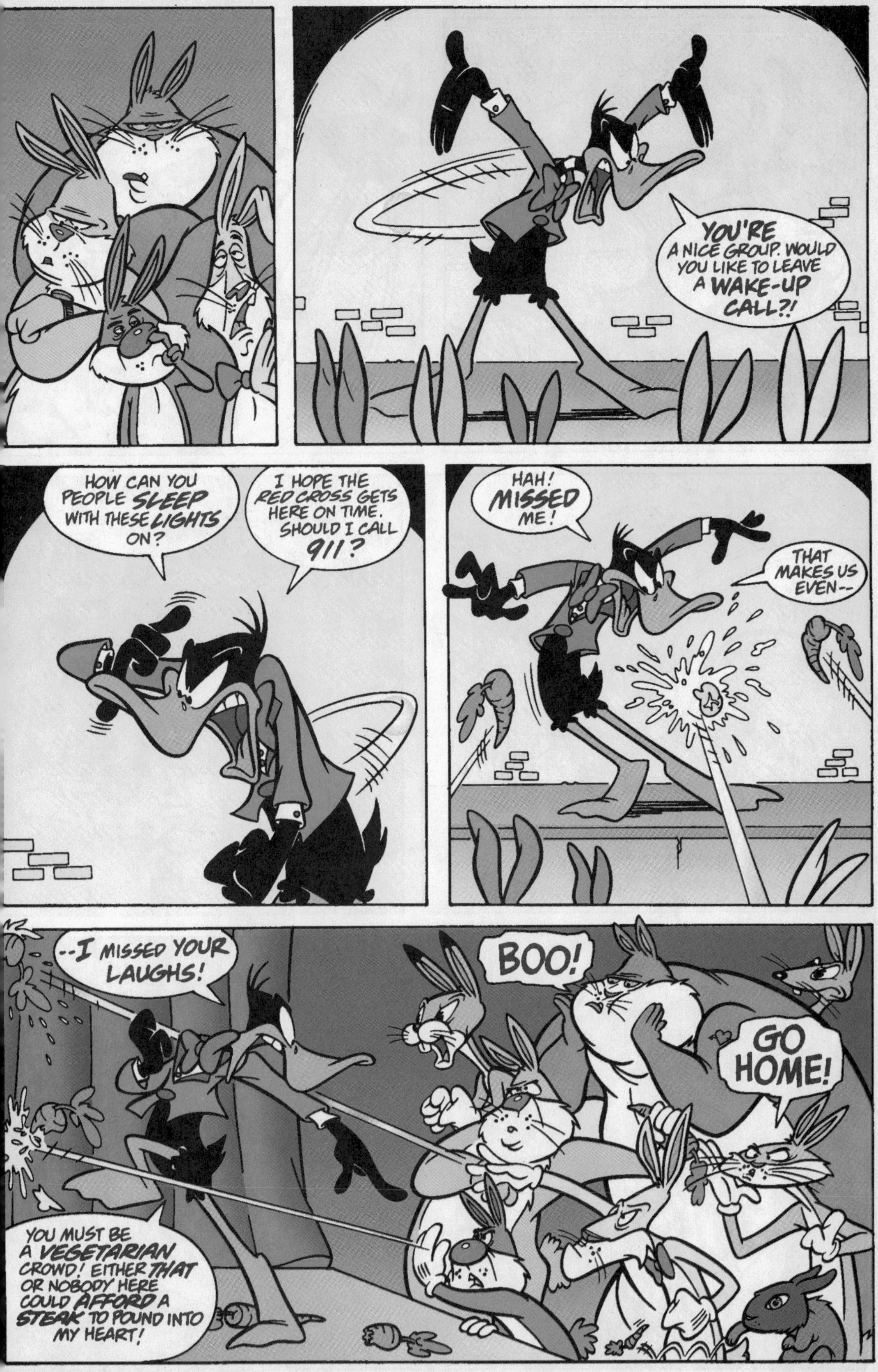
YOU'RE A NICE GROUP. WOULD YOU LIKE TO LEAVE A WAKE-UP CALL?!
HOW CAN YOU PEOPLE SLEEP WITH THESE LIGHTS ON?
I HOPE THE RED CROSS GETS HERE ON TIME. SHOULD I CALL 911?
HAH! MISSED ME!
THAT MAKES US EVEN--
--I MISSED YOUR LAUGHS!
BOO!
GO HOME!
YOU MUST BE A VEGETARIAN CROWD! EITHER THAT OR NOBODY HERE COULD AFFORD A STEAK TO POUND INTO MY HEART!

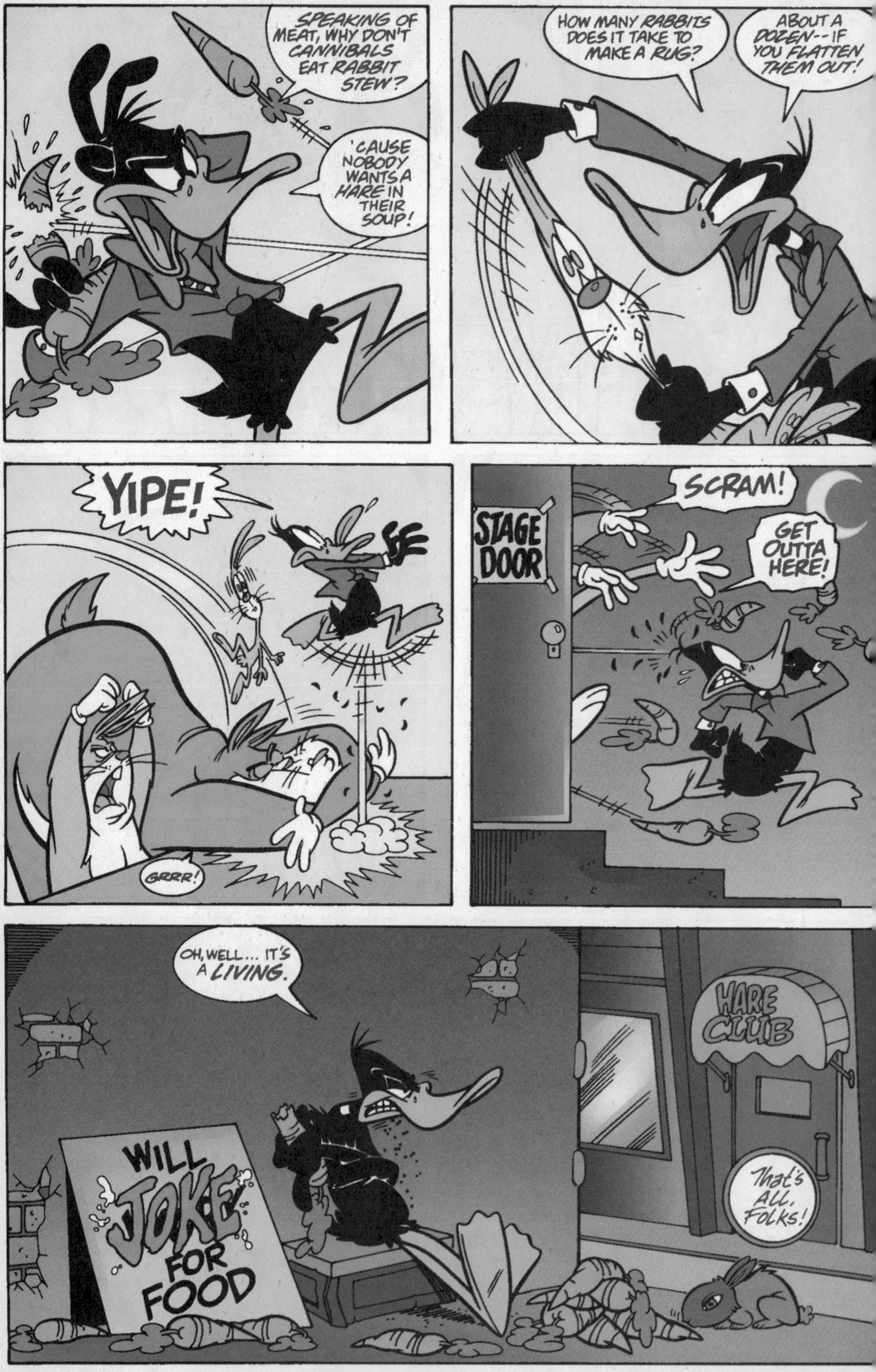
SPEAKING OF MEAT, WHY DON'T CANNIBALS EAT RABBIT STEW?
'CAUSE NOBODY WANTS A HARE IN THEIR SOUP!
HOW MANY RABBITS DOES IT TAKE TO MAKE A RUG?
ABOUT A DOZEN-- IF YOU FLATTEN THEM OUT!
YIPE!
GRRR!
SCRAM!
GET OUTTA HERE!
STAGE DOOR
OH, WELL... IT'S A LIVING.
WILL JOKE FOR FOOD
HARE CLUB
That's All, Folks!

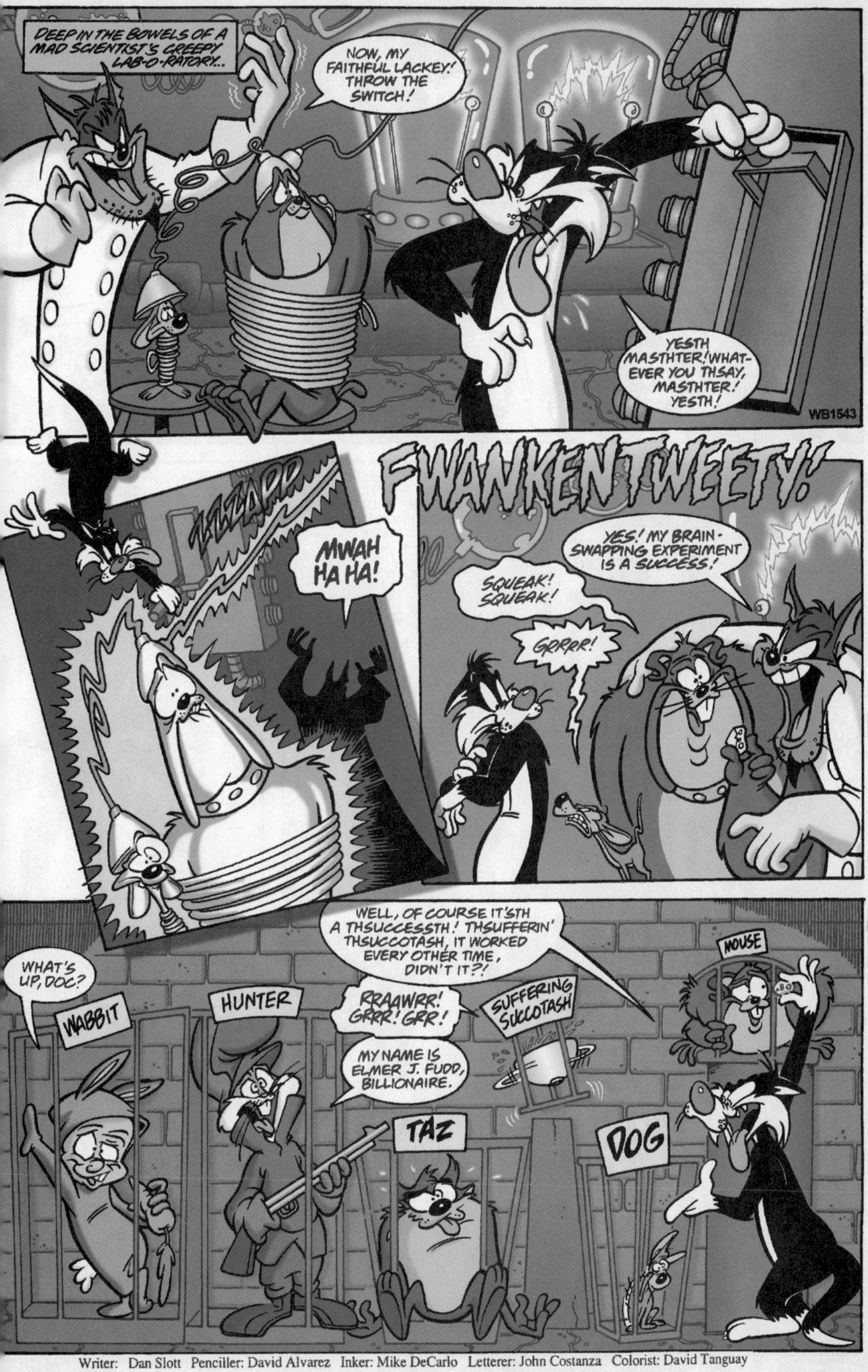
DEEP IN THE BOWELS OF A MAD SCIENTIST'S CREEPY LAB-O-RATORY...
NOW, MY FAITHFUL LACKEY! THROW THE SWITCH!
YESTH MASTHTER! WHATEVER YOU THSAY, MASTHTER! YESTH!
WB1543
FWANKENTWEETY!
ZZZAPP
MWAH HA HA!
YES! MY BRAIN-SWAPPING EXPERIMENT IS A SUCCESS!
SQUEAK! SQUEAK!
GRRRR!
WELL, OF COURSE IT'STH A THSUCCESSTH! THSUFFERIN' THSUCCOTASH, IT WORKED EVERY OTHER TIME, DIDN'T IT?!
WHAT'S UP, DOC?
WABBIT
HUNTER
RRAAWRR! GRRR! GRR!
MY NAME IS ELMER J. FUDD, BILLIONAIRE.
SUFFERING SUCCOTASH
MOUSE
TAZ
DOG

Writer: Dan Slott Penciller: David Alvarez Inker: Mike DeCarlo Letterer: John Costanza Colorist: David Tanguay

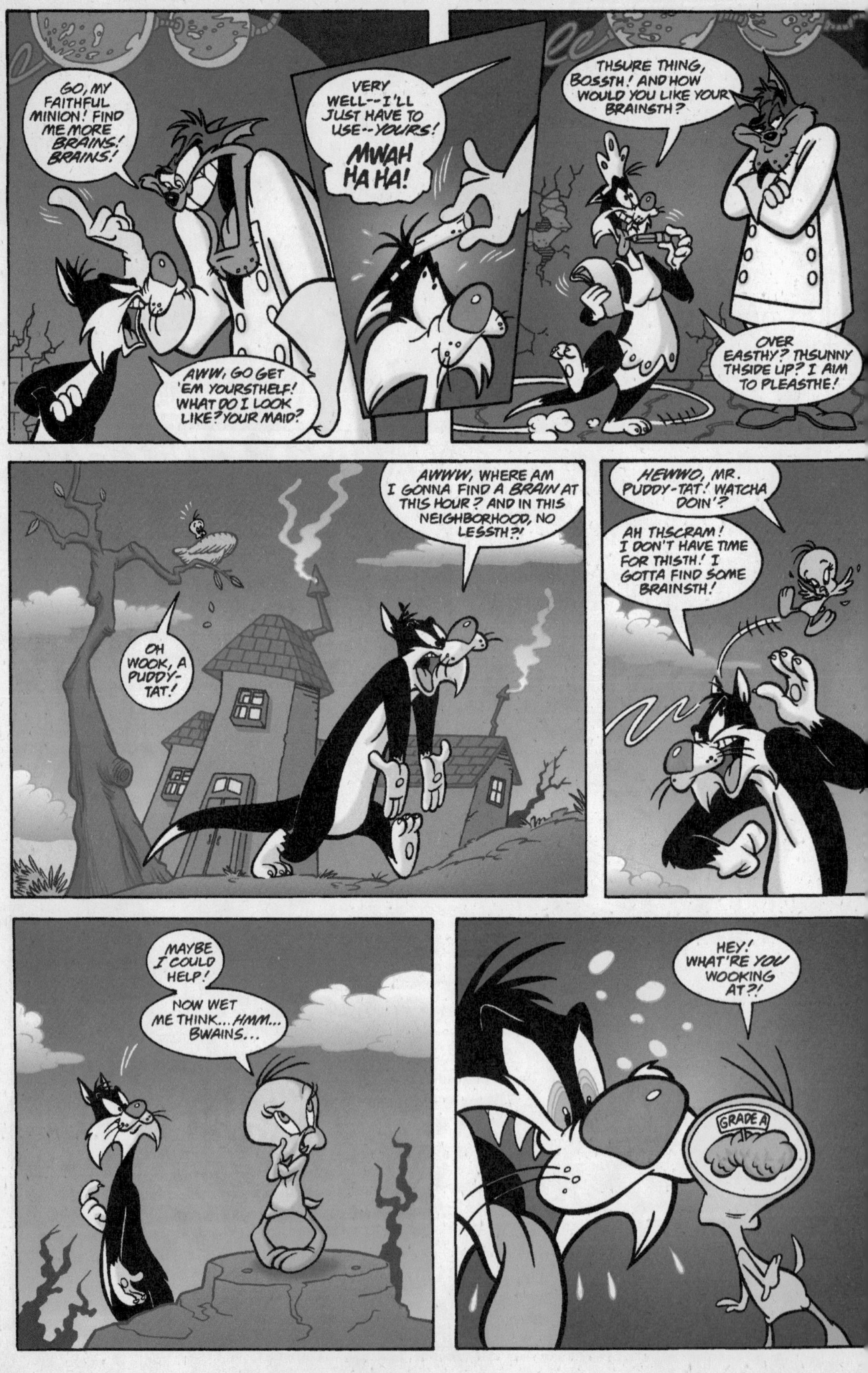
GO, MY FAITHFUL MINION! FIND ME MORE BRAINS! BRAINS!
AWW, GO GET 'EM YOURSTHELF! WHAT DO I LOOK LIKE? YOUR MAID?
VERY WELL--I'LL JUST HAVE TO USE--YOURS!
MWAH HA HA!
THSURE THING, BOSSTH! AND HOW WOULD YOU LIKE YOUR BRAINSTH?
OVER EASTHY? THSUNNY THSIDE UP? I AIM TO PLEASTHE!
AWWW, WHERE AM I GONNA FIND A BRAIN AT THIS HOUR? AND IN THIS NEIGHBORHOOD, NO LESSTH?!
OH WOOK, A PUDDY-TAT!
HEWWO, MR. PUDDY-TAT! WATCHA DOIN'?
AH THSCRAM! I DON'T HAVE TIME FOR THISTH! I GOTTA FIND SOME BRAINSTH!
MAYBE I COULD HELP!
NOW WET ME THINK... HMM... BWAINS...
HEY! WHAT'RE YOU WOOKING AT?!
GRADE A

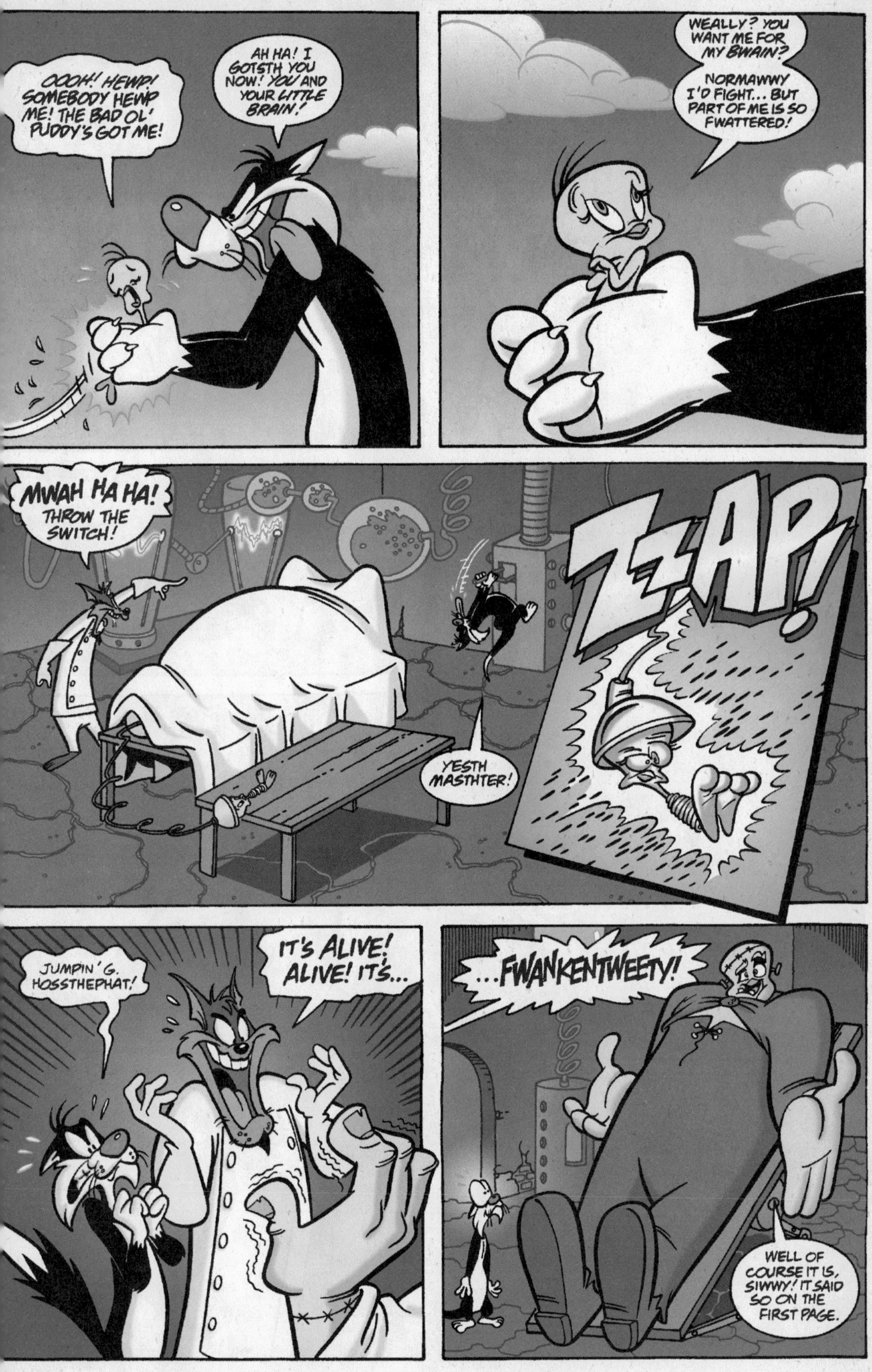
OOOH! HEWP! SOMEBODY HEWP ME! THE BAD OL' PUDDY'S GOT ME!
AH HA! I GOTSTH YOU NOW! YOU AND YOUR LITTLE BRAIN!
WEALLY? YOU WANT ME FOR MY BWAIN?
NORMAWWY I'D FIGHT... BUT PART OF ME IS SO FWATTERED!
MWAH HA HA! THROW THE SWITCH!
YESTH MASTHTER!
ZZAP!
JUMPIN' G. HOSSTHEPHAT!
IT'S ALIVE! ALIVE! IT'S...
...FWANKENTWEETY!
WELL OF COURSE IT IS, SIWWY! IT SAID SO ON THE FIRST PAGE.

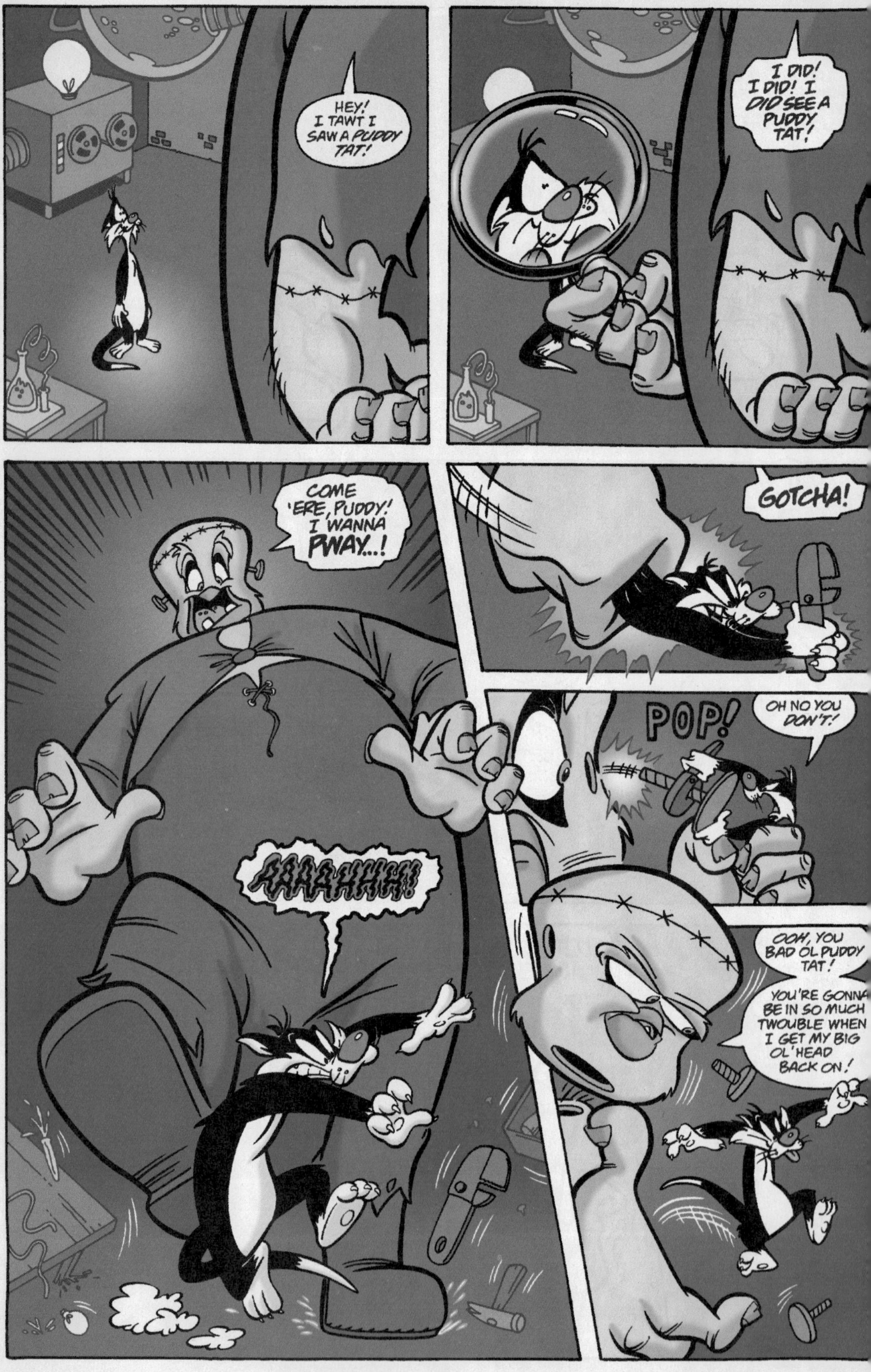
HEY! I TAWT I SAW A PUDDY TAT!
I DID! I DID! I DID SEE A PUDDY TAT!
COME 'ERE, PUDDY! I WANNA PWAY...!
GOTCHA!
AAAAHHH!!
POP!
OH NO YOU DON'T!
OOH, YOU BAD OL PUDDY TAT!
YOU'RE GONNA BE IN SO MUCH TWOUBLE WHEN I GET MY BIG OL' HEAD BACK ON!

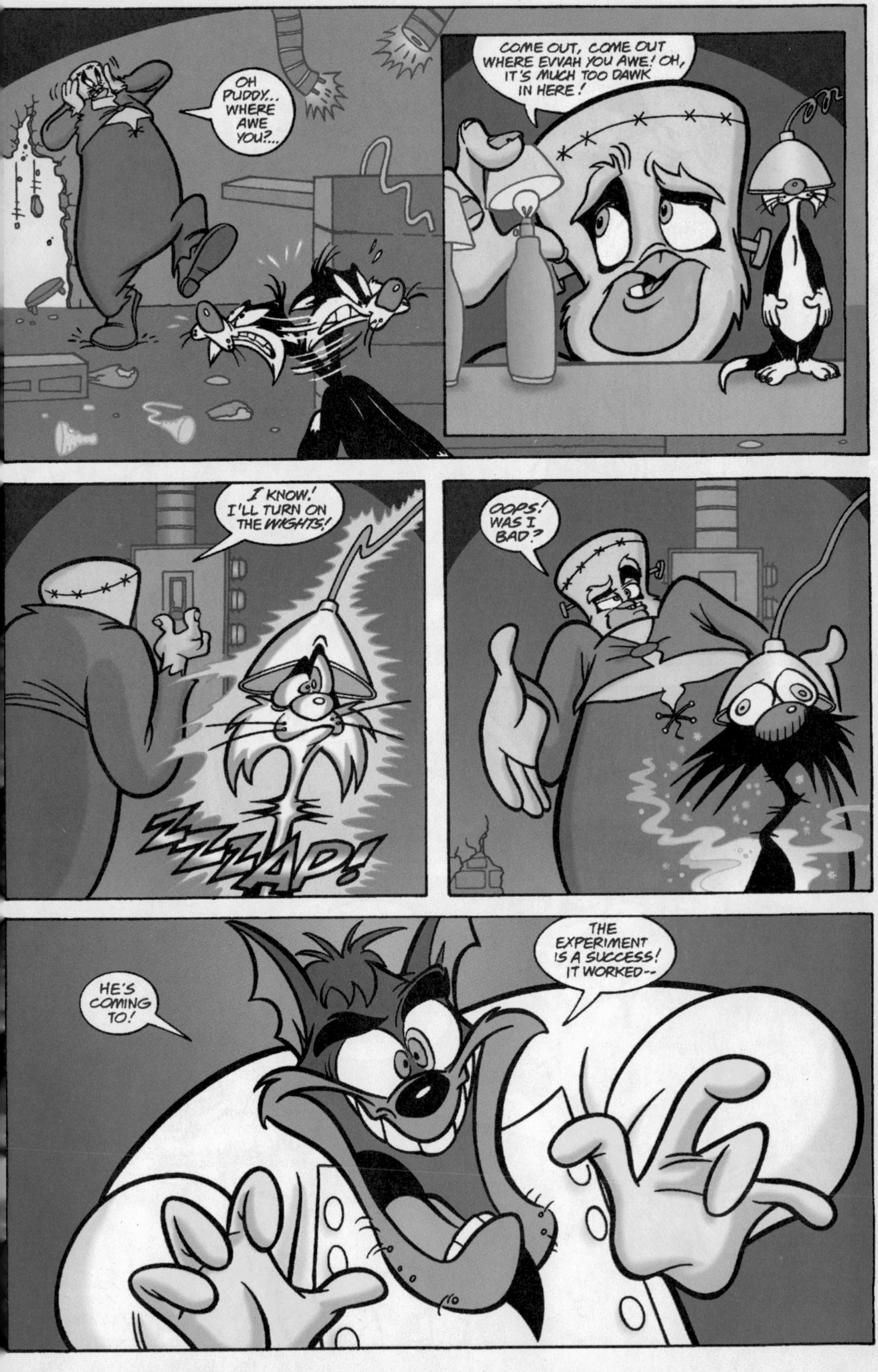
OH PUDDY... WHERE AWE YOU?...
COME OUT, COME OUT WHERE EVVAH YOU AWE! OH, IT'S MUCH TOO DAWK IN HERE!
I KNOW! I'LL TURN ON THE WIGHTS!
ZZZZAP!
OOPS! WAS I BAD?
HE'S COMING TO!
THE EXPERIMENT IS A SUCCESS! IT WORKED--

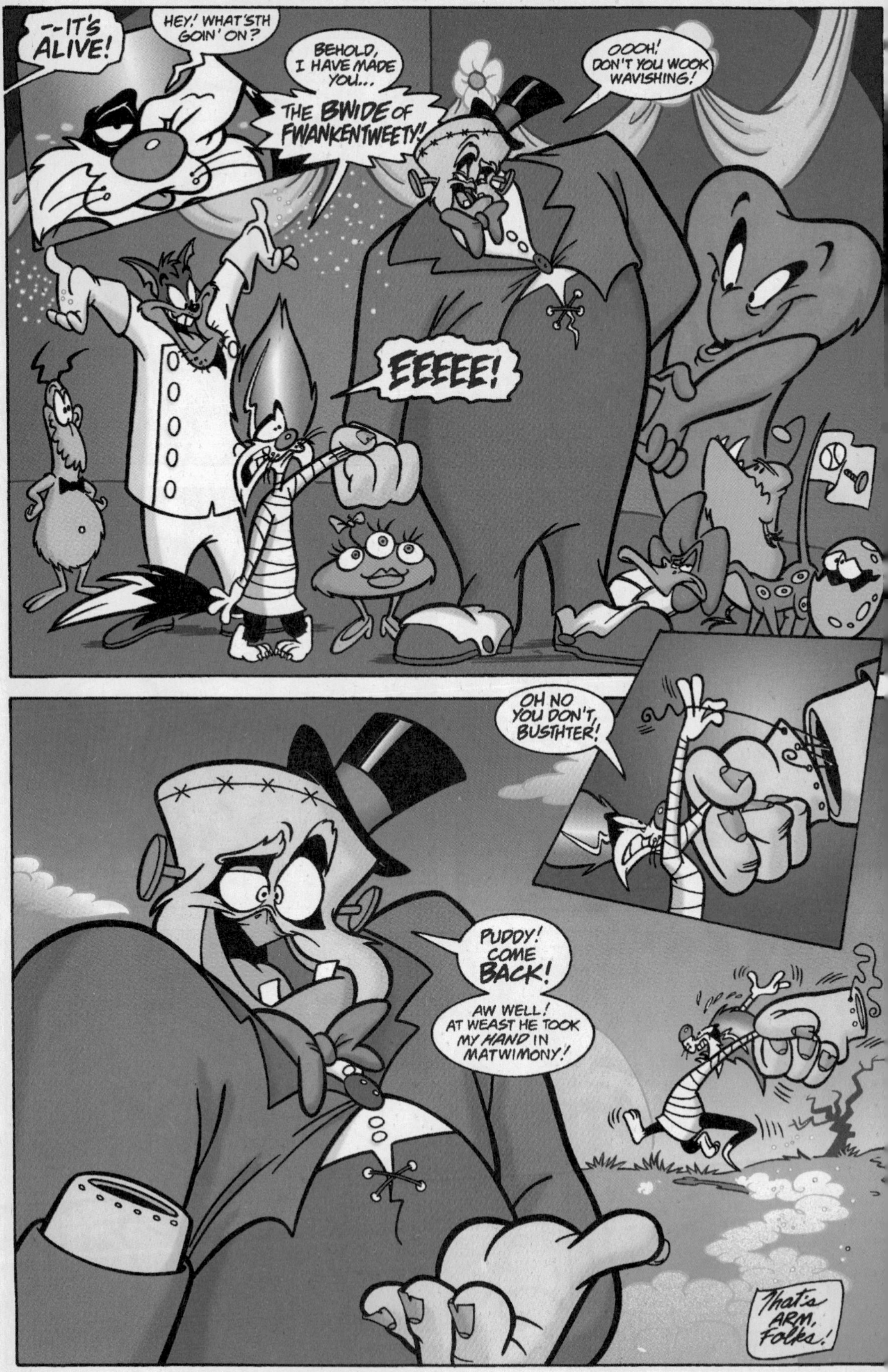

--IT'S ALIVE!
HEY! WHAT'STH GOIN' ON?
BEHOLD, I HAVE MADE YOU...
THE BWIDE OF FWANKENTWEETY!
OOOH! DON'T YOU WOOK WAVISHING!
EEEEE!
OH NO YOU DON'T, BUSTHTER!
PUDDY! COME BACK!
AW WELL! AT WEAST HE TOOK MY HAND IN MATWIMONY!
That's ARM, Folks!

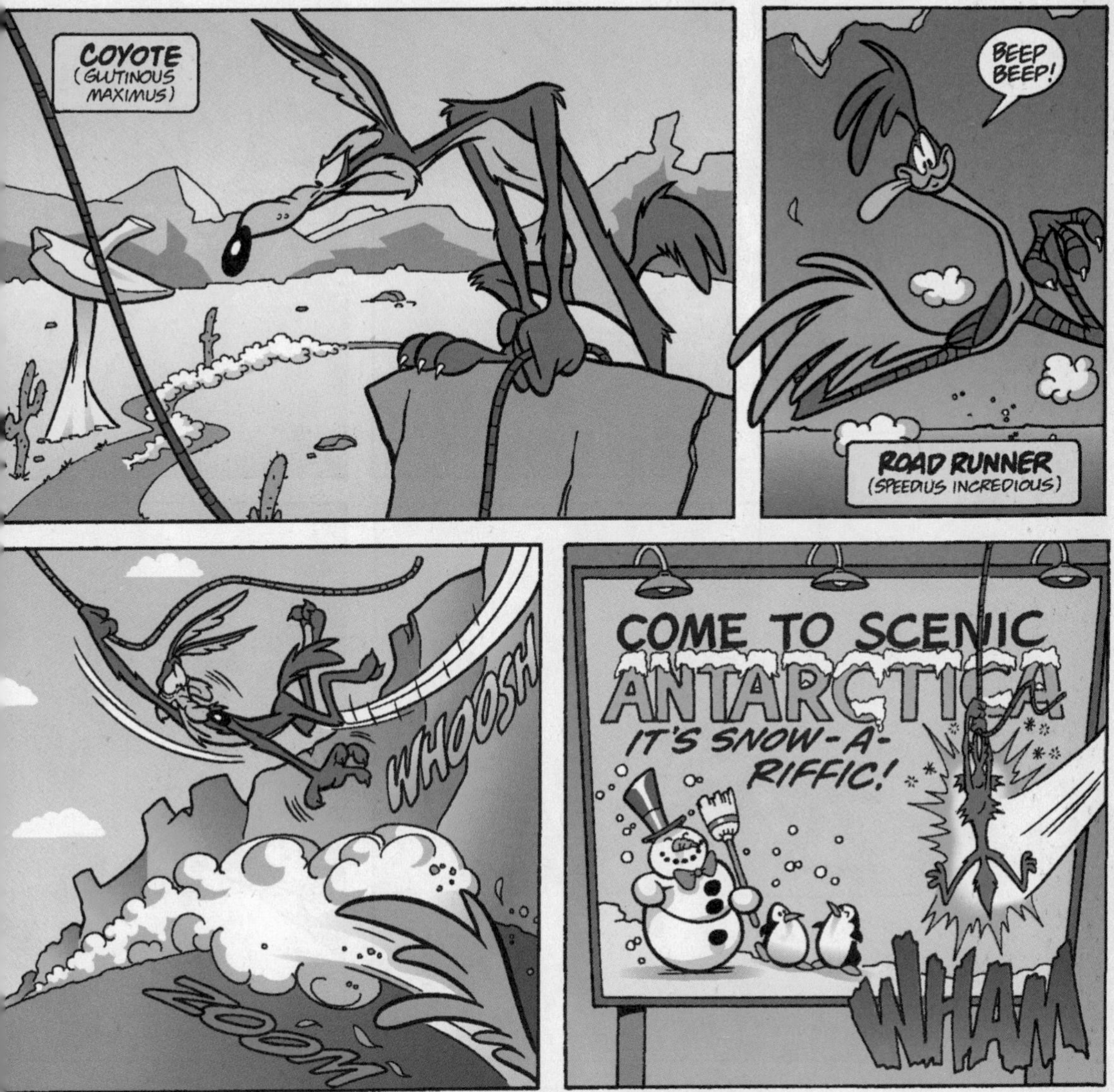
COYOTE
(GLUTINOUS MAXIMUS)
BEEP BEEP!
ROAD RUNNER
(SPEEDIUS INCREDIOUS)
WHOOSH
ZOOM
COME TO SCENIC
ANTARCTICA
IT'S SNOW-A-RIFFIC!
WHAM

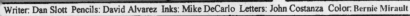

Writer: Dan Slott Pencils: David Alvarez Inks: Mike DeCarlo Letters: John Costanza Color: Bernie Mirault

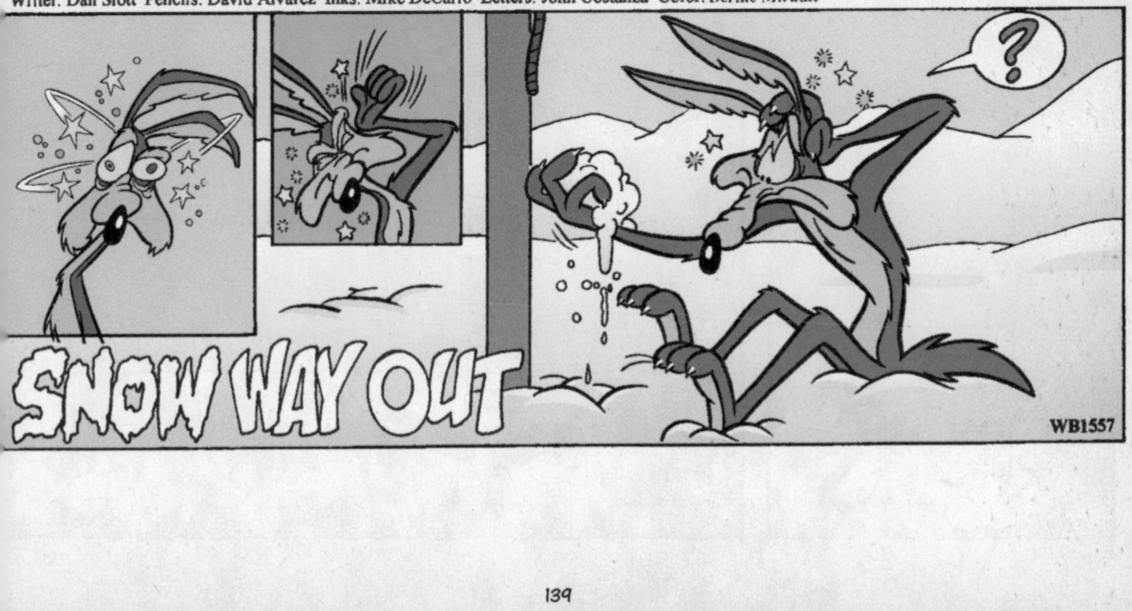
?
SNOW WAY OUT
WB1557

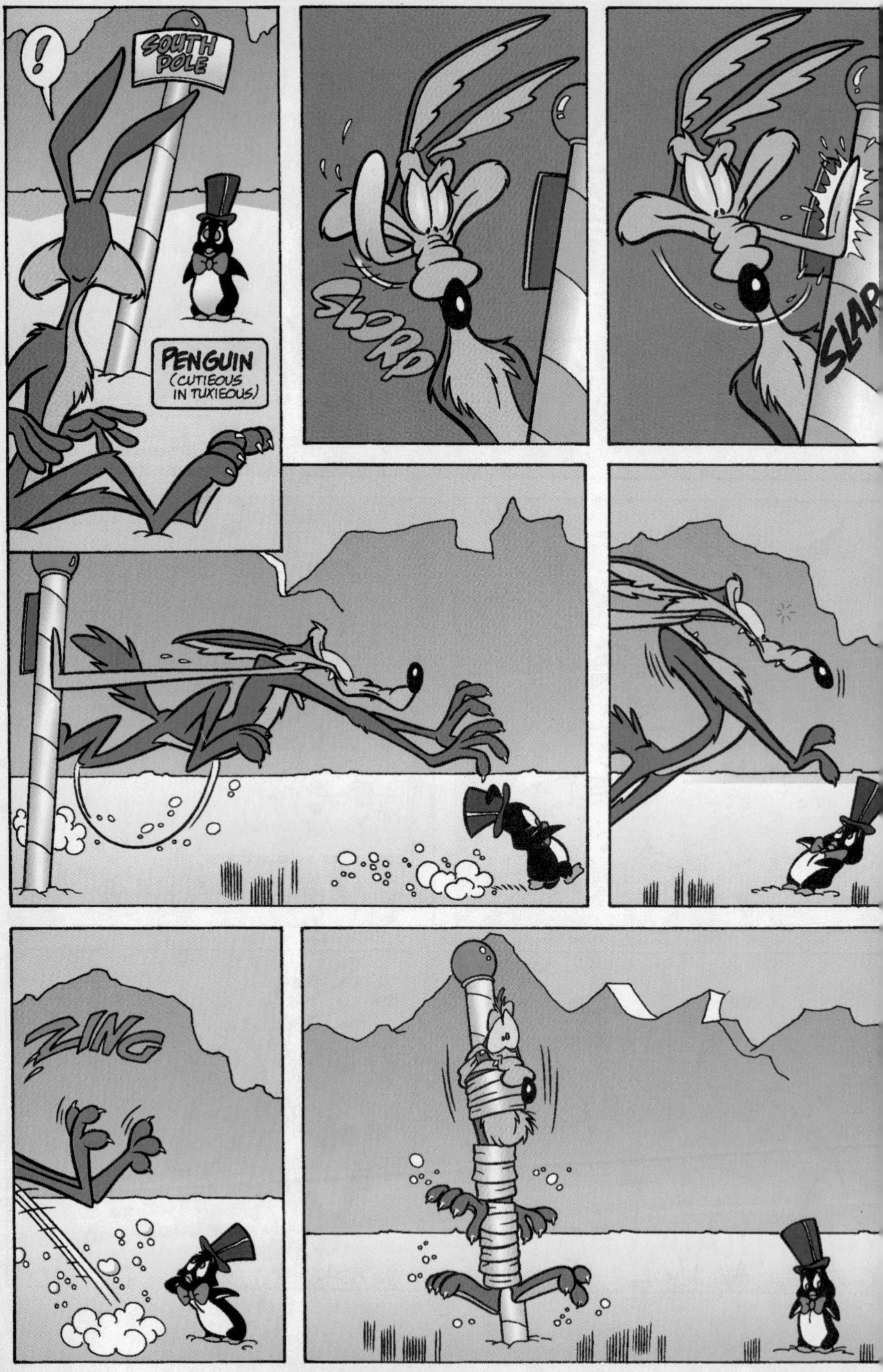
!
SOUTH POLE
PENGUIN (CUTIEOUS IN TUXIEOUS)
SLORP
SLAP
ZING

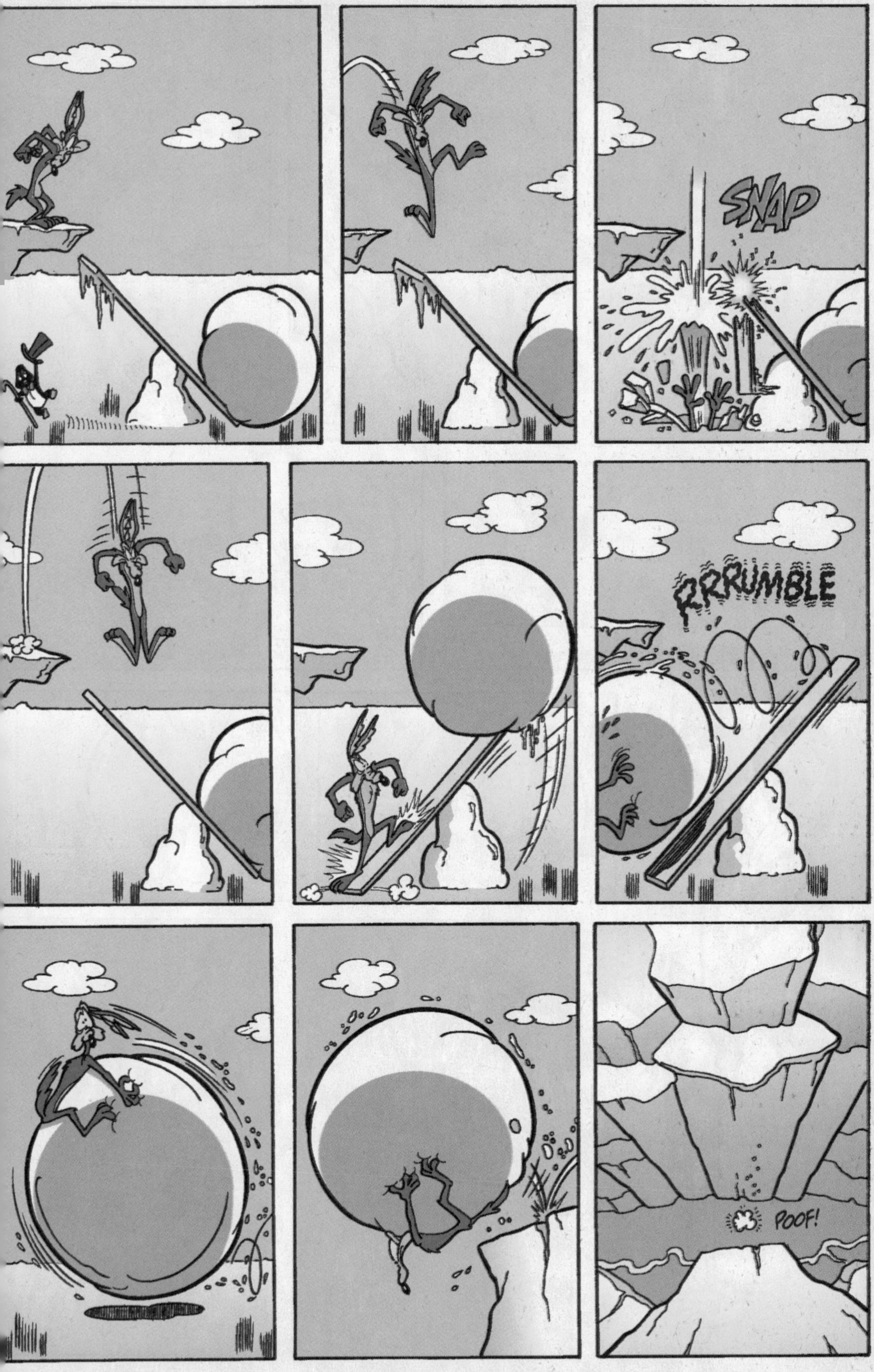
SNAP
RRRUMBLE
POOF!

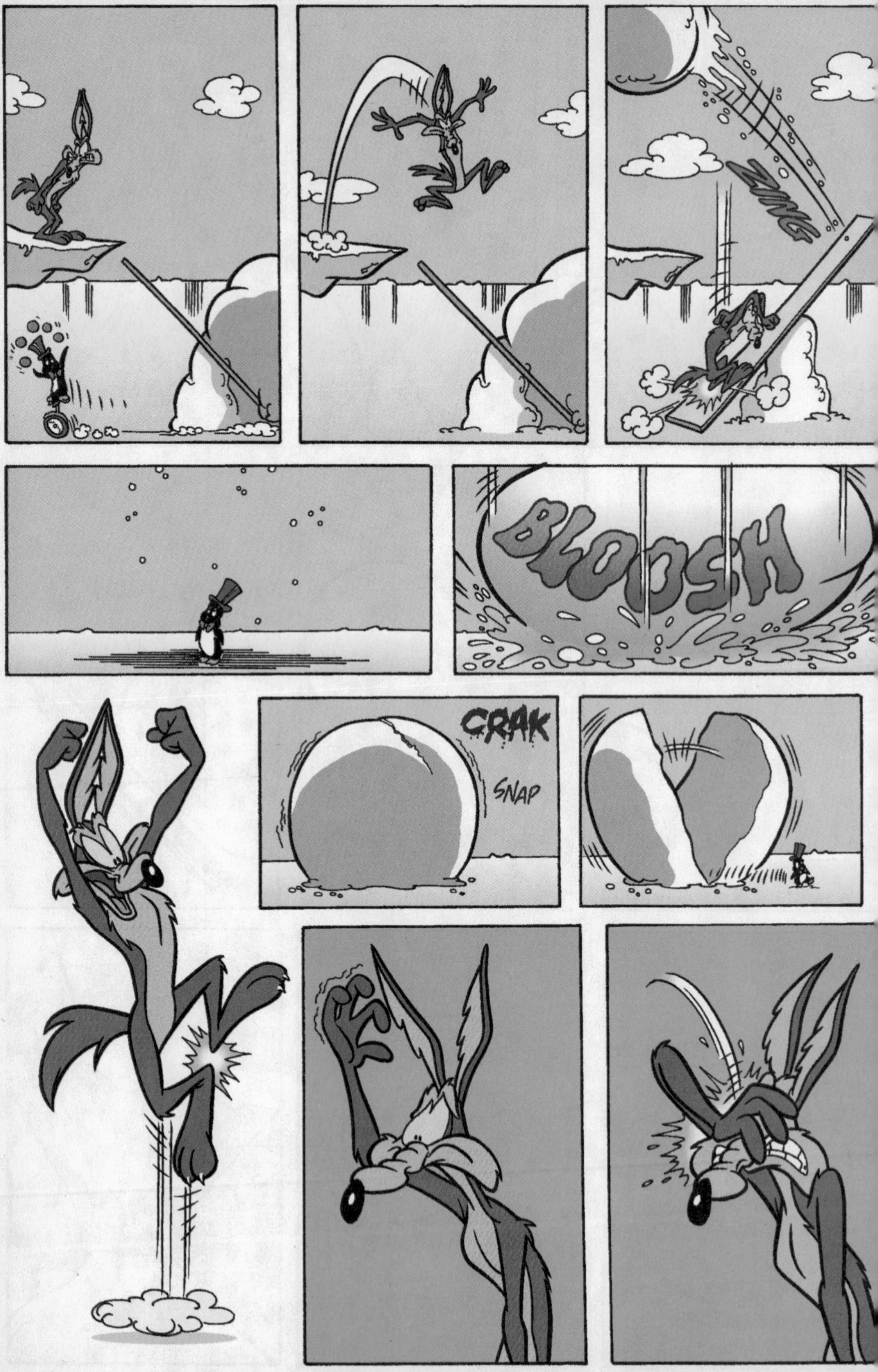
ZING
BLOOSH
CRAK
SNAP

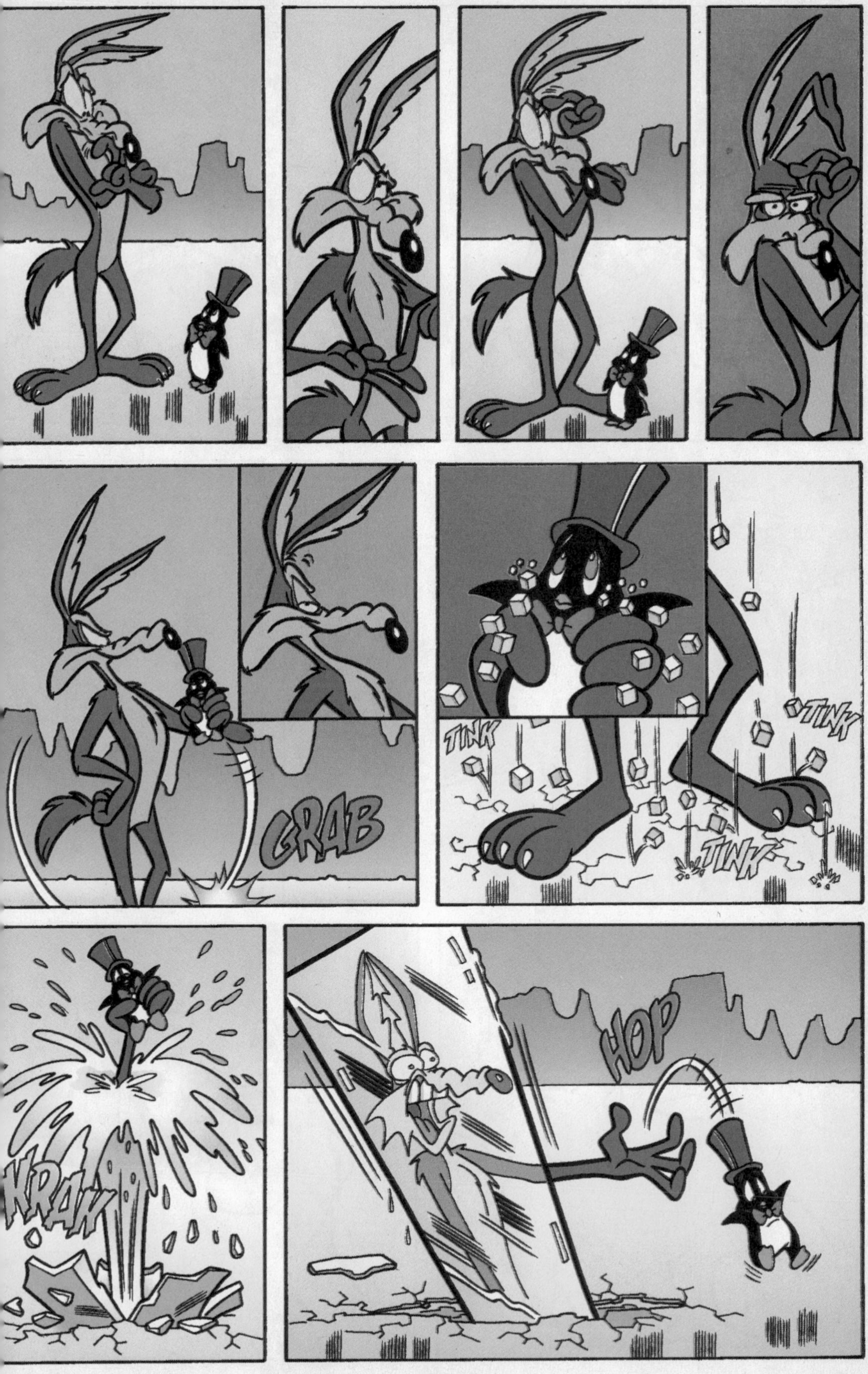
GRAB
TINK
TINK
TINK
KRAK
HOP

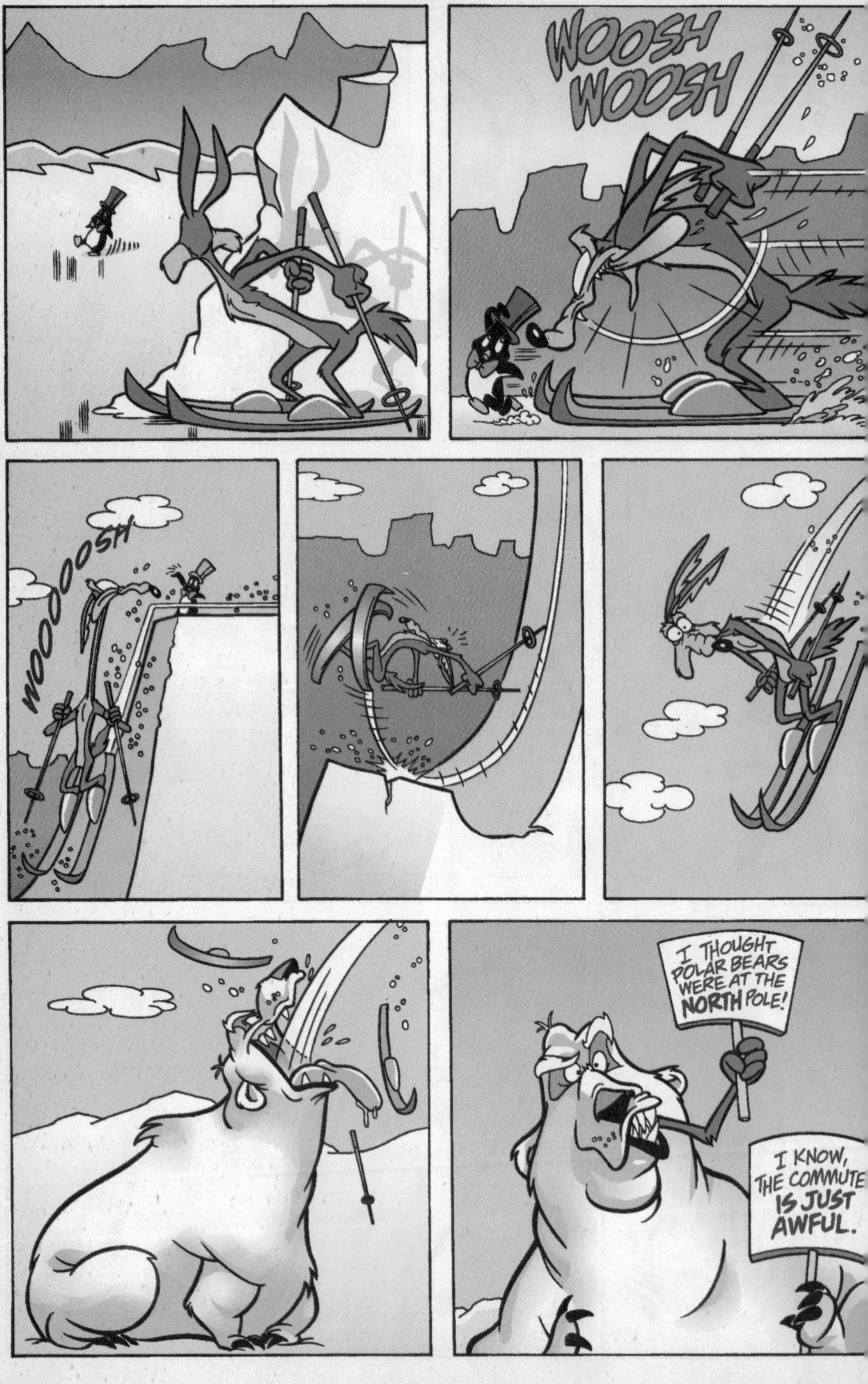
WOOSH
WOOSH
WOOOOOOSH
I THOUGHT POLAR BEARS WERE AT THE NORTH POLE!
I KNOW, THE COMMUTE IS JUST AWFUL.

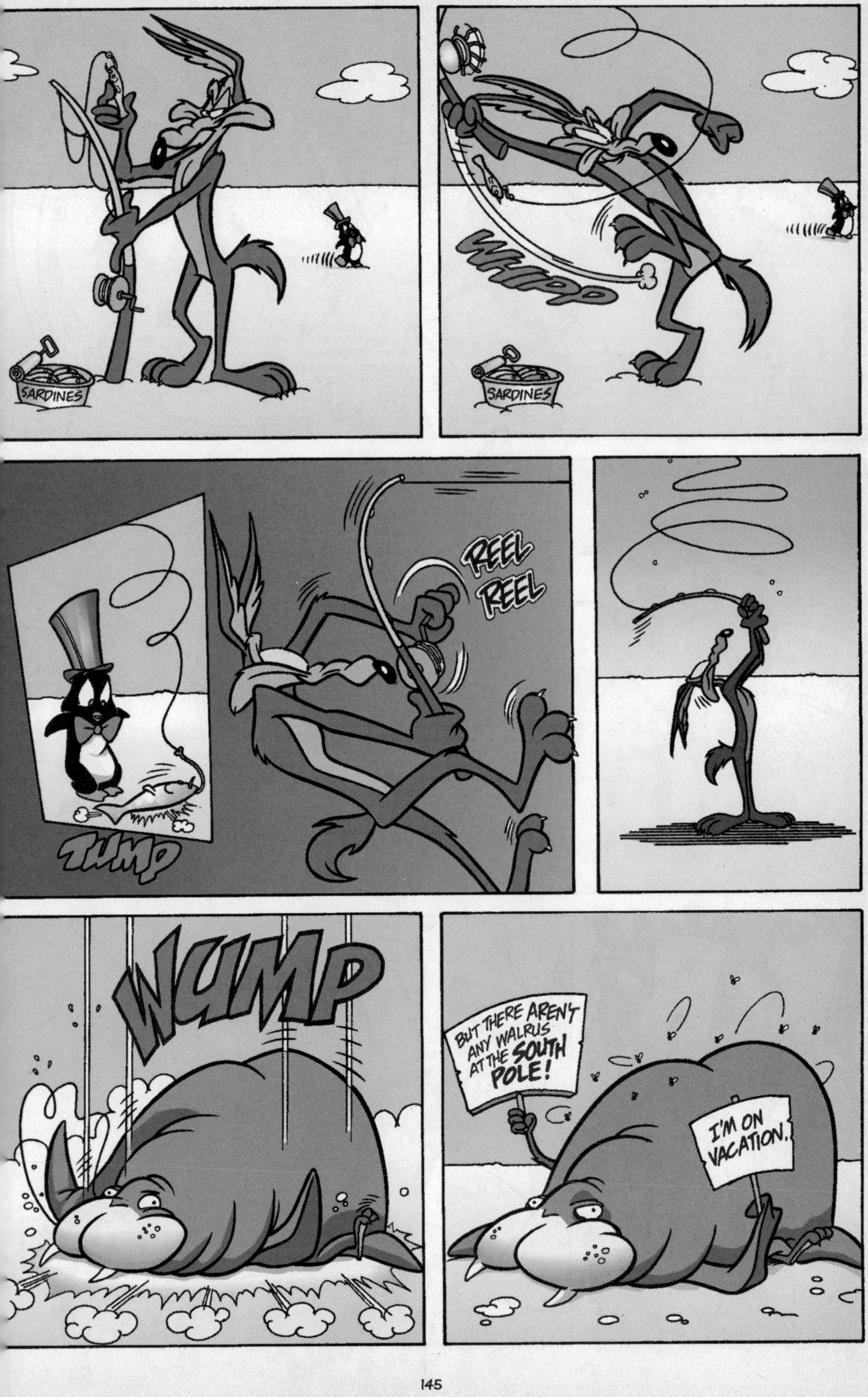
SARDINES
SARDINES
WHIPP
REEL
REEL
THMP
WUMP
BUT THERE AREN'T ANY WALRUS AT THE SOUTH POLE!
I'M ON VACATION.

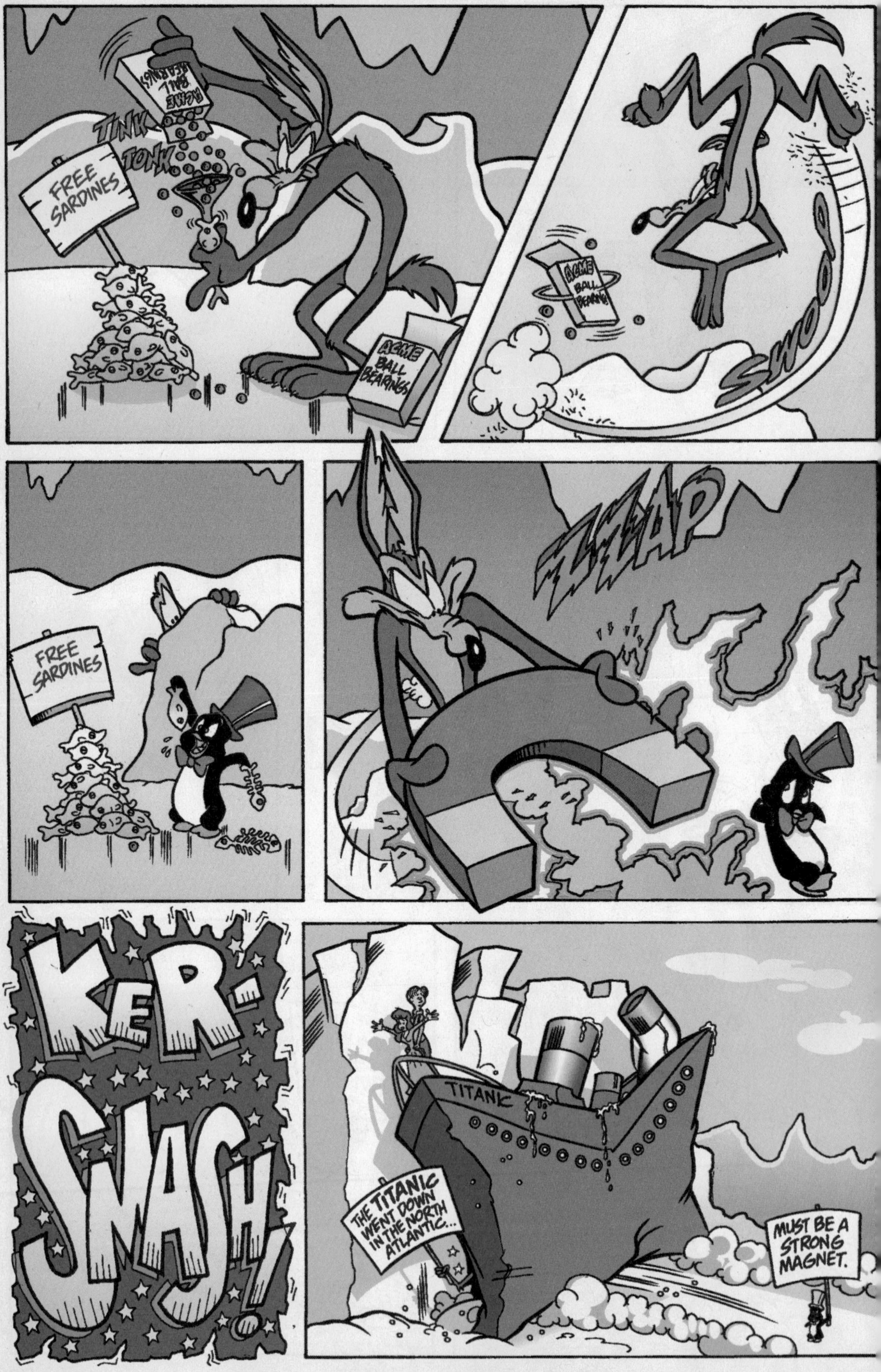
ACME BALL BEARINGS
TINK
TONK
FREE SARDINES
ACME BALL BEARINGS
ACME BALL BEARINGS
SWOOP
FREE SARDINES
ZZZAP
KER-SMASH!
TITANIC
THE TITANIC WENT DOWN IN THE NORTH ATLANTIC...
MUST BE A STRONG MAGNET.

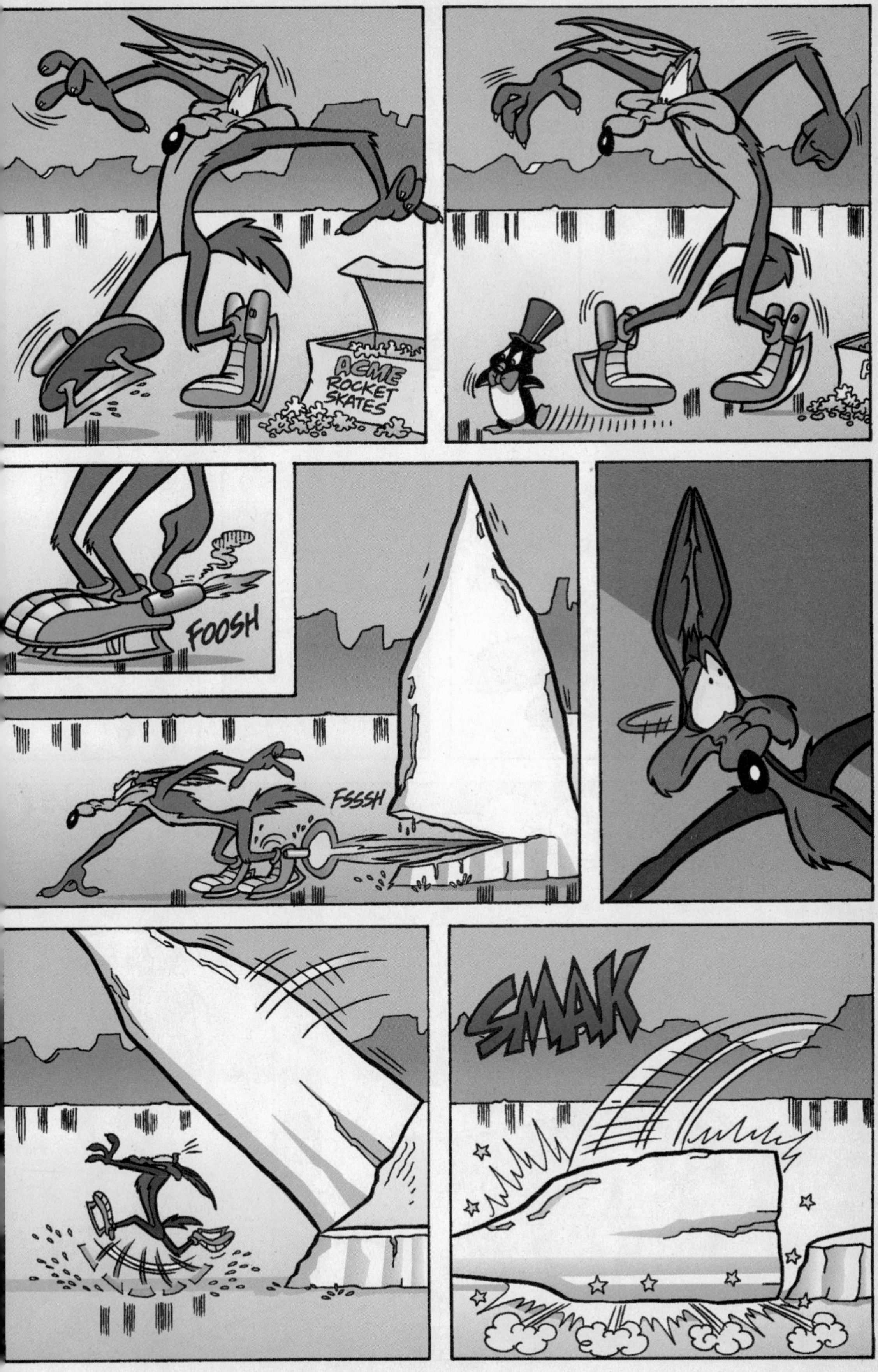
ACME
ROCKET
SKATES
FOOSH
FSSSH
SMAK

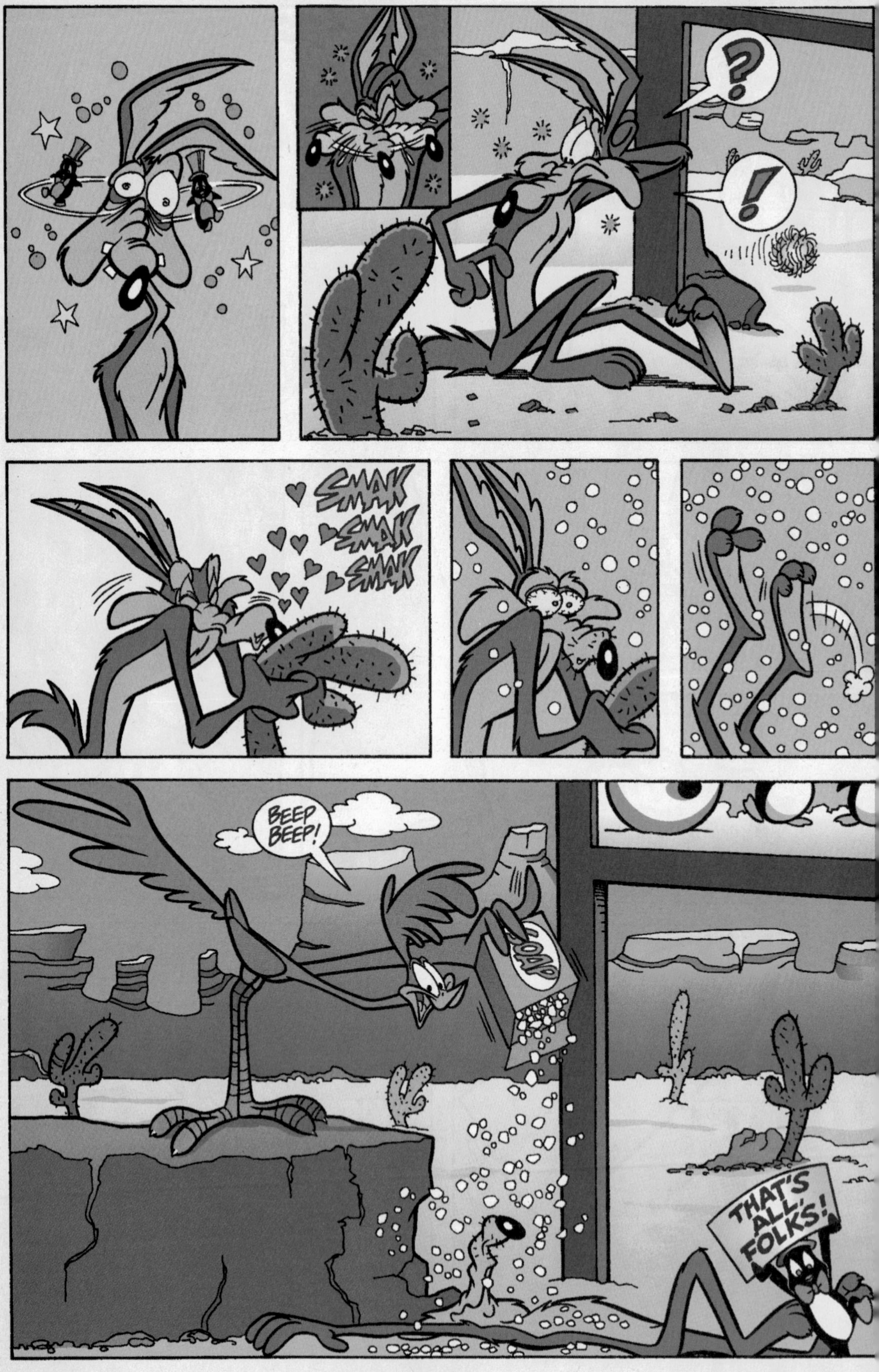
?
!
SMAK
SMAK
SMAK
BEEP BEEP!
SOAP
THAT'S ALL, FOLKS!

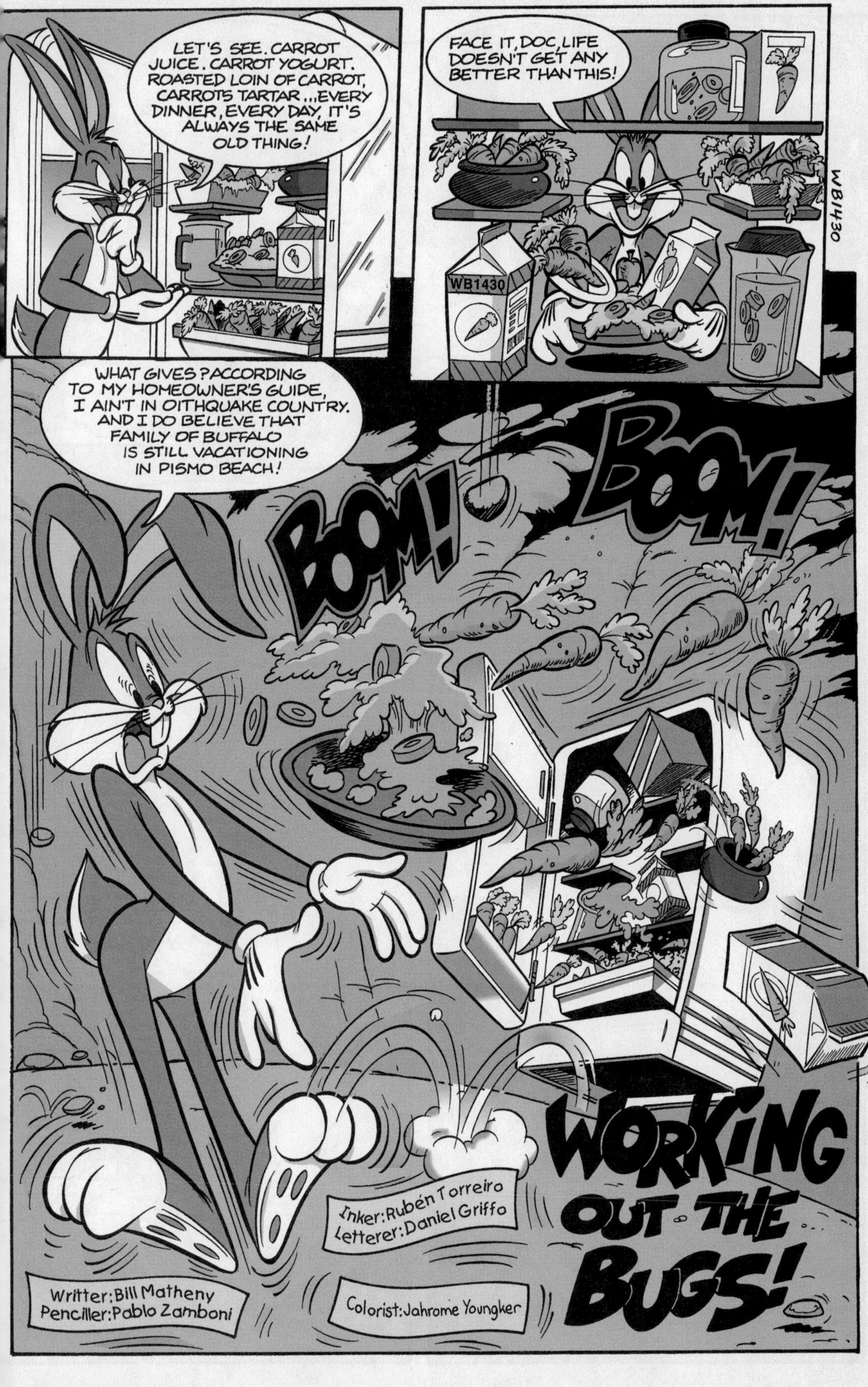
LET'S SEE. CARROT JUICE. CARROT YOGURT. ROASTED LOIN OF CARROT, CARROTS TARTAR ...EVERY DINNER, EVERY DAY, IT'S ALWAYS THE SAME OLD THING!
FACE IT, DOC, LIFE DOESN'T GET ANY BETTER THAN THIS!
WB1430
WB1430
WHAT GIVES? ACCORDING TO MY HOMEOWNER'S GUIDE, I AIN'T IN OITHQUAKE COUNTRY. AND I DO BELIEVE THAT FAMILY OF BUFFALO IS STILL VACATIONING IN PISMO BEACH!
BOOM!
BOOM!
WORKING OUT THE BUGS!
Inker: Rubén Torreiro
Letterer: Daniel Griffo
Writter: Bill Matheny
Penciller: Pablo Zamboni
Colorist: Jahrome Youngker

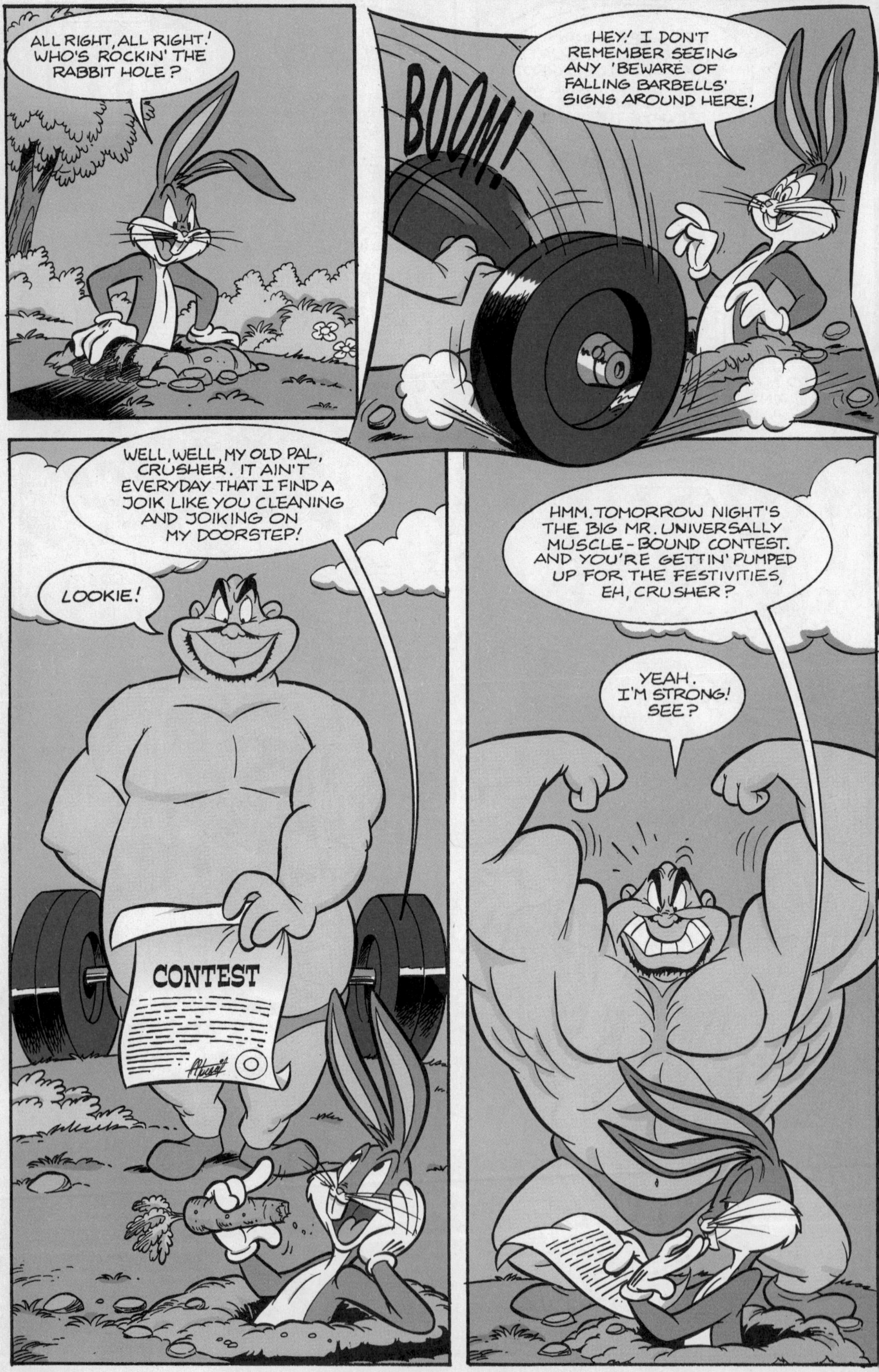
ALL RIGHT, ALL RIGHT! WHO'S ROCKIN' THE RABBIT HOLE?
BOOM!
HEY! I DON'T REMEMBER SEEING ANY 'BEWARE OF FALLING BARBELLS' SIGNS AROUND HERE!
WELL, WELL, MY OLD PAL, CRUSHER. IT AIN'T EVERYDAY THAT I FIND A JOIK LIKE YOU CLEANING AND JOIKING ON MY DOORSTEP!
LOOKIE!
CONTEST
HMM. TOMORROW NIGHT'S THE BIG MR. UNIVERSALLY MUSCLE-BOUND CONTEST. AND YOU'RE GETTIN' PUMPED UP FOR THE FESTIVITIES, EH, CRUSHER?
YEAH. I'M STRONG! SEE?

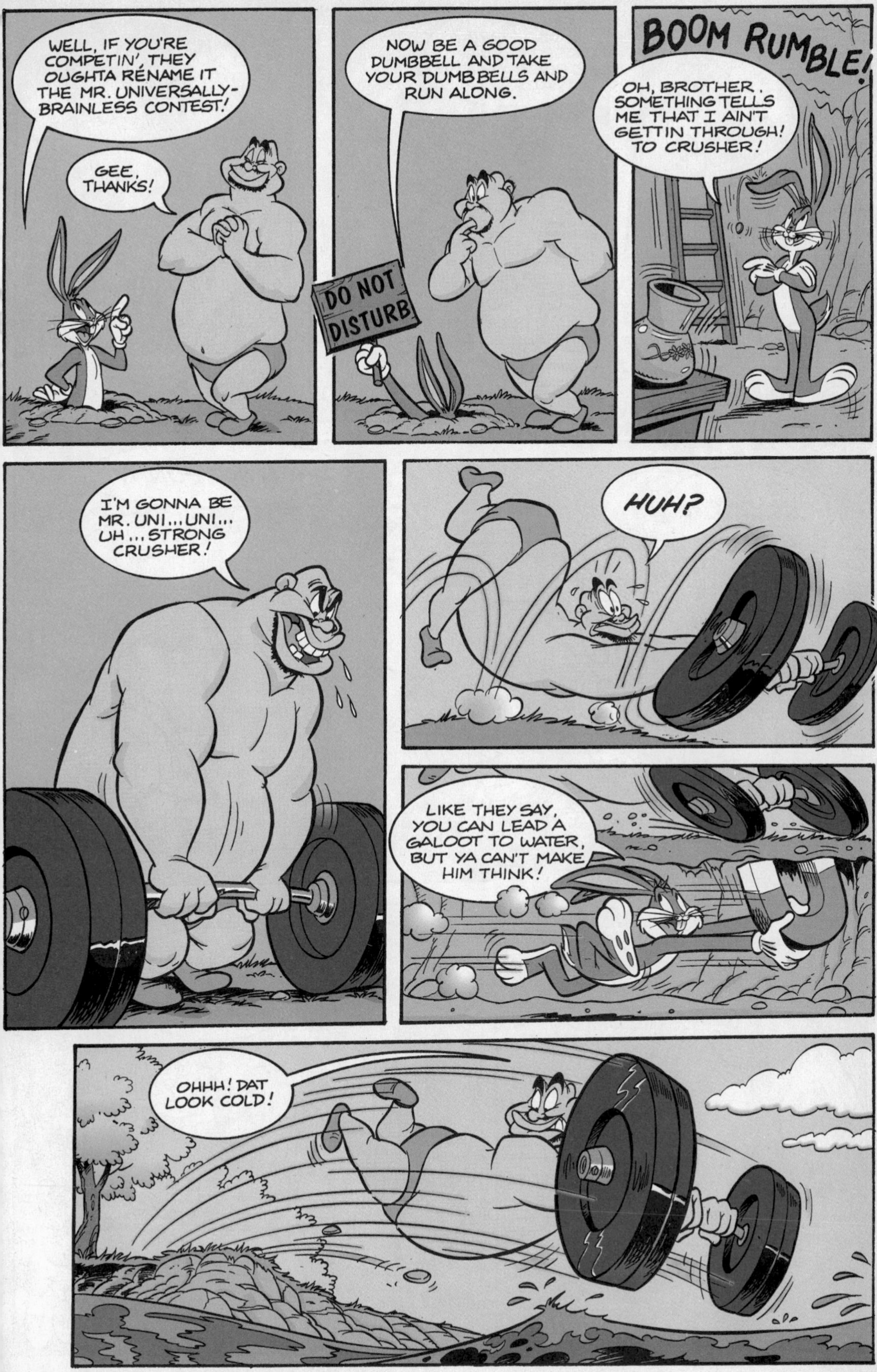
WELL, IF YOU'RE COMPETIN', THEY OUGHTA RENAME IT THE MR. UNIVERSALLY-BRAINLESS CONTEST!
GEE, THANKS!
DO NOT DISTURB
NOW BE A GOOD DUMBBELL AND TAKE YOUR DUMBBELLS AND RUN ALONG.
BOOM RUMBLE!
OH, BROTHER. SOMETHING TELLS ME THAT I AIN'T GETTIN THROUGH! TO CRUSHER!
I'M GONNA BE MR. UNI...UNI... UH...STRONG CRUSHER!
HUH?
LIKE THEY SAY, YOU CAN LEAD A GALOOT TO WATER, BUT YA CAN'T MAKE HIM THINK!
OHHH! DAT LOOK COLD!

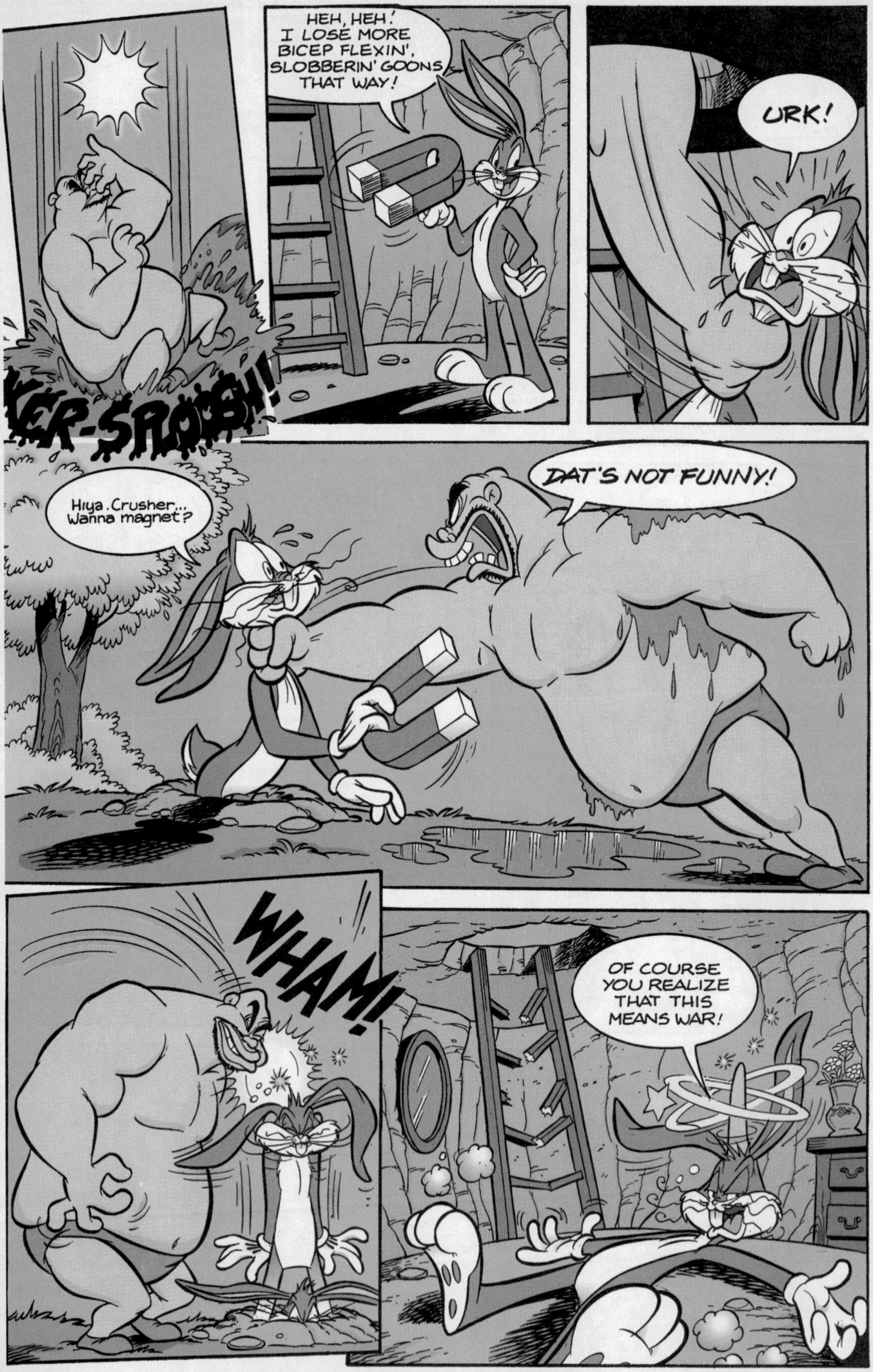
KER-SPLOOSH!!
HEH, HEH! I LOSE MORE BICEP FLEXIN', SLOBBERIN' GOONS THAT WAY!
URK!
Hiya. Crusher... Wanna magnet?
DAT'S NOT FUNNY!
WHAM!
OF COURSE YOU REALIZE THAT THIS MEANS WAR!

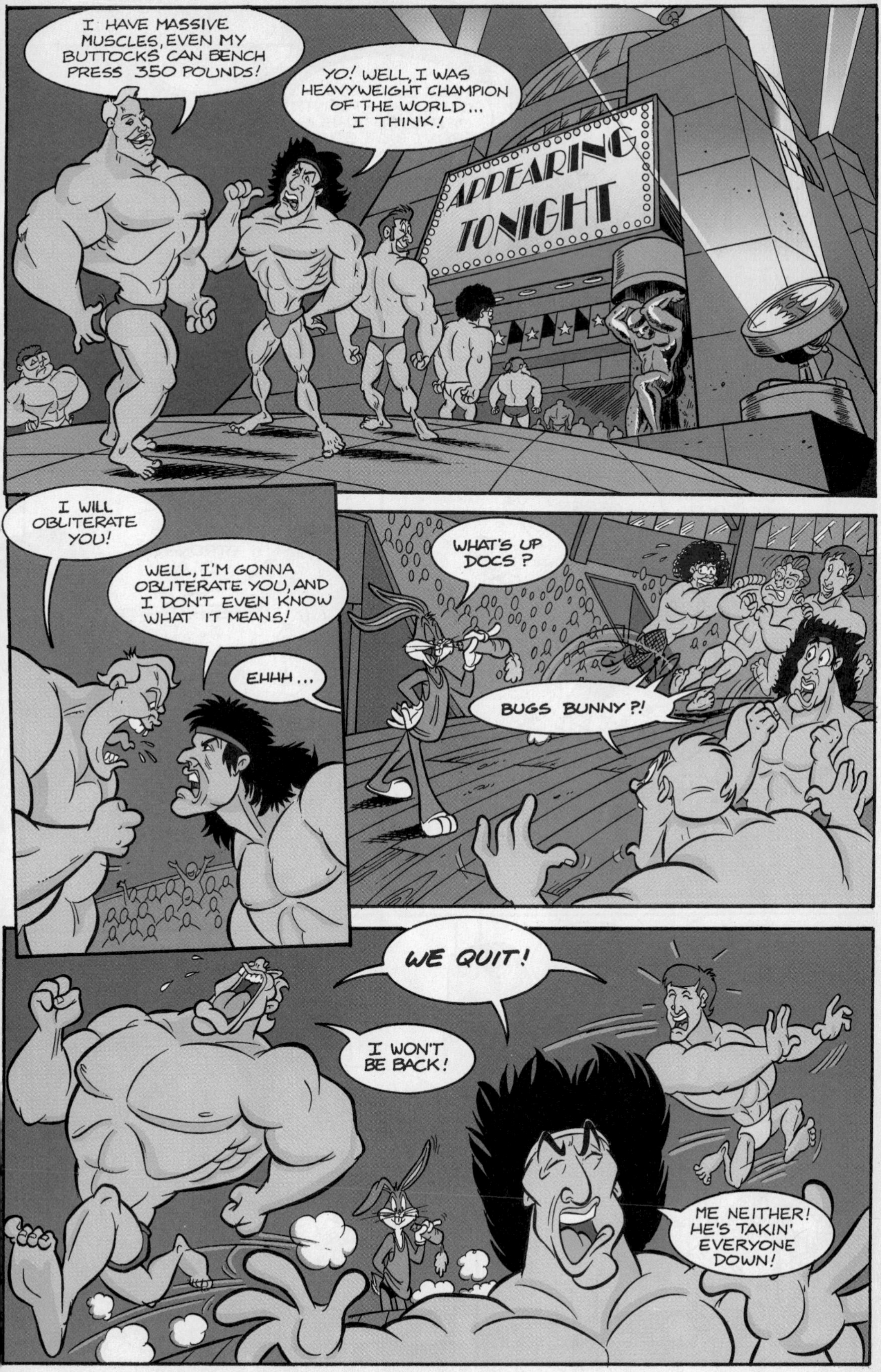
I HAVE MASSIVE MUSCLES, EVEN MY BUTTOCKS CAN BENCH PRESS 350 POUNDS!
YO! WELL, I WAS HEAVYWEIGHT CHAMPION OF THE WORLD... I THINK!
APPEARING TONIGHT
I WILL OBLITERATE YOU!
WELL, I'M GONNA OBLITERATE YOU, AND I DON'T EVEN KNOW WHAT IT MEANS!
EHHH...
WHAT'S UP DOCS ?
BUGS BUNNY ?!
WE QUIT!
I WON'T BE BACK!
ME NEITHER! HE'S TAKIN' EVERYONE DOWN!

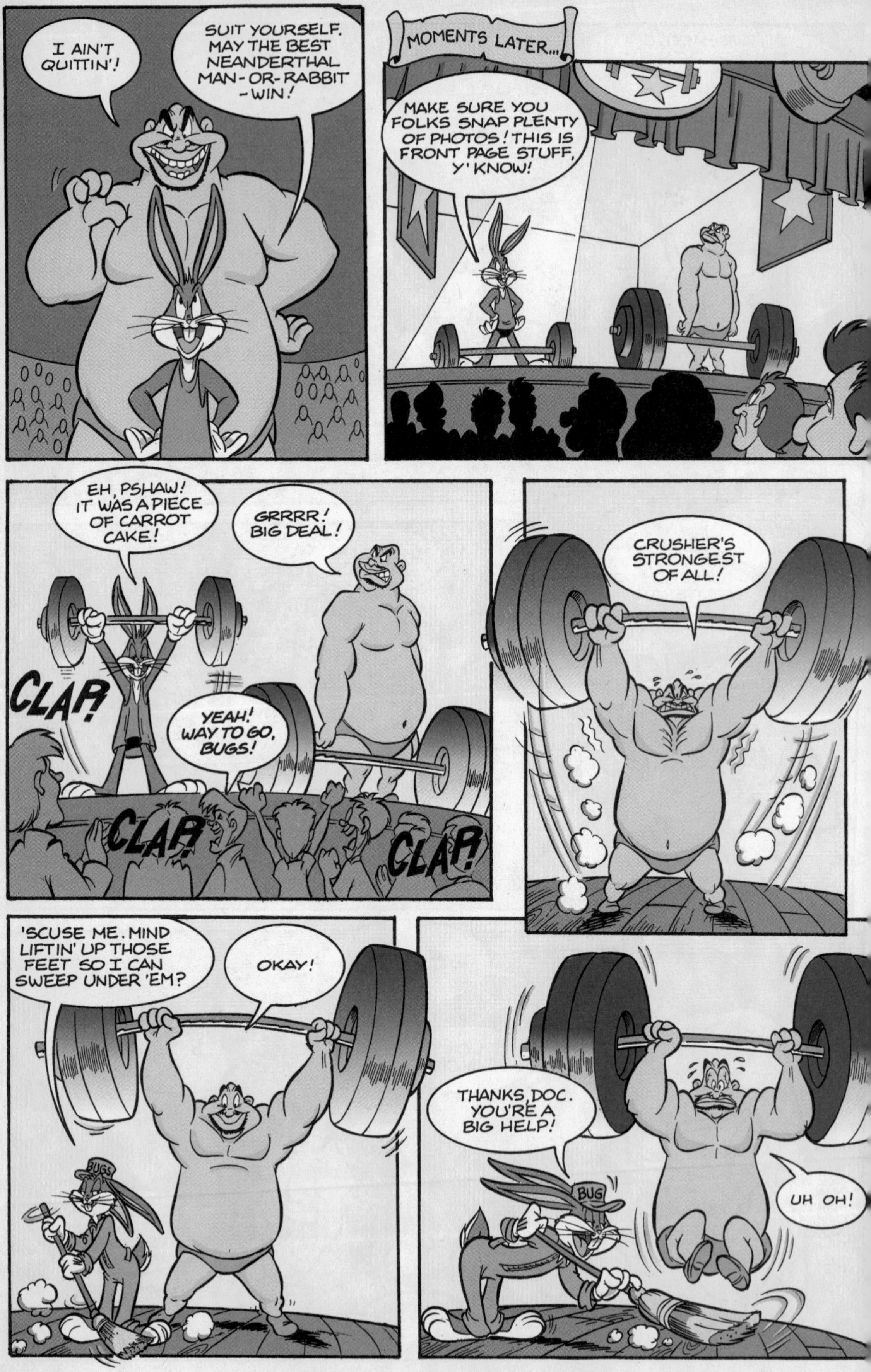
I AIN'T QUITTIN'!
SUIT YOURSELF. MAY THE BEST NEANDERTHAL MAN-OR-RABBIT -WIN!
MOMENTS LATER...
MAKE SURE YOU FOLKS SNAP PLENTY OF PHOTOS! THIS IS FRONT PAGE STUFF, Y'KNOW!
EH, PSHAW! IT WAS A PIECE OF CARROT CAKE!
GRRRR! BIG DEAL!
CLAP!
YEAH! WAY TO GO, BUGS!
CLAP!
CLAP!
CRUSHER'S STRONGEST OF ALL!
'SCUSE ME. MIND LIFTIN' UP THOSE FEET SO I CAN SWEEP UNDER 'EM?
OKAY!
BUGS
THANKS, DOC. YOU'RE A BIG HELP!
BUG
UH OH!

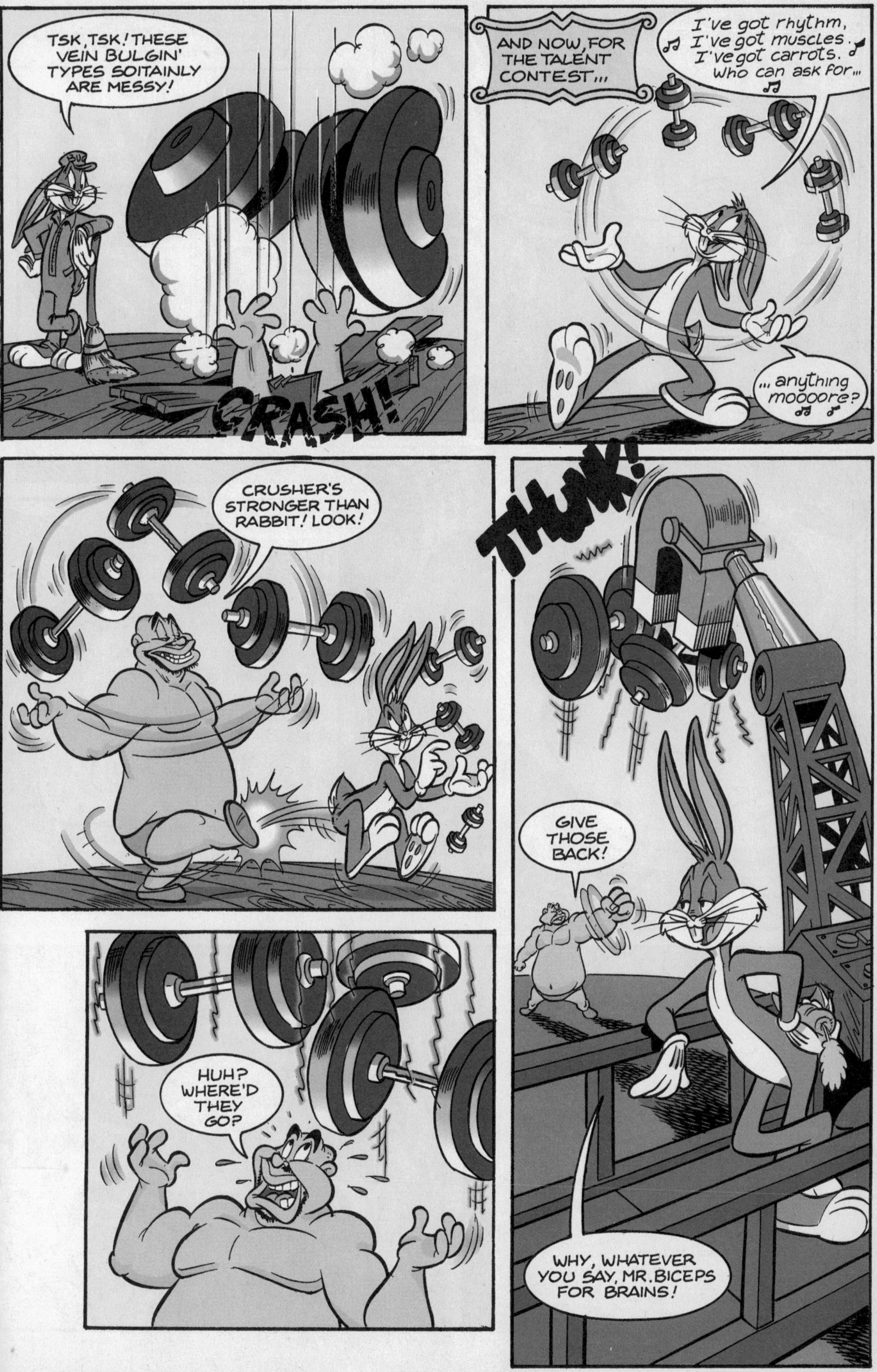
TSK, TSK! THESE VEIN BULGIN' TYPES SOITAINLY ARE MESSY!
CRASH!
AND NOW, FOR THE TALENT CONTEST...
I've got rhythm, I've got muscles. I've got carrots. Who can ask for...
... anything moooore?
CRUSHER'S STRONGER THAN RABBIT! LOOK!
THUK!
GIVE THOSE BACK!
WHY, WHATEVER YOU SAY, MR. BICEPS FOR BRAINS!
HUH? WHERE'D THEY GO?

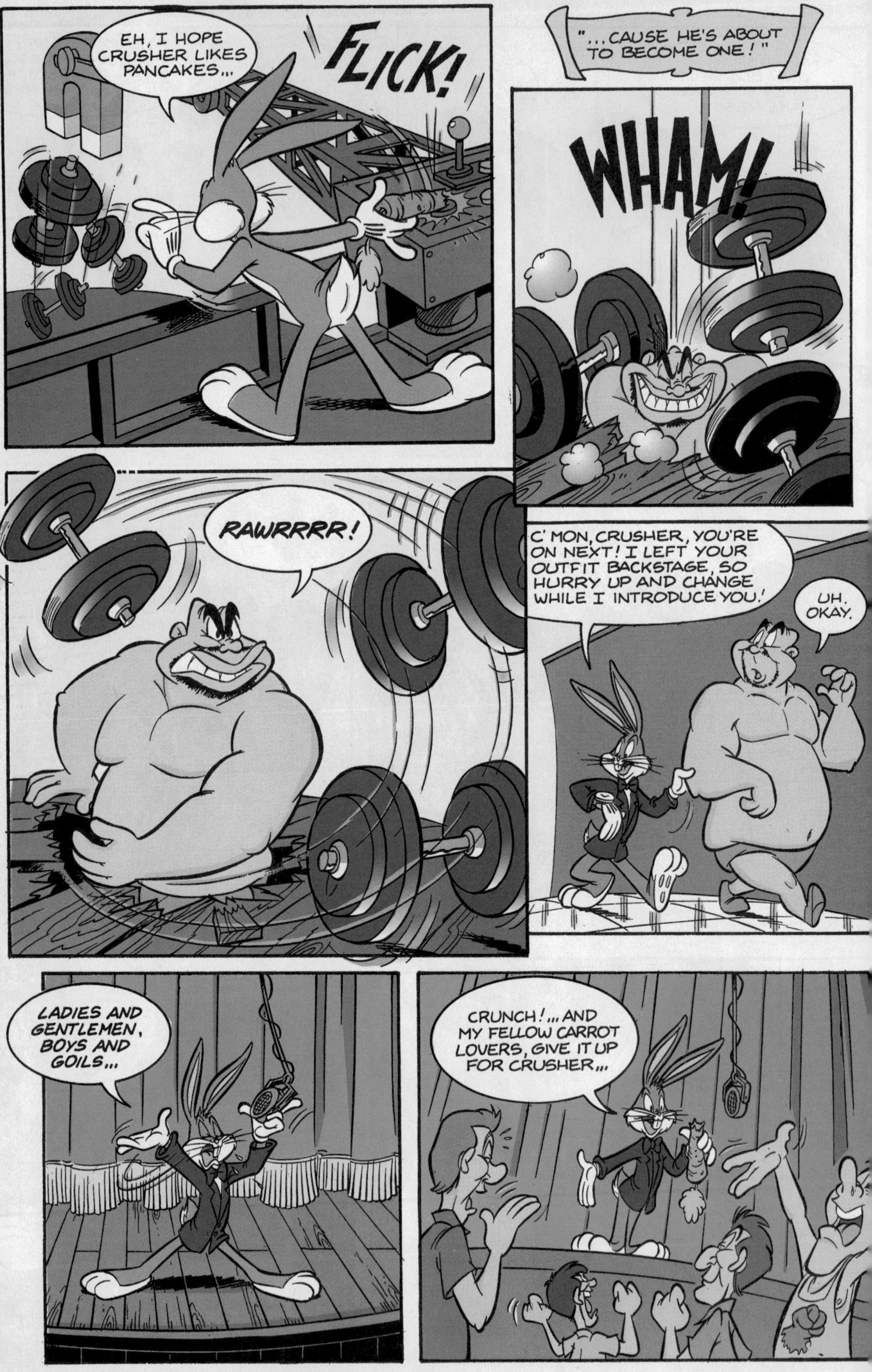
EH, I HOPE CRUSHER LIKES PANCAKES...
FLICK!
"...CAUSE HE'S ABOUT TO BECOME ONE!"
WHAM!
RAWRRRR!
C' MON, CRUSHER, YOU'RE ON NEXT! I LEFT YOUR OUTFIT BACKSTAGE, SO HURRY UP AND CHANGE WHILE I INTRODUCE YOU!
UH. OKAY.
LADIES AND GENTLEMEN, BOYS AND GOILS...
CRUNCH!... AND MY FELLOW CARROT LOVERS, GIVE IT UP FOR CRUSHER...

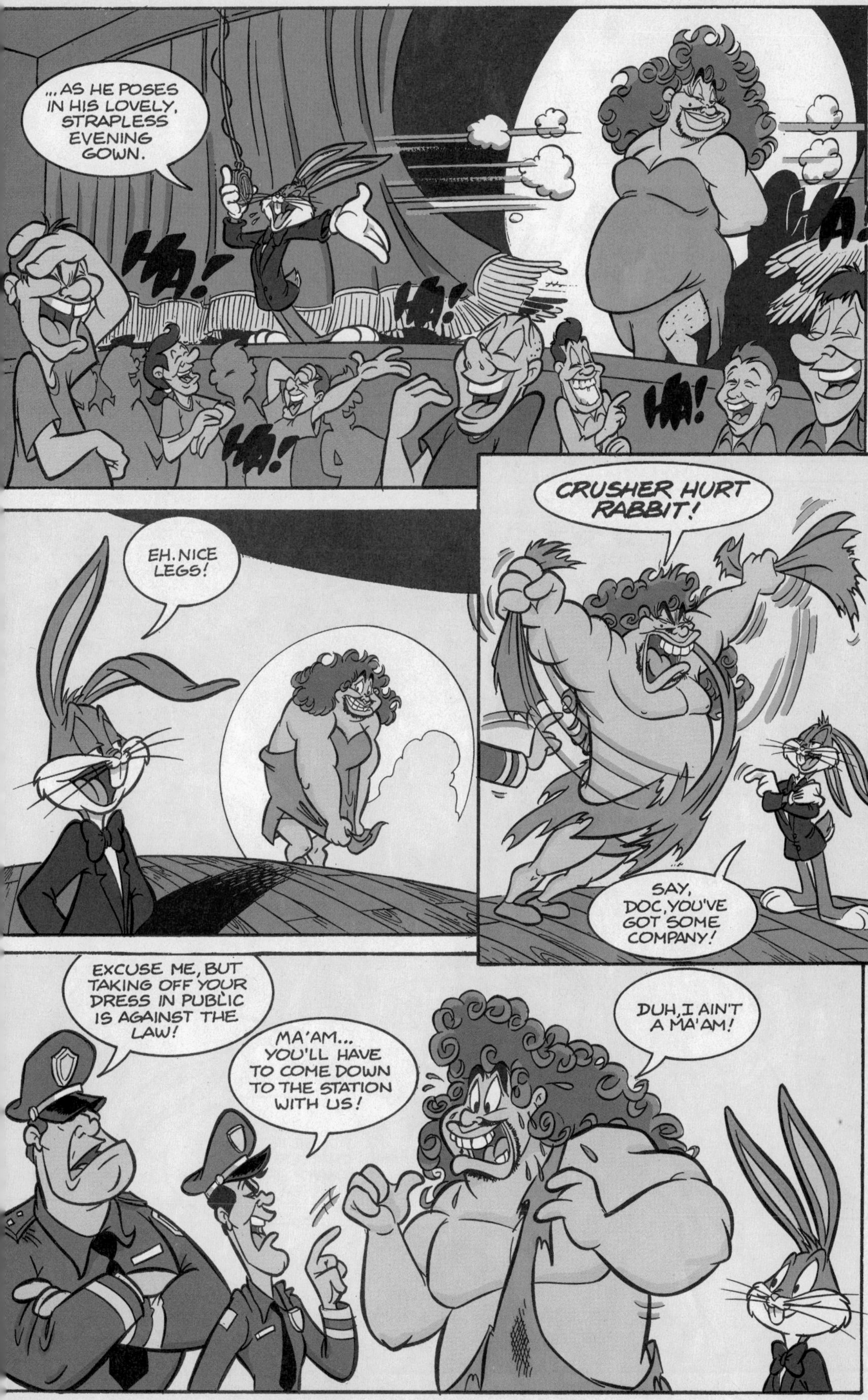
...AS HE POSES IN HIS LOVELY, STRAPLESS EVENING GOWN.
HA!
HA!
HA!
HA!
HA!
EH. NICE LEGS!
CRUSHER HURT RABBIT!
SAY, DOC, YOU'VE GOT SOME COMPANY!
EXCUSE ME, BUT TAKING OFF YOUR DRESS IN PUBLIC IS AGAINST THE LAW!
MA'AM... YOU'LL HAVE TO COME DOWN TO THE STATION WITH US!
DUH, I AIN'T A MA'AM!

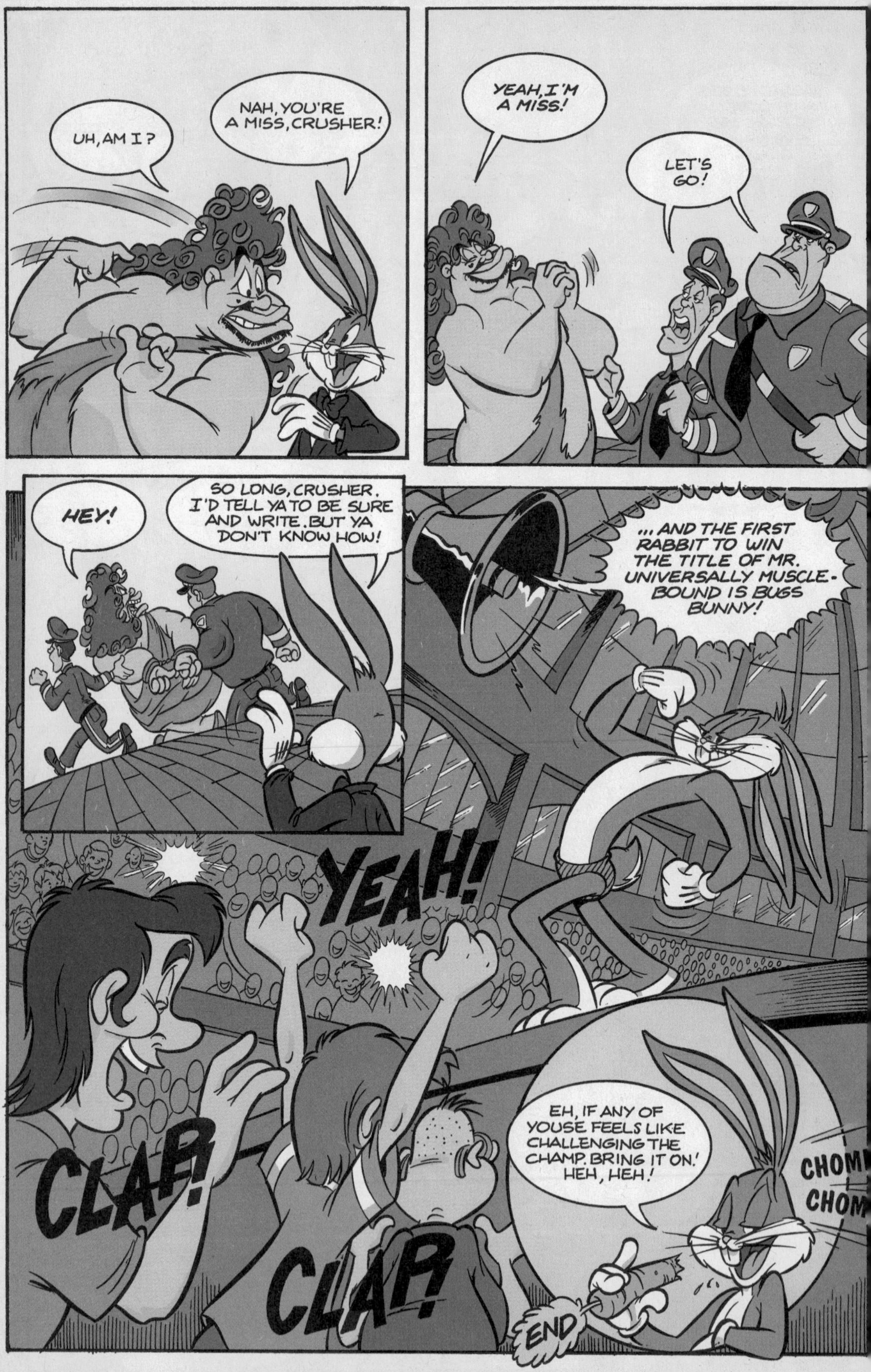
UH, AM I?
NAH, YOU'RE A MISS, CRUSHER!
YEAH, I'M A MISS!
LET'S GO!
HEY!
SO LONG, CRUSHER. I'D TELL YA TO BE SURE AND WRITE. BUT YA DON'T KNOW HOW!
...AND THE FIRST RABBIT TO WIN THE TITLE OF MR. UNIVERSALLY MUSCLE-BOUND IS BUGS BUNNY!
YEAH!
CLAP!
CLAP!
EH, IF ANY OF YOUSE FEELS LIKE CHALLENGING THE CHAMP, BRING IT ON! HEH, HEH!
CHOMP
CHOMP
END